Harlequin Marrying the Boss Collection

Being good at the job is one thing. Falling for the boss...? That's not what these heroines intend. They're here to do their work as best they can.

But those intentions are complicated when their bosses prove *they* have more than work on their minds! When these men set their sights on pursuing these heroines, keeping business separate from pleasure is impossible. And the chase can end in only one place—the altar.

Join us for this special 2-in-1 collection of classic stories where employee and boss trade in their job titles for those of bride and groom!

If you enjoy these two stories, look for more marrying-the-boss themed books in other Harlequin series.

CARA COLTER

shares ten acres in British Columbia with her real-life hero, Rob, ten horses, a dog and a cat. She has three grown children and a grandson. Cara is a recipient of the Career Achievement Award in the Love and Laughter category from *RT Book Reviews.* Cara invites you to visit her on Facebook or contact her through her website, cara-colter.com.

Be sure to look for other books by Cara Colter in Harlequin Romance—the ultimate destination for stories from the heart, for the heart! There are new Harlequin Romance titles available every month. Check one out today!

HIRED: NANNY BRIDE

AND

RESCUED IN A WEDDING DRESS

CARA COLTER

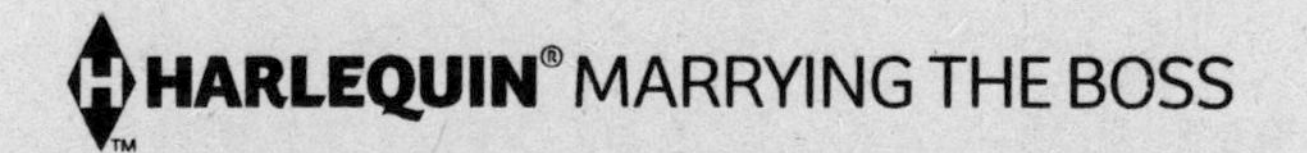

Recycling programs for this product may not exist in your area.

ISBN-13: 978-0-373-60663-4

Hired: Nanny Bride and Rescued in a Wedding Dress

This edition published by arrangement with Harlequin Books S.A.

For questions and comments about the quality of this book, please contact us at CustomerService@Harlequin.com.

Printed in U.S.A.

CONTENTS

HIRED: NANNY BRIDE

To Mike Kepke and Aline Pihl

"Love fills a lifetime"

August 9, 2008

CHAPTER ONE

JOSHUA COLE HEARD the unfamiliar sound and felt a quiver of pure feeling snake up and down his spine. So rare was that particular sensation that it took him a split second to identify it.

Fear.

He was a man who prided himself on moving forward, rather than back, in any kind of stressful situation. It had turned out to be a strategy for success in the high-powered world he moved in.

Joshua hit the intercom that connected his office to his secretary's desk in the outer lair. His office underscored who he had become with its floor-to-ceiling glass windows that overlooked the spectacular view of Vancouver, downtown skyscrapers in the foreground, majestic white-capped mountains as the backdrop.

But if his surroundings reflected his confidence, at this moment his voice did not. "Tell me that wasn't what I thought it was."

But the sound came again, through his closed, carved, solid walnut door. Now it was amplified by the intercom.

There was absolutely no mistaking it for anything but what it was: a baby crying, the initial hesitant sobs building quickly to strident shrieking.

"They say you are expecting them," said his receptionist, Amber, her own tone rising, in panic or in an effort to be heard above the baby, he couldn't quite be sure.

Of course he was expecting them. Just not today. Not here. Children, and particularly squalling babies, would be as out of place in the corporate offices of the company he had founded as a hippo at Victoria's Empress Hotel's high tea.

Joshua Cole had built his fortune and his company, Sun, around the precise lack of that sound in each of his exclusive adult-only resorts.

His office replicated the atmosphere that made the resorts so successful: tasteful, expensive, luxurious, no detail overlooked. The art was original, the antiques were authentic, the rugs came from the best bazaars in Turkey.

The skillful use of rich colors and subtle, exotic textures made Joshua Cole's office mirror the man, masculine, confident, charismatic. His desk faced a wall that showcased his career rise with beautifully framed magazine covers, *Forbes, Business, Business Weekly.*

But this morning, as always, his surroundings had faded as he intently studied what he hoped would become his next project. The surface of his desk was littered with photos of a run-down resort in the wilderness of the British Columbia interior.

He'd had *that* feeling as soon as he'd seen the photos. Moose Lake Lodge could be turned into an adventure destination for the busy young professionals who trusted his company to give them exactly what they wanted in a vacation experience. His clients demanded grown-up adventure plus five-star meals, spalike luxuries and all against the backdrop of a boutique hotel atmosphere.

The initial overture to Moose Lake Lodge had not gone particularly well. The owners were reluctant to talk to him, let alone sell to him. He had sensed they were wary of his reputation as a playboy, concerned about the effect of a Sun resort in the middle of cottage country. The Moose Lake Lodge had run as a family-oriented lakeside retreat since the 1930s, and the owners had sentimental attachments to it.

But sentiment did not pay the bills, and Joshua Cole did his homework. He knew buyers were not lining up for the place, and he was already strategizing his next move. He would up his offer tantalizingly. He'd convince the Baker family he could turn Moose Lake Lodge into a place they would always feel proud of. He'd visit them personally, win them over. Joshua Cole was very good at winning people over.

And he was passionate about this game, in all its stages: acquiring, renovating, opening, operating.

To that end Joshua had a resort in the Amazon jungle that offered rainforest canopy excursions, and one on the African savannah featuring photo safaris. And, of course, he still had his original small hotel in Italy, in the heart of Tuscany, where it had all started, offering a very grown-up winery and tasting tours.

Most recently Sun had opened a floating five-star destination for water lovers off the Kona Coast, on the Big Island of Hawaii.

Water lovers and kid haters.

Well, not all kid *haters*. Some of his best clients were just busy parents who desperately needed a break from the demands of children.

"WAHHHHH."

As if that sound didn't explain it all. Even his own sister, Melanie, domestic diva that she had become, had accepted his offer to give her and her hubbie a much-needed break at the newly opened Sun in Kona.

No wonder, with a kid whose howls could register off the decibel chart.

How could his niece and nephew be here? His crammed calendar clearly said tomorrow. The plane was arriving at ten in the morning. Joshua planned, out of respect to his sister, to meet the plane, pat his niece on the head and make appropriate noises over the relatively new baby nephew, hopefully without actually touching him. Then he was planning on putting them, and the nanny they were traveling with, in a limo and waving goodbye as they were whisked off to a kid-friendly holiday experience at Whistler.

Holiday for Mom and Dad at the exclusive Kona Sun; holiday for the kids; Uncle Josh, hero-of-the-hour.

The baby screamed nonstop in the outer office, and Joshua's head began to throb. He'd given his sister and brother-in-law, Ryan, the adult-getaway package after the birth of the baby, stunned that his sister, via their Web cam conversations, always so vital in the past, could suddenly look so worn-out. Somehow, he hadn't exactly foreseen *this* moment, though he probably should have when Melanie had started worrying about her kids within seconds of agreeing to go to the Kona Sun for a week. Naturally, her brother, the hero, had volunteered to look after that, too.

He should have remembered that things never went quite as he planned them when his sister was involved.

"What is going on?" Joshua asked in a low voice into his intercom. His legendary confidence abandoned him around children, even ones he was related to.

"There's a, um, woman here. With a baby and another, er, small thing."

"I know *who* they are," Joshua said. "Why is the baby making that noise?"

"You know who they are?" Amber asked, clearly feeling betrayed that they hadn't wandered in off the street, thereby making disposing of them so much easier!

"They aren't supposed to be here. They're supposed to be—"

"Miss! Excuse me! You can't just go in there!"

But before Amber could protect him, his office door opened.

For all the noise that baby was making, Joshua was struck by a sudden sensation of quiet as he pressed the off button on the intercom and studied the woman who stood at the doorway to his enclave.

Despite the screaming red-faced baby at her bosom, and his four-year-old niece attached to the hem of her coat, the woman carried herself with a calm dignity, a sturdy sea vessel, innately sure of her abilities in a storm, which, Joshua felt, the screaming baby qualified as.

His niece was looking at him with dark dislike, which took him aback. Like cats, children were adept at attaching themselves to those with an aversion, and he had spent his last visit to his sister's home in Toronto trying to escape his niece's frightening affection. At that time the baby had been an enormous lump under his sister's sweater, and there had been no nanny in residence.

The distraction of the baby and his niece's withering look aside, he was aware of feeling he had not seen a woman like the one who accompanied his niece and nephew for a very long time.

No, Joshua Cole had become blissfully accustomed to perfection in the opposite sex. His world had become populated with women with thin, gym-sculpted bodies, dentist-whitened teeth, unfurrowed brows, perfect makeup, stunning hair, clothing that *breathed* wealth and assurance.

The woman before him was, in some ways, the epitome of what he expected a nanny to be: fresh-scrubbed; no makeup; sensible shoes; a plain black skirt showing from underneath a hideously rumpled coat. One black stocking had a run in it from knee to ankle. All that was missing was the umbrella.

She was exactly the type of woman he might dismiss without a second look: frumpalumpa, a woman who had given up on herself in favor of her tedious child-watching duties. She was younger than he would have imagined, though, and carried herself with a careful dignity that the clothes did not hide, and that did not allow for easy dismissal.

A locket, gold and fragile, entirely out of keeping with the rest of her outfit, winked at her neck, making him aware of the pure creaminess of her skin.

Then Joshua noticed her hair. Wavy and jet black, it was refreshingly uncolored, caught back with a clip it was slipping free from. The escaped tendrils of hair should have added to her generally unruly appearance, but they didn't. Instead they hinted at something he wasn't seeing. Something wilder, maybe even exotic.

Her eyes, when he met them, underscored that feeling. They were a stunning shade of turquoise, fringed with lashes that didn't need one smidgen of mascara to add to their lushness. Unfortunately, he detected his niece's disapproval mirrored in her nanny's expression.

Her face might, at first glance, be mistaken for plain. And yet there was something in it—freshness, perhaps—that intrigued.

It was as if, somehow, she was *real* in the world of fantasy that he had so carefully crafted, a world that had rewarded him with riches beyond his wildest dreams, and which suddenly seemed lacking in *something,* and that *something* just as suddenly seemed essential.

He shrugged off the uncharacteristic thoughts, put their intrusion in his perfect world down to the yelps of the baby. He had only to look around himself to know he was the man who already had everything, including the admiration and attention of women a thousand times more polished than the one in front of him.

"My uncle hates us," his niece, Susie, announced just as Joshua was contemplating trying out his most charming smile on the nanny. He was pretty confident he was up to the challenge of melting the faintly contemptuous look from her eyes. Pitting his charm against someone so wholesome would be good practice for when he met with the Bakers about acquiring their beloved Moose Lake Lodge.

"Susie, that was extremely rude," the nanny said. Her voice was husky, low, as real as she was. And it hinted at something tantalizingly sensual below the frump-alumpa exterior.

"Of course I don't hate you," Joshua said, annoyed at being put on the defensive by a child who had plagued him with xoxo notes less than a year ago, explaining to him carefully each x stood for a kiss and each o stood for a hug. "I'm terrified of you. There's a difference."

He tried his smile.

The nanny's lips twitched, her free hand reached up and touched the locket. If a smile had been developing, it never materialized. In fact, Joshua wasn't quite sure if he'd amused her or annoyed her. If he'd amused her, her amusement was reluctant! He was not accustomed to ambiguous reactions when he dealt with the fairer sex.

"You hate us," Susie said firmly. "Why would Mommy and Daddy need a holiday from *us?*"

Then her nose crunched up, her eyes closed tight, she sniffled and buried her face in the folds of the nanny's voluminous jacket and howled. The baby seemed to regard that as a challenge to make himself heard above his sister.

"Why, indeed?" he asked dryly. The children had been in his office approximately thirty seconds, and he already needed a holiday from them.

"She's just tired," the nanny said. "Susie, shush."

He was unwillingly captivated by the hand that she rested lightly on Susie's head, by the exquisite tenderness in that faint touch, by the way her voice calmed the child, who quit howling but hiccupped sadly.

"I think there's a tiny abandonment issue," the nanny said, "that was not in the least helped by your leaving us stranded at the airport."

He found himself hoping that, when he explained there had been a misunderstanding, he would see her without the disapproving furrow in her forehead.

"There seems to have been a mix-up about the dates. If you had called, I would have had someone pick you up."

"I did call." The frown line deepened. "Apparently only very important people are preapproved to speak to you."

He could see how all those security measures intended to protect his time and his privacy were just evidence to her of an overly inflated ego. He was probably going to have to accept that the furrowed brow line would be permanent.

"I'm terribly sorry," he said, which did not soften the look on her face at all.

"Are those women naked?" Susie asked, midhiccup, having removed her head from the folds of her nanny's coat. Unfortunately.

He followed her gaze and sighed inwardly. She was staring at the Lalique bowl that adorned his coffee table. Exquisitely crafted in blue glass, and worth about forty thousand dollars, it was one of several items in the room that he didn't even want his niece to breathe on, though to say so might confirm for the nanny, who already had a low opinion of him, that he really did hate children.

He realized that the bowl, shimmering in the light from the window, was nearly the same shades of blue as the nanny's eyes.

"Susie, that's enough," the nanny said firmly.

"Well, they are naked, Miss Pringy," Susie muttered, unrepentant.

Miss Pringy. A stodgy, solid, librarian spinster kind of name that should have suited her to a T, but didn't.

"In your uncle's circles, I'm sure that bowl would be considered appropriate decor."

"And what circles are those?" Joshua asked, raising an eyebrow at her.

"I had the pleasure of reading all about you on the plane, Mr. Cole. *People to Watch.* You are quite the celebrity it would seem."

Her tone said it all: superficial, playboy, hedonist. Even before he'd missed her at the airport, he'd been tried and found guilty.

Joshua Cole had, unfortunately, been discovered by a world hungry for celebrity, and the fascination with his lifestyle was escalating alarmingly. It meant he was often prejudged, but so far he'd remained confident of his ability to overcome misperceptions.

Though he could already tell that Miss Pringy, of

all people, looked as if she was going to be immune to his considerable charisma. He found himself feeling defensive again.

"I'm a businessman," he said shortly, "not a celebrity."

In fact, Joshua Cole disliked almost everything about his newly arising status, but the more he rejected media attention, the more the media hounded him. That article in *People to Watch* had been unauthorized and totally embarrassing.

World's Sexiest Bachelor was a ridiculous title. It perturbed him that the magazine had gotten so many pictures of him, when he felt he'd become quite deft at protecting his privacy.

Where had all those pictures of him with his shirt off come from? Or relaxing, for that matter? Both were rare events.

To look at those pictures, anyone would think he was younger than his thirty years, and also that he spent his days half naked in sand and sunshine, the wind, waves and sun streaking his dark hair to golden brown. The article had waxed poetic about his "buff" build and sea-green eyes. It was enough to make a grown man sick.

Joshua was learning being in the spotlight had a good side: free publicity for Sun for one. For another, the label *playboy* that was frequently attached to him meant he was rarely bothered by women who had apple-pie, picket-fence kind of dreams. No, his constantly shifting lineup of companions were happy with lifestyle-of-the-rich-and-famous outings and expensive trinkets; in other words, no *real* investment on his part.

The downside was that people like the mom-and-pop owners of Moose Lake Lodge weren't comfortable with his notoriety coming to their neck of the woods.

And sometimes, usually when he least expected it, he would be struck with a sensation of loneliness, as if no one truly knew him, though usually a phone call to his sister fixed that pretty quickly!

Maybe it was because the nanny represented his sister's household that he disliked being prejudged by her, that he felt strangely driven to try to make a good impression.

Just underneath that odd desire was an even odder one to know if she was evaluating him as the World's Sexiest Bachelor. If she was, she approved of the title even less than he did. In fact, she looked as if she might want to see the criteria that had won him the title!

Was it possible she didn't find him attractive? That she didn't agree with the magazine's assessment of his status? For a crazy moment he actually cared! He found himself feeling defensive again, saying in his head, *Miss Pringy wouldn't know sexy if it stepped on her.*

Or walked up to her and kissed her.

Which, unfortunately, made him look at her lips. They were pursed in a stern line, which he should have found off-putting. Not challenging! But the tightness around her lips only accentuated how full they were, puffy, *kissable.*

She reached up and touched the locket again, as if it was an amulet and he was a werewolf, as if she was totally aware of his inappropriate assessment of the kissability of her lips and needed to protect herself.

"I'm Danielle Springer, Dannie," the woman announced formally, the woman least likely to have her lips evaluated as kissable. She was still unfazed by the shrill cries of the baby. Again, he couldn't help but notice her voice was husky, as sensuous as a touch. Under different circumstances—very different circumstances—he was pretty sure he would have found it sexy.

At least as sexy as her damned disapproving lips.

"I was told you'd meet us at the plane."

"There seems to have been a mix-up," he said for the second time. "Not uncommon when my sister is involved."

"It's not easy to get children ready for a trip!" She was instantly defensive of her employer, which, under different circumstances, he would have found more admirable.

"That's why you're there to help, isn't it?" he asked mildly.

Her chin lifted and her eyes snapped. "Somehow I am unsurprised that you would think it was just about packing a bag and catching a flight."

She was obviously a woman of spirit, which he found intriguing, so he goaded her a bit. "Isn't it?"

"There's more to raising a child than attending to their physical needs," she said sharply. "And your sister knows that."

"Saint Melanie," he said dryly.

"Meaning?" she asked regally.

"I am constantly on the receiving end of lectures from my dear sister about the state of my emotional bankruptcy," he said pleasantly. "But despite my notoriously cavalier attitudes, I really did think you were arriving tomorrow. I'm sorry. I especially wouldn't want to hurt Susie."

Susie shot him a suspicious look, popped her thumb in her mouth and sucked. Hard.

Dannie juggled the baby from one arm to the other and gently removed Susie's thumb. He could suddenly see that despite the nanny's outward composure, the baby was heavy and Dannie was tired.

Was there slight forgiveness in her eyes, did the stern line around her mouth relax ever so slightly? He studied her and decided he was being optimistic.

He could read what was going to happen before it did, and he shot up from behind his desk, hoping Dannie would get the message and change course. Instead she moved behind the desk with easy confidence, right into his space, and held out the baby.

"Could you? Just for a moment? I think he's in need of a change. I'll just see if I can find his things in my bag."

For a moment, Joshua Cole, self-made billionaire, was completely frozen. He was stunned by the predicament he was in. Before he could brace himself or prepare himself properly in any way, he was holding a squirming, puttylike chunk of humanity.

Joshua shut his eyes against the warmth that crept through him as his eight-month-old nephew, Jake, settled into his arms.

A memory he thought he'd divorced himself from a long, long time ago returned with such force his throat closed.

Bereft.

"Don't worry. It's not what you think," Dannie said. Joshua opened his eyes and saw her looking at him quizzically. "He's just wet. Not, um, you know."

Joshua became aware of a large warm spot soaking through his silk tie and onto his pristine designer shirt. He was happy to let her think his reaction to holding the baby was caused by an incorrect assumption about what Jake was depositing on his shirt.

The baby, as stunned by finding himself in his uncle's arms as his uncle himself, was shocked into sudden blessed silence and regarded him with huge sapphire eyes.

The Buddha-like expression of contentment lasted for a blink. And then the baby frowned. Turned red. Strained. Made a terrifying grunting sound.

"What's wrong with him?" Joshua asked, appalled.

"I'm afraid now it is, um, you know."

If he didn't know, the sudden explosion of odor let the secret out.

"Amber," he called. The man who reacted to stress with aplomb, at least until this moment, said, "Amber, call 911."

Dannie Springer's delectable lips twitched. A twinkle lit the depths of those astonishing eyes. She struggled, lost, started to laugh. And if he hadn't needed 911 before, he did now.

For a time-suspended moment, looking into those amazing blue depths, listening to the brook-clear sound of her laughter, it was as if disaster was not unfolding around him. It was as if his office, last sanctuary of the single male, had not been invaded by the enemy that represented domestic bliss. He might have laughed himself, if he wasn't so close to gagging.

"Amber," he said, trying to regain his legendary control in this situation that seemed to be unraveling dismally, "forget 911."

Amber hovered in the doorway. "What would you like me to do?"

"The children haven't eaten," Miss Pringy said, as if she was in charge. "Do you think you could find us some lunch?"

How could anyone think of lunch at a time like this?

Or put Amber in charge of it? Even though Amber

disappeared, Josh was fairly certain food was a question lost on her. As far as Joshua could see, his secretary survived on celery sticks.

Did babies eat celery sticks?

For a moment he felt amazed at how a few seconds could change a man's whole world. If somebody had told him when he walked into his office, he would be asking himself questions about babies and celery sticks before the morning was out, he would not have believed it.

He would particularly not have believed he would be contemplating celery sticks with that odor now permeating every luxurious corner of his office.

But he, of all people, should know. A few seconds could change everything, forever. A baby, wrapped in a blue hospital blanket, his face tiny and wrinkled, his brow furrowed, his tiny, perfect hand—

Stop! Joshua ordered himself.

And yet even as he resented memories of a long-ago hurt being triggered so easily by the babe nestled in his arms now, he was also aware of something else.

He felt surprised by life, for the first time in a very, very long time. He slid his visitor a glance and was painfully aware of how lushly she was curved, as if *she* ate more than celery sticks. In fact, he could picture her digging into spaghetti, eating with robust and unapologetic appetite. The picture was startlingly sensual.

"I'll just change the baby while we wait for lunch."

"In here?" he sputtered.

"Unless you have a designated area in the building?" she said, raising an eyebrow at him.

Joshua could clearly see she was the kind of woman you did not want to surrender control to. In no time flat, she would have the Lalique bowl moved and the change station set up where the bowl had been.

It was time to take control, not to be weakened by his memories but strengthened by them. It was time to put things back on track. The nanny and the children had arrived early. The thought of how his sister would have delighted in his current predicament firmed his resolve to get things to exactly where he had planned them, quickly.

"The washroom is down the hall," Joshua said, collecting himself as best he could with the putty baby trying to insert its pudgy fingers in his nose. "If you'd care to take the baby there, Miss Pringy—"

"Springer—" she reminded him. "Perhaps while I take care of this, you could do something about, er, that?"

A hand fluttered toward the Lalique. He knew it! She was eyeing the table for its diaper changing potential!

"It's art," he said stubbornly.

"Well, it's art the children aren't old enough for."

Precisely one of his many reservations about children. Everything had to be rearranged around them. Naturally, he needed to set her straight. It was his office, his business, his life. No one, but no one, told him how to run it. She and the children were departing as soon as he could arrange the limo and reschedule their reservations by a day.

But when she took the evilly aromatic baby back, after having fished a diaper out of a huge carpetbag she was traveling with, he was so grateful he decided not to set her straight about who the boss was. After she looked after the baby change, there would be plenty of time for that.

Dannie left the room, Susie on her heels. In a gesture he was not going to consider surrender, Joshua went and retrieved his suit jacket from where it hung on the back of his chair, and gently and protectively draped it over the bowl.

"Thank you," the nanny said primly, noticing as soon as she came back in the room. A cloud of baby-fresh scent entered with her, and Jake was now gurgling joyously.

"Naked is not nice," Susie informed him.

"Well, that depends on—" A look from the nanny made him take a deep breath and change tack. "As soon as we've had some lunch, I'll see to changing the arrangements I've made for you. You'll love Whistler."

"Whistler?" Miss Pringy said. "Melanie never said anything about Whistler. She said we were staying with you."

"I'm not staying with him," Susie huffed. "He hates us. I can tell."

He wondered if he should show her all those little x and o notes, placed carefully in the top drawer of his desk. No, the nanny might see it as a vulnerability. And somehow, as intriguing—and exasperating—as he found her, he had no intention of appearing vulnerable in front of her.

"Don't worry," Joshua told Susie, firmly, "No one is staying with me, because I don't want—"

"Don't you dare finish that sentence," Miss Springer told him in a tight undertone. "Don't you dare."

Well, as if his life was not surprising enough today! He regarded her thoughtfully, tried to remember when the last time anyone had told him what to do was, and came up blank.

And that tone. No one ever dared use that tone on him. Probably not since grade school, anyway.

"Amber," he called.

She appeared at the doorway, looking mutinous, as

if one more demand would finish her. "Lunch is on the way up."

"Take the children for a moment. Miss Pringy and I have a few things to say privately."

Amber stared at him astounded. "Take them where?"

"Just your office will do."

Her lips moved soundlessly, like a fish floundering, but then wordlessly she came in and took the baby, holding him out carefully at arm's length.

"You go, too," Miss Pringy said gently to Susie.

It was a mark of her influence on those children, that with one warning look shot at him, Susie traipsed out of the room behind Amber, shutting the door with unnecessary noisiness behind her.

"You weren't going to say you didn't want them in front of them, were you?" Miss Pringy asked, before the door was barely shut.

It bothered him that she knew precisely how he had planned to finish that sentence. It bothered him the way she was looking at him, her gaze solemn and stripping and seemingly becoming less awed by him by the second.

Much as he disliked his fledgling celebrity status, Joshua had to admit he was growing rather accustomed to awe. And admiration. Women *liked* him, and they had thousands of delightful ways of letting him know that.

But no, Miss Pringy looked, well, *disapproving*, again, but then she shook her hair. It was not the flirtatious flick of locks that he was used to, and yet he found himself captivated. He found himself thinking she was really a wild-spirited gypsy dancer disguised, and unpleasantly so, as a straitlaced nanny.

"Look," he said doggedly, "I've made arrangements

for you to stay at a lovely resort in Whistler. They organize child activities all day long! Play-Doh sculpture. Movies. Nature walks. I just have to change everything up a day. You should be out of here and on your way in less than an hour."

"No," she said, and shook her hair again. Definitely not flirtatious. She was *aggravated.*

"No?" he repeated, stunned.

"That's not what Melanie told me, and she is, after all, my employer, not you."

Until the moment his sense of betrayal in his sister increased, Joshua had been pleasantly unaware he still harbored it.

His older sister had been with him in those exhilarating early days of the business, but then she'd broken the cardinal rule. It was okay to date the clients; it was not okay to fall head over heels in love with them!

Then she'd decided, after all these years of wholeheartedly endorsing the principles and mission of Sun, that she *wanted* kids.

That was okay. He felt as if he'd forgiven her even though over the past few years it felt as if he had been under siege by her, trying to make him see things her way. His sister had made it her mission to get him to see how great a relationship would be, how miraculous children were, how empty a life without commitment and a relationship and a family was.

She sent him e-mails and cell phone videos of Susie, singing a song, cuddling with her kitty, pirouetting at her ballet classes. Lately, Jake starred in the impromptu productions. The last one had shown him being particularly disgusting in his desperate attempts to hit his own mouth with a steadily deteriorating piece of chocolate cake gripped in his pudgy hands.

Mel's husband, Ryan, a busy and successful building contractor, a man among men, fearless and macho, was often in the background looking practically teary-eyed with pride over the giftedness of his progeny.

For the most part, Joshua had managed to resist his sister's efforts to involve him in her idea of a perfect life. Was the arrival of her children some new twist in her never-ending plot to convince him the life he'd chosen for himself was a sad and lonely place compared to the life she had chosen for herself?

"Why did you invite the children here just to send them away?" Dannie demanded.

"Play-Doh sculpture is nothing to be scoffed at," he insisted.

"We could have done that at home."

"Then why did you come?"

"Melanie had this idea that you were going to spend some time with them."

Joshua snorted.

"She was so delighted that they were going to get to know you better."

"I don't see why," he said.

"Frankly, neither do I!" She sank down on the couch, and he suddenly could see how tired she was. "What a mess. Melanie said I could trust you with the lives of her children. But you couldn't even make it to the airport!"

"She gave me the wrong day!"

"Nothing is more important to your sister than the well-being of Susie and Jake. Surely she couldn't have made a mistake?" This last was said quietly, as if she was thinking out loud.

Joshua Cole heard the doubt in her voice, and he really didn't know whether to be delighted by it or insulted.

"A mistake?" he said smoothly. "Of course not. I said I'd make arrangements for you and the children's accommodations immediately."

Rather than looking properly appreciative, Miss Pringy was getting that formidable look on her face again.

"Mr. Cole," she said sternly, "I'm afraid that won't do."

Joshua Cole lived in a world where he called the shots. "Won't do?" he repeated, incredulous.

"No," she said firmly. "Packing the children off to a hotel in Whistler will not do. That's no kind of a vacation for a child or a baby."

"Well, what is a vacation for them?" he asked. Inwardly he thought, *anything*. If she wanted tickets to Disneyworld, he'd get them. If they wanted to meet a pop star, he'd arrange it. If they wanted to swim with dolphins, he'd find out how to make that happen. No cost was too high, no effort too great.

"They just want to be around people who love them," she said softly. "In a place where they feel safe and cared about. That is what Melanie thought they were coming to or she would never have sent them."

Or gone herself, he thought, and suddenly, unwillingly, he remembered his sister's tired face. No cost was too high? How about the cost of putting himself out?

Had he led Melanie to believe he was finally going to spend some quality time with her kids? He didn't think so. She hadn't really asked for details, and he hadn't provided any. He wasn't responsible for her assumptions.

But Joshua was suddenly very aware that a man could be one of the world's most successful entrepreneurs, moving in a world of power and wealth, controlling an empire, but still feel like a kid around his older sister, still *want* her approval in some secret part of himself.

Or maybe what he wanted was to be worthy of her trust. Something in him whispered, *Be the better man.*

Out loud he heard himself saying, without one ounce of enthusiasm, "I guess they could come stay with me."

Danielle Springer looked, understandably, skeptical of his commitment.

Too late he realized the full ramifications of his invitation.

Miss Pringy, the formidable nanny with the sensual lips and mysterious eyes would be coming to stay with him, too.

And if that wasn't bad enough, he was opening himself up to a world that might have been his, had he hung on instead of letting go of a different baby boy in a lifetime he had left behind himself.

His son.

He wanted to be a better man, worthy of his sister's trust, but who was he kidding? He'd lost faith in himself, in his ability to do the right thing, a long time ago. His sister didn't even know about the college pregnancy of his girlfriend.

He found himself holding his breath, hoping Dannie Springer would not be foolish enough to say yes to his impulsive invitation, wishing he could take it back, before it drew him into places he did not want to go.

"Obviously, we have to stay somewhere for now," she said, her enthusiasm, or lack thereof, matching his exactly. "I'm not subjecting the children to any more travel or uncertainty today."

But his whole world suddenly had a quality of the

uncertain about it. And Joshua Cole did not like it when things in his well-ordered world shifted out of his control. He didn't like it one little bit.

CHAPTER TWO

DANNIE SAT IN the backseat of the cab, fuming. *The next time I see Melanie, I'm going to kill her,* she decided.

Thinking such a thought felt like a terrible defeat for a woman who prided herself on her steady nature and unflappable calm, at least professionally. To think it toward Melanie showed how truly rattled Dannie was. Melanie, in just a few short months, had become so much more than an employer.

But the truth was that a steady nature was not any kind of defense against a man like Joshua Cole. He was a complete masculine, sexy package, with that brilliant smile, the jade of those eyes, the perfect masculine cut of his facial features, the way he carried himself, the exquisitely expensive clothing over the sleek muscle of a toned body. All of it put together would have been enough to rattle Mother Theresa!

Dannie had known Melanie's brother was attractive. She had seen two pictures of him in the Maynards' home. Not that those pictures could have prepared her for Joshua Cole in the flesh.

Melanie's two framed photos showed her brother through the lens of an ordinary family. Nothing extraordinary about Joshua at twelve, on the beach, scrawny, white, not even a hint of the man he would become. In fact, whatever had been behind that impish grin seemed to be gone from him entirely.

The other picture showed Joshua in a college football uniform, posed, looking annoyingly cocky and confident, again some mischief in him that now seemed to be gone. Though he was undeniably good-looking, that photo showed only a glimmer of the self-possessed man he now was.

"He never finished college," Melanie had said, with a hint of sadness, when she had seen Dannie looking at that picture. For some reason Dannie had assumed that sadness was for her brother's lost potential.

Melanie had seemed to see Joshua as the exasperating kid brother who was an expert at thwarting her every effort to interfere in his life with her wise and well-meaning sisterly guidance. From Melanie's infrequent mentions of her brother, Dannie had thought he managed a hotel or a travel agency, not that he was the president and CEO of one of the world's most up-and-coming companies!

So, the article in *People to Watch* had been a shocker. First, the photos had come a little closer to capturing the pure animal magnetism of the man. The little-boy mischief captured in his sister's snapshots was gone from those amazing smoky-jade eyes, replaced with an intensity that was decidedly sensual.

That sensuality was underscored in the revealing photos of him: muscled, masculine, at ease with his body, oozing a self-certainty that few men would ever master.

Melanie had certainly never indicated her brother was a candidate for the World's Sexiest Bachelor, though his unmarried status seemed to grate on her continually.

Again, the magazine portrayal seemed to be more accurate than the casual remarks Melanie had tossed out about him. The magazine described him as powerful, engaging and lethally charming. And that was just personally. Professionally he was described as driven. The timing of the openings of his adventure-based adult-only resorts was seen as brilliant.

In the article, his name had also been paired with some of the world's wealthiest and most beautiful women, including actress Monique Belliveau, singer Carla Kensington and heiress Stephanie Winger-Stone.

By the time he'd stood them up at the airport, Danielle Springer, the steady one, had already been feeling nervous about meeting Joshua Cole, World's Sexiest Bachelor, and had developed a feeling of dislike for him, just *knowing* he would exude all the superficial charm and arrogance of a man who had the world at his feet. He would move through life effortlessly, piling up successes, traveling the globe, causing heartbreaks but never suffering them.

She had already known, before the plane landed, that Melanie had made a terrible mistake in judgment sending them all here. That knowledge had only been underscored by the fact the Great One had not put in an appearance at the airport, and she had not been able to penetrate the golden walls that protected him from the annoyances of real life.

Which begged the question: Why *hadn't* she jumped at the opportunity to go to Whistler when he had offered it? It was more than the fact small children and hotels rarely made a good combination, no matter how "child-friendly" they claimed to be.

It was more than the fact that the children were exhausted and so was she, not a good time to be making decisions!

It was that something about him had been unexpected.

He had not been all arrogance and charm. Something ran deeper in him. She had seen it in that unguarded moment when she had thrust Jake upon him, something in his face that said his life had not been without heartbreak, after all.

Stop it, she told herself sternly. They would spend the evening with him. Tomorrow, rested, she would regroup and decide what to do next. The original plan no longer seemed feasible. Spend a week with him? Good grief!

What she was not going to do was call Melanie and Ryan, who needed this time together desperately. At a whisper of trouble, Melanie would come home.

Still, could it really be in the best interests of the children to spend time with their uncle? He'd made it clear he was uncomfortable with children. In fact, his success was based on the creation of a child-free world! There was no sense seeing anything noble in his sudden whim to play the hero and spend time with the niece and nephew he'd invited here in the first place.

And how about herself? How much time could any woman with blood flowing through her veins spend with a man like that without succumbing?

Not, she reminded herself sourly, that there would be anything to *succumb* to. He was rich and powerful and definitely lethally charming. There had been no pictures in the article of him accompanied by women like her.

Women like her: unprocessed, unsophisticated, slightly plump.

She touched the locket on her neck and felt the ache. Only a few weeks ago, the locket would have protected her. *Taken.*

Brent had given it to her before leaving for Europe. "A promise," he'd said, "I will return to you."

Perhaps it would be better to take the locket off, now that it represented a promise broken. On the other hand perhaps it protected her still, reminding her of the fickleness of the human heart, and especially of the fickleness of the *male* human heart.

And besides, she wasn't ready to take it off. She still looked at the photo inside it each night and felt the ache of loss and the stirring of hope that he would realize he had made a mistake....

Though all along maybe the worst mistake had been hers. Believing in what she felt for Brent, even after what she had grown up with. Her own parents' split up had been venomous, their passion had metamorphosed into full-blown hatred that was destructive to all it had touched, including their children. Maybe especially their children.

Thank God, Dannie thought, for the Maynards, for Melanie and Ryan, for Susie and Jake. Thank God she had already been welcomed into the fold of their household when this hurricane of heartbreak had hit her. She would survive because they gave her a sense of family and of belonging, a safe place to fall when her world had fallen apart.

Bonus: loving them didn't involve one little bit of risk!

Though since Brent's call from London, "I'm so sorry, there's someone else," now when Dannie saw the way that Melanie and Ryan looked at each other, she felt a startling stab of envy.

"Hey, lady, are we going somewhere, or are we just sitting here?" the cabbie asked her, waiting for her instructions, impatient.

"When you see the horrible yellow car, follow it," Dannie said. Delivering the variation on the line "Follow that car" gave her absolutely no pleasure.

"A yellow car?" he said, bemused. "Do you think you could be a little more specific?"

Dannie looked over her shoulder. "It's coming now."

The cabbie whistled. "Okay, lady, though in what world a Lamborghini is horrible, I'm not sure."

"Totally unsuited for children's car seats," she informed him. The horrible yellow car, with its horrible gorgeous driver passed them slowly.

A man like that could make a woman rip a locket right off her neck!

She snorted to herself. A man like that could cause a heart to break just by being in the same room, a single glance, green eyes lingering a touch too long on her lips… Joshua's eyes were probably always making promises he had no intention of keeping.

Unattainable to mere mortals, she reminded herself with a sniff. Not that she was a mortal in the market! Done. Brent had finished her. She had given love a chance, nurtured her hopes and dreams over the year he'd been away, *lived* for his cards and notes and e-mails and been betrayed for all her trouble.

Terrible how that vow of being *done* could be rattled so easily by one lingering look from Joshua Cole! How could his gaze have made her wish, after her terrible Brent breakup, that she had not made herself over quite so completely? Gone was the makeup, the fussing over the hair, the colorful wardrobe. On was about fifteen pounds, the result of intensive chocolate therapy!

She was *done,* intent on making herself invisible and therefore safe. How could she possibly feel as if Joshua

Cole had *seen* her in a way Brent, whom she had pulled out all the makeover tricks for, never had?

The sports car was so low, she could look in the window and see Jake, his brand-new car seat strapped in securely, facing backward, his black hair standing straight up like dark dandelion fluff.

She refused to soften her view of Joshua Cole because he had insisted on the car seat to get the baby home. Once you softened your view of a man who was lethally charming, you were finished. That's what *lethally* meant.

Besides, there hadn't been enough room in that ridiculous car to put her and Susie to ride with him.

A car like that said a lot about a man. Fast and flashy. Self-centered. Single and planning to stay that way.

Since she was also single and very much planning to stay that way *for the rest of her life, a poor spinster nanny in the basement room*, it was probably unfair to see that as a flaw in him.

Except the car meant he was a *hunter,* on the prowl. Didn't it?

"What does a car like that mean to you?" she asked the cab driver, just in case she had it wrong.

"That you can have any girl you want," he muttered.

Bingo.

"If he opens her up, I'm not going to be able to keep up with him," the cabbie warned.

"If he opens her up, I'm going to kill him," she said. "He has a baby in there." *My baby.* Of course, Jake was not officially her baby. Unofficially he had won her heart and soul from the first gurgle. Now, post-Brent, she had decided Jake might be the only baby she ever had.

Emotion could capsize her unexpectedly since Brent

had hit her with his announcement, and she felt it claw at her throat now, defended against it by telling herself that sweet little baby boy was probably going to be lethally charming someday, just like his uncle.

Twice, in the space of five minutes, steady, dependable Dannie had thought of killing people.

That's what heartbreak did: turned normal, reliable people into bitter survivors, turned them into what they least wanted to be. In fact, it seemed to her, her recent tragedy had the potential to turn her into her parents, who had spent their entire married lives trying to kill each other.

Figuratively. Mostly.

"You shouldn't say you're going to kill people," Susie told her, a confirmation of what Dannie already knew. Susie was hugging the new teddy bear that had arrived in her uncle's office along with the car seat. The teddy bear did not seem to have softened the child's view of her uncle at all.

In Susie's view, Uncle Josh was the villain who had torn her mother away from her. A teddy bear was not going to fix that.

A lesson Uncle Josh no doubt needed to learn! You could not buy back affection.

The car seat and the teddy bear had arrived within minutes of a quiet phone call. Dannie had heard him giving instructions to have a baby crib set up at his apartment. In the guest room with the Jacuzzi. Which begged the question not only how many guest rooms were there, but why did you need a guest room with a Jacuzzi?

Obviously, for the same reason you needed a car like that. Entertaining.

Still, she had gotten the message. He spoke; people jumped.

And he'd better not even think of trying that with her! She might have been the kind of person who jumped before Brent's betrayal. She was no longer!

They arrived at a condominium complex not far from his office building, and Dannie tried very hard not to be awed, even though a guest room with a Jacuzzi should have given her ample time to prepare herself for something spectacular.

She was awed, anyway. Even though Melanie and Ryan certainly had no financial difficulties, she knew she was now moving in an entirely different league.

The high-rise building appeared to be constructed of white marble, glass and water. The landscaping in front of the main door was exquisite: lush grass, exotic flowers, a black onyx fountain shooting up pillars of gurgling foam.

She was fumbling with her wallet when Joshua appeared at the driver's window, baby already on his hip, and paid the driver. He juggled the baby so he could open the door for her. There was no sense noticing his growing comfort with the baby!

Instead, she focused on the fact that if the great Joshua Cole was aware he had parked the horrible yellow thing in a clearly marked no-parking zone, it didn't concern him.

But she'd do well to remember that: rules were for others.

A doorman came out of the building to move the car almost instantly. Another unloaded her luggage from the trunk of the cab.

Joshua greeted both men by name, with a sincere warmth that surprised her. And then he was leading her through a lobby that reminded her of the one and only five-star hotel she had ever stayed at. The lobby had soaring ceilings, deep carpets over marble tile, distressed leather furniture.

For all that, why did it feel as if the most beautiful thing in the room was that self-assured man carrying a baby, his strength easy, his manner unforced?

Few men, in Dannie's experience, were really comfortable with children. Brent had claimed to like them, but she had noticed he had that condescending, overly enthusiastic way of being around them that children *hated.*

She hoped it was a sign of healing that she had remembered this flaw in her perfect man!

It was a strange irony that, while Joshua Cole had not made any claims about liking children and in fact radiated unapologetic discomfort around them, he was carrying that baby on his hip as if it was the most natural thing in the world to be doing.

Joshua chose that moment to glance down at the bundle in his arms. She caught his look of unguarded tenderness and felt her throat close. Had she just caught a glimpse of something so real about him that it made her question every other judgment she had made?

What if the World's Sexiest Bachelor was a lie? What if the sports car and clothes and office were just a role he'd assumed? What if he was really a man who had been born to be a daddy?

Danger zone, she told herself. What was wrong with her? She had just been terribly disappointed by one man! Why would she be reading such qualities into another that she barely knew?

Besides, there was no doubt exactly why men like

Joshua Cole were so successful with women. They had charm down to a science.

It made it so easy to place them in the center of a fantasy, it was so easy to give them a starring role in a dream that she had to convince herself she did not believe in anymore.

Enough of fantasies, she told herself. She had spent the entire year Brent was away building a fantasy around his stupid cards and e-mails, reading into them growing love, when in fact his love had been diminishing. She was a woman pathetic enough to have spent her entire meager savings on a wedding dress on the basis of a vague promise.

Joshua went to a door off the bank of elevators and inserted a key.

The door glided open, and Dannie tried not to gawk at the unbelievable decadence of a private glass elevator. How was a girl supposed to give up on fantasy in a world where fantasy became reality?

The glass-encased elevator eased silently upward, and even Susie forgot to be mad at her uncle and squealed with delight as they glided smoothly higher and higher, the view becoming more panoramic by the second.

The problem with elevators, especially for a woman trying desperately to regain control of suddenly undisciplined thoughts, of her *fantasies,* was that everything was too close in them. She could smell the tantalizing aroma of Joshua, expensive cologne, mixed with soap. His shoulder, enormously broad under the exquisite tailoring of his suit jacket, brushed hers as he turned to let the baby see the view, and she felt a shiver of animal awareness so strong that it shook her to the core.

The reality of being in this elevator with a *real* man

made her aware that for a year Brent had not been real at all, but a faraway dream that she could make into anything she wanted him to be.

Had she ever been this aware of Brent? So aware that his scent, the merest brush of his shoulder, could make her dizzy?

She forced her attention to the view, all too aware it had nothing to do with the rapid beating of her heart. She could see the deep navy blue of an ocean bay. It was dotted with sailboats. Wet-suited sailboarders danced with the white capped waves. Outside of the bay a cruise ship slid by.

All she could think was that she had made a terrible mistake insisting on coming here with him. She touched her locket. *Its* powers to protect seemed measly and inadequate.

To be so *aware* of another human being, even in light of her recent romantic catastrophe, was terrible. To add to how terrible it was, she knew he would not be that aware of her. Since the breakup call, she had stripped herself of makeup, put away her wardrobe of decent clothes, determined to be invisible, to find the comfort of anonymity in her role as the nanny.

The elevator stopped, the doors slid open, and Dannie turned away from the view to enter directly into an apartment. To her left, floor-to-ceiling glass doors that spanned the entire length of the apartment were open to a terraced deck. Exotic flowering plants surrounded dark rattan furniture, the deep cushions upholstered in shades of lime and white. White curtains, so transparent they could only be silk, waved gracefully in the slightly salt-scented breeze.

Inside were long, sleek ultramodern white leather sofas, casually draped with sheepskins. They formed a conversation area around a fireplace framed in stainless steel, the hearth beaded in copper-colored glass tile. The themes of leather, glass and steel repeated themselves, the eye moving naturally from the conversation area to a bar that separated the living area from a kitchen.

The kitchen was magazine-layout perfect, black cabinets and granite countertops, more stainless steel, more copper-colored glass tiles. A wine cooler, state-of-the-art appliances, everything subtle and sexy.

"Don't tell me you cook," she said, the statement coming out more pleading than she wanted.

He laughed. "Does opening wine count?"

Oh, it counted, right up there with the car and the Jacuzzi, as a big strike against him.

Thankfully, it really confirmed what she already knew. She was way out of her league, but vulnerable, too. And the apartment gave her the perfect excuse.

Was he watching her to see her reaction?

"Obviously," she said tightly, "we can't stay here. I'm sorry. I should never have insisted. If you can book us a flight, I need to take the children home."

But the very thought made her want to cry. She told herself it wasn't because his apartment was like something out of a dream, that it called to the part of her that wanted, dearly, to be pampered, that wanted, despite her every effort, to embrace fantasy instead of reject it.

No. She was tired. The children were tired. She couldn't put them all back on a plane today. Maybe tomorrow.

"A motel for tonight," she said wearily. "Tomorrow we can go home."

"What's wrong?"

Everything suddenly seemed wrong. Her whole damned life. She had never wanted anything like the elegance of this apartment, but only because it was beyond the humble dreams she had nurtured for Brent's and her future.

So why did it feel so terrible, a yawning emptiness that could never be filled, that she realized she could never have this? Or a man like him? She hadn't even been able to hold the interest of Brent, pudgy, owlish, *safe*.

Joshua Cole had the baby stuffed under his arm like a football, and was looking at her with what could very easily be mistaken for genuine concern by the hopelessly naive. At least she could thank Brent for that. She wasn't. Hopelessly naive. Anymore.

"Obviously, I can't stay here with the children. They could wreck a place like this in about twenty minutes." The fantasy was about being pampered, enjoying these lush surroundings; the reality was the children wrecking the place and her being frazzled, trying to keep everything in order.

Reality. Fantasy. As long as she could keep the two straight, she should be able to survive this awkward situation.

"That's ridiculous," he said, but uncertainly.

"Dic-u-lous," Susie agreed, her eyes lighting on a pure crystal sculpture of a dolphin in the center of the coffee table.

Dannie took a tighter hold on Susie's hand as the child tried to squirm free. She could already imagine little jam-covered fingerprints on the drapes, crayon marks on the sofas, wine being pulled out of the cooler.

"No," she said. "It's obvious you aren't set up for children. I'd have a nervous breakdown trying to guard all your possessions."

"They're just possessions," he said softly.

Of course he didn't mean that. She'd already seen what he drove. She'd seen him eyeing that bowl in his office with grave concern every time Susie had even glanced in its direction. It was time to call him on it.

"You're less attached to all this than the bowl in your office?" She congratulated herself on just the right tone of disbelief.

"I can move anything that is that breakable."

"Start with the wine," she said, just to give him an idea how big a job it was.

"The cooler locks. I'll do it now." As he moved across the room, he said over his shoulder, "I'll send for some toys as a distraction."

She had to pull herself together. She had to make the best decision for the children. The thought of moving them again, of cooping them up in a hotel room for the night suddenly seemed nearly unbearable.

They would stay here the night. One night. Rested, she would make good decisions tomorrow. Rested, she would be less susceptible to the temptations of his beautiful world. And his drop-dead-gorgeous eyes. And the brilliant wattage of his smile.

Which was directed at her right now. "What kind of toys should I get?" he asked her. He came over and gave her the key to the wine cooler, folded her hand around it.

She desperately wished he had not done that. His touch, warm and strong, filled with confidence, made her more confused about reality and fantasy. How could a simple touch make her feel as if she'd received an electric jolt from fingertip to elbow?

She'd given him an out, but he wasn't taking it. She could see he was the kind of man who made up his mind and then was not swayed.

There was no point in seeing that as admirable. It was mule-stubbornness, nothing more.

"What toys?" he asked her again. He was smiling wickedly, as if he knew the touch of his hand had affected her.

Of course he knew! He radiated the conceited confidence of a man who had played this game with many women. Played. That's why they called them playboys. It was all just a game to him.

"Princess Tasonja!" Susie crowed her toy suggestion. "And the camping play set. I have to have the tent and the backpack. And the dog, Royal Robert." Seeing her uncle look amenable, she added a piece she coveted from a totally different play set. "And the royal wedding carriage. Don't get Jake anything. He's a baby."

He took his cell phone out of his pocket and tried to dial with his thumb while still holding the baby. Apparently, he was going to have someone round up all the toys his niece had demanded.

"I wouldn't bother with Princess Tasonja, if I were you," Dannie managed, in a clipped undertone as Susie slipped free of her hand and skipped over to the sofa where she buried her face in a copper-colored silk pillow. Dannie was pretty sure the remnants of lunch were on that face.

"Why not?"

Why bother telling him that Susie's attention would be held by the Princess Tasonja doll and her entire entourage for about thirty seconds? Why not let him find out on his own that attempts to buy children's affection usually ended miserably? Susie would become a monster of demands once the first one was met.

That was a lesson he probably needed to learn about the car, too. Any woman who would be impressed with such a childish display of wealth was probably not worth knowing.

Her own awed reaction to this apartment probably spoke volumes about her own lack of character!

"I suspect you think it's going to keep her occupied— Susie do not touch the dolphin. But it won't. Unless you are interested in playing princess doll dress up with her, the appeal will be strictly limited."

He clicked the cell phone shut. "What do I do with her if I don't buy her toys?" he asked.

"You are a sad man," she blurted out, and then blushed at her own audacity.

"I don't do kids well. That doesn't make me *sad*." He regarded her thoughtfully and for way too long.

Swooning length.

"You don't just work for my sister," he guessed. "You hang out with her, sharing ideas. Scary. I'm surprised she doesn't have you married off." He looked suddenly suspicious. "Unless that's why you're here."

"Excuse me?"

"My sister has been on this 'decent girl' kick for a while. She better not be matchmaking."

"Me?" Dannie squeaked. "You?" But suddenly she had a rather sickening memory of Melanie looking at her so sadly as she'd dealt with her news about Brent, as if everyone had expected it *except* her.

Joshua's look grew very dark. "Do you have a boyfriend?"

"Not at the moment," she said coolly, as if she'd had dozens of them, when she'd had only one serious relationship, and the greatest part of that had been by long distance. "But you needn't worry, Mr. Cole. Your sister would know me well enough to know that you are not my type!"

He had the nerve to look offended, as if he just naturally assumed he was every woman's type, the title of World's Sexiest Bachelor obviously having gone straight to his handsome head. "Really? And what is your type?"

She could feel heat staining her cheeks to a color she just knew would be the most unflattering shade of red ever. "Not you!"

"That isn't really an answer."

"Studious, serious about life, not necessarily a sharp dresser, certainly not materialistic." She was speaking too fast, and in her panic describing a man she knew was less than ideal to a T.

"Priests aren't generally available," he said dryly.

"I meant someone like a college professor." Which was what Brent had been. Rumpled. Academic. Faintly preoccupied all the time. Which she had thought was adorable!

"Your ideal man is a college professor?"

"Yes!" How dare he say it with such scorn?

"Miss Dannie Springer, don't ever take up poker. You can't lie. You're terrible at it."

"As it happens, I don't like poker, and neither does my ideal man." With whom her whole relationship, in retrospect, had been a lie, concocted entirely by her, sitting at home by herself making up a man who had never existed.

"The college professor," he said dryly.

"Yes! Now, if you'll entertain Susie for a bit, it's time for Jake to have a bath." Of course, it wasn't anywhere near time Jake had a bath, but she had to get out of this room and this conversation. She doubted Mr. Playboy of the World knew anything about baby bath times. Or college professors for that matter! But he seemed to know just a little too much about women, and his look was piercing.

"Entertain Susie?" he said, distracted just as she had hoped. "How? Since you've nixed Princess Tasonja."

"Try noughts and crosses."

He frowned. "Like those notes she used to give me? Before she hated me? That were covered with x's and o's that meant hugs and kisses?"

Dannie steeled herself. He was not *really* distressed that he had fallen into his niece's disfavor. His world was way too big that he could be brought down by the little things.

"Noughts and crosses," she said. "Tic-tac-toe."

He looked baffled, underscoring how very far apart their worlds were, and always would be.

"Get a piece of paper and a pencil, Susie will be happy to show you how it works," she said.

"You mean a piece of paper and a pencil will keep her as entertained as the princess?"

"More."

"Do I let her win?" he asked in a whisper. He shot his niece a worried look.

"Would that be honest?"

"For God's sake, I'm not interested in honest."

"I'm sure truer words were never spoken," she said meanly, getting back at him for being so scornful of her college professor.

"I'm interested in not making a little girl cry."

"It's about spending time with her. That's the important part. Not winning or losing."

"I have a lot to learn."

"Yes, you do, Mr. Cole," she said, aware of a snippy little edge to her voice.

"You have a lot to learn, too," he said, quietly, looking at her with an unsettling intensity that she would have done anything to escape.

"Such as?" she said, holding her ground even though she wanted to bolt.

"The college professor. Not for you."

"How would you know?"

"I'm an astute judge of people."

"You aren't! You didn't even know whether or not to be honest playing noughts and crosses."

"Not miniature people, the under-five set. But you, I know something about you. I wonder if you even know it yourself."

"You know nothing about me that I don't know about myself!" she said recklessly. To her detriment, part of her wanted to hear what he had to say. How often, after all, did an invisible nanny get to hear love advice from the World's Sexiest Bachelor?

But he didn't say a word, just proved exactly why he was the World's Sexiest Bachelor. He lifted her chin with the tip of his finger and looked deep into her eyes. Then he touched her lip with his thumb.

If it was possible to melt she would have. She felt like chocolate exposed to flame. She felt every single lie she had ever told herself about Brent. Dannie yanked away from him, but he nodded, satisfied that he did know something she didn't know herself.

Except now she had an idea.

That she was as weak as every other damn woman he'd ever met. Not that he ever had to know that!

"You're in the bedroom at the end of the hall," he said, as if he hadn't shaken her right to the core. "I had the crib set up in there. Is that okay?"

"Perfect," she said tightly, and she meant it. A pint-size chaperone for weaklings, not that she needed to worry about this man sneaking into her room in the dead of night. That was fantasy.

Of the X-rated variety, and she didn't mean tic-tac-toe, either.

"Hey, Susie," he said turning from her, after one last look that seemed more troubled than triumphant, "do you want to play noughts and crosses?"

Susie glared at him, clearly torn between personal dislike and the temptation of her favorite game. "All right," she said grudgingly.

Danielle marched down the hall with the baby. The room at the end had the same spectacular views and windows as the rest of the apartment.

The decorating was so romantic it was decadent, the whole room done in shades of brown, except for the bed linens that were seductively and lushly cream colored, inviting in that sea of rich dark chocolate.

Her suitcases were on the bed. How that had happened she wasn't quite sure. A crib had been set up for Jake, too.

Through a closed door was a bathroom, with the Jacuzzi.

A jetted tub built for two.

"We have to get out of here," she confided in the baby as she took his plump, dimpled limbs out of his clothes. The fact that Joshua thought his sister might be matchmaking—and that she could not say with one hundred per cent certainty that Melanie was not—just added an element of humiliation to the urgency she felt to go.

Was Melanie matchmaking? She frowned, thinking back over her conversations with her employer. As eager as Mel was to have everyone in the world enjoy the same state of wedded bliss she lived in, she had always been reserved about Brent.

Dannie assumed because she had never met him.

She had assumed Mel's eagerness to have her join her children with their uncle had only been her effort to help her nanny over her heartbreak, to give her a change of scenery. A hidden agenda? Wouldn't that be humiliating?

But Mel had never alluded, even subtly, to the possibility she considered her nanny and her brother to be anything of a match.

Because we so obviously are not, Dannie thought, and detected just a trace of sulkiness in that conclusion.

As always, the baby worked his magic on her sour mood, her tendency toward dour introspection. Dannie put about two inches of water in the gigantic tub, and Jake surrendered his little naked self gleefully into the watery playpen.

When the baby began to laugh out loud, she was drawn in, and she laughed back, splashing his little round tummy with warm water until he was nearly hysterical with joy.

"Do I take myself and life way too seriously, Mr. Jake?"

What if Mel *had* sent her here with some kind of hidden agenda? So what? What if she just played along?

"Oh, Dannie," she chided herself, "that would be like playing patty-cake with a powder keg."

Jake recognized the term, cooperatively held out his hands and crowed.

Relax, she ordered herself. *If you still know how,* and then sadly, *if you ever knew how.*

CHAPTER THREE

"PATTY CAKE, PATTY CAKE, baker's man, bake me a cake as fast as you can."

Dannie's voice and her laughter, intermingled with happy shouts from the baby and splashing noises, floated down the hallway to where Joshua sat opposite Susie on the couch.

Who would have imagined the serious, rather uptight nanny could sound like that? So intriguingly carefree?

Not that that was the truth about her. No, the truth was what he had *felt* when he had touched her lip—

"Tic, tac, toe," Susie cried and drew a triumphant line through her row of crosses.

Susie was trouncing him at noughts and crosses.

Something unexpected was happening to him. Given that his carefully executed schedule had gone out the window, he felt unexpectedly relaxed, as if a tightly wound coil inside of him was unwinding. Watching his niece, whose tongue was caught between her teeth in fierce concentration, listening to Dannie and the baby, he felt a *feeling* unfurling inside him.

It couldn't possibly be yearning.

He had the life every man worked toward, success beyond his wildest dreams, the great car, the fabulous apartment, gorgeous women as abundant in his life as apples on a tree. Just as ready to be picked, too.

And yet all of that paled in comparison to a baby's

laughter and a little girl playing noughts and crosses. All that paled in comparison to the softness of a woman's lip beneath his thumb.

His sister, diabolical schemer that she was, would be thrilled by this turn of events.

What had he been thinking when he had touched Dannie's lip? When he had said to her with such ridiculous confidence, "I know something about you. I wonder if you even know it yourself."

The truth was he hadn't been thinking at all. Thinking belonged to that other world: of deals, successes, planning. That other world of accumulating more and more of the stuff.

The stuff that had failed to make him feel as full as he felt in this moment.

No, the truth was that thought had abandoned him when he touched her. Something deeper had temporarily possessed him.

He had seen her, not through his mind, but with his heart. He had seen her and *felt* the lie she had told him about the college professor. How could she even kid herself that she would ever be happy with a staid life?

From the second she had appeared in his office, she had presented the perfect picture of a nanny. Calm, controlled, prissy.

And from the beginning, he had seen something else. A gypsy soul, wanting to dance. That is what he knew about her that she did not know about herself.

That the right man—and probably not a college professor—was going to make her wild. Would make her toss out everything she thought she believed about herself. Under that costume of respectability she wore beat the drum of passion.

Stop, he told himself. *What is wrong with me?*

"I win," Susie said, carefully checking the placement of her crosses. "Again. You're dumb."

He stared at her, and then started to laugh. Yesterday he would have disagreed, probably argued, but today, since he had done one extremely dumb thing after another, starting with inviting them here, and ending with touching Dannie Springer's most delectable lip, he knew Susie was right.

"Let this be a lesson to you," he said. "Don't drop out of school."

"I don't even go to school yet," Susie informed him. "But when I do, I will love it. I will never ever stop going. I will go to school until I am one hundred."

That was precisely how he had felt about college. From the first day, he'd had a sense of arrival. This was where he belonged. He loved learning things. He loved playing football. He loved the girls, the parties, all of it.

And then, in his senior year, along came Sarah. They were "the" couple on campus. The cool ones. The ones everyone wanted to be. She played queen to his king. Looking back, something he rarely did, what they had called love seemed ridiculously superficial.

And in the end it had been. It had not stood up to the test life had thrown at it. Despite the fact they had taken every precaution, Sarah was pregnant.

Funny how, when he'd found out, he'd felt a rush, not of fear, but of excitement. He'd been willing to do whatever it took to give his baby a family, a good life.

Sarah had been stunned by his enthusiasm. "I'm not keeping it."

To this day, he could feel the bitterness, a force so real and so strong, he could nearly taste it on his tongue, when he remembered those words and the look on her face when she'd said them. "It."

He'd actually, briefly and desperately, considered keeping the baby himself. But reality had set in, and reluctantly he had gone along with Sarah. He'd stuck with her through the pregnancy and the birth.

It was a boy.

And then he'd made the mistake.

He'd held his son in his arms. He had felt the incredible surge of love and protectiveness. He had felt that moment of connection so intense that it seemed nothing else in his life but that moment had ever mattered.

He had known, *I was born to do this.*

But it was too late. He'd held his baby, his son, his light, for about five minutes. And then he'd let go. He had not met the adoptive parents.

Every other reality had faded after that. Nothing mattered to him, not school, not life, not anything at all. His grief was real and debilitating.

Sarah, on the other hand, had chosen not to see the baby, and she moved on eagerly, as if nothing had happened. He was part of what she left behind, but really, he had continued with her throughout the pregnancy out of a sense of honor and decency. But he had never forgiven her the "it."

He dropped out of college a month before he was supposed to graduate, packed a backpack, bought a ticket to anywhere. He'd traveled. Over time, he had come to dislike going to places with children. The sound of their laughter, their energy, reminded him of what he was supposed to be and was not.

When he'd come across Sarah's obituary a few years ago, killed in a ski accident in Switzerland, he had taken his lack of emotion as a sign he'd been a man unworthy of raising that child, anyway.

"Are you all right?"

He hadn't seen her come down the hallway, but now Dannie was standing in the doorway, Jake wrapped up in a pure white towel, only his round, rosy face peeking out, and a few spikes of dark hair.

Her blouse was soaked, showing off full, lush curves, and she looked as rosy as the baby.

Dannie looked at home with Jake, comfortable with her life. Why was she content to raise other people's children, when she looked as if she'd been born to hold freshly bathed babies of her own?

"All right?" he stammered, getting up from the couch. "Yeah. Of course."

But he wasn't. He was acutely aware that being around these kids, around Dannie, was making him feel things he had been content not to feel, revisit places he had been relieved to leave behind.

All he had to do was get through the rest of tonight. Tomorrow he'd figure out how to get rid of them, or maybe she would decide to go.

That would be best for everyone involved, and to hell with his sister's disapproval.

Though what if Mel cut her own vacation short? She needed it.

"Are you sure you're all right?" Dannie asked, frowning.

He pulled himself together, vowed he was not going back to the memory of holding his baby. He could not revisit the pain of letting that little guy go and survive. He couldn't.

He was going to focus totally and intensely on this moment.

He said, with forced cheer, "As all right as a guy can be whose been beaten at noughts and crosses by a four-year-old, thirty-three times in a row."

Because of his vow to focus on the moment, he became acutely aware of what it held. Dannie. Her hair was curling from the moistness, her cheeks were on fire, her blouse was sticking to her in all the right places.

He glanced at Susie, who was drawing a picture on the back of a used piece of paper, bored with the lack of competition.

Her picture showed a mommy, a daddy, a child suspended between their stick arms, big smiles on their oversize heads.

Despite his vow, the thought hit him like a slug. The world he had walked away from.

His son would have been three years older than his niece. Did he look like Susie? Worse, did he look like him?

He swore under his breath, running a hand through his hair.

"Mr. Cole!"

Susie snickered, delighted at the tone of voice he'd earned from her nanny.

"Sorry," he muttered, "Let's go get something to eat." His mind wandered to the thought of Danielle eating spaghetti. "There's a great Italian restaurant around the corner. Five-star."

Dannie rolled her eyes. "Have you ever taken a baby and a four-year-old to a restaurant?"

No, he wanted to scream at her, *because I walked away from that life.*

"So, we'll order pizza," he snapped.

"Pizza," Susie breathed, "my favorite."

"Pizza, small children and white leather. Hmm," Dannie said.

"I don't care about the goddamned leather!" he said.

He expected another reprimand, but she was looking at him closely, way too closely. Just as he had seen things about her that she might have been unaware of, he got the same feeling she saw things like that about him.

"Pizza sounds great," she said soothingly.

Glad to be able to move away from her, to take charge, even of something so simple, he went and got a menu out of the drawer by the phone.

"What kind?" he asked.

"Cheese," Susie told him.

"Just cheese?"

"I hate everything else."

"And what about you, Miss Pringy? Can we order an adult pizza for us? The works?"

"Does that include anchovies?"

"It does."

"I think I'm in heaven," she said.

He looked at her wet shirt, the beautiful swelling roundness of a real woman. He thought maybe he could be in heaven, too, if he let himself go there. But he wasn't going to.

She glanced down at where he was looking and turned bright, bright red. She waltzed across the space between them, and placed the towel-wrapped baby in his arms.

"I need to go put on something dry."

The baby was warm, the towel slightly damp. A smell tickled his nostrils: something so pure it stung his eyes.

He realized he'd had no idea what heaven was until that moment. He realized the survival of his world probably depended on getting these children, and her, back out of his life.

She wanted to go. He wanted her to go.

So what was the problem?

The problem was, he suspected, both of them knew what they wanted, and neither of them knew what they needed.

Dannie reemerged just as the pizza was brought to the front desk. She was dressed casually, in black yoga pants and a matching hoodie, which, he suspected, was intended to hide her assets, and which did nothing of the sort. Her figure, minus the ugly black skirt, was amazing, lush.

Her complexion was still rosy from the bath. Or she was blushing under his frank look.

He had to remember she was not the kind of woman he'd become accustomed to. Sophisticated. Experienced. *Expecting* male admiration.

"I'll just run down to the lobby and pick up the pizzas," he said. He glanced at her feet. They were bare, each toenail painted hot, exotic pink.

He turned away quickly. College professor, indeed! He'd *known* that's what she was hiding. What he hadn't known was how he, a man who spent time with women who were quite comfortable sunbathing topless, would find her naked toes so appealing.

Would have a sudden vision of chasing her through this apartment until she was breathless with laughter.

What would he do with her when he caught her?

He almost said the swear word out loud again. Instead he spun on his heel and took the elevator down to the lobby. He took his time getting back, cooling down, trying to talk sense to himself.

He might as well not have bothered. When he returned to the apartment, she was in the kitchen, scowling at his fridge.

"This is pathetic," she told him.

"I know." He brushed by her and set the pizza down. He tried not to look at her feet, snuck a peek, felt a funny rush, the kind he used to feel a long time ago, in high school, when Mary Beth McKay, two grades older than him, had smiled at him.

It was obviously a lust for the unobtainable.

She was studying his fridge. "No milk. No juice. No ketchup."

"Ketchup on pizza?" he asked.

"I'm just making a point."

"Which is?"

"Your fridge is empty." But it sounded more like she had said his life was empty.

Ridiculous. His life was full to overflowing. He worked twelve-hour days regularly and sixteen-hour days often. His life was filled with constant meetings, international travel, thousands of decisions that could be made only by him.

His life was million-dollar resorts and grand openings. The livelihoods of hundreds of people depended on him doing his work well. His life was flashy cars and flashier women, good restaurants, the fast lane. So why was he taking her disapproving inventory of his fridge as an indictment?

"Do you have peanut butter?" she asked, closing the fridge and opening a cabinet.

"On pizza?" he asked, a bit defensively. "Or are you making a point again?"

"Just thinking ahead," she said. "Breakfast, lunch." She took a sudden interest in a sack of gourmet coffee, took it out and read the label. "Until you make arrangements for us to go. Which you probably will, immediately after you've seen the children eat pizza."

"Give me some credit," he said, though of course that

was exactly what he wanted to do. Feed them pizza, talk to his assistant who made all his travel arrangements, get them gone. "Do you want wine? As you've seen, my beverage choices are limited."

"No, thank you," she said. *Primly.*

Good for her. A glass of wine would be the wrong thing to add to the mix. Especially for her. She'd probably get drunk on a whiff of the cork.

They had no high chair, so he held the baby on his lap and fed him tidbits of crust and cheese. She'd been right about the mess. Despite his efforts, Jake looked as if he'd been cooked inside the pizza.

His cell phone rang during dinner, Susie, her lips ringed in bright-red tomato sauce, scowled at him when he fished it out of his pocket.

"My Daddy doesn't answer his phone when we eat," she informed him.

"I'm not—" he swallowed *your daddy* at the warning look on Miss Pringy's face and shut his phone off "—going to, either, then."

When was the last time he'd done anything for approval? But there was something about the way those two females were beaming at him that made him think he'd better get back in the driver's seat. Soon.

Maybe after supper.

Immediately, whoever had tried his cell phone tried his landline. The answering machine picked up.

"Mr. Cole, it's Michael Baker. If you could get back to me as soon as—"

He practically tossed the tomato-sauce stained baby to Dannie. Susie, noticing the nanny's hands were full, decided she had to have a pencil, right then. She jumped up from her seat.

"No," Dannie called. "Susie, watch your hands."

But it was too late. A pizza handprint decorated his white sofa.

"Michael," he said to the owner of Moose Lake Lodge, "good to hear from you."

Susie was staring at the pizza smudge on his couch. She picked up the hem of her shirt and tried to wipe it off. Out of the corner of her eye, she saw Dannie moving toward her.

"I can fix it myself!" she screamed. "I didn't mean to."

"Just a sec," he put the phone close to his chest. "It's nothing," he told the little girl. "Forget it."

But Susie had decided it was something. Or something was something. She began to howl. Every time Dannie got near her, she darted away, screaming and spreading tomato sauce disaster. Dannie, encumbered by the baby, didn't have a hope of catching her.

"Sorry," he said into the phone. How could one little girl make it sound like World War III was occurring? How could one little girl be spreading a gallon of pizza sauce when he could have sworn the pizza contained a few tablespoons of it at the most? The baby, focused on his sister, started to cry, too. Loudly.

He was going to take the phone and disappear into his den with it, but somehow he couldn't leave Dannie to deal with this mess. He sighed.

Regretfully he said, "I'll have to call you back. A few minutes."

He went and took the baby back from Dannie, and sat on the couch, never mind that the baby was like a pizza sauce squeeze bottle. His shirt was pretty much toast, anyway.

"I want my mommy," Susie screamed. And then

again, as if he might have missed the message the first time. "I want my mommy!"

He didn't know where the words came from.

He said, "Of course you want your mommy, honey." He probably spoke with such sincerity because he dearly wanted her mommy right now, too. Here, not soaking up the sun in Kona, but right here, guiding him through this sticky situation.

Something in his voice, probably the sincerity, stopped Susie midhowl. She stared at him, and then she came and sat on the couch beside him.

He held his breath. The baby took his cue from his sister, quieted, watched her intently, deciding what his next move would be.

Susie leaned her head on Joshua's arm, sighed, popped her thumb in her mouth, and the room was suddenly silent except for the sound of her breathing, which became deeper and deeper. Her eyes fluttered, popped open and then fell shut again. This time they didn't reopen.

The baby regarded his sleeping sister, sighed, burrowed into his uncle's chest and slept, too.

"What was that?" Joshua whispered to Dannie.

"Two very tired kids," she said. "Susie has been acting up a bit ever since she heard her parents were planning a vacation that did not include her."

His fault. Sometimes even when a guy had the best of intentions, things went drastically wrong.

"I'm sorry," he said.

"I actually think it's good for them to experience a little separation now and then. It'll help them figure out the world doesn't end if Mel and Ryan go away."

"What now?" he said.

"Well, if you don't mind a few more pizza stains, I

suggest we just pop them into their beds. I can clean them up in the morning."

She held out her arms for the baby, who snored solidly through the transfer. Then he picked up his niece.

Who was just a little younger than his son would be.

And for the first time in his life, he put a child to bed. Tucked clean sheets around little Susie, so tiny in sleep. So vulnerable.

Who was tucking his son in tonight? Was the family who adopted him good enough? Kind? Decent? Fun-loving? People with old-fashioned values and virtues?

These were the thoughts he hated having, that he could outrun if he kept busy enough, if he never let himself get too tired or have too many drinks.

He left Susie's room as if his feet were on fire, bumped into Dannie in the hall outside her room where she had just settled Jake.

"Are you okay?" she asked.

"Oh. Sure. Fine. Why wouldn't I be okay?"

She regarded him with those huge blue eyes, the eyes that *expected* honesty, and he had the feeling if you spent enough time around someone like her, you wouldn't be able to keep the mask up that kept people out.

"You just look," she tilted her head, studied him, "as if you've seen a ghost."

A ghost. Not quite.

"A kind of a ghost," he said, forcing lightness into his tone. "I'm remembering what my home looked like before pizza."

She smiled. "I tried to warn you. I'll have it cleaned up in a jiff."

"No, we'll clean it up." In a jiff. Who said things

like that? Probably people with old-fashioned values and virtues.

A little later he tossed a damp dishcloth in the sink. He was a man who had trekked in Africa and spelunked in Peru. He had snorkeled off the coast of Kona and bungee jumped off the New River Gorge Bridge in West Virginia.

How was it something so simple—tracking down all the stains and moving all the items that were delicate and breakable—seemed oddly *fun,* as if he was fully engaged, fully alive for the first time in a long time?

Is that what a woman like her would make life like? Fun when you least expected it? Engaging without any trinkets or toys?

Was it time to find out?

"Do you want that glass of wine now?" he asked her, when she threw a tomato-sauce-covered rag into the sink beside his. "You're off duty, aren't you?"

"I'm never off duty," she said, but not sanctimoniously. Still, she was treating the offer with caution.

Which was smart. As his niece had pointed out to him earlier, he wasn't smart. Plain old dumb.

"It's more than a job for you, isn't it?" he asked, even though he knew he should just let her get away to do whatever nannies did once the kids were asleep.

She blinked, nodded, looked away and then said in a low, husky voice, filled with reverence, "I love them."

He felt her words as much as heard them. He felt the sacredness of her bond with his niece and nephew and knew how lucky his sister was to have found this woman.

But how had it happened that Dannie loved the children enough, apparently, to put her own college-professor dreams on hold, her own dreams for her life, her own ambitions?

He wanted to say something, and he didn't. He didn't want to know anymore about what she was giving up for other people's children.

"I think we should go tomorrow," she said, taking a deep breath. "I know your intentions are good, but the children really need to be someplace where they can romp. Someplace not so highly vulnerable to small hands, pizza sauce, the other daily catastrophes of all that energy."

Her eyes said, *I need to be away from you.*

And he needed to be away from her. *Fast.* Before he asked more questions that would reveal to him a depth of love that shone like water in a desert, beckoning, calling.

"I'll go make the arrangements," he said coolly. "I have to return a phone call, anyway."

"I'll say good-night, then, and talk to you in the morning."

He nodded, noticing she did not go back to her room but slipped out onto the terrace. He watched her for a moment as she stood looking out at darkness broken by lights reflecting in the water, stars winking on overhead. The sea breeze picked up her hair, and he yearned to stand beside her, immerse himself in one more simple moment with her.

Moments, he reminded himself harshly, that were bringing up memories and thoughts he didn't want to deal with.

Unaware she was being watched, she turned slightly. He saw her lift the chain from around her neck, open the locket and look at it.

There was no mistaking, from the look on her face,

that she had memories of her own to deal with. And he didn't want to know what they were!

He walked away from the open patio doors, and moments later he shut the door of his home office. He waited for the familiar surroundings to act as a balm on him, to draw him back into his own world.

But they didn't. He thought of her standing on the deck with the wind lifting her hair. The fact that he suddenly didn't want her to go was all the more reason to make the arrangements immediately. Thinking of them leaving filled him with relief. And regret. In nearly equal proportions.

He glanced at his watch. It had been less than eight hours since she had arrived in his office.

His whole world had been turned topsy-turvy. He had revisited a past he thought was well behind him. He was feeling uncertainties he didn't want to feel.

He needed the safety and comfort of his own world back.

He dialed Michael Baker's number.

Michael sounded less guarded than he had in the past, almost jovial.

"It sounded like you had your hands full," he said to Joshua.

"My niece and nephew are here for a visit."

"My wife and I were under the impression you didn't like children," Michael said.

"Don't believe everything you read," Joshua said carefully, sensing the slightest opening of a door that had been firmly closed.

"We had decided to just tell you no," Michael said. "Moose Lake Lodge is not at all like any of your other resorts."

Baker said that in a different way than he had said it

before, in a way that left Joshua thinking the door was open again. Just a little bit. Just enough for a shrewd salesman to slip his foot in.

"None of my resorts are ever anything like the other ones. They're all unique."

"This is a family resort. We're kind of hoping it always will be. Does that fit into your plans?"

To just say *no* would close the door irrevocably. He needed to meet with the Bakers. He needed them to trust and like him. He was certain he could make them see his vision for Moose Lake Lodge. Hikes. Canoe and kayak adventures. Rock climbing. The old retreat alive with activity and energy and excitement.

Whether that vision held children or not—it didn't—was not something Joshua felt he had to reveal right now.

"I could fly up tomorrow," Joshua said. "Just meet with me. I'm not quite the superficial cad the press makes me out to be. We'll talk. You don't have to agree to anything."

"You might be making the trip for nothing."

"I'm willing to risk it. I'd love to see it. It's a beautiful place in the pictures." He always did his homework. "Just being able to have a look at the lodge would be great. I understand your grandfather logged the trees for it and built it nearly single-handedly, with a block and tackle."

Hesitation. "Maybe we have been hasty in our judgments. We really don't know anything about you."

"No, you don't."

"It probably couldn't hurt to talk."

"That's how I feel."

"No lawyers, though. No team. Unless—"

"Unless what?"

"How long are your niece and nephew with you?"

A few more hours. "It hasn't quite been decided."

"Look, why don't you bring them up for a few days? Sally and I will get to know you, and a little about your plans for Moose Lake. The kids can enjoy the place. This is the first year we haven't booked in families, because we're trying to sell and we didn't want to disappoint anyone if it sold. We're missing the sound of kids."

It was an answer to a prayer, really, though how anybody could miss the sound that had just filled his apartment, Joshua wasn't quite sure.

Still, the situation was shaping up to be win-win. He could give the kids the vacation he'd promised his sister. He could woo the owners of the Moose Lake Lodge.

It occurred to him he should ask the nanny if she thought the trip would be in the kids' best interests, but she had a way of doing the unpredictable, and she probably had not the least bit of concern in forwarding his business concerns.

She might even see it as using the children.

Was he using the children?

The little devil that sat on every man's shoulder, that poked him with its pitchfork and clouded his motives, told him of course not!

Told him he did not have to consult the nanny. He was the children's uncle! Susie had wanted a camping toy. This was even better! A real camping experience.

"We'll be there tomorrow," he said smoothly. "I'll land at the strip beside the lake around one." He was juggling his schedule in his head. "Would two days be too much of an inconvenience?"

"Two days? You mean fly in one day, and leave the next? That's hardly worth the trip. Why don't you make it four?"

He couldn't make it four. His schedule was impossible to squeeze four days out of. On the other hand, if he stayed four days, he could send the kids home knowing their mother and father would be only a day or two behind them. He could claim he had given them a real holiday.

Plus he could have four whole days to convince the Bakers that their lodge would be safe in the hands of Sun.

"Four days," he agreed smoothly. "It sounds perfect."

"We'll be at the runway to pick you up."

Joshua put down the phone and regarded it thoughtfully. The usual excitement he felt as he moved closer to closing a deal was strangely absent. Somehow he thought maybe he had just created more problems than he had solved.

CHAPTER FOUR

DANNIE WOKE UP and stretched luxuriously. The bed was phenomenal, the linens absolutely decadent. She snuggled deeper under the down comforter, strangely content, until she remembered the day held nothing but uncertainty.

Had Joshua booked them tickets for home? Why did she feel sad instead of happy? Was she falling under the charm of all the *stuff?* The luxurious rooms, the million-dollar views?

Or was it his charm she was falling under? She thought of the smoke and jade green of those eyes, the deep self-assuredness in his voice, the way his thumb had felt, on her lip.

Whatever remained of her contentment evaporated. She felt, instead, a certain queasiness in her stomach, similar to what she felt on a roller coaster as it creaked upward toward its free fall back to earth. Was it anxiety or excitement or some diabolical mixture of both?

She touched her locket, reminding herself where these kinds of thought led. She was not even over Brent. How could she possibly be thinking about a roller-coaster ride with another man?

"Fantasy," she reminded herself sharply. "Whatever is going on in your thoughts with Joshua Cole is not real, even if he did touch your lip." Sadly, she suspected the same was true of her relationship with Brent.

Created largely in her own mind. Was that why Melanie had sometimes looked at her with ill-disguised sympathy, as Dannie had added yet another picture to her "possible honeymoon" file? Had everyone known, long before she had, that a good relationship was not conducted from three thousand miles away and oceans apart?

Normally she would have looked in her locket when she first woke up and allowed herself to feel a longing for what was not going to be, but today she just let it settle back in the hollow of her neck, unopened.

Jake gurgled from his crib, she sat up on her elbows and watched him pull himself to his feet, begin his joyous morning bounce.

The wonderful thing about children was they did not allow one to dwell for too long in the realm of mind, they called you out of those twisting, complicated caverns of thought. They invited you to dance with the now, to laugh, to enjoy every simple pleasure. Jake was especially good at this, gurgling at her, holding out his arms, practicing a new song.

"Ba, bab, da, da, boo, boo, doo."

She could not resist. It was the first morning in a long time that she did not feel like crying. Maybe she'd start opening that locket less often! In fact, Dannie threw back the covers, went and hefted Jake from his crib, danced around the room to his music. Her bedroom door burst open and in flew Susie in her Princess Tasonja pajamas, the new bear tucked under her arm. She made for the bed and began jumping.

Normally Dannie would not encourage jumping on the bed, but the children were on holidays. For another few hours, anyway. This might be as good as it got.

She threw her own caution to the wind, and baby in

arms, jumped on the bed with Susie. They jumped and then all fell down in a heap of helpless giggles.

The room grew very quiet. She realized they were no longer alone. Dannie, upside down in the bed, tilted her head just a little bit.

Joshua Cole stood in the doorway, a faint smile tickling his lips. Unlike them, he was not in pajamas, though dressed more casually than he had been yesterday, in crisp khaki hiking pants, a pressed shirt. He had obviously showered and shaved, his golden-brown hair was darkened by the damp, his face had that smooth look of a recent close encounter with a razor that made Dannie want to touch it, to see if it felt as soft as it looked.

He took a sip of steaming coffee, drawing her eyes to his lips. She wondered how he'd feel if she waltzed over and put her thumb on his lips!

She wondered how *she'd* feel.

Like an idiot, probably. World's Sexiest Bachelor could pull off such nonsense with panache. World's Frumpiest Nanny, not so much.

Naturally, he had caught her at her frumpy best.

Her pajamas were baggy red flannel trousers with a drawstring waistline. She had on a too-large man's white T-shirt that fit comfortably over her extra protective padding. Too late, she remembered the shirt claimed she'd gotten lei'd in Hawaii.

His eyes lingered there for a touch too long. "Have you been to Hawaii?" he asked.

"No, I'm afraid I haven't. This was a gift from a friend."

"Ah. You'd love it there."

How would you know what I'd love? she thought grumpily. No two worlds had probably ever been further apart than his and hers. However, if Hawaii was even a fraction as gorgeous as this apartment, he was probably right.

"The air there smells like your perfume," he said softly.

She went very still. It was a line, obviously. The lame line of a guy whose lame lines had scored him lots of points with women a lot more sophisticated than her.

"I'm not wearing perfume," she said, letting the grumpiness out.

"Really?" He looked genuinely astounded, as if he'd meant it about Hawaii smelling like her.

She resisted an impulse to give her armpits a quick, subtle sniff. And then she realized that she was having this intimate conversation while lying upside down with a baby on her tummy.

She scrambled to sitting, juggling Jake. Her hair was flying all over the place, hissing with static, and she ran a self-conscious hand through it, trying to tame it.

He took another sip of his coffee. "Maybe it's your hair that made me think of Hawaii."

The flattery was making her flustered. A different woman, which she suddenly found herself wishing she was, would know how to respond to that. A different woman might giggle and blink her eyes and talk about skinny-dipping in the warm waters of the Pacific. With him.

Even *thinking* about skinny-dipping made her blush. Thinking of skinny-dipping anywhere in the vicinity of him made her feel as if she should go to confession. And she wasn't even Catholic!

Besides, she was sworn off men. And romance. And most certainly off skinny-dipping! Though it did seem like a bit of a shame to swear off something before even trying it.

Having thoroughly rattled her, he smiled with cat-that-got-the-cream satisfaction.

"I'm having some breakfast sent up," he said. "Fruit, yogurt. Any other requests?"

"I have to have Huggi Bears for breakfast," Susie told him.

"She doesn't," Dannie said firmly. "Yogurt is just fine. If you'll excuse us for a minute, I'll make myself presentable. And the children. Of course."

"I thought you were quite presentable. Don't feel you have to dress for breakfast. I want you to feel at home here."

"Why? We're leaving."

"Until you do," he said smoothly, and then shut the door quietly and left them alone.

A few minutes later she had the children washed and dressed. Dannie actually found herself lamenting the lack of choice in the clothing she had brought, but wore the nicest things she had packed, a pinstripe navy blue blazer and matching slacks. Like most of her clothes, the slacks were protesting her weight gain and were just a touch too snug. Thankfully the blazer covered the worst of it! The outfit was decidedly businesslike, almost in defiance of his invitation to make themselves at home. At the last moment she added a hint of makeup, ridiculously grateful there was some in her bag left over from her last trip.

He was being particularly charming this morning. That would come naturally to him. She needn't be flattered by it. Or worse, wonder what he wanted. She had nothing a man like that would want, even with the addition of mascara!

When she came out, the breakfast bar had been set up with platters of fresh fruit and croissants. Several child-size boxes of cereal, including Huggi Bears were available. There were choices of milk, chocolate milk or juice, the coffee smelled absolutely heavenly.

What would it be like to live like this? To just snap your fingers and have a feast including Huggi Bears delivered instantly?

It would make a person spoiled rotten, she thought. Emphasis on the *rotten.*

Or make them feel as if they had died and gone to heaven, she thought as she took a sip of the coffee. It was even richer and more satisfying than it had smelled.

It renewed her commitment to taking the children home. Before she was spoiled for real life. Before she started wanting and expecting luxuries she was never going to have.

"Let's take it out on the terrace," he suggested. He took the baby from her with more ease than she would have expected after just one day. When she joined him outside, he was spooning yogurt into Jake who was co-operatively opening his mouth like a baby bird waiting for a worm.

Susie had chosen one of the tiny boxes of Huggi Bears. It was the annoying kind that claimed it could be used as a bowl, but never quite worked properly. Still, Susie insisted she had to have it out of the box, and by the time Dannie had it opened along all the dotted lines and had poured the milk, she was cursing Joshua's charm and good looks, which made her feel as clumsy as if she were trying to open the box with elephants' feet instead of hands!

She made herself focus on the view, which was spectacular in the early morning light. The sea breeze was fresh and scented. She wondered what Hawaii smelled like.

She ordered herself just to enjoy this place and this moment, but it proved to be impossible. She needed to know what happened next. It was just her nature.

"So, may I ask what arrangements you've made for the children and me?" The thought of traveling again so soon exhausted her. The thought of staying here with him was terrifying.

It gave new meaning to being caught between a rock and a hard place.

"Well," he said, and smiled widely, "I have a surprise for you."

Danielle was one of those people who did not care much for surprises. It was part of being the kind of person who liked to know what was going to happen next.

"I'm flying out to look at a property for a few days. It's called the Moose Lake Lodge. Susie mentioned camping, so I thought she'd love it. All of us. A vacation in the British Columbia wilderness."

"We're going camping?" Susie breathed. "I love camping!"

"You don't know the first thing about camping," Dannie said.

"I do so!"

She was staring at Joshua with a growing feeling of anger. So this was why he'd been so charming this morning! Smelled like Hawaii, indeed. Her hair made him think of Hawaii. Sure it did!

"Are you telling me or consulting me?" she asked dangerously.

He pondered that for a moment. "I'd really like for you to come."

It was an evasive answer. It meant he hadn't booked them tickets home.

"The real question is *why* would you want to drag two children and a nanny along on a business trip?"

"It's not strictly business."

She raised an eyebrow and waited.

"You know as well as I do Melanie will kill me if I send the kids home after I promised her I'd give them a holiday."

It still wasn't the whole truth. She could feel it.

"Say yes," Susie said, slipping her hand into Dannie's and blinking at her with her most adorable expression. "Please say yes. Camping."

Everything in her screamed no.

Except for the part of her that screamed yes.

The part of her that *begged* her to, just once, say yes to the unexpected. Just once to not know what the day held. To not have a clue. To just once embrace a surprise instead of rejecting it.

To leave the safe haven of her predictable, controlled world.

What had her controlled world given her so far? Despite her best efforts, she had ended up with her heart broken, anyway.

"What do you mean, *you're* flying?" she asked, looking for a way to ease into accepting, not wanting to say an out-and-out yes as if the promise of an adventure was more than poor, boring her could refuse.

Not wanting to appear like a staid nanny who'd been offered a rare chance to be spontaneous.

"I have a pilot's license," he said. "I fly my own plane."

There was that feeling in her stomach again, of a roller coaster chugging up the steep incline. "Is that safe?" she demanded.

"More safe than getting in your car every day," he

said. "Did you know that you have more chance of dying in your own bathroom than you do of dying on an airplane?"

Who could argue with something like that? Who could ever look at their own bathroom in the same way after hearing something like that?

That was the problem with a man like Joshua Cole. He could turn everything around: make what had always seemed safe appear to be the most dangerous thing of all.

For wasn't the most dangerous thing of all to have died without ever having lived? Wasn't the most dangerous thing to move through life as if on automatic pilot, not challenged, not thrilled, not engaged?

Engaged. She hated that word with its multitude of meanings. She thought she had been engaged. For the first time she did not touch her locket when she thought about it.

She took a deep breath, squeezed Susie's hand. "All right," she said. "When would you like us to be ready?"

DANNIE HAD NEVER flown in a small plane before. Up until getting on the plane, her stomach had been in knots about it. But watching Joshua conduct extremely precise preflight checks on the aircraft calmed her. The man radiated confidence, ease, certainty of his own abilities.

The feeling of calm increased as she settled the children, Jake in his car seat, and then she took the passenger seat right beside Joshua.

She loved the look on his face as he got ready to fly, intensely focused and relaxed at the very same time. He had the air of a man a person could trust with their life, which of course was exactly what she was doing.

The level of trust surprised her. At this time yesterday, getting off an airplane after having read about him, she had been prepared to dislike him. When he hadn't arrived at the airport, she had upgraded to intense dislike.

But after seeing him in his own environment, and now in charge of this plane, she realized the mix-up at the airport probably had been Melanie's. Joshua gave the impression of a man who took everything he did seriously and did everything he did well.

Still, to go from being prepared to dislike someone to feeling this kind of trust in less than twenty-four hours might not be a good thing. She might be falling under his legendary, lethal charm, just like everyone else.

Of course she was! Why else had she agreed to fly off into the unknown with a man who was, well, unknown?

She did touch her locket then, a reminder that even the known could become unknown, even the predictable could fail.

Before she really had time to prepare herself, the plane was rumbling along the airstrip and then it was lifting, leaving the bonds of gravity, taking flight.

Dannie was surprised, and pleasantly so, to discover she liked small airplanes better than big ones. She could watch her pilot's face, she could feel his energy, he did not feel unknown at all. In fact, she had a sense of knowing him deeply as she watched his confident hands on the controls, as she studied his face.

He glanced at her, suddenly, and grinned.

For a second he was that boy she had seen in the photo on the beach, full of mischief and delight in life. For a second he was that football player in the other photo, confident, sure of his ability to tackle whatever the world threw at him.

Something had changed him since those photos were taken. She had not been aware he carried a burden until she saw it fall away as they soared into the infinite blue of the sky.

"You love this," she guessed.

"It's the best," he said, and returned his attention to what he was doing. And she turned hers to the world he had opened up for her. A world of such freedom and beauty it could hardly be imagined. Joshua pointed out landmarks to her, explained some of the simpler things he was doing.

An hour or so later he circled a lake, the water dark denim blue, lovely cabins on spacious tree-filled lots encircling it. Wharves reached out on the water. Except for the fact it was too early in the year for people to be here, it looked like a poster for a perfect summer. Still, she was actually sorry when the flight was over.

A car waited for them at the end of the runway, and introductions were made. Sally and Michael Baker were an older couple, the lines of living outdoors deeply etched in both their faces. They were unpretentious, dressed casually in jeans and lumber jackets. Dannie liked them immediately.

And she liked it that Joshua did not introduce her as a nanny, but said instead that his sister had sent her along because she didn't trust him completely with her children!

The Bakers had that forthright and friendly way about them that made children feel instantly comfortable. Jake went into Sally's arms eagerly.

"I think he's been waiting all his short life to have a grandmother," Joshua said.

"He doesn't have a grandmother?" Sally asked, appalled.

"The kids paternal grandparents are in Australia. My mom and dad were killed in an accident when I was growing up."

Melanie had told Dannie her parents were gone, but never the circumstances. Dannie had assumed they were older, and that they had died of natural causes. Now she wondered if that was the burden he carried, and she also noted how quickly he had revealed that to the Bakers.

There was a great deal to know about this man. But to know it was to invite trouble. Because even knowing that he'd lost his parents when he was young caused a growing softness toward him.

"That must have been very hard," Sally clucked, her brown eyes so genuinely full of concern.

"Probably harder on my sister than me," he said. "She was older."

Suddenly Dannie saw Melanie's attitude toward her brother, as if he was a kid, instead of a very successful man, in a totally different light.

Michael packed their things in the back of an SUV, and they drove toward the lake. Soon they were on a beautiful road that wound around the water, trees on one side, the lake, sparkling with light, on the other.

Then they came into a clearing. A beautiful, ancient log lodge was facing the lake at one end of it, gorgeous lawns and flower beds sweeping down to the sandy shores. Scattered in on the hill behind it were tiny log cabins of about the same vintage.

"It's beautiful," Dannie breathed. More than beautiful. Somehow this place captured a feeling: summer laughter, campfires, water games, children playing tag in the twilight.

A children's playground was on part of the huge

expanse of lawn before the beach, and Susie began squirming as soon as she saw it.

"Is that a tree fort?" she demanded. "I want to play!"

Sally laughed. "Of course you want to play. You've been cooped up in a plane. Why don't I watch the kids at the park, while Michael helps you two get settled?"

Dannie expected some kind of protest from Susie, but there was none. As soon as the car door opened, she bolted for the playground.

Michael and Joshua unloaded their bags, and they followed Michael up a lovely wooden boardwalk that started behind the main lodge, wound through whispering aspens, spruce and fur. The smell alone, sweet, pure, tangy, nearly took Dannie's breath away. The boardwalk came to a series of stone stairs set in the side of the hill, and at the top of that was the first of about a dozen cabins that looked through the trees to the glittering surface of the lake.

The cabin had a name burned on a wooden plaque that hung above the stairs to the porch.

Angel's Rest.

There were a pair of rocking chairs on the covered, screened-in front porch. The logs and flooring were gray with age, the chinking and the trim around the paned window was painted white. A window box was sadly empty. Dannie could imagine bright red geraniums blooming there. A worn carpet in front of a screen door said Welcome.

Michael opened the door, which squeaked outrageously and somehow only added to the rustic charm. He set their bags inside.

It occurred to her she and Joshua were staying together, under the same roof. Why was it different from how staying under the same roof had been last night?

The cabin was smaller, for one thing, everything about it more intimate than the posh interior of Joshua's apartment. This was a space that was real. The decades of laughter, of family, soaked right into the cozy atmosphere.

"This is our biggest cabin," Michael said. "There's two bedrooms down and the loft up. Sometimes the kids sleep on the porch on hot nights, though it's not quite warm enough for that, yet."

"How wonderful there's a place left in the world where it's safe enough for the kids to sleep out on an unlocked porch," Dannie said.

Michael nodded. "My daughter and her kids usually take it for the whole summer, but—" He stopped abruptly and cleared his throat. "Dinner is at the main lodge. See you there around six. There's always snacks available in the kitchen if you need something before then."

And then he closed the door and left them.

Alone.

The cabin was more than quaint, it was as if it was a painting entitled *Home*. There were colorful Finnish rag rugs over plank flooring. An old couch, with large faded cabbage roses on the upholstery, dominated the living room decor. Inside, where the logs had not been exposed to the weather, they were golden, glowing with age and warmth. A river rock fireplace, the face blackened from use, had two rocking chairs painted bright sunshine yellow, in front of it.

Maybe it was that feeling of home that made her venture into very personal territory. Standing in this place, with him, made her feel connected to him, as if all the warmth and love of the families who had gathered in this place had infused it with a spirit of caring.

"I can't believe I've worked for Melanie for months and didn't know about your parents. I knew they had passed, but I didn't know the circumstances."

"It was a car accident. She doesn't talk about it."

"Do you?"

He shrugged. "We aren't really talkers in our family."

"Doers," she guessed.

"You got it." Without apology, almost with warning. No sympathy allowed. Don't go there. To prove the point, he began exploring the cabin, and she could tell his assessment of the place was somewhat clinical, as if he was deliberately closing himself off to the whispers of its charm.

He was studying the window casings, which were showing slight signs of rot, scowling at the floors that looked decidedly splintery. He went up the stairs to the loft.

"I'll take this room," he called.

She knew she shouldn't go up there, but she did. She went and stood behind him. The loft room was massive. The stone chimney from downstairs continued up the far wall, and there was another fireplace. A huge four-poster bed, antique, with a hand-crafted quilt took up the greater part of the space.

He was looking under the bed.

"Boogeymen?" she asked.

He hit his head pulling out from under the bed, surprised that she was up here. "Mice."

The shabby romance of the place was obviously lost on him. "And?"

"Mouse free. Or cleaned recently."

She was afraid of mice. He was afraid of caring. Maybe it was time for at least one of them to confront their fears.

"Joshua, I'm sorry about your parents. That must have been incredibly hard on you." She said it even though he had let her know it was off-limits.

He went over and opened a closet door, peered in. She had a feeling he was already making architectural drawings, plans, notes.

"Thanks," he said. "It was a long time ago."

"What are your plans for this place?" she said, trying to respect his obvious desire not to go there. "If you acquire it?"

"I want to turn it into a Sun resort. So that means completely revamping the interiors of these cabins, if we kept them at all. Think posh hunting lodge, deep, distressed leather furniture, a bar, good art, bearskin rugs."

She actually felt a sense of loss when he said that.

"For activities," he continued, "overnight camping trips, rock climbing, hiking, a row of jet skis tied to a new wharf."

She winced at that.

"Five-star dining in the main lodge, a lounge, some of the cabins with their own hot tubs."

"Adult only?" She felt her heart sinking. How could he be so indifferent to what this place was meant to be?

"That's what we do."

"What a shame. This place is crying for families. It feels so empty without them."

"Well, that's not what Sun does."

"Is it because of your own family?" she asked softly, having to say it, even if it did cross the boundaries in his eyes. "Is that why you cater to people who don't have families around them? Because it's too painful for you to go there?"

He stopped, came out of the closet, looked at her with

deep irritation. "I don't need to be psychoanalyzed. You sound like my sister."

She had hit a nerve. She saw that. And she saw that he was right. Staying at his place, seeing him with the children, riding in his airplane, being alone in this cabin with him had all created a false sense of intimacy.

She was the nanny, the employee. She had no right to probe into his personal life. She had no right to think of him on a personal level.

But she already was! How did you backpedal from that?

"I'm sorry, Mr. Cole," she said stiffly.

The remote look left his face immediately. He crossed the room to her, she was aware how much taller he was when he looked down at her.

"Hey, I didn't mean to hurt your feelings."

"You didn't."

"Yes, I did. I can see it in your face."

"I'm sure you're imagining things."

"No, I'm not."

"Now you're being too personal, Mr. Cole."

He stared at her. "Are we having a fight?"

"I think so." Though after what she'd grown up with, this wouldn't even qualify as a squabble.

He started to laugh, and then surprisingly so did she, and the sudden tension between them dissipated, only to be replaced with a different kind of tension. Hot and aware. She could feel his breath on her cheek.

"Please don't call me Mr. Cole again."

"All right, Joshua."

"Just for the record, I didn't start running adult only resorts because of my parents." For a moment there was a pain so great in his eyes she thought they would both drown in it.

It seemed like the most reasonable thing in the world to reach out and touch his cheek, to cup his jawline in her palm and to rest her fingertips along the hard plain of his cheekbones.

His cheek was beginning to be ever so slightly whisker roughened. His skin felt unexpectedly sensual, cool and taut, beneath the palm of her hand.

He leaned toward her. For a stunning moment she thought he was going to tell her something. Something important. Maybe even the most important thing about him.

And then, the veil came down in his eyes, and something dangerous stirred in that jade surface. He was going to kiss her. She knew she should pull away, but she was helpless to do so. And then he reeled back as if he had received an electric shock, looked embarrassed, turned back to his inspection of the cabin.

She was way too aware of that big bed in this room, of the fireplace, of the pure and rugged romance of it.

"Uncle! Dannie!" Susie burst through the door downstairs. "Isn't this place the best? The best ever? You have to come see the tree fort. Sally said maybe I could sleep in it. Do you want to sleep in it with me?"

Now, that would be so much better than sleeping in here, with him. Even though she would be in a different room, this loft space was so open to the rest of the cabin below it. She would be able to imagine him here even as she slept in another room. She might even be pulled here, in the darkest night, when the heart spoke instead of the head.

Her eyes went once more to the bed. She was aware that Joshua had stopped and was watching her.

"Where are you?" Susie called.

"Up here. But coming down." Away from temptation.

Dannie ran down the steps, relieved by the distraction of the children.

Her job, she reminded herself sternly, her priority.

"Do you want to pick a bedroom?' she asked Susie.

"No, I want to *camp* in the tree fort. It's the best," Susie said, hugging herself and turning in delirious circles. "Moose Lake Lodge is the best!"

"The best," Dannie agreed halfheartedly, knowing the future of Moose Lake Lodge rested with someone who had quite a different vision of what *best* was.

But why did she feel that underneath that exterior of a cool, professional, hard-hearted businessman, Joshua was something quite different?

"I have to change," Dannie said, suddenly aware her suit was hopelessly wrong for this place. Luckily, in anticipation of a holiday, she had packed some casual slacks and T's. "Pick a room," she told Susie, "just in case you don't like camping in the tree fort."

Susie rolled her eyes at that impossibility but picked out a room. Then Dannie grabbed her suitcase and ducked into the other one.

Her mind went to that encounter with Joshua in the loft. If that kiss had been completed would she know who Joshua *really* was? Or would she be more confused than ever?

She saw herself in the old, faintly warped mirror. The first thing she noticed was not the extra ten or fifteen pounds of sadness that she carried, but the locket winking at her neck.

She touched it, then on impulse took it off and tucked it into the pocket of her suitcase. She told herself the gesture had no meaning. The locket was just too delicate for this kind of excursion.

Unwelcome, the thought blasted through her mind

that she was also way too delicate for this—still fragile, still hurting.

And despite that, she would have kissed him if he had not pulled away! She put on a fresh pair of yoga pants and a matching T-shirt, regarded her reflection and was a little surprised to feel voluptuous rather than fat.

That assessment should have convinced her to put the locket back on, a constant reminder of the pain of engaging.

But she didn't. She left it right where it was.

CHAPTER FIVE

THE THING JOSHUA Cole loved about flying was that it was a world accessed only through absolute control, through a precision of thought and through self-discipline that only other pilots fully understood. Flying gave a sense of absolute freedom, but only after the strictest set of rules had been adhered to.

Business was much the same way. Hard work, discipline, precision of thought, all led to a predictable end result, a tremendous feeling of satisfaction, of accomplishment.

But relationships—that was a different territory altogether. They never seemed to unfold with anything like predictability. There was no hard-and-fast set of rules to follow to keep you out of trouble. No matter what you did, the safety net was simply not there.

Take the nanny, for instance. Not that he was having a relationship with her. But a man could become as enraptured by the blue of her eyes as he was held captive by the call of the sky.

He had seen something in her when they flew that he had glimpsed, too, when she had come out of her bedroom at his apartment, with Jake wrapped in that pure white towel, her blouse sticking to her, the laughter still shining in her eyes. Dannie Springer had a rare ability to experience wonder, to lose herself in the moment.

Something about her contradictions, stern and playful, pragmatic and sensitive, made him feel vulnerable. And off course. And it seemed the harder he tried to exert his control over the situation the more off course he became.

For instance, when he could feel her probing the tragedy of his parents' deaths, he had done what he always did: erected the wall.

But the fact that he had hurt her, while trying to protect himself, had knocked that wall back down as if it was constructed of paper and Popsicle sticks, not brick and mortar and steel, not any of the impenetrable materials he had always assumed it was constructed of.

In the blink of an eye, in as long as it took to draw a breath, he had gone from trying to push her away to very nearly telling her his deepest truth. He'd almost told her about his son. He had never told anyone about that. Not even his sister. To nearly confide in a woman who was virtually a stranger, despite the light of wonder that had turned her eyes to turquoise jewels while they flew, was humbling. He prided himself on control.

And it had gone from bad to worse, from humbling to humiliating. Because that flash moment of vulnerability had made him desperate to change the subject.

And he had almost done so. With his lips.

And though he had backed away at exactly the right moment, what he felt wasn't self-congratulatory smugness at his great discipline. No, he felt regret.

That he hadn't tasted the fullness of those lips, even if his motives had been all wrong.

"Just to get it over with," he muttered out loud.

He heard her come back into the main room below him and was drawn to the railing that overlooked it.

She had changed into flared, stretchy pants that rode

low on the womanly curves of her hips. She was wearing sandals that showed off those adorable toes.

Just to get it over with? Who was he kidding? He suspected a person never got over a woman like Dannie, especially if he made the mistake of tasting her, touching his lips to the cool fullness of hers. If he ever got tired of her lips—fat chance—there would be her delectable little toes to explore. And her ears. And her hair, and her eyes.

Just like a baby, wrapped in a blue blanket, those eyes of hers, turquoise and haunting, would find their way into his mind for a long, long time after she was the merest of memories.

Only, though, if he took it to the next level. Which *he* wasn't going to. No more leaning toward her, no more even thinking of sharing his deepest secrets with her.

He barely knew her.

She was his niece and nephew's nanny. Getting to know her on a different level wouldn't even be appropriate. There were things that were extremely attractive about her. So what? He'd been around a lot of very attractive women. And he'd successfully avoided entanglement with them all.

Of course, with all those others he had the whole bag of tricks that money could buy to give the illusion of involvement, without ever really investing anything. It had been a happy arrangement in every case, the women delighted with his superficial offerings, he delighted with the emotional distance he maintained.

Dannie Springer would ask more of him, expect more, deserve more. Which was why it was such a good thing he had pulled back from the temptation of her lips at exactly the right moment!

He hauled his bag up to the loft, changed into more-casual clothes and then went back down the stairs and outside without bothering to unpack. He paused for a moment on the porch, drinking it in.

The quiet, the forest smells, the lap of waves on the beach stilled his thoughts. There was an island in the lake, heavily timbered, a tiny cabin visible on the shore. It was a million-dollar view.

Which was about what it was going to take—a million dollars—take or give a few hundred thousand, to bring Moose Lake Lodge up to the Sun standard.

He had seen in Dannie's face that his plans appalled her. But she was clearly ruled by emotion, rather than a good sense of business.

Maybe her emotion was influencing him, because preserving these old structures would be more costly than burning them to the ground and starting again. And yet he wanted to preserve them, refurbish them, keep some of that character and solidness.

The playground would have to go, though. He could picture an outdoor bar there, lounge chairs scattered around it. A heated pool and a hot tub would lengthen the seasons that the resort could be used. A helicopter landing pad would be good, too.

And then the squeal of Susie, floating up from the playground he wanted to destroy, was followed by the laughter of Dannie. He looked toward the playground. He could clearly see the nanny was immersing herself in the moment again, chasing Susie up the ladder into the tree fort, those long legs strong and nimble. Susie burst out the other side of the fort and slid back to the ground, Dannie didn't even hesitate, sliding behind his niece.

If he knew women with more to offer than her, he suddenly couldn't think of one. He could not think of one woman he knew who would be so comfortable, so happy, flying down a children's slide!

A little distance away from Dannie and Susie, Sally was sitting on a bench with Jake at her feet. He had a little shovel in his hand, and was engrossed in filling a pail with fine sand.

Joshua wondered how he was going to tear the playground down now. Without feeling the pang of this memory. That was the problem with emotion. He should have stuck to business. He should never have brought the children here. Of course, without the children he doubted he would have been invited here himself.

For a moment, watching the activity at the playground, Joshua felt acutely the loss of his parents and the kind of moment they would never share with him. He felt his vision blurring as he looked at the scene, listened to the shouts of laughter.

He missed them, maybe more than he had allowed himself to miss them since they had died. He remembered moments like the one below him: days at the beach in particular, endless days of carefree laughter and sunshine, sand and water.

He had a moment of clarity that felt like a punch to his solar plexus.

I wanted to keep my son so I could feel that way again. A sense of family. Of belonging. Of love.

The thought had lived somewhere deep within him, waiting for this exact moment of vulnerability to burst into his consciousness. When he had given up his son, he had given up that dream. Put it behind him. Shut the door on it. Tried to fill that empty place with other things.

And not until this very moment was he aware of how badly he had failed. He snorted with self-derision,

He was one of the world's most successful men. How could he see himself as a failure?

His sister knew what he really was.

And so did he. A man who had lost something of himself.

He shook off the unwanted moment of introspection. Though he had planned to move away from the group at the playground and go in search of Michael to begin to discuss business, he found himself moving toward them instead.

With something to prove.

Just like kissing Dannie might get it out of his system, might prove the fantasy was much more delightful than the reality could ever be, so was that scene down there.

That happy little scene was just begging to be seen with the filters removed: the baby stinking, Susie cranky and demanding.

Sally looked up and smiled at him as he crossed the lawn toward them. "Glad you arrived," she said. "I was just going to see about dinner."

And then she got up and strolled away, leaving him with Jake. After a moment considering his options, Joshua sat down on the ground beside his nephew. Just as he'd suspected: reality was cold and gritty, not comfortable at all.

And then he looked through a plastic tub of toys, found another shovel and helped Jake fill a bucket.

Just as he'd suspected: boring.

And then he tipped the bucket over and saw the beginning of a sand castle. Jake took his little shovel and smashed it, chortling with glee.

Susie arrived, breathless. "Are you making something?"

Dannie's long length of leg moved into his range of vision. She was hanging back just a bit. Sensing, just as he did, that something dangerous was brewing here.

He looked up at her. He didn't know why he noticed, but the locket was missing. Just in case he hadn't already figured out something dangerous was brewing here.

He handed her a bucket, as if he was project manager on a huge construction site. *Thatta boy,* he congratulated himself. *Take charge.* "Do you and Susie want to haul up some water from the lake? We'll make a sand castle."

Before he knew it, he wasn't bored, but he was still plenty uncomfortable. Take charge? Working this closely with Dannie, he was finding it hard to even take a breath, he was so aware of her! She kept casting quick glances at him, too. It was so junior high! Building a Popsicle bridge for the science fair with the girl you had a secret crush on!

Not that he had a secret crush on her!

The castle was taking shape, multiturreted, Dannie carefully carving windows in the wet sand, shaping the walls of the turrets.

She had the cutest way of catching her tongue between her teeth as she concentrated. Her hair kept falling forward, and she kept shoving it impatiently back. It made him wonder what his fingers would feel like in her hair, a thought he quickly dismissed in favor of helping Susie build the moat and defending the castle from Jake's happy efforts to smash it with his shovel.

Before he knew it, his discomfort had disappeared, and happiness, that sneakiest of human emotions, had slipped around them, obscuring all else. It was as if fog, turned golden by morning sun, had wrapped them in a world of their own. Before he knew it, he was laughing.

And Dannie was laughing with him, and then Susie was in his arms with her thumb in her mouth, all wet and dirty and sandy, and the baby smelled bad, and reality was strangely and wonderfully better than any fantasy he had ever harbored.

Something in him let go, he put business on the back burner. For some reason, though he was undeserving of it, he had been given this gift. A few days to spend with his niece and nephew in one of the most beautiful places he had ever seen or been.

A few days to spend with a woman who intrigued him.

By the next day, he and Dannie settled into a routine that felt decidedly domestic. It should have felt awkward playing that role with her, but it didn't. It felt just like walking into the cottage Angel's Rest had felt, like coming home.

Sally prepared the most wonderful food he had ever eaten: old-fashioned food, stew and buns for supper the evening before, biscuits and jam for breakfast, thick sandwiches on homemade bread for lunch.

The lodge, magnificently constructed, always smelled of bread rising and baking and of fresh-brewed coffee. In the chill of the evening last night, there had been a fire going, children's board games and toys spread out on the floor in front of it.

The second day unfolded in endless spring sunshine. They played in the sand, they went on a nature walk, he rowed the kids around in the rowboat. When the kids settled in for their afternoon naps, he and Dannie sat on the front porch of Angel's Rest.

"Kids are exhausting," he told her, settling back in

his chair, glad to be still, looking at the view of the little cabin on the island. "I need a nap more than them."

"You are doing a great job of being an uncle. World's Best Builder of Sand Castles."

Somehow that meant more to him than being bestowed with the title of World's Sexiest Bachelor.

"Thanks. You're doing a great job of...being yourself." That made her blush. He liked it. He decided to make her blush more. "World's Best Set of Toes."

"You're being silly," she said, and tried to hide her naked toes behind her shapely calves.

Today she was wearing sawed-off pants he thought were called capris. They hugged her delicious curves in the most delightful way.

"I know. Imagine that. Come on. Be a sport. Give me a peek of those toes."

She hesitated, took her foot out from behind her leg, and wiggled her toes at him.

He laughed at her daring, and then so did she. He thought it would be easy to make it a mission to make her laugh...and blush.

"I love the view from here," Dannie told him, hugging herself, tucking her toes back under her chair. "Especially that cabin. If I ever had a honeymoon, that's where." She broke off, blushing wildly.

If there was one thing a guy as devoted to being single as he was did not ever discuss it was weddings. Or honeymoons. But his love of seeing her blush got the better of him.

"What do you mean *if?*" he teased her. "If ever toes were made to fit a glass slipper, it's those ones. Some guy is going to fall for your feet, and at your feet, and marry you. You'll spend your whole honeymoon getting chased around with him trying to get a nibble of them. I'm surprised it hasn't happened already."

Even though the teasing worked, her cheeks staining to the color of crushed raspberries, the thought of some lucky guy chasing her around made him feel miserable.

"Oh," she said, her voice strangled, even as she tried to act casual, "I've given up Cinderella dreams. Men are mostly cads in sheep's clothing."

Her attempt at being casual missed, and then she touched her neck, where the locket used to be.

"How right you are," he said, but he felt very sorry about it, and he knew he was exactly the wrong guy to correct her misconceptions. Who had lured her and the kids here veiling another motive, after all?

Who looked at her lips and her toes and her hair and fought an increasingly hard battle not to steal a little taste, no matter what the consequences?

He knew he shouldn't ask. But he did, anyway. "Did he hurt you badly?"

"Who?" she croaked, wide-eyed.

He sighed. "The professor."

Her hand dropped away from her neck. "I'm embarrassed to be so transparent."

"Good. I hope it makes you blush again. Did he?"

She contemplated that for a moment and then said quietly, "No, I hurt myself."

But he doubted if that was completely true, and he felt a sudden murderous desire to meet the jerk that had hurt her. And another desire to see if he could chase the sudden sadness from her eyes. With his lips.

But something kept him from giving in to the little devil that sat on his shoulder, prodding him with the proverbial pitchfork and saying with increasing force and frequency, *Kiss her. No one will get hurt.*

The thought was in such contrast to the innocence of playing tag in the trees until they were breathless with laughter, in such contrast to the wholesome fun of wading and splashing along the shorelines of a lake too cold yet to swim in.

He was not looking forward to another night in the cabin with her, once the children were in bed, but the angel that sat on her shoulder must have been stronger than the devil on his.

Because after another incredible supper, fresh lake trout cooked by Sally, Dannie announced she and Susie would be sleeping in the tree fort. Ridiculously, he heard himself saying he would join them.

He had the worst sleep of his life in the tree fort, with Susie between his and Dannie's sleeping bags, the baby in a huge wicker basket at their heads, cooing happily from his nest of warm blankets.

Dannie was so close, he could touch that incredible hair, but he didn't. She was so close he could smell the Hawaiian flower scent of her. He lay awake looking at the incredible array of stars overhead, and listening to her breathing, and in the morning, he felt cold and cramped and more alive than he had felt in a long, long time.

He woke up looking into Dannie's sleep-dazed turquoise eyes, and wondered how on earth he was ever going to go back to life as he had known it.

The carefree stay here at Moose Lake Lodge was about as far from his high-powered life as he could have gotten. He didn't check his Blackberry, there was no TV to watch. No Internet.

He had a new reality and so much of it was about Dannie: her eyes and her lips and the way she tossed her hair. How she looked with her slacks rolled up and smudged with dirt, hugging the womanliness of her curves, her bare toes curling in warm sand.

He saw the way she was with those kids: patient, loving, genuine. He came to look forward to her intelligence, the playful sting of exchanged insults.

He was acutely aware Dannie was the kind of woman that men, superficial creatures that they were, overlooked. But if a man was looking for a life partner—which he thankfully was not—could he do any better than her?

That morning, after the exquisite pleasure of a hot shower after a cold night, over pancakes and syrup, Sally told them she and Michael would mind the kids for the day.

"The only one who hasn't had any kind of a holiday, a break from responsibility, is Dannie. This is your last full day here. Go have some fun, you two."

His niece had been so right about him, Joshua thought. He was just plain dumb.

He turned to Dannie, humbled by Sally's consideration of her. This morning Dannie was wearing a red sweatshirt that hid some of the features that made his mouth go dry, but the jeans made up for it.

The dark denim hugged her. It occurred to him that skinny butts were highly overrated. It occurred to him that was a naughty thought for a man who was going to try his hand at being considerate.

"The whole time I've been thinking how enjoyable this experience is," Joshua admitted, "you've been doing your job, minding children."

"Oh, no," Dannie protested, "I don't feel like that at all. I once heard if you do a job you love, you'll never work a day in your life, and that's how I feel about being with Susie and Jake."

Again, Joshua was taken with what a prize she was going to make for someone. And again he was taken aback by his own reaction to that thought. Misery.

Before someone else snapped her up, could he put his own priorities on hold long enough to show her a good time? Could he trust himself, not forever, but for one day? To put her needs ahead of his own? To be considerate, instead of a self-centered jerk?

"Sally's right," he decided firmly. "It's time for your holiday."

Dannie was looking wildly uncomfortable, as if she didn't really want to spend time with him without the buffer zone of two lively and demanding children.

Which was only sensible. He was tired of her sensible side. He was annoyed at being bucked when he'd made the decision to be a better man, to be considerate and a gentleman.

"I have had a holiday, really," she insisted. "How can I eat food like Sally's, and stay in a place as beautiful as Angel's Rest and not feel as if I've had a holiday? I loved it better than a stay at a five-star resort. No offense to five-star resort owners in the vicinity."

"No," Sally said, firmly. "Today it's your turn. You have some grown-up time. Why don't you and Josh take a canoe over to the island? I'll pack you a picnic. Josh should look at it anyway, since it's part of the Moose Lake Lodge property. Many a honeymoon has taken place at that cabin!"

Despite Dannie claiming to be cynical about relationships, he did not miss the wistful look in her eyes when she heard that she had been so right about the island being an idyllic setting for a honeymoon! Joshua, good intentions aside, wasn't sure he was up to grown-up time with Dannie on an island where people had their honeymoons!

Still, he didn't miss the fact that Sally and Michael, though no business had been discussed, must be opening just a little bit to the idea of him acquiring the Lodge for Sun since they were encouraging him to see all that comprised it.

In search of perfect adventures for the clients of Sun, and in keeping with his fast-paced single lifestyle, Joshua had tried many activities, including some that might be considered hair-raising like bungee jumping and parasailing.

None of those activities had ever really fazed him, but an hour later, out in the canoe with Michael, brushing up on his canoeing skills, Joshua felt the weight of responsibility. He had canoed before, but never in waters that could kill you with cold if you capsized and had to stay in them for any length of time.

Michael assured him the island was only a twenty-minute paddle across quiet waters.

"I'll keep an eye on you," he promised. "If something goes wrong, I'll rescue you in the powerboat."

Joshua was not sure he could imagine anything that would be more humiliating than that, especially with Dannie sharing the boat with him. He was also aware Dannie's presence, besides making him aware of not wanting a rescue, made him feel responsible for another human being, something that was also new in his free-wheeling bachelor existence.

In a way it was ironic, because he shouldered tremendous responsibility. The business decisions he made literally affected the lives and livelihoods of hundreds of people.

That kind of responsibility didn't even seem real

compared to having a life in his hands. Naturally he'd had his own life in his hands many times before, but if he got himself in trouble, he was the only one who suffered the consequences. Maybe the truth was he didn't really even care.

Strangely, both feelings—of not wanting to make a fool of himself in front of her and of feeling responsible for her safety—made him feel not weakened, but strengthened. Like he was manning up, assuming the ancient role of the protector, the warrior. He would never have guessed that role could feel so satisfying.

Trust Dannie not to let him relish the role for too long! He got her settled in the front of the boat—the non-control position in a canoe—and gave her a paddle for decorative purposes. He issued dire warnings about the tipiness of the contraption they were setting out in, and then he settled into his own position of navigator, course setter, and head paddler.

He was so intent on his duties, he noticed only peripherally that her red sweatshirt matched the red of the canoe, and that her rear in those jeans was something worth manning up for!

But before they were even out of the protected bay that sheltered the lodge, she turned to him in annoyance. Her cheeks were flushed with exertion, which she was bringing on herself by trying to pull the boat single-handedly through the water with her paddle!

"Look, I think this is a team activity. I'm not really the kind of girl who wants to sit in the front of the boat and look pretty, but I think we're paddling out of sync."

In other words she wasn't the kind of girl he'd gotten accustomed to.

In other words, maybe he'd been going it alone a

little too much. He wasn't even sure he could play on a team anymore.

But to his surprise, as soon as he relaxed control, as soon as he began to work with her instead of trying to do it all himself, the canoe began to cut through the water with silent speed and grace, an arrow headed straight for that island.

"That's better," she said, looking over her shoulder and grinning at him.

He wasn't quite sure when she had transformed, but somewhere in the last few days she had gone from plain to beautiful. The sun had kissed pale skin to golden, she had given up all effort to tame her luscious hair, and it curled wildly around her face, her expression seemed to become more relaxed each second that they left the children behind them.

"You are pretty," he stammered, and was amazed how he sounded. He, who had escorted some of the world's most beautiful and accomplished women, sounded like a schoolboy on his first date.

In answer, she scraped her paddle across the surface of the water, and deliberately splashed him with the icy cold lake water.

Now he could see the gypsy he had glimpsed in her before, dancing to life, especially when she laughed at his chagrin. Dannie said, with patent insincerity, "Oops."

Now, in this moment, he could see the truth of who she was, shining around her. This is what he had glimpsed when he had touched her lip with this thumb, a very long time ago, it seemed. This is what he had known about her that she had not known about herself. That she was made to dance with life, to shine with laughter, to blossom.

And in that he recognized another truth.

It was not her who was becoming transformed. It was him.

"Don't rock the boat," he said grumpily. And somehow it sounded like a metaphor for his life. Joshua Cole, entrepreneur who performed feats of daring and innovation in business, and who embraced adventure in the scant amount of time he allowed for play, did not rock the boat in that one all-important area.

Relationships. He did not even risk real involvement. He saw women a few times, and at the first hint they wanted more he made an exit. At the first sign of true intimacy of the emotional variety he was out of there. He was willing to play the game with his wallet, but he did not take chances with his heart.

Because his heart had been battered and bruised. When his parents had died, people had told him time would heal all wounds. When he had agreed with Sarah that the best thing for that baby would be to allow him to go to a loving family who were emotionally and financially mature, who were prepared for a child in every way, he had thought time would eventually lessen the ache he felt over that decision.

Maybe he had even believed that time *had* eased the pain. But he had only been kidding himself.

Outrunning something was not the same as healing. Not even close.

"Land ho," Dannie called, as they drew close to the island.

He looked at her face, shining with enthusiasm for the day, and he felt his guard slip away. He made a decision, just for today, he would engage as completely as he was able.

For her. So she could enjoy one day of being irresponsible, of having fun without the kids.

They landed the canoe, gracelessly, coming as close to tipping it as they had come yet, though thankfully the waters off the island were shallow enough that he didn't have to worry about her dying of hypothermia in them if they did capsize. Still, even with her jeans rolled up, she was wet to her knees.

He lifted the picnic basket Sally had packed for them and followed Dannie up the shoreline and left the basket there.

"I can't wait to see it," she said, and started up the path that led to the cabin. She stumbled on a root, and he reached out his hand to steady her. Somehow he never took his hand away. Hers folded into his as if it was absolutely meant to be there.

There was a well-worn path to the cabin, which was as quaint up close as it had been from far away. Like Angel's Rest, it had a name plaque hanging at the entrance to the covered, vine-twined porch.

"Love's Rhapsody," she read out loud. "Isn't that lovely?"

"Corny," he said, deciding then and there the sign was coming down the minute he owned the place

"Should we go in?" she asked. There was something about her wide-eyed wonder in the little cabin that was making him feel edgy.

"Well, yeah, it's not a church. Besides, I might own it one day. I might as well see how much money I'd have to throw at it to keep it."

She reacted as he had hoped, by glaring at him as if he had desecrated a sacred site. It was important that she know that distinction existed between them. He cynical and pragmatic, she soft and dreamy. It was important she know that that distinction existed between them, so the wall was up.

And a man needed a wall up in a place like this! He needed a wall up when he was beginning to feel all enthused about playing the protector and warrior. When he felt strangely uncertain if they should enter that sanctuary. What if whatever was in there—the spirit of romance—overcame them? What if he was helpless against it?

Annoyed with himself for so quickly breaking his vow to make the day about her instead of about him, Joshua pushed past her and shoved open the door.

His first reaction to the interior was one of relief, because the cabin was dark and musty smelling. There was absolutely nothing in it to speak of. An old antique bed, with the mattress rolled up, and the linens stored, a little table, a threadbare couch and a stone fireplace just like the one at Angel's Rest.

And yet, the fact there was so little in here, seemed to highlight that there was something in here, unseen.

"Look," she whispered, wandering over to one of the walls. "Oh, Joshua, look."

Carved lovingly into the walls, were names. Mildred and Manny, April 3, 1947, Penelope and Alfred, June 9, 1932. Sometimes it was just the couple's name, other times a heart and arrow surrounded it, sometimes a poem had been painstakingly cut out in the wall. It seemed each couple who had ever honeymooned here had left their mark on those walls.

It was hard not to be moved by the testament to love, to commitment. There really was nothing at all of material value in this cabin.

And yet there was something here so valuable it

evaded being named: a history of people saying yes to the adventure of beginning a life together.

In this funny little cabin, it felt as if it was the only adventure that counted.

Cynicism would protect him from the light shining in her eyes. But what of his vow to let her have the day she wanted?

So, when they left the cabin he took her hand again, despite the fact he wanted to shove his into his pockets, defending against what had been in there. Strangely, holding her hand seemed to still the uncertainty in him.

The island was small. They walked around the whole thing in an hour. He soon forgot his discomfort in the cabin, and found himself making it about her with amazing ease. But then, that's what being with her was like: easy and comfortable.

With just the faintest hint of sexual awareness, tingling, that added to rather than detracted from the experience of being together.

Finally they returned to the beach and opened Sally's picnic basket. She had sent them hot dogs and buns, matches and fire starter.

They gathered wood, and he lit the fire, feeling that *thing* again, the shouldering of the ancient role: *I will start the fire that will warm you.*

Obviously, the corniness from the cabin was catching!

With hot dogs blackening on sticks over an open fire, and the magic of the cabin behind him, he found himself taking a tentative step forward, wanting to be more but also to know more. Soon she would go her own way, and he would go his. It made the exchange seem risk-free.

"Tell me why you're content to raise other people's

children," he said, touching the mustard at the edge of her mouth with his finger, putting that finger to his own lips, watching her eyes go as wide as if he had kissed her.

"I told you, it's a job I love. I never feel as if I'm working."

"But doesn't that make you think you are ideally suited to be a mother yourself, of your own children?"

Maybe that was too personal, because Dannie blushed wildly, as if he had asked her to be the mother of his children!

He loved that blush! Before her, when was the last time he had even met a woman who still blushed?

"It's because of the heartbreak," he guessed softly, looking at the way she was focusing on her hot dog with sudden intensity. "Will you tell me about it?"

This was exactly the kind of question he *never* asked. But suddenly he really wanted to know. He knew about things you kept inside. You thought they'd gone away, when in fact they were eating you from the inside out.

"No," she said. "You're burning your hot dog."

"That's how I like them. What was his name?"

She glared at him. Her expression said, *leave it.* But her voice said, reluctantly, "Brent."

"Just for the record, I've always hated that name. Let me guess. A college professor?"

"It's not even an interesting story."

"All stories are interesting."

"Okay. You asked for it. Here is the full pathetic truth. Brent was a college professor. I was a student. He waited until I wasn't in any of his classes to ask me out. We dated for a few months. I fell in love and thought he did, too. He had a trip planned to Europe, a year's sabbatical from teaching, and he went."

"He didn't ask you to go?"

"He asked me to wait. He made me a promise."

Joshua groaned.

"What are you making noises for?"

"If he loved you he would never, ever have gone to Europe without you."

"Thank you. Where were you when I needed you? He promised he would come back, and we'd get married. I took the nanny position temporarily."

"No ring, though," Joshua guessed cynically.

"He gave me a locket!"

"With his own picture inside? Thought pretty highly of himself, did he?" It was the locket she'd worn when he first met her. That she'd put away. What did it mean that she had taken it off?

That it was a good time for her to have this conversation? He knew himself to be a very superficial man, the wrong person to be navigating the terrifying waters of a woman's heartbreak. What moment of insanity had gripped him, encouraged her confidences? But now that she'd got started, it was like a dam bursting.

"At first he e-mailed every day, and I got a flood of postcards. It made me do really dumb things. I…I used all my savings and bought a wedding gown."

Her face was screwing up. She blinked hard. Maybe wheedling this confession out of her hadn't been such a good idea after all.

"It's like something out of a fantasy," she whispered. "Lace and silk." She was choking now. "It was all a fantasy. Such a safe way to love somebody, from a distance, anticipating the next contact, but never having to deal with reality.

"Can I tell you something truly awful? Something I don't even think I knew until just now? The longer he stayed away, the more elaborate and satisfying my fantasy love for him became."

She was crying now. No mascara, thank God. He patted her awkwardly on the shoulder, and when that didn't seem to give her any comfort, or him either, he threw caution to the wind, and his hot dog into the fire. He pulled her into his chest.

Felt her hair, finally.

It felt as he had known it would feel, like the most expensive and exquisite of silks.

It smelled of Hawaii, exotic and floral. This was why he was so undeserving of her trust: she was baring her soul, he was being intoxicated by the scent of her hair.

"Actually," she sniffed, "Brent was the final crack in my romantic illusions. My parents had a terrible relationship, constant tension that spilled over into fighting. When I met Brent, I hoped there was something else, and there was, but it turned out to be even more painful. Oh, I hope I don't sound pathetic. The I-had-a-bad-childhood kind of person."

"Did you?" he asked, against his better judgment. Of course the smell of her hair and her soft curves pressed into his body made him feel as if he had no judgment at all, wiped out by sensory overload. And yet even for that, he registered her saying she'd had a bad childhood and he ached for her. There were things even a warrior could not hope to make right.

"Terrible," she said with a defeated sigh. "Filled with fighting and uncertainty, making up that always filled us kids with such hope and never lasted. It was terrible."

"Maybe that's why you're so invested in children. Giving them the gift of happiness that you didn't have. You do have that gift, you know. So engaged with them, so genuinely interested in them."

"Did you have a good childhood?" she asked, and her wistfulness tore through the barriers around his heart that usually kept him from sharing too deeply with anyone.

"Camelot," he said. "I can't remember one bad thing. I often wonder if every family is only allotted so much luck, and we used ours up."

"Oh, Joshua," she said softly.

"My parents were crazy about each other. And about us. We were the fun family on the block—my dad coaching the Little League team, my mom filling the rubber swimming pool for all the neighborhood kids. And it was all so genuine. I see parents sometimes who I think are following a rule book, thinking about how it all looks to other people, but my folks weren't like that. They did these things with us because they loved to do it, not because they wanted to *look* like great parents."

"And because of that they were great parents."

"The best," he remembered softly. "Every year for three weeks they rented a cottage on the seashore. We had these long days of swimming and playing in the sand, we had bonfires out front on the beach every night. There wasn't even a TV set. If it rained, we played Monopoly or Sorry or cards."

He realized he had never felt that way again. Ever. Not until he had come here.

And to feel that way was to leave yourself open to a terrible hurt.

Was he ready?

A sudden sound made him jerk up from her. Without his noticing, so engrossed in protecting her and comforting her, and sharing his own secret memories with her, the wind had come up on the lake.

Some warrior. Some protector! He had not tied the

canoe properly. It had yanked free of its mooring, the sound he had heard was it crashing into a rock as it bounced away from the small island.

He ran for the water, plunged in, could not believe the cold and stopped.

"Leave it," Dannie cried.

Good advice. He should let the canoe go, but everything about Moose Lake Lodge said the Bakers were operating on a shoestring. He'd been entrusted with their canoe.

"I can't," he shouted at her, moving deeper into the water. "Can you imagine how the Bakers will react if the canoe drifts back there, empty? What about Susie?"

He took a deep breath and moved deeper into the water, felt her movement on the beach behind him.

"Stay there," he called. "I've got it under control."

He was used to speaking, and people listened. Naturally, Dannie did not. He heard her splash into the water, her shocked gasp as the icy water filled her shoes.

It made him desperate to get that canoe before they were both in deep trouble. He was up to his waist, he lunged forward, and just managed to get the rope that trailed off the bow of the boat.

He pulled it back toward shore, grabbed her elbow as he moved by, steering her in the right direction.

"I told you not to come in," he said.

"I was trying to help!" she said, unrepentant.

"Now we're both wet." But what he was thinking was it had been a long time since he had been with the kind of woman who would plunge into that water with him. He knew a lot of women who would have stood on shore, unhelpfully hysterical or more worried about her haute couture than him!

Still, they both could have got in trouble and it would

have been his fault. He was aware of freezing water squeezing out of his shoes and that, wet up to his chest, his teeth were chattering wildly and in a most unmanly way.

Except for the fact it might save the Bakers some distress, his rescue was wasted. When he inspected the canoe it had a hole the size of his fist in the bottom of it from where it had smashed into a rock.

He inspected her, too. She was wet past her waist, had her arms wrapped around herself. She was reacting to the cold in a very womanly way, and he did his best not to whistle with low appreciation.

Think, Joshua snapped at himself.

He was stranded on an island. With a beautiful woman. Who was shivering, and who had hair that smelled of Hawaii.

They were both going to have to get these wet clothes off quickly. And not in the way any red-blooded man wanted to have the first disrobing happen.

But because the May wind was like ice as the spring day lengthened and chilled, if they didn't get out of these wet clothes, there was a real chance of hypothermia.

There was only one option.

They were going to have to seek shelter in the honeymoon cabin.

Just his luck that he was going to end up half-naked in the honeymoon cabin with Dannie Springer. Maybe it was because he was shaking with cold that he couldn't quite figure out if he had landed in the middle of a dream or a nightmare.

CHAPTER SIX

DANIELLE SPRINGER HAD been in a few awkward situations, but this one definitely rated as Most Embarrassing, especially given the fact she was in the company of Most Sexy. If she hadn't known that about him before, she certainly couldn't miss it now that she had seen his soaked clothes mold every inch of his fine male body.

What had started off as a day full of potential, was now quickly declining toward disastrous, as quickly as darkness was sweeping over the small island.

She had broken down in front of him, shared confidences she never should have shared. When the canoe had ripped away, she'd been devastated. He had been in the middle of telling her important things, *real* things about himself. Thankfully, his own confidences had snapped her out of her self-pitying recital of woe.

Watching him push out into the water to save the canoe, she had thought sadly, only Dannie Springer would be alone on an island with a man like that, lamenting her last, lost boyfriend. It was no excuse that Joshua had encouraged her. That's what men who were successful with women did. That was their secret weapon. They listened.

Except it was becoming increasingly difficult to see Joshua in the light of his playboy reputation.

Especially after the way he had looked talking about his family, the tenderness in his voice, he seemed like the most real man she had ever met. Poor Brent seemed like a comic book character in comparison. Joshua Cole seemed genuine. That's why the *trust* element was there, despite the fact she had known him only a matter of days. That's why she had let her guard down, when she of all people, jilted, should have her guard up higher.

When had she decided it would be okay to trust him with her heart? It was the way he looked at her, compassionate intensity darkening the shade of green of his eyes. Something she interpreted as *interest,* hot, male and intoxicating was brewing just beneath the calm surface.

Yet for all that male energy—sure and strong—the way he had conducted himself over the past few days was nothing short of admirable. He was a man navigating a foreign land with the children, and yet he was doing it with grace and openness.

Even the way he plunged into the water after that canoe spoke to character. It was him, supposedly the self-centered bachelor, not her, the supposedly compassionate nanny, who had considered how others would react to the empty canoe showing up somewhere.

Dumb to plunge into the water after him, because what was she going to do? But somehow, ever since they'd gotten in that canoe together, she had felt the delicious sense of teamwork. She had plunged into the water almost on instinct. They were in this *together.*

But she was paying for her altruism now.

They were in the honeymoon cottage where hundreds of couples had shyly taken off their clothes for each other for the very first time.

And not a single one of them like this, she thought dourly. Not a single one of them because they were in imminent danger of shivering to death.

"Embarrassing," she muttered out loud.

"Forget embarrassment," he said, glancing back at her from where he was crouched in front of the fireplace, feeding little sticks into it, coaxing a bright blaze to life.

He had peeled off his sodden trousers as if it was the most natural thing in the world. Of course, for him, World's Sexiest Bachelor, it probably was.

Except for the part where he'd warned her he was doing it, giving her time to turn around.

Except for the part where he'd unearthed a container full of bedding, snapped off the lid, and tucked a blanket around himself.

He should have looked like an idiot with his flowing red tartan blanket tied in a knot at his taut stomach. Instead he looked like a chieftain, his shoulders and chest bare, his arms rippling with sinewy strength. There was a warrior cast to his face, remote and focused, as he had turned his attention to getting a fire going in the old stone fireplace.

"I can't get my jeans off," she wailed.

"What?"

"I can't get them off," she said, annoyed he was making her say it again. He had heard her the first time!

The soaked denim, which had probably been a touch snug to begin with, was stuck to her now. Her hands were so cold she couldn't make them do one thing she wanted them to do.

He turned and looked at her. "Are you asking me to help you get your pants off, Miss Pringy?"

"No!" Then with sudden rueful understanding, she said, "You like making me blush, don't you?"

"If I was considering a new hobby that would be it.

I could while away hours at a time thinking up things like—"

"Now is not the time for games, Joshua! I'm just telling you I'm stuck. Just hand me a blanket."

He came across the room toward her, without the covering she had ordered, and his own blanket slipped. She held her breath, shamelessly hopeful, but he stopped and reknotted it, moved toward her.

"Just relax," he said soothingly, looking at the situation with what struck her as an annoying bent toward the analytical. She had the button undone on her jeans, and the zipper down. She had wrested the uncooperative, sodden, freezing fabric about three inches down her hips and there it was stuck, hard.

"It's because you're tense," he decided.

Taking off my pants in a room with the World's Sexiest Bachelor, and I'm tense. Go figure.

"It's because my hands are too cold." It was true her hands felt as if they had turned into icy basketballs at the ends of her wrists. But there was another problem. She was just going to have to admit it and get it over with.

"The jeans might have been a little too tight to begin with. Marginally."

"They looked fine to me," he said, apparently thinking about it. "More than fine. Great." She might have been thrilled that he'd noticed in different circumstances.

As it was, the jeans had been a bit of a challenge to get on, and that's when they'd been dry. What little devil of vanity had made her think her rear end looked good enough in them to put up with a tiny bit of discomfort?

"Look, no matter how reasonable a choice they were when they were dry, they won't come off now. They won't fit over my hips. There, am I blushing enough for you?"

His lips twitched.

"Don't laugh," she warned him.

"I won't," he said, but she could tell he was biting the inside of his cheek. Hard. He didn't speak for a minute, containing himself. "Let me help," he finally managed, and then choked. "I sound like a butler."

"Only one of us here would know what that sounded like," she warned him, but it was too late.

He was laughing, moving toward her with singleness of purpose written all over him.

"Don't touch me!" There. Self-preservation finally rising to the occasion. Where had that fine attribute of character been when she had been sobbing her heart out in his seemingly sympathetic ear?

"I can't help you without touching you."

"I don't need your help." That was a lie obvious to both of them. "You're laughing at me."

"I'm trying not to."

"Try harder."

"Okay." He crouched down, and was looking at the area where the soaked jeans were bound up around the wideness of her hips. Oddly enough, the way his eyes rested there, briefly and with heat, before returning to her face did not make her feel like a whale. At all. In fact, his laughter seemed to have died, too.

"Yes, you do," he said firmly, "need my help."

"Okay, then." She was shaking too hard to deny it any longer. She closed her eyes hard against her humiliation. "Just be quick."

"That's the first time I've ever heard that in this particular situation," he muttered.

"We are not in a *situation,*" she warned him, "or not one you've ever been in before."

"You're absolutely right about that," he said.

His hands settled around the jeans. Her skin was so cold she actually felt scorched from the heat of his hands. She had to resist an impulse to wiggle into that warmth. Instead she made herself stand rigidly still. She opened her eyes just enough to squint at him undetected through the veil of her lashes.

He yanked with considerable strength, enough that she saw that lovely triceps muscle in his arm jump into gorgeous relief. Unfortunately the jeans did not budge, not a single, solitary fraction of an inch.

"Your skin feels like ice-cold marble," he noted clinically.

Somehow in her imagination, she had imagined him saying softly, *Your skin is like silk that's been heating in the sun, soft and sensual.*

When had she imagined such a thing? Practically every damn minute since she had met him, a dialogue of lust and wanting running just below her prim surface.

"Can't you relax?"

"I doubt it," she moaned, and then made the confession that made her humiliation complete. "You're going to have hurry. I think I have to go to the bathroom."

"Dannie, it would be really inadvisable for you to get us laughing right now. Really."

"Believe me, I am nowhere close to laughing." But his lips were twitching again. How had she ever thought he was handsome? He wasn't. He was like an evil leprechaun.

"Someday you'll see the humor in this," he assured her. "You'll tell your kids about it."

No, she wouldn't. Because a story like that would begin with, "Did I ever tell you how I met your dad?"

And he was not going to be the father of her children. Though suddenly she was aware she had a secret self that not only conducted entire conversations just out of range of her conscious mind, but *wished* things. Impossible things.

Green-eyed babies.

She told herself she had just gotten over another man. This was rebound lust, nothing more. But she was very aware of quite a different truth. There never had been another man, really, just a convenient fantasy, a risk-free way to play at love, a safe way to withdraw from the game while pretending to be engaged in it.

Joshua tugged again. The wet, cold, thick fabric shifted a mean half inch or so.

"Ouch. Who invented denim? What a ridiculous material," she complained.

"There's a reason they don't make swimsuits out of it," he agreed, and then broke it to her gently. "You're going to have to lie down on the bed. Hang on. I'll cut the mattress open."

He found a knife and cut the strings that were wrapped tightly around the mattress, a defense against mice.

Mice, which had probably been her greatest fear until about thirty seconds ago. Now her greatest fear was herself!

"Maybe you could just cut the jeans off," she said. She shuffled over to the bed, the jeans just down enough to impair her mobility, no dignified waltz across the cold cabin floor for her. She left great puddling footsteps in her wake.

"I'll keep that in mind as a last resort, but I might cut you by accident, so we'll try this first. Lie down."

Why didn't her fantasies *ever* work out? Every woman in the world would die to hear those words from his lips. "Don't get bossy," she said, so he'd never guess how great her disappointment was at the *way* he said that.

"Hey, if you could have followed simple instructions in the first place, you wouldn't be in this predicament."

She turned around and flopped down on the mattress, her knees hanging over. "I wasn't letting you go in that water by yourself."

"Why not?"

The truth blasted through her. *I think I'm falling in love with you. For real, damn it, not some romantic illusion I can take home and satisfy with buying dresses and planning honeymoons I know are never going to happen.*

Out loud she said, "The team thing. Okay, pull. Pull hard."

Real, she scoffed at herself. She was getting more pathetic by the day. You did not fall in love with a man in four days. Unless you were a Hollywood celebrity, which she most definitely was not.

She felt his hands, scorching hot again against the soft flesh of her hips and looked at the frown of concentration marring his handsome features.

It felt real, even if it wasn't. Of course, people who heard little voices swore that was real, too.

"Hang on," he said. He took a grip and pulled. The jeans inched down. Finally he was past the horrible hip obstacle, but now his hands rested on the top of her thighs, his thumbs brushing that delicate tissue of pure sensitivity on her inner leg. Thankfully, the skin was nearly frozen, not nearly sensitive enough to make her reach up, grab his ears and order him huskily to make her warm.

He tugged again. His hands moved from the thigh area and the jeans reluctantly parted from her frozen, pebbled skin. He yanked them free triumphantly, held them up for her to see, as if he was a hunter holding up a snake he had killed and skinned just for her.

"My skin looks like lard, doesn't it?" she demanded, watching his face for signs of revulsion. If she had seen any, she would have gotten up and marched straight back into that lake!

He was silent for a long moment. "Alabaster," he said softly.

"Huh!" Nonetheless, she was mollified for a half second or so until she thought of something else. "I hope I don't have on the panties that say Tuesday."

"Uh, no, you don't."

Suddenly she saw why he delighted so in making her blush, because when she saw that brick red rise up from his neck and suffuse his cheeks, she felt gleeful.

"Wednesday?" she asked, shocked at herself.

"I am trying to be a gentleman!"

Of course he was. And it didn't come naturally to him, either. One little push, and he wouldn't be a gentleman at all.

But did she know how to handle that?

"Here's a blanket," he said, sternly, handing it to her.

She glanced down before she took the blanket from him. Plain white, the perfect underwear for the nanny to have her encounter with the billionaire playboy! Of course the encounter was tragic, rather than romantic. She really didn't have what it took to start a fire that she didn't know how to put out!

She wrapped the blanket around herself, lurched off the bed, nearly tripped in the folds.

He reached out to steady her. "It's okay," he said softly. "Don't be embarrassed."

She looked at where his hand rested on her arm. There was that potential for fire again. She pulled her arm away. "I have to go to the bathroom. Now can I be embarrassed?"

"Yeah, okay. Everybody on the planet has to go to the bathroom about four times a day, but if you want to be embarrassed about it be my guest." And then he grinned at her in a way that made embarrassment ease instead of grow worse, because when he grinned like that she saw the person he *really* was.

Not a billionaire playboy riding the helm of a very successful company. Not the owner of a grand apartment, and the pilot of his own airplane,

The kid in the picture on the beach, long ago.

And in her wildest fantasies, she could see herself sitting around a campfire, wrapped in a blanket like this one, her children shoulder to shoulder with her, saying, "Tell us again how you met Daddy."

She bolted out of the cabin, then took her time trying to regain her composure. Finally she went back in.

He had pulled the couch in front of the fire and patted the place beside him. "Nice and warm."

Cottage. Fire. Gorgeous man.

In anyone else's life this would be a good equation! She squeezed herself into the far corner of the couch, as far away from him as she could get.

He passed her half a chocolate bar.

She swore quietly. Cottage. Fire. Gorgeous man. Chocolate.

"Nannys aren't allowed to swear," he reprimanded her lightly.

"Under duress!"

"What kind of duress?" he asked innocently.

She closed her eyes. *Don't tell him, idiot.* Naturally her mouth started moving before it received the strict instructions from her brain to shut up. "You'll probably think this is hilarious, but I'm finding you very attractive."

At least it wasn't a declaration of love.

"It's probably a symptom of getting too cold," she added in a rush. "Lack of oxygen to the brain. Or something."

"It's probably the way I look in a blanket," he said, deadpan.

"I suppose there is that," she agreed reluctantly, and then with a certain desperation, "Is there any more chocolate?"

"I find you attractive, too, Dannie."

She blew out a disbelieving snort.

He leaned across the distance between them and touched her hair. "I can't tell you how long I've wanted to do this." His hands stroked her hair, his fingers a comb going through the tangles gently pulling them free. He moved closer to her, buried his face in her hair, inhaled.

She was so aware this was his game, his territory, he *knew* just how to make a woman melt. Spineless creature that she was, she didn't care. In her mind she took that stupid locket and threw it way out into Moose Lake.

What kind of fire she could or could not put out suddenly didn't matter. So close to him, so engulfed in the sensation of his hands claiming her hair, she didn't care if she burned up on the fires of passion!

She turned her head, caught the side of his lip, touched it with her tongue. He froze, leaned back, stared at her, golden light from the fire flickering across the handsome features of his face.

And then he surrendered. Only it was not a surrender at all. He met her tentativeness with boldness that took her breath away. He plundered her lips, took them captive, tasted them with hunger and welcome.

She knew then the totality of the lie she had told herself about loving another, about pining for another.

Because she had never felt this intensity of feeling before, as if fireworks were exploding against a night sky, as if her heart had started to beat after a long slumber, as if her blood had turned to fire. There was not a remnant of cold left in her.

Burn, she told herself blissfully, *burn.*

"I've wanted to do that for a long time, too," he whispered, his voice sexy, low and hoarse. "You taste of rain. Your hair smells of flowers, you do not disappoint, Danielle."

She tasted him, rubbed her lips over the raspiness of whiskers, back to the softness of his mouth, along the column of his neck. She gave herself permission to let go.

And felt the exquisite pull of complete freedom. She went back to his mouth, greedy for his taste and for the sensation of him. She let her hands roam his bare skin, felt the exquisite texture of it, soft, the hardness of male muscle and bone just beneath that surface softness.

His breathing was coming in hard gasps, almost as if she knew what she was doing.

She both did and didn't. The part of her that was knowledge knew nothing of this, she was an explorer in unmapped terrain. But the part of her that was instinct, animal and primal, knew everything about this, knew just how to make him crazy.

She loved it when she felt him begin to tremble as her lips followed the path scorched out first across his naked chest with her hand.

"Stop," he said hoarsely.

She laughed, loving this new wicked side to herself. "No."

But he pulled away from her, back to his own side of the couch. As she watched him with narrowed eyes, he ran a hand through the spikiness of his hair that looked bronze in the firelight.

"We aren't doing this," he said, low in his throat, not looking at her.

She laughed again, feeling the exquisiteness of her power.

"I'm not kidding, Dannie. My sister would kill me."

"You're going to mention your sister *now?*"

"She always comes to mind when I'm trying to do the decent thing," he said sourly.

"I'm a grown woman," she said. "I make my own decisions."

"Yeah, good ones, like following me into the water when it was completely unnecessary." She moved across the couch toward him. He leaped out of it.

"Dannie, don't make this hard on me."

"I plan to make it very hard on you," she said dangerously, gathering her own blanket around her, sliding off the couch.

"Hey, I hear something."

She smiled. "Sure you do."

"It's a powerboat!"

She froze, tilted her head, could not believe the stinginess of the gods. They were stealing her moment from her! She had *chosen* to burn.

And now the choice was being taken away from her!

There was no missing his expression of relief as the sound of the motor grew louder out there in the darkness. With one last look at her—gratitude over a near miss, wistful, too, he grabbed his blanket tighter with one fist, and bolted out the door.

As soon as he was gone, the feeling of power left her with a slam. She flopped back on the couch and contemplated what had just transpired.

She, Danielle Springer, had become the tigress.

"Shameless hussy, more like," she told herself.

She was not being rescued in a blanket! Her state of undress suddenly felt like a neon Shameless Hussy sign! She tossed it down and grabbed her jeans from where he had hung them on a line beside the fire.

They were only marginally drier than before, and now beginning to stiffen as if someone had accidentally dropped a box of starch in with the laundry.

Nonetheless, she lay back down on the bed and tried valiantly to squeeze them back on.

She had just gotten to that awful hip part when he came back in the door.

"Don't look," she said huffily. "I'm getting dressed. I plan to maintain my dignity." As if it wasn't way too late for that!

He made a noise she didn't like.

She let go of her jeans and rolled up on her elbow to look at him. "What?"

"That was Michael in the boat. The bottom of the lake is really rocky here and he can't see because it's too dark. He said if we'd be okay for the night, he'd come back in the morning."

"And you told him we'd be okay for the night?" she said incredulously. It was so obvious things were not okay, that her self-discipline had unraveled like a spool of yarn beneath the claws of a determined kitten.

"That's what I told him."

"Without asking me?"

"Sorry, I'm used to making executive decisions."

She picked up a pillow and hurled it at him. He ducked. She hurled every pillow on that bed, and didn't hit him once. If there had been anything else to pick up and throw, she would have done that, too.

But there was nothing left, not within reach, and she was not going to get up with her jeans half on and half off to go searching. Instead she picked up her discarded blanket, and pulled it over herself, even over her head.

"Go away," she said, muffled.

It occurred to her, her thirty seconds of passion had done the worst possible thing: turned her into her parents! Loss of control happened that fast.

And had such dire consequences, too. Look at her mom and dad. A perfect example of people prepared to burn in the name of love.

She peeked up from the blanket.

In the murky darkness of the cabin, she saw he had not gone away completely. He had found a stub of a candle and lit it. Now he was going through the rough cabinets, pulling out cans.

"You want something to eat?" he asked, as if she hadn't just been a complete shrew, made a complete fool of herself.

Of course she wanted something to eat! That's how she handled pain. That's why the jeans didn't fit in the first place. She yanked them back off, wrapped herself tightly in the blanket and crossed the room to him. If he could pretend nothing had happened, so could she.

"This looks good," she said, picking up a can of tinned spaghetti. If he noticed her enthusiasm was forced, he didn't say a word.

"Delicious," he agreed, looking everywhere but at her, as if somehow spaghetti was forbidden food, like the apple in the garden of Eden.

CHAPTER SEVEN

"DELICIOUS," DANNIE SAID woodenly. "Thank you for preparing dinner."

Hell hath no fury like a woman scorned, Joshua thought, trying not to look at Dannie. He'd been right about her and spaghetti. Her mouth formed the most delectable little *O* as she sucked it back. No twisting the spaghetti around her fork using a spoon for her.

The ancient stove in the cabin was propane fired, and either the tanks had not been filled, because there was going to be no season this year at Moose Lake, or it had just given out in old age. He'd tried his luck with a frying pan and a pot over the fire, and the result was about as far from delicious as he could have made it. Even on purpose.

"Everything's scorched," he pointed out.

Something flashed in her eyes, vulnerable, and then closed up again. Truthfully it wouldn't have mattered if it was lobster tails and truffles. Everything he put in his mouth tasted like sawdust. Burnt sawdust.

The world was tasteless because he'd hurt her. Insulted her. Rejected her.

It was for her own bloody good! And if she didn't quit doing that to the spaghetti his resolve would melt like sugar in boiling water.

He made the mistake of looking at her, her features softened by the golden light of the fire and the tiny, guttering candles, but her expression hardened into indifference and he could see straight through to the hurt that lay underneath.

She plucked a noodle from her bowl, and he felt that surge of heat, of pure wanting. He knew himself. Part of it was because she was such a good girl, prim and prissy, a bit of a plain Jane.

It was the librarian fantasy, where a beautiful hellcat lurked just under the surface of the mask of respectability.

Except that part wasn't a fantasy. Unleashed, Danielle Springer was a hellcat! And the beauty part just deepened and deepened and deepened.

He wanted back what he had lost. Not the heated kisses; he'd had plenty of those and would have plenty more.

No, what he wanted back was the rare trust he felt for her and had gained from her. What he wanted back was the ease that had developed between them over the past few days, the sense of companionship.

"Want to play cards?" he asked her.

The look she gave him could have wilted newly budded roses. "No, thanks."

"Charades?"

No answer.

"Do you want dessert?"

The faintest glimmer of interest that was quickly doused.

"It's going to be a long evening, Dannie."

"God forbid you should ever be bored."

"As if anybody could ever be bored around you," he muttered. "Aggravating, annoying, doesn't listen, doesn't appreciate when sacrifices have been made for her own good—"

She cut him off. "What were the dessert options?"

"Chocolate cake. No oven, but chocolate cake." Just to get away from the condemnation in her eyes, he got up, his blanket held up tightly, and went and looked at the cake mix box he had found in one of the cupboards.

He fumbled around in the poor light until he found another pot, dumped the cake mix in and added water from a container he had filled at the lake. He went and crouched in front of the fire, holding the pot over the embers, stirring, waiting, stirring.

Then he went and got a spoon, and sat on the couch. "You want some?" he asked.

"Sure. The girl who can't even squeeze into her jeans will forgive anything for cake," she said. "Even bad cake. Fried cake. I bet it's gross."

"It isn't," he lied. "You looked great in those jeans. Stop it." And then, cautiously, he said, "What's to forgive?"

"I wanted to keep kissing. You didn't."

"I need a friend more than I need someone to kiss. Do you know how fast things can blow up when people go there?" He almost added *before they're ready.* But that implied he was going to be ready someday, and he wasn't sure that was true. You couldn't say things to Dannie Springer until you were sure they were true.

Silence.

"Come on," he said softly. "Forgive me. Come eat cake." He wasn't aware his heart had stopped beating until it started again when she flopped down on the couch beside him.

He filled up the spoon with goo and passed it to her, tried not to look at how her lips closed around that spoon. Then he looked anyway, feeling regret and yearning in equal amounts. He'd thought watching her eat spaghetti was sexy? The girl made sharing a spoon seem like something out of the *Kama Sutra.*

The cake was like a horrible, soggy pudding with lumps in it, but they ate it all, passing the spoon back and forth, and it tasted to him of ambrosia.

"Tell me something about you that no one knows," he invited her, wanting that trust back, longing for the intimacy they had shared on the lakeshore. Even if it had been dangerous. It couldn't be any more dangerous than sharing a spoon with her. "Just one thing."

"Is that one of your playboy lines?" she asked.

"No." And it was true. He had never said that to a single person before.

Still, she seemed suspicious and probably rightly so. "You first."

When I put that spoon in my mouth, all I can think is that it has been in your mouth first.

"I was a ninety-pound weakling up until the tenth grade."

"I already knew that. Your sister has a picture of you."

"Out where anyone can see it?" he asked, pretending to be galled.

"Probably posted on the Internet," she said. "Try again."

There was one thing no one knew about him, and for a moment it rose up in him begging to be released. To her. For a moment, the thought of not carrying that burden anymore was intoxicating in its temptation.

"Sometimes I pass gas in elevators," he said, trying for a light note, trying to be superficial and funny and irreverent, trying to fight the demon that wanted out.

"You do not! That's gross."

"Real men often are," he said. "You heard it here first."

"Wow. I don't even think I want to kiss you again."

"That's good."

"Was it that terrible?" she demanded.

Could she really believe it had been terrible? That made the temptation to show her almost too great to bear. Instead, he gnawed on the now empty spoon. "No," he said gruffly, "It wasn't terrible at all. Your turn."

"Um, in ninth grade I sent Leonard Burnside a rose. I put that it was from Miss Marchand, the French teacher."

"You liked him?"

"Hated him," she said. "Full-of-himself jock. He actually went to the library and learned a phrase in French that he tried out on her. Got kicked out of school for three days."

"Note to self—do not get on Danielle Springer's bad side."

"I never told anyone. It was such a guilty pleasure. Your turn."

"I don't floss, ever."

"You *are* gross."

"You mean you could tell I didn't floss?" he asked sulkily. "I knew if you really knew me, you wouldn't want to kiss me."

And then the best thing happened. She was laughing. And he was laughing. And they were planning cruel sequences that she could have played on full-of-himself Lennie Burnside.

It grew very quiet. The fire sputtered, and he felt warm and content, drowsy. She shifted over, he felt her head fall onto his shoulder. Even though he knew better, he reached out and fiddled with her hair.

"The part I don't get about you," she said, after a long time that made him wonder if she'd spent all that time thinking of him, "is if you had such a good time with your family on family holidays, why is your own company geared to the young and restless crowd?"

The battle within him was surprisingly short. He had carried it long enough. The burden was too heavy.

He was shocked that he *wanted* to tell her. And only her.

Shocked that he wanted her to know him completely. With all his flaws and with all his weaknesses. He wanted her to know he was a man capable of making dreadful errors. He wanted to know if the unvarnished truth about him would douse that look in her eyes when she looked at him, dewy, yearning.

"When I was in college," he said softly, "the girl I was dating became pregnant. We had a son. We agreed to put him up for adoption."

For a long time she was absolutely silent, and then she looked at him. In the faint light of the fire, it was as if she was unmasked.

What he saw in her eyes was not condemnation. Or anything close to it.

Love.

Her hand touched his face, stroked, comforting.

"You didn't want to," Dannie guessed softly. "Oh, Joshua."

He glanced at her through the golden light of the dying fire. She was looking at him intently, as if she was holding her breath. Her hand was still on his cheek. He could turn his head just a touch and nibble her thumb. But it would be wrong. A lie. Trying to distract them both from the real intimacy that was happening here, and from her deepest secret, which he had just seen in her eyes.

"No, I didn't want to. I guess I wanted what I'd had before, a family to call my own again, that *feeling*. I cannot tell you how I missed that feeling after Mom and Dad died. Of belonging, of having a place to go to where people knew you, clean through. Of being held to a certain standard by the people who knew you best and knew what you were capable of."

He was shocked by how much he had said, and also shocked by how easily the words came, as if all these years they had just waited below the surface to be given voice.

"What happened to the baby?" Dannie asked quietly.

"Sarah didn't want to be tied down. She wasn't ready to settle down. I considered, briefly, trying to go it on my own, as a single dad, but Sarah thought that was stupid. A single dad, just starting in life, when all these established families who could give that baby so much stability and love were just waiting to adopt? My head agreed with her. My heart—"

He stopped, composing himself, while she did the perfect thing and said nothing. He went on, "My heart never did. Some men could be unchanged by that. I wasn't. I couldn't even finish school. I tried to run away from what I was feeling. I had abandoned my own son to the keeping of strangers. What kind of person did a thing like that?

"I traveled the world and developed an aversion for places that catered to families. Wasn't there anywhere a guy like me could get away from all that love? I kind of just fell into the resort business, bought a run-down hotel in Italy, started catering to the young and hip and single, and became a runaway success before I knew what had hit me."

Her hand, where it touched his cheek, was tender. It felt like absolution. But he knew the truth. She could not absolve him.

Silence for a long, long time.

And then she said, "Funny, that your company is called Sun. If you say it, instead of spell it, it's kind of like you carried him with you, isn't it? Your son. Into every single day."

That was the problem with showing your heart to someone like Dannie. She saw it so clearly.

And then she said, "Have you considered the possibility that what you did was best for him? That he did get a family who were desperate for a child to love? Who could give him exactly what you missed so much after your parents died?"

"On those rare occasions that I allow myself to think about it, that is my hope. No, more than a hope. A prayer. And I'm a man who doesn't pray much, Dannie."

"Have you ever thought of finding him?" she asked softly.

"Now and then."

"And what stops you?"

"How complicated it all seems. Just go on the Internet and type in *adoption* to see what a mess of options there are, red tape, legal ramifications, ethical dilemmas."

Dannie wasn't buying it, seeing straight through him. "You must have a team of lawyers who could cut to the quick in about ten minutes. If you haven't done it, there's another reason."

"Fear, then, I guess," he said, relieved to make his truth complete, wanting her to know who he really was.

Maybe wanting himself to know, too. "Fear of being rejected. Fear of opening up a wanting that will never be satisfied, searching the earth for what I can't have or can't find."

"Oh, Joshua," she said sadly, "you don't get it at all, do you?"

"I don't?" He had told her his deepest truth, and though the light of love that shone in her eyes did not lessen, her words made him feel the arrow of her disappointment.

A woman like Dannie could show a man who was lost how to find his way home. Like being in a family, she would never accept anything but his best. Like being in a family, she would show him how to get there when he couldn't find his way by himself.

For the first time in a very, very long time, the sense of loneliness within him eased, the sense that no one really knew him dissipated.

"When you gave your son up for adoption, it wasn't really about what you needed or wanted, Joshua," she said gently. "And it isn't now, either. It's about what he needs and wants. What if he wants to know who his biological father is?"

And suddenly he saw how terribly self-centered he had always been. He had become more so, not less, after he had walked away from his baby seven years ago. He had layered himself in self-protective self-centeredness.

And he was so glad he had not taken that kiss with Dannie to where it wanted to go.

Because he had things he needed to do, roads he needed to travel down, places he needed to visit. Places of the heart.

For a moment, sitting here by the fire, exchanging laughter and confidences, eating off the same spoon, slurping spaghetti, he had thought it felt like homecoming.

Now he saw he could not have that feeling, not with her and not with anyone else, not until he had made peace with who he was and what he had done.

A long time ago he had given his own flesh and blood into the keeping of strangers. He had tried to convince himself it was the right decision. He had rationalized all the reasons it was okay. But in the back of his mind, he had still been a man, self-centered and egotistical, *knowing* that child would have disrupted his plans and his life and his dreams.

Ironically, even after he'd made the decision that would supposedly set him free, he had been a prisoner of it.

Dannie had seen that right away. *Sun. Son.*

A nibbling sense of failure, of having made a mistake in an area where it really counted, had chased him, and chased him hard. He had barely paused to catch a breath at each of his successes before beginning to run again. He had lost faith in himself because of that decision.

And no amount of success, money, power or acquisition had ever absolved him.

But Dannie was right. It was about the child, not about him. If he found out if his boy was okay, then would the demons rest? If he was able to put the needs of that babe ahead of his own, then was he the man worthy of what he saw in Dannie's eyes?

Joshua realized when he had come back into this cabin, after Michael had roared away in the motorboat, leaving them here together until morning, he had thought his mission was to get her to trust him again, the way she had when she had told him about her disastrous nonrelationship with the college professor. The way she had when she had told him about a wedding gown that she had spent all her money on and that she would never wear.

But now he saw that mission for what it was: impossible.

He could not ask anyone else to place their trust in him until he had restored his trust in himself, his belief that he could be counted on to do the right thing.

Where did that start? Maybe his journey had begun already, with saying yes to the needs of his niece and nephew. And then again, maybe that didn't count, since he'd had an ulterior motive.

Maybe his journey had begun when he had backed away from Dannie, backed away from the soft invitation of her lips and the hot invitation of her eyes, because he had known he was not ready and neither was she.

And maybe he could win back his trust in himself by taking one tiny step at a time. Was it as simple—and as difficult—as adding his name to an adoption registry, so that his son would know if he ever wanted him, he would be there for him?

"Thank you for trusting me," Dannie said softly.

The last of the embers were dying, and her voice came at him out of the darkness.

"Dannie, you are completely trustworthy," he said. And he wondered if someday he was going to be a man worthy of that.

But he had a lot of work to do before he was. The darkness claimed him, and when he woke in the morning, it was to the sound of a powerboat moving across the lake. His neck hurt from sleeping on the couch; he could not believe how good it felt to have her cuddled into him.

Trusting.

He sighed, put her away from him, got up and pulled his stiff slacks from where they were strung in front of the now-dead fire.

Trust. He could not even trust himself to look at her, did not think he was strong enough to fight the desire to say good morning to her with a kiss.

Dannie barely spoke on the way back across the water. Neither did he. There was something so deep between them now it didn't even need words. That was what he wanted to be worthy of.

They had barely landed when Susie greeted them, by dancing between the two of them, and throwing her sturdy arms around their knees, screeching as if it was Christmas morning. Even the baby seemed thrilled to see them.

Worthy of this kind of love.

"Were you okay over there?" Sally asked. "What a terrible thing to happen."

"We were fine, but I think the canoe is beyond repair," Joshua said. "I'll replace it."

Sally made a noise that sounded suspiciously close to disgust. "I'm not worried about *stuff,*" she said annoyed. "Stuff can be replaced. People can't."

A little boy in a blue blanket. Never replaced. Not with all the stuff.

"I've made a farewell breakfast," Sally said, turning away from them and leading the way back to the lodge. "Come."

With Susie holding his one hand, as if he completely deserved her love and devotion, and the baby in the crook of his arm, he followed Sally up to the lodge. Dannie trailed behind, lost in her own thoughts.

Sally had made a wonderful feast: bacon, eggs, pancakes, fresh-squeezed juice. For them. For people she barely knew. Still, she looked a little sad and Joshua realized that was part of the magic of this place. It made everyone who came here into family, it made every farewell difficult.

He had not once discussed business with Michael, and suddenly he was glad. He had not made any promises he could not keep.

Trust. It was time to be a man he could be proud of. That Dannie would be proud of. That maybe his son would be proud of one day.

"I have a confession to make," he said, when the remnants of breakfast had been cleared away. Susie was in front of the fire, playing with an old wooden fire engine, out of earshot.

He looked Michael in the eye. "Michael, I was trying to get rid of my niece and nephew when you called. They'd arrived in my life because of an error in dates. I didn't want them there. They made me feel inadequate and uncomfortable. But when I got the feeling that they might improve my chances of acquiring the lodge, I jumped at your invitation and I brought them with me. I was going to play devoted uncle to manipulate your impressions of me."

He glanced at Dannie, could not read the expression on her face. Had he disappointed her again?

"Instead of *using* them, as I'd intended," he continued, "the lodge gave me a chance to spend time with them and really enjoy them, and I'm very thankful to you and Sally for that opportunity."

No one looked at all surprised by his confession, as if he had been totally transparent all along. No one looked angry or betrayed or hurt.

Somehow he had stumbled on the place that was *family,* where everyone saw you as you were, and while they hoped the best for you, always saw the potential, they never seemed to judge where you were at in this moment.

"So, Joshua, what are your plans for the lodge if you acquire it?" Michael asked, but his voice conveyed a certain reluctance to discuss business.

Joshua was silent. Then he said words he did not think he had said in his entire business career. "I thought I knew. But I don't. I can't make you any promises. I don't know what direction Sun is moving in."

He glanced at Dannie. He knew she had heard the truth. It was not about Sun right now. It was about son.

Michael sighed and looked at his hands, Joshua could clearly see he was a man with the weight of the world on his shoulders.

Dannie, always intuitive, saw it, too.

"Why are you selling Moose Lake Lodge?" Dannie asked. "You obviously love this place so much. To be frank, I can't even picture the place without you two here."

It was the kind of question Joshua would never have asked in the past. It was the kind of question that blurred the lines between professional and personal.

On the other hand, hadn't those lines been blurring for days now? He felt grateful it had been asked. He felt as if the right decision on his part needed the full story and all the facts.

Sally shot Joshua a look, clearly wondering if he would use any weakness against them. She glanced at her husband. He shrugged, and she covered his big work-worn hand with hers.

It was a gesture of such tenderness, some connection between them so strong and so bright, that Joshua felt his eyes smart.

Or maybe it was just from the fire smoking in the hearth. Or from several days so far out of his element. Or from falling in love with Dannie Springer.

He looked at her again, saw her watching Sally with such enormous compassion. Remembered her over the past few days, laughing, playing with the kids, running into the lake right behind him when the boat had broken free.

A woman a man could share the burdens with, just as Sally and Michael so obviously had shared theirs over the years. A woman a man could go to as himself, flawed, and still feel valued. *Worthy.*

He had said it in his own mind. He was falling in love with her. He waited for the terror to come.

But it didn't. Instead what came was a sense of peace such as he had not felt for a very long time.

"We're selling, or trying to sell, for a number of reasons," Sally said, her voice soft with emotion. "Partly that we're too old to do the place justice anymore." She stopped, distressed, and he watched Michael's hand tighten over hers.

"It's mostly that our daughter is sick," Michael said gruffly. "Darlene has an aggressive form of a degenerative muscle disorder. She practically grew up here, but she can't come here anymore. She's got three little kids and she's a single mom.

"Pretty soon she's going to need a wheelchair. And if she's going to stay in her own home, everything has to be changed, from the cabinets to the door handles. She's going to need a special lift system to get in the bathtub. She's going to need a modified van. She's going to need us."

Joshua heard the unspoken: it was going to take more

money than they knew how to raise to take care of their daughter as her health deteriorated.

Michael got up abruptly and walked out into the clear brightness of the morning, a man prepared to do the right thing, no matter how hard it was, no matter what it cost him, no matter what he had to let go of.

"Sorry," Sally said, watching him go, pain and love equal in her eyes. "It's hard for a man to care as much as he does and to find himself helpless."

It really confirmed everything Joshua already knew about love. It could slay the strongest man. It could tear the flesh from his bones. It could leave him trembling and unsure of the world.

He looked at Dannie. She was staring into the fire.

He saw her hand had crept into Sally's. Such a small thing. Such a right thing.

He felt sick to his stomach. He wanted the Moose Lake Lodge, and he wanted it badly. But he wasn't going to take advantage of these fine people's misery.

Except they needed the money.

And they only had one way to get it.

To sell what they loved most. Their history. Their memories.

Why did his whole life feel all wrong ever since the nanny had put in an appearance?

Only a few days ago, Joshua Cole had been sure of his identity: businessman, entrepreneur. Maybe he'd even embraced the playboy part of it a little bit because it had allowed him to fill up his life with superficial fun but never required anything *real* of him.

Today he was sure of nothing at all, least of all his identity.

Later that morning, his bags packed beside him, Joshua watched Dannie and the kids from the safety of the porch on Angel's Rest. They were walking the beach one last time with Sally, Dannie carrying the baby, her feet bare in the cold sand. He acutely felt, watching that scene, the emptiness of his own life.

He had filled it with stuff instead of substance.

He watched Dannie pull something from her pocket. He saw her reach inside herself for strength, and then she sent that small object hurtling out into the water, further than he could have imagined she could throw.

He saw the glint of gold catching in the sun, before the object completed its upward arch and then plummeted to the lake and slipped beneath the surface with nary a ripple.

From here he could hear Dannie's laughter. And understood that she was free.

He was glad to get on the plane an hour later. His world. Precision. Control. He hoped for freedom as great as he had heard in Dannie's laughter.

But instead of feeling a joyous release as the plane took off, he was acutely aware there would be no more running. He could not fly away from the truths he had to face. They would just be waiting when he landed.

It occurred to him that maybe he would never find his own son. Or maybe he would find him, and the family would choose not to have contact.

But he was aware that he could reclaim his faith in himself in other ways.

Joshua Cole knew his heart was ready.

And he was surprised to find he did have a simple faith, after all. It was that once a heart was ready, the opportunities would come. And once a man was ready, he would take them.

CHAPTER EIGHT

THEY WERE SAYING GOODBYE. Dannie couldn't believe it had happened this fast. She had wanted to tell Joshua she admired him for telling Sally and Michael the truth. She wanted to ask him how he planned to help them, for surely he did.

And she had wanted to thank him for telling her about his son.

But somehow, during that short flight back to Vancouver from Moose Lake Lodge, the opportunity had never come. Aside from the fact his expression had been remote and focused, not inviting any kind of conversation, Jake had been terribly fussy.

Susie had a delayed reaction to the fact they had left her for the night without consulting her, and her upset had intensified when she had not been able to find Michael to tell him goodbye.

Now she was behaving outrageously. Bits of stuffing from the teddy bear Joshua had given her on their first day with him was soon floating in the air, landing in handfuls in the front seats of the aircraft.

Joshua didn't even seem to notice, but no wonder when he landed, he asked them to wait, and then disappeared into the terminal.

When he came back out he told them he had arranged their flight home. A chartered plane would take them to Toronto, a car and driver would meet them and take them to his sister's house.

He took Dannie's hands in both his own. For a moment she thought he was going to kiss her, but he didn't. In some ways the look in his eyes was better than a kiss.

Trusting. Forthright.

"I'll be in touch as soon as I can," he said. "I have some things I need to look after first. I don't know how long it will take, but when it is done, I promise, I will come for you."

Words eerily like those Brent had spoken.

Would she do it again? Build a fantasy around a few words, a vague promise? But when she returned his look, she found herself believing. This time it was real.

But the lifestyles-of-the-rich-and-famous flight home, the growing geographical distance between them, played with her mind. Nothing about this private plane ride seemed *real*.

Was it possible Joshua Cole had divested her from his life?

Was it possible he had left the story in the middle? Was it possible Dannie might never know what happened to Sally and Michael? To Sun and Moose Lake Lodge?

Was it possible he would make that journey of the heart, his decisions about his son, alone? By himself?

He was the playboy. Lethally charming. Had she fallen, hook, line and sinker, for that lethal charm, or had she really seen the genuine Joshua Cole, the one he showed no one else?

Melanie and Ryan arrived home a day later, tanned and relaxed, more in love than ever.

Their affection and respect for each other seemed, impossibly, to have deepened. Susie's behavioral problems evaporated instantly once her secure family unit was back the way she wanted it to be.

Dannie had never felt on the outside of that family quite so much. She had never felt so uncertain of her own choices.

Part of her waited, on pins and needles, jumping every time the phone rang. Because when she thought back on her time with Joshua, it seemed as if it had been exquisitely solid, an island in the land of mist that her life had been. It seemed as if those days at Moose Lake Lodge might have been the most real thing about her entire life.

It felt as if what she had been when she was with him, alive and strong and connected to life, had been the genuine deal. She was sure he had felt it, too.

He had shared his secret self with her. He had told her about his son. Every time she thought of the way he had looked as he told that story, lost and forlorn, and yet so brave and so determined, she felt like weeping. She felt as if she wanted to be there for him as he took the next steps, whatever he decided those would be.

She had been sure he would call. Positive that his promise meant something. She had felt as if he needed her to navigate the waters he was entering, as if she could be on his team as surely as when they had paddled the canoe together.

When he did not call, for one day and then another, her self-doubt returned in force. When a week passed with no call, Dannie condemned herself as the woman who could spin a romance, a fantasy out of the flimsiest of fabrics.

Brent had given her a locket with his picture in it. He had made vague promises. Naturally he was coming home to marry her.

Joshua Cole, World's Sexiest Bachelor, in a moment of complete vulnerability had told her his deepest secret. Naturally that meant he was throwing over all the women he'd been paired with in the past!

He was giving up actresses and singers and heiresses for the nanny! Of course he was! Dannie even took her wedding dress out of its wrapper and laid it on her bed, allowed herself to look at it wistfully and imagine herself gliding down the aisle, *him* waiting for her.

But as the days passed and it became increasingly apparent he wasn't, Dannie found comfort in chocolate rather than her wedding dress!

"Okay," Mel said finally. "Tell me what on earth happened to you, Dannie?"

"What do you mean?"

"You're gaining about a pound a day! You're not the same with the children as you were before. It's as if you've decided to be an employee instead of a member of our family. I miss you! What's going on?"

"It's the whole Brent thing," Dannie lied. *The whole romance thing. The whole life thing.*

But Melanie stared at her, and understanding, totally unwanted, dawned in her eyes.

"It's not Brent," she guessed softly. "It's my brother. What has Josh done to you?"

"Nothing," Dannie said, quickly. Obviously way too quickly.

"I'm going to kill him," Mel said.

Dannie had a sudden humiliating picture of Mel phoning her brother and reaming him out for having done something to her nanny.

The one he had probably forgotten existed as soon as he'd divested himself of her at the airport!

"You didn't do a bit of matchmaking, did you? You

didn't think your brother and I would make a good pair, did you?" Dannie asked, remembering Joshua's embarrassing conclusion on their first meeting.

"Of course not," Melanie said quickly and vehemently, her eyes sliding all over the place and landing everywhere but on her nanny's face.

"You did!" Dannie breathed.

"I didn't. I mean not officially."

"But unofficially?"

"Oh, Dannie, I just love you so. And him. And you both seemed so lonely and so lost and so devoted to making absolutely the wrong choices for yourselves. I thought it couldn't hurt to put you together and just see what happened. I thought it couldn't do any harm. But it did, didn't it?"

Harm? Dannie thought of her days with Joshua, of the delight of getting to know him, and herself. Even if he never called, could those days be taken away from her? Could what she had glimpsed in herself fade away?

Only if she let it.

"I'm going to kill him," Melanie said again, but with no real force.

"You know what, Melanie?" Dannie said slowly, as understanding dawned in her. "Your brother didn't do anything to me. I do things to myself."

"What does that mean?" Melanie asked, skeptical.

"It means I have an imagination that fills in the gaps where reality leaves off."

As she said it, Dannie's understanding of herself grew. She was too willing to give her emotions into the keeping of other people. She was too willing to rearrange her whole world around a possibility, to put her whole life on hold while she *waited* for someone else to call the shots.

It was not admirable that she was willing to put her whole world and her whole life on hold in anticipation of some great love, some great event in the future! She'd done it with Brent on very little evidence, and now on even less evidence—only four days—she was going to waste time mooning over Joshua Cole?

No, he could have his car and his airplane and his fancy apartment and his five-star resorts. He could have heiresses and actresses and rock stars, if that was what made him happy. Love wanted the beloved to be happy. It didn't demand ownership!

Besides, Dannie missed the girl she had been, ever so briefly, in that canoe. Not a girl who *waited* for life to happen, but someone who participated fully, someone who had discovered her own strength and insisted on pulling her own weight.

While Melanie watched her, Dannie took the ice cream she was eating and washed it down the sink.

"That's it," she told her friend and employer. "No more self-pity. No more being victimized. I have a life to live!"

"I'm still going to kill him," Melanie muttered.

"Not for my benefit, you're not," Dannie said firmly.

The next day, her day off, she took the wedding gown to a local theatrical company and donated it to their costume department. They were thrilled to have it, and frankly she was thrilled to see it go. That's where that fantasy concoction of silk and lace belonged, in a world of make-believe. And that's where she was living no longer.

And then she went and signed up for canoe lessons at a place called Wilderness Ways Center. And while she was there, she noticed they had a class in rock climbing, and their own rock wall, so she signed up for that, too.

She took to her activities intensively, spending every free minute at the centre.

The loveliest and most unexpected thing happened. Danielle Springer had been waiting her whole life to fall in love. And she did.

She fell in love with herself.

She fell in love with the laughter-filled woman who attacked climbing walls and finicky canoes with a complete sense of adventure. She fell in love with the woman, whom she recognized had always been afraid of life, suddenly embracing its uncertainties.

She had always been a good nanny, and she knew that, but suddenly she felt as if she was a great nanny, because she was passing on this new and incredible sense of adventure and discovery to the children.

As the cool, fresh days of spring turned to the hot, humid days of summer, she found herself right out there jumping through the sprinkler with Susie, immersed in the wading pool with Jake.

She was teaching her young charges what she was learning: that life was a gift. An imperfect life, a life that did not go as planned, was no less a gift. Maybe a surprising life was even more of one.

The strangest thing was the more she danced with the gypsy spirit she was discovering in herself, the less she needed a man to validate her! When Joshua Cole had touched her lip with his thumb, he had told her he knew something of her that she did not know of herself.

But now she did! She knew she was strong and independent and capable. And fun loving. And full of mischief. And ready to dance with life! The irony, of course, was that men, who had always treated her as invisible, liked her. They flocked to her! They flirted with her.

The phone started ringing for her all the time. Now that she could have anything she wanted, and anyone, she was surprised how much herself was enough. She liked how uncomplicated it was to live her own life, pursue her own interests, immerse herself in her job and her everyday pleasures. Something as simple as lying on the fragrant back lawn at night looking with wonder at the stars filled her to the top.

She was just coming in the door from her kayak lesson, when Melanie told her she had a phone call.

"It's Joshua," Melanie said, eyebrows raised, not even trying to hide her hope and delight that her brother might be coming to his senses.

Dannie picked up the phone. Despite how she had made herself over, her heart was hammering in her throat.

"How are you?" he asked.

Such a simple question. And yet the sound of his voice, alone, familiar, deep, masculine, tender, made her call him, in her own mind, "beloved."

"I'm fine, Joshua." Before she could ask how he was, he started talking again.

"Mel says you've been keeping really busy. Canoeing and rock climbing."

"I've been staying busy," she said, keeping her voice carefully neutral so he would not hear the unspoken, *I wish you could do it with me.*

"She says the guys are calling there all the time for you."

Was that faint jealousy in the World's Sexiest Bachelor's voice? Dannie laughed. "Not *all* the time."

His voice went very low. "She says you don't go out with any of them. Not on dates, anyway."

"Joshua! Your sister shouldn't be telling you anything about my private life."

"She can't resist me when I beg," he said.

Who could? "Why are you begging for information about me?"

"You know why."

Yes. She said nothing, afraid to speak, afraid to believe, afraid this was a test of all her resolve to not live in her fantasies but to create a dynamic reality for herself in the here and the now.

"Dannie, I couldn't call you until I had looked after certain things. Until I had done my very best to clear away any baggage, any heartache that would have kept me from being the man you deserve."

She wanted to tell him he was wrong, that he had always been the man she deserved, but something in her asked her to wait, to listen, and most of all, to believe.

"When I got back from Moose Lake Lodge, I thought of what you had said, about putting the ball in my son's court. Doing what he needed, instead of what I thought I needed or wanted. I discussed the options with one of my lawyers. After a lot of discussion we finally agreed to register with an agency that specializes in triad reunions. That means all three parties, the child, the adoptive family and the birth parents, have to want a contact or a meeting or a reunion. Until all three pieces are in place, nothing happens."

She could hear the emotion in his voice. She felt so proud of him. She felt as if she had never loved him more.

There was a long, long silence. Finally he spoke, whispered a single word.

"Dannie."

He couldn't possibly be crying. He couldn't. Not the

strong, totally in control playboy. Not the World's Sexiest Bachelor. Not one of the world's most successful entrepreneurs and resort visionaries.

Her Joshua, the one she had always seen, while the rest of the world bought the role he was playing, was capable of this great tenderness, this great vulnerability, this final unmasking.

"Dannie," Joshua choked out, "they were waiting for me."

"Oh, Joshua," she breathed his name, and then again in confirmation that he was exactly who she had known he was. "Oh, Joshua."

The tears of joy were coursing down her own cheeks.

"I've spoken to his parents on the phone. And him. It's funny, I had not grieved the death of his mother, until I had to tell him she was gone."

"Joshua." Again his name came from her lips like a celebration, like a prayer.

"I've arranged to meet my son and his adoptive parents this weekend. They live in Calgary. His name's Jared. I—" he stopped, hesitated, his voice still hoarse with emotion "—I'd like you to come with me."

"Why?" she said. It was a hard question to ask, when everything in her just wanted to say *yes*. Scream yes.

But his answer was everything. Everything. If he wanted her to come with him because of her skills as a nanny, it didn't count. It wasn't what she wanted. It wasn't even close. The seconds before he answered were easily the longest of her life.

"I want you to come with me because this is the most important thing I've ever done, and I cannot imagine doing it without you. I want you to come with me because I trust you more than I trust myself," he said, and then softly, ever so softly, "I want you to come because

I think I could fall in love with you. I think I'm half-way there, already."

She couldn't speak through the tears.

"Dannie, are you there?"

"Yes."

"Will you?"

The question asked more than whether she would accompany him to meet his son for the first time.

It asked her to take a chance on this crazy, unpredictable, potential-for-heartbreak thing called love all over again.

"Will I? Oh, Joshua, I'm just like them." She took a deep breath. It did not stop her voice from shaking. "I've been waiting for you."

She didn't even know how true that was until she spoke the words. She hadn't even realized all of it—the canoeing and rock climbing, the boldly saying yes to life, all of it had been about being ready.

Being the kind of woman ready to fall in love—sure of herself and her place in the world first.

Not being *needy*, but being strong. Not needing another person to complete her, but bringing her whole self to a union.

It was true, she had been waiting for Joshua. It was just as true that she had been waiting for herself.

CHAPTER NINE

I've been waiting for you.

The words, and his memory of them, had been like a lifeline through the past few days. He held on to them, he held on to the beauty of what he had heard in Dannie's voice.

Joshua Cole had been the prime player in million-dollar deals. He had taken a company from nothing and turned it into something. He single-handedly ran an empire valued in billions, not millions.

And yet all that paled in comparison to how he felt about meeting his son. And about seeing Dannie again.

It was as if, in all his world, only two things mattered. Only two things had become important.

And both those things were all about *the* thing. Love.

He waited at the Calgary International airport for Dannie, nervously holding a bouquet of flowers for her. He had purchased flowers for dozens of women, and it had never caused him so much anxiety, choosing each bloom personally, debating over daisies or roses, baby's breath or lily of the valley.

He saw Dannie coming through the door of the security area, and was astonished by the changes in her, knew that daisies were *exactly* right, unpretentious, simple, earthy, beautiful, hardy.

Dannie looked as if she was twenty pounds lighter than she had been the first time he'd seen her. Gone was any vestige of the frumpalumpa. Today she was dressed in a white tailored silk shirt, a blazer, amazing low-riding jeans. He was aware he wouldn't have any problem peeling those jeans off her if they got wet!

Not that he wanted his mind to be going there since he was working so hard at being the man she deserved. Decent. Considerate. Strong. A man of integrity and honor.

Her hair was, thankfully, the same jet-black gypsy tangle. She had made no effort to tame it, and it sprang around her head in sexy, unruly curls that his fingers ached to touch. She was tanned and healthy looking, her turquoise eyes subtly shaded with makeup that made them pop.

He saw the man who came out the door ahead of her glance back, knew enough about male body language to know he was interested.

Hey, buddy, I saw her first.

And that was the truth. He had *seen* her, even before she had done one single thing to be seen.

Joshua saw that though Dannie had always radiated calm, a ship confident of riding out the storm, now there were layers to that calm. He saw the confidence in her. And the purity of her strength. And he knew he had never needed it more.

She saw him, and he didn't think for as long as he lived, he would ever forget the look in her eyes. More than welcome. More than joy. Bigger.

Homecoming.

She flew into his arms, no reservations, and he picked her up and swung her around, felt his own welcoming answer to the look in her eyes, felt how right her sweet weight was in his arms, as if she belonged there, her softness melting into the firmness of his chest.

Finally, he put her down and gazed at her, silent, wonder filled. He touched her hair, just to make it real.

"Tonight is just you and me," he said, picking up her bag, realizing he couldn't just stand there staring at her forever, even if that's what he wanted to do. "We're going to meet Jared and his mom and dad for lunch tomorrow at their house, and if that goes okay, we're going to go to the zoo."

"How are you doing?" she asked, seeing right through the illusion of control reciting the itinerary was supposed to give him!

He smiled at how she could see right through the confidence of the designer suit, and the take-control businessman attitude.

Just as he had seen her before anyone else had, she had seen him.

"Terrified," he whispered. Not just about Jared, either, but about making a mistake with her. Funny, he who had been classified as a playboy, felt he had no skill at being real. But he needn't have worried.

"What do you want to do tonight?" he asked, his voice faintly strangled.

It sounded hilarious, like a teenage boy fumbling his way through his first date. He felt like a teenage boy, as if he wanted to get this so right. Before her arrival, he'd picked up the newspaper and been scanning it, looking for exactly the activity that would bring them back to the people they had been on that island several weeks ago.

There were a number of live shows in town. Five-star restaurants had been recommended to him. But he had not bought tickets or made reservations because he didn't want it to have that awkward-first-date feeling.

Even though that's probably what it was, he felt way past that.

"Let's order a pizza in the hotel," she said, burying her nose in the bouquet, "and watch a movie in your room."

So simple. So perfect. Like daisies. Like her.

"Um," he actually felt shy, embarrassed. "I booked you a separate room. I didn't think—" He was actually blushing, he could feel it.

She threw back her head and laughed. "You were right, Joshua, you are going to have to woo me. I'm not like the other girls."

"You aren't," he said ruefully. "Not a single soul I know could use the word *woo* seriously like that."

"Well, I intend to be wooed. I'm not just falling into the sack with you."

It was his turn to laugh, to tell the little devil on his shoulder to forget peeling off those pants anytime soon.

That night they sprawled out on his bed in his room, eating pizza and watching movies, and he remembered how it had been that night with her in the cabin.

Exhilarating. But comfortable, too.

At eleven she kissed him good-night, her lips tender and full of promise. But then she went to her own room.

The next morning she insisted they find a rock-climbing wall, because she said the tension was boiling off him.

By the time she'd beaten him to the top of that wall three times, he didn't have any energy left, never mind any tension.

They went shopping together. He was going to buy Jared a teddy bear, but she rolled her eyes at that, and told him seven-year-old boys did not like teddy bears.

Which was a relief, because then he got to look at the

really fun stuff like remote control cars and footballs, skateboards and video games. He wanted to buy everything. Dannie, guiding him calmly through the jagged mountain terrain of the heart, told him to choose one.

And so they arrived at Jared's house at lunchtime, he with one remote control car, wishing he had a box-load full of toys to hide behind. He looked at the house, gathering evidence that somehow, despite himself, all those years ago, he had managed to do the right thing.

It was an ordinary house on an ordinary street, well kept, tidy, *loved.* Behind the picket fence, peeping through the leaves of a mature maple tree, he could see a platform in a tree, looking over the yard. A bicycle leaned up against the side of the house. A volleyball lay in the neat grass.

It pleased Joshua more than he could have said that the yard and the house indicated his son had enjoyed an ordinary life, an ordinary family, a life very different than the one Joshua could have given him if he'd hung on instead of letting go.

A better life, he thought, surveying the yard one more time, feeling Dannie's hand tightening in his, a life where everyone had put Jared first. Even the man who had been unaware that he had done so.

Joshua had never in his life been as afraid as he was when he rang that doorbell. A dog barked from inside. A golden retriever, delirious with happiness greeted them first. A lovely woman came to the door, in her early thirties, a redhead with an impish grin and warm green eyes. Behind her stood her husband, as wholesome looking as apple pie, the guy next door who built the tree house and threw the baseballs until dark, and who probably got up predawn to coach the peewee hockey team.

And then the world went still.

Jared ran into the room, all energy and joy. By now, Joshua had seen his son's picture, but it did not prepare him for how he felt. It seemed as if energy streamed off the boy, pure as sunshine. Jared was sturdy, with auburn hair and green eyes that danced with mischief, the confidence of a child who had known only love.

He skidded to a halt, ruffed the dog's ears, gazed at Joshua with intent curiosity.

"You look like me," he decided, "I couldn't really tell from the picture. Hey, Mom, can I get a frog?"

Until that moment, it felt to Joshua as if his life had been a puzzle, the pieces scattered all over the place.

But with those words, *Hey, Mom, can I get a frog* and the sudden laughter that chased the awkwardness from the room, it was as if the pieces drew together and slid firmly into place.

It seemed as if that moment, and all of life, was infused with light, as if, in spite of the efforts of people, rather than because of them, everything had turned out exactly as it was meant to be.

Introductions were made, but they were an odd formality in this group of people that somehow already were, and always would be a family.

The entire weekend, they did nothing special, and yet everything was special. Eating barbecued burgers in the Morgans' backyard, playing Frisbee with the dog, touring the zoo, sitting on the edge of his son's bed, trying to read him a story through the lump in his throat.

Joshua Cole, who had specialized in giving ordinary people spectacular experiences made the humbling discovery that ordinary experiences were made spectacular by the people you shared them with, by the addition of one secret ingredient.

Love.

He discovered that sometimes a man had to work at love.

But most of the time it was just brought to him, even though he might be completely undeserving of it.

"I can't think when I've had a more perfect weekend," Joshua said as he strolled through the airport with Dannie on Sunday night. Her hand in his felt perfect, too.

"Me, neither," she said.

In a few moments, the miles would separate them. How could he make the ache less, take away the sense of loss? Not just for himself, which was the way the old Joshua thought, but for her?

He stopped in front of a jewelry store counter, and they looked at a display of sparkling diamond necklaces together. "Pick one," he said. "Any one. To remember this weekend by."

"No," she said.

"Come on," he said. "To remember me. To show you how much I care for you and am going to miss you until we meet again."

"No," she said, more firmly than the first time.

Too expensive, he thought, not appropriate for their first weekend together, though he had given far more expensive gifts for far less.

"How about one of those, then?" he said, pointing to a glittering display of diamond tennis bracelets.

"Joshua, no!"

"Hey," he said, "I'm wooing you!"

"No," she said, almost gently, as if she was explaining the timetables to a three year old. "That's wowing. There's a difference. I don't need anything to remember this weekend by, Joshua."

"How am I supposed to woo you with an attitude like that?" he asked, pretending to be grouchy.

"For you, Joshua, the easiest thing would be to shower me with gifts, with all the *stuff* money can buy. But that's not what I want. I want the hardest things from you. I want your time. I want your energy. I want you fully engaged. I want *you.* You can't win me by throwing your wealth at me."

He scowled at that. The weekend had gone so well he thought he'd already won her. He could now clearly see that wasn't true.

That she was going to make him work for her heart, and that she planned to give him a run for his money. He could clearly see that he was going to have to win her the old-fashioned way.

And suddenly it felt like the most exciting challenge of his whole life. Better than any of it. Better than buying resorts, better than flying airplanes, better than thrill seeking, better than traveling to the seven wonders of the world.

She was trying to tell him there was no destination. It was all about the trip. And the truth was, he couldn't wait. He felt as if she was leading him to the eighth wonder of the world.

Which existed for each man within the unexplored and unmapped territories of his own heart.

"DANNIE," MELANIE SAID, "could you just say yes? My brother is driving me crazy."

They were both standing at her picture window, looking out at the front lawn. Overnight three hundred plastic pink flamingos had appeared on it, splashes of color against the first winter's snow. They spelled out, more or less, DANNIE.

"It's been six months," Melanie said. "He's more insanely in love with you every day. Just say yes."

"I don't really know if the flamingos fit the criteria. He used money."

"He had to have rented them! Or borrowed them. Maybe he even stole them. He didn't buy them. And I bet he was out there himself in the freezing cold spelling your name in tacky plastic birds. If that isn't love, nothing is. Say yes."

"To what?" Dannie said innocently. "He hasn't asked me anything yet."

Dannie smiled at Melanie, allowed herself to feel the tenderness of the flamingos planted in a declaration of love for her. When she had challenged Joshua to woo her, without great displays of wealth and power, nothing could have prepared her for how that man rose to a challenge!

The only exception she had made to her proviso about his using his wealth was plane tickets. Even she had to admit that it was pretty hard to woo someone unless you saw them.

So, he flew to Toronto, and he flew her to Vancouver, or they met in Calgary to have time with Jared and the Morgans.

Melanie was right. Her brother was crazy, but in the most phenomenal way. Never had a woman been wooed the way Danielle Springer was being wooed.

While the weather had still been good, they had attended rock-climbing and canoeing schools together. To his consternation, Dannie insisted on paying her own tuition. She asked him to donate his offering to the classes Wilderness Ways offered to the Boys & Girls Club.

He had found a guitar—he claimed it had been given

to him, so that it was still within her rules of wooing—and sang to her outside his sister's house. He neither knew how to play or how to sing. Listening to him murder a love song had been more endearing than him offering to take her to a concert in Vancouver, which she had said no to, firmly, when he had flashed the very expensive tickets in front of her.

He had made her a cedar chest with his own hands, when she had refused the one he had wanted to buy for her after she had admired it at an antique store they had been browsing through. He didn't know how to build anymore than he knew how to sing, the chest a lopsided testament to his love.

He was slowly filling it with treasures, not a single one that money could buy. The chest held his mother's wedding ring and his grandmother's handmade lace. It held a bronzed baby shoe—his—and a baby picture of Jared. He was giving her his history.

He had made her a locket to replace the one she had thrown away, only his was made out of paper maché and contained his thumb print. She had worn it until it threatened to disintegrate, and then she had put it in the chest with her other treasures.

He had baked her cookies shaped like haphazard hearts and that had tasted strongly of baking soda. One of their most romantic evenings had been over his home-cooked spaghetti, perfecting the art of eating the same noodle, both of them sucking one end of it until their lips met in the middle.

He had sent her dental floss, special delivery, claiming he was a reformed man.

"Is that used?" Melanie had asked, horrified when Danielle had opened the package.

"Never mind," Danielle had said, tucking the envelope in her chest of treasures. "I will show it to my children one day. I will say, 'Your father gave me plaque.'"

"You're as disgusting as him," Melanie griped. "What children? Has he asked you?"

"Not yet."

"He better get on with it. I'm reporting him to the post office if he sends anything else like that."

When he flew in for the weekends, he taught her how to fish on a little canal near Melanie and Ryan's house, and when it froze over, he taught her how to skate. They never caught a single fish, though they caught a frog for Jared, and then had to figure out how to get it to him. Joshua ended up chartering a plane so he didn't have to smuggle the little green creature through airport security.

Dannie never was able to skate without him holding her up, and it just didn't matter. They went for long walks and on star-gazing expeditions. When they passed some children with kittens in a box outside a grocery store, under a huge sign that said Free, he picked out the cutest one for her.

She named it Rhapsody.

When he flew her to Vancouver, she brought him terrible poems that she had written herself, and cooked him disastrous meals. She admired the flowers he was growing for her on his terrace, since he wasn't allowed to buy her anything. They rode the Skytrain, and explored Stanley Park. They spent evenings in the Jacuzzi, in bathing suits.

When they went to Calgary they went on picnics with the Morgans and rode bicycles with Jared on the network of trails. They threw baseballs in the backyard and built a roof on the tree platform so they could sleep out there at night. Joshua proved again he was no builder. That roof leaked like a sieve, which only added to the fun!

They took Jared to the public pools that had waves and waterslides, and they hung out at the libraries that offered story time. They caught bugs for his frog, Simon, and took the golden retriever to obedience class.

Joshua and Jared took ski lessons at the Olympic Park, and she perfected the art of drinking hot chocolate in the ski lodge.

"There he is," Melanie said, looking past the flamingos. She snorted with affection. "The great playboy arrives. If he doesn't ask you this weekend, I'm disowning him."

"You said that last weekend," Dannie reminded her.

"The difference is this weekend I mean it."

"Look, Melanie," Dannie said softly, "he brought you a surprise."

Joshua was getting out of a small sports car, obviously a rental, trying to convince an eight-foot-long toboggan to get out with him. And then a little boy tumbled out of the front seat.

"Ohmygod," Melanie said, and turned wide tear-filled eyes to Dannie. "Is that my nephew?" She didn't wait for an answer, but went out the front door in her sock feet, tripping over pink flamingos in her haste to meet the little boy who looked just like her brother had once looked.

Every day they spent together seemed magical, but that one more so. They took the kids tobogganing, Susie had an instant case of hero-worship for her older cousin.

When they got home, Melanie took the kids under her wing, then handed her brother an envelope. "Enough's enough," she said sternly. "I'll mind the children."

Joshua opened the envelope. Inside it was a map.

Danielle could hardly look at him, suddenly shy, wondering if he, too, remembered the last time someone had offered to mind the children for them.

They followed the map outside of the city, through the ever deepening darkness and the countryside to a little cabin.

It was inside the cabin that Dannie realized he was in on it. How else could it be completely stocked with tinned spaghetti and boxed cake mix?

He made her a dinner, and then as the fire roared in the stone hearth, he poured the cake mix into a pot, mixed it with water, and cooked it over the fire.

"I don't want any of that," she said.

"Come on. You're just way too skinny."

It was true, but for the first time in her life, she wasn't skinny on purpose. She was skinny because she was so happy there was not a single space in her that food could fill.

Tonight, she thought, looking through the door to the bedroom of the tiny cabin. Tonight would be the night. She leaned forward and kissed him.

Normally he would have kissed her back, but tonight he didn't.

"I can't do it anymore," he said. "I can't kiss you and not have you."

"I know," she said. "It's okay. I'm wooed. Let's go to bed."

"Ah, no."

"What do you mean, no?" she asked stunned.

"Dannie, that's not how an old-fashioned wooing ends."

"It isn't?"

"No," he said and got down on one knee in front of her. "It ends like this." He freed a ring box stuck in his pocket. "Dannie, will you marry me? Will you be mine forever? Will you have my children and be a part of the family that includes my son? And my niece and nephew?"

"Yes," she whispered.

Then he kissed her, but when she tried to get him into that bedroom he wouldn't allow it.

"Nope. You have to wait until the wedding night."

"I do?"

"Yeah."

"Give me the fried cake," she said glumly. She shared the spoon with him. It didn't taste half bad.

"Don't you want to see what's in the box?" he teased.

She'd actually forgotten to look at the ring. The truth was the ring did not mean anything to her. How could it compare to the ring he'd made her out of tinfoil and glue that was in her box of treasures? How could it have the same value as these wonderful days of wooing? Oh, she was going to miss this.

Of course, being married meant it was all going to be replaced. With something better. Much better. She realized she was *starved* for him. For more of him. For his body and for his tongue and for his lips and for his hands all over her.

Her eyes skittered to that bedroom door again. Was he really going to make her wait?

"Open it," he insisted handing her the box.

The lid was very hard to pry open. When she did get it open, she saw why. Instead of a ring, there was a piece of paper folded up to fit in there. Carefully, she unfolded it, tried to understand the legal terms printed on it.

Finally, she got it. Joshua had given her the deed to Moose Lake Lodge.

"I cannot imagine not having you as a full partner in

every single thing I do, my confidante, my equal. This is yours, Dannie, to run as you see fit."

She was smiling through her tears.

"How long is it going to take you to plan a wedding?" he asked. "I want you to have it all. The dress, the flower girls, the cathedral, the—"

"No," she said. "No, I don't want any of that. That's all about a wedding, and nothing about a marriage." She began to blush. "Joshua, I can't wait much longer."

"For what?" he said with evil knowing.

"You know."

"Tell me."

So she whispered her secret longings in his ear.

"You're right," he said. "I think we need to do something fast. My honor is at stake. What do you have in mind, then?"

"A quick civil ceremony. As soon as we can get the documents in place."

He laughed. "I forgot you already have a dress."

"I don't," she said. "I'm marrying you in a snowsuit so that we can go straight to our honeymoon."

"You've given that some thought?" he asked, raising a wicked eyebrow at her.

"I'm afraid I have," she confessed, blushing. "I want to have our honeymoon at Moose Lake Lodge at the honeymoon cabin."

"It's snowing up there!" he said.

She smiled. She could not think of one thing—not one—that she would love better than being snowbound in a little cabin with him.

"I know," she said happily. "I know."

"I don't even know how you get to the cabin in the winter. I'm not canoeing you across the lake in the snow!"

"Joshua?"

"Yes?"

"I trust you to think of something." She paused, and whispered, "I trust you."

"You wouldn't if you knew the perverted thoughts I was having about your toes."

But she saw the words were her gift to him. The one he needed and wanted more than any other. She put her head on his shoulder and found the warmth of his hand.

"I trust you," she whispered again. "With my forever after."

EPILOGUE

JOSHUA COLE STOOD behind Angel's Rest at Moose Lake Lodge. It was a rare moment alone, and the sounds of summer—a vigorous game of football, laughter, the shouts of children down on the beach— drifted up to him.

He held a rose to plant and a spade, and he looked for the perfect place in the rugged garden that had been started there. Four years had passed since he had first laid eyes on this place, and first acknowledged the stirrings of his own heart.

Four years had not changed much about Moose Lake Lodge. It remained stable while all around it changed.

Dannie had an innate sense for what the world wanted: a family place, a home away from home, a place basically untouched by modern conveniences, by technology, by all those things like TV sets and computers that put distance between people who shared the same homes.

Moose Lake Lodge had become Sun's first family resort. It was not a runaway financial success, but it stood for something way more important than financial success. It was his favorite of all the Sun resorts.

"Susie, Susie Blue-Toes."

His son, Jared, now eleven, was down there tormenting his niece, refusing her command to be called Susan now that she had reached the mature age of eight. His nephew, Jake, now four, had the same contempt for the new baby that his sister had once had for him. Sally and Michael managed the place, their three grandchildren had come to live here with them since the death of Sally and Michael's daughter, Darlene, in the spring.

Moose Lake Lodge seemed a natural place for those children, since they had been able to spend so much time here with their mother. The only real change Sun had ever made to the lodge was to make Angel's Rest completely wheelchair accessible, so that Darlene could spend her last few summers here.

In the folds of what had become a family.

His son, Jared, and the Morgans, came every year for the whole summer. Joshua never stopped learning from the Morgans' generosity of spirit, from how they had included him in their lives without a moment's pause or hesitation. From them he had learned that love expanded to include; if it contracted to exclude it was no longer love.

Melanie and Ryan had fallen in love with Moose Lake Lodge from their first visit. They were entrenched in the cabin called Piper's Hollow for every long weekend and every summer. Susie and Jake acted as if they owned the whole place.

No one wanted a pool. Or a new wharf. Or jet skis. No one wanted new furniture or an outdoor bar.

No one who came here wanted anything to change.

This summer was the baby's first year here. Joshua had worried his daughter, only four months old, was too young for cold nights and onslaughts of mosquitoes, for late nights around the campfire, for noisy children all wanting to hold her. Dannie had laughed at him.

Dannie, who had come into her own in ways he had not even imagined a woman could come into her own:

shining with beauty and light, with laughter and compassion. Somehow Dannie was always at the center of all this love, the spokes around which the wheel turned.

As he thought of her, he heard her shout, turned for a moment from the flower bed, to see if he could catch a glimpse of her.

And there she was, hair flying, feet bare, slender and strong, those long legs flashing in the sun, with every kid in the place trying to catch her and wrest that football from her.

Sometimes he wished her curves back. He remembered her lush full figure when he had first met her.

But she said that once a woman had known love, chocolate just didn't do it anymore. Only four months after the baby, she was back to her normal self.

He turned again to the flower garden that Sally had just planted in Darlene's memory and found an empty place in the rich dark soil. He got down on his hands and knees and began to dig, the sounds of shouting and laughter like music in the background.

Every life, he thought, had a period of Camelot in it, a time overflowing with youth and energy, a time that shimmered with creation and abundance and love.

Joshua had experienced that in his boyhood, and thought he'd lost his chance to have it again, for good, when he had given up Jared.

He'd chased it, tried to manufacture its feeling through the Sun resorts.

But in the end Camelot came to those who did not chase it. It came through grace.

Joshua put the rose in the hole he had made in the ground, tenderly patted the dirt back into place around it, sat back on his heels and admired the buds that promised pure white blooms. To get to Camelot, an ordinary man had to become a knight, to ride into the unknown with only one weapon: a brave heart.

A heart that had faith that all would be good in the end, even if there was plenty of evidence to the contrary.

A heart that knew a man could not always trust circumstances would go his way, but if he was true, he would always be able to trust himself to deal with those circumstances.

In Camelot, there was only one truth. Money did not heal wounds. Nor did possessions. The biggest lie of all was that time did.

No, here in Camelot, Joshua found comfort in the greatest truth of all: love healed all wounds.

When a man's world burned down and there was nothing left, out of the ashes of despair and hurt and fear, love grew roses.

"Dad-O." The voice drifted up the hill, the name his son Jared had chosen to call him. "Are you coming? Our team needs you."

Joshua gave the rose one final pat, got to his feet, looked across the lake to where a little cabin, Love's Rhapsody, waited. It would probably have to wait awhile yet for them to return there, but just looking at it, he remembered.

Chasing Dannie. Kissing her toes until they were both breathless with wanting. Fusing together to create the boundless miracle that was life.

"Dad-O!" Jared had an eleven-year-old's impatience. And he would never say what he really meant. That he was anxious to spend every second he could with his father before summer ended.

"Coming," Joshua called, and went down the creaking old boardwalk stairs, two at a time, to a world that was beyond anything he could have ever dreamed of for himself. To a world that was better than any man had a right to dream of for himself.

It was a world that had waited for him when he was lost. Sometimes he called it Camelot.

But he knew its real name was Love.

* * * * *

RESCUED IN A WEDDING DRESS

CHAPTER ONE

MOLLY MICHAELS STARED at the contents of the large rectangular box that had been set haphazardly on top of the clutter on her desk. The box contained a wedding gown.

Over the weekend donations that were intended for one of the three New York City secondhand clothing shops that were owned and operated by Second Chances Charity Inc—and that provided the funding for their community programs—often ended up here, stacked outside the doorstep of their main office.

It did seem like a cruel irony, though, that this donation would end up on *her* desk.

"Sworn off love," Molly told herself, firmly, and shut the box. "Allergic to amour. Lessons learned. Doors closed."

She turned and hung up her coat in the closet of her tiny office, then returned to her desk. She snuck the box lid open, just a crack, then opened it just a little more. The dress was a confection. It looked like it had been spun out of dreams and silk.

"Pained by passion," Molly reminded herself, but even as she did, her hand stole into the box, and her fingers touched the delicate delight of the gloriously rich fabric.

What would it hurt to *look?* It could even be a good exercise for her. Her relationship with Chuck, her broken engagement, was six months in the past. The dress was probably ridiculous. Looking at it, and feeling *nothing,* better yet *judging* it, would be a good test of the new her.

Molly Michaels was one hundred percent career woman now, absolutely dedicated to her work here as the project manager at Second Chances. It was her job to select, implement and maintain the programs the charity funded that helped people in some of New York's most challenged neighborhoods.

"Love my career. Totally satisfied," she muttered. "Completely fulfilled!"

She slipped the pure white dress out of the box, felt the sensuous slide of the fabric across her palms as she shook it out.

The dress *was* ridiculous. And the total embodiment of romance. Ethereal as a puff of smoke, soft as a whisper, the layers and layers of ruffles glittered with hundreds of hand-sewn pearls and tiny silk flowers. The designer label attested to the fact that someone had spent a fortune on it.

And the fact it had shown up here was a reminder that all those romantic dreams had a treacherous tendency to go sideways. Who sent their dress, their most poignant reminder of their special day, to a charity that specialized in secondhand sales, if things had gone well?

So, it wasn't just *her* who had been burned by love. *Au contraire!* It was the way of the world.

Still, despite her efforts to talk sense to herself, there was no denying the little twist of wistfulness in her tummy as Molly looked at the dress, *felt* all a dress like that could stand for. *Love. Souls joined. Laughter shared. Long conversations. Lonely no more.*

Molly was disappointed in herself for entertaining

the hopelessly naive thoughts, even briefly. She wanted to kill that renegade longing that stirred in her. The logical way to do that would be to put the dress back in the box, and have the receptionist, Tish, send it off to the best of Second Chances stores, Wow and Then, on the Upper West Side. That store specialized in high-end gently used fashions. Everything with a designer label in it ended up there.

But, sadly, Molly had never been logical. Sadly, she had not missed the fact the dress was *exactly* her size.

On impulse, she decided the best way to face her shattered dreams head-on would be to put on the dress. She would face the bride she was never going to be in the mirror. She would regain her power over those ever so foolish and hopelessly old-fashioned dreams of *ever after*.

How could she, of all people, believe such nonsense? Why was it that the constant squabbling of her parents, the eventual dissolution of her family, her mother remarrying *often*, had not prepared Molly for real life? No, rather than making her put aside her belief in love, her dreams of a family, her disappointment-filled childhood had instead made her *yearn* for those things.

That yearning had been drastic enough to make her ignore every warning sign Chuck had given her. And there had been plenty of them! Not at first, of course. At first, it had been all delight and devotion. But then, Molly had caught her intended in increasingly frequent insults: little white lies, lateness, dates not kept.

She had forgiven him, allowing herself to believe that a loving heart overlooked the small slights, the inconsiderations, the occasional surliness, the lack of enthusiasm for the things she liked to do. She had managed to minimize the fact that the engagement ring had been embarrassingly tiny, and efforts to address setting a date had been rebuffed.

In other words, Molly had been so engrossed in her fantasy about love, had been so focused on a day and a dress just like this one, that she had excused and tolerated and dismissed behavior that, in retrospect, had been humiliatingly unacceptable.

Now she was anxious to prove to herself that a dress like this one had no power over her at all. None! Her days of being a hopeless dreamer, of being naive, of being romantic to the point of being pathetic, were over.

Over and done. Molly Michaels was a new woman, one who could put on a dress like this and *scoff* at the beliefs it represented. *Round-faced babies, a bassinet beside the bed, seaside holidays, chasing children through the sand, cuddling around a roaring fire with him, the dream man, beside you singing songs and toasting marshmallows.*

"Dream man is right," she scolded herself. "Because that's where such a man exists. In dreams."

The dress proved harder to get on than Molly could have imagined, which should have made her give it up. Instead, it made her more determined, which formed an unfortunate parallel to her past relationship.

The harder it had been with Chuck, the more she had tried to make it work.

That desperate-for-love woman was being left behind her, and putting on this dress was going to be one more step in helping her do it!

But first she got tangled in the sewn-in lining, and spent a few helpless moments lost in the voluminous sea of white fabric. When her head finally popped out the correct opening, her hair was caught hard in one of the pearls that encrusted the neckline. After she had got free of that, fate made one more last-ditch effort to get her to stop this nonsense. The back of the dress was not designed to be done up single-handedly.

Still, having come this far, with much determination and contortion, Molly somehow managed to get every single fastener closed, though it felt as if she had pulled the muscle in her left shoulder in the process.

Now she took a deep breath, girded her cynical loins, and turned slowly to look at herself in the full-length mirror hung on the back of her office door.

She closed her eyes. *Goodbye, romantic fool.* Then she took a deep breath and opened them.

Molly felt her attempt at cynicism dissolve with all the resistance of instant coffee granules meeting hot water. In fact everything dissolved: the clutter around her, the files that needed to be dealt with, the colorful sounds of the East Village awaking outside her open transom window, something called out harshly in Polish or Ukrainian, the sound of a delivery truck stopped nearby, a horn honking.

Molly stared at herself in the mirror. She had fully expected to see her romantic *fantasy* debunked. It would just be her, too tall, too skinny, redheaded and pale-faced Molly Michaels, in a fancy dress. Not changed by it. Certainly not *completed* by it.

Instead, a princess looked solemnly back at her. Her red hair, pulled out of its very professional upsweep by the entrapment inside the dress and the brief fray with the pearl, was stirred up, hissing with static, fiery and free. Her pale skin looked not washed out as she had thought it would against the sea of white but flawless, like porcelain. And her eyes shimmered green as Irish fields in springtime.

The cut of the dress had seemed virginal before she

put it on. Now she could see the neckline was sinful and the rich fabric was designed to cling to every curve, making her look sensuous, red-hot and somehow *ready.*

"This is not the lesson I was hoping for," she told herself, the stern tone doing nothing to help her drag her eyes away from the vision in the mirror. She ordered herself to take off the dress, in that same easily ignored stern tone. Instead, she did an experimental pose, and then another.

"I would have made a beautiful bride!" she cried mournfully.

Annoyed with herself, and with her weakness—eager to get away from all the feelings of loss for dreams not fulfilled that this dress was stirring up in her—she reached back to undo the fastener that held the zipper shut. It was stuck fast.

And much as she did not like what she had just discovered about herself—romantic notions apparently hopelessly engrained in her character—she could not bring herself to damage the dress in order to get it off.

Molly tried to pull it over her head without the benefit of the zipper, but it was too tight to slip off and when she lowered it again, all she had accomplished was her hair caught hard in the seed pearls that encrusted the neckline of the dress again.

It was as if the dress—and her romantic notions—were letting her know their hold on her was not going to be so easily dismissed!

Her phone rang; the two distinct beeps of Vivian Saint Pierre, known to one and all as Miss Viv, beloved founder of Second Chances. Miss Viv and Molly were always the first two into the office in the morning.

Instead of answering the phone, Molly headed out

of her own office and down the hall to her boss's office to be rescued.

From myself, she acknowledged wryly.

Miss Viv would look at this latest predicament Molly had gotten herself into, know instantly *why* Molly had been compelled to put on the dress and then as she was undoing the zip she would say something wise and comforting about Molly's shattered romantic hopes.

Miss Viv had never liked Chuck Howard, Molly's fiancé. When Molly had arrived at work that day six months ago with her ring finger empty, Miss Viv had nodded approvingly and said, "You're well rid of that ne'er-do-well."

And that was even before Molly had admitted that her bank account was as empty as her ring finger!

That was exactly the kind of pragmatic attention Molly needed when a dress like this one was trying to undo all the lessons she was determined to take from her broken engagement!

With any luck, by the end of the day her getting stuck in the dress would be nothing more than an office joke.

Determined to carry off the lighthearted laugh at herself, she burst through the door of Miss Viv's office after a single knock, the wedding march humming across her lips.

But a look at Miss Viv, sitting behind her desk, stopped Molly in her tracks. The hum died midnote. Miss Viv did not look entertained by the theatrical entrance. She looked horrified.

And when her gaze slid away from where Molly stood in the doorway to where a chair was nearly hidden behind the open door, Molly's breath caught and she slowly turned her head.

Despite the earliness of the hour, Miss Viv was not alone!

A man sat in the chair behind the door, the only available space for visitors in Miss Viv's hopelessly disorganized office.

No, not just a man. The kind of man that every woman dreamed of walking down the aisle toward.

The man sitting in Miss Viv's office was not just handsome, he was breathtaking. In a glance, Molly saw neat hair as rich as dark chocolate, firm lips, a strong chin with the faintest hint of a cleft, a nose saved from perfection—but made unreasonably more attractive—by the slight crook of an old break and a thin scar running across the bridge of it.

The aura of confidence, of *success,* was underscored by how exquisitely he was dressed. He was in a suit of coal-gray, obviously custom tailored. He had on an ivory shirt, a silk tie also in shades of gray. The ensemble would have been totally conservative had it not been for how it all matched the gray shades of his eyes. The cut of the clothes emphasized rather than hid the pure power of his build.

The power was underscored in the lines of his face. And especially in the light in his eyes. The surprise that widened them did not cover the fact he radiated a kind of self-certainty, a cool confidence, that despite the veneer of civilization he wore so well, reminded Molly of a gunslinger.

In fact, that was the color of those eyes, *exactly,* gunmetal-gray, something in them watchful, *waiting.* She shivered with awareness. Despite the custom suit, the Berluti shoes, the Rolex that glinted at his wrist, he was the kind of man who sat with his back to the wall, always facing the door.

The man radiated power and the set of his shoulders telegraphed the fact that, unlike Chuck, this man was pure strength. The word *excuse* would not appear in his vocabulary.

No, Molly could tell by the fire in his eyes that if the ship was going down, or the building was on fire—if the town needed saving and he had just ridden in on his horse—he was the one you would follow, he was the one you would rely on to save you.

An aggravating conclusion since she was so newly committed to relying on herself, her career and her co-workers to save her from a disastrous life of unremitting loneliness. The little featherless budgie she had at home—the latest in a long list of loving strays that had populated her life—also helped.

The little *swish* of attraction she felt for the stranger made her current situation even more annoying. It didn't matter how much he looked like the perfect person to cast in the center of a romantic fantasy! She had given up on such twaddle! She was well on her way to becoming one of those women perfectly comfortable sitting at an outdoor café, alone, sipping a fine glass of wine and reading a book. Not even slipping a look at the male passers-by!

Of course, this handsome devil appearing without warning in her boss's office on a Monday morning was a test, just like the dress. It was a test of her commitment to the new and independent Molly Michaels, a test of her ability to separate her imaginings from reality.

Look at her deciding he was the one you would follow in a catastrophe when she knew absolutely nothing about him except that he had an exceedingly handsome face. Molly reminded herself, extra sternly, that all the catastrophes in her life had been of her own making.

Besides, with the kind of image he portrayed—all easy self-assurance and leashed sexuality—probably more than one woman had built fantasies of hope and forever around him. He was of an age where if he wanted to be taken he would be. And if his ring finger—and the expression on his face as he looked at the dress—was any indication, he was not!

"Sorry," Molly said to Miss Viv, "I thought you were alone." She gave a quick, curt nod of acknowledgment to the stranger, making sure to strip any remaining *hopeless dreamer* from herself before she met his eyes.

"But, Molly, when I rang your office, I wanted you to come, and you must have wanted something?" Miss Viv asked her before she made her escape.

Usually imaginative, Molly drew a blank for explaining away her attire and she could think of not a single reason to be here except the truth.

"The zip is stuck, but I can manage. Really. Excuse me." She was trying to slide back out the door when his eyes narrowed on her.

"Is your hair caught in the dress?"

His voice was at least as sensual as the silk where the dress caressed her naked skin.

Molly could feel her cheeks turning a shade of red that was probably going to put her hair to shame.

"A little," she said proudly. "It's nothing. Excuse me." She tried to lift her chin, to prove how *nothing* it was, but her hair was caught hard enough that she could not, and she also could not prevent a little wince of pain as the movement caused the stuck hair to yank at her tender scalp.

"That looks painful," he said quietly, getting to his feet with that casual grace one associated with athletes, the kind of ease of movement that disguised how swift they really were. But he was swift, because he was standing in front of her before she could gather her wits and make good her escape.

The smart thing to do would be to step back as he took that final step toward her. But she was astounded to find herself rooted to the spot, paralyzed, helpless to move away from him.

The world went very still. It seemed as if all the busy activity on the street outside ceased, the noises faded, the background and Miss Viv melted into a fuzzy kaleidoscope as the stranger leaned in close to her.

With the ease born of supreme confidence in himself—as if he performed this kind of rescue on a daily basis—he lifted the pressure of the dress up off her shoulder with one hand, and with the other, he carefully unwound her hair from the pearls they were caught in.

Given that outlaw remoteness in his eyes, he was unbelievably gentle, his fingers unhurried in her hair.

Molly's awareness of him was nothing less than shocking, his nearness tingling along her skin, his touch melting parts of her that she had hoped were turned to ice permanently.

The moment took way too long. And not nearly long enough. His concentration was complete, the intensity of his steely-gray gaze as he dealt with her tangled hair, his unsettling nearness, the graze of his fingers along her neck, stealing her breath.

At least Molly didn't feel as if she was breathing, but then she realized she must, indeed, be pulling air in and out, because she could smell him.

His scent was wonderful, bitingly masculine, good aftershave, expensive soap, freshly pressed linen.

Molly gazed helplessly into his face, unwillingly marveling at the chiseled perfection of his features, the intrigue of the faint crook in his nose, the white line of that scar, the brilliance of his eyes. He, however, was pure focus, as if the only task that mattered to him was freeing her hair from the remaining pearl that held it captive.

Apparently he was not marveling at the circumstances that had brought his hands to her hair and the soft place on her neck just below her ear, apparently he was not swamped by their scents mingling nor was he fighting a deep awareness that a move of a mere half inch would bring them together, full frontal contact, the swell of her breast pressing into the hard line of his chest…

The dress, suddenly freed, fell back onto her shoulder. He actually smiled then, the faintest quirk of a gorgeous mouth, and she felt herself floundering in the depths of stormy sea eyes, the chill gray suddenly illuminated by the sun.

"Did you say the zipper was stuck as well?" he asked.

Oh, God. Had she said that? She could not prolong this encounter! It was much more of a test of the new confidently-sitting-at-the-café-alone her than she was ready for!

But mutely, caught in a spell, she turned her back to him and stood stock-still, waiting. She shivered at the thought of a wedding night, what this moment meant, and at the same time that unwanted thought seeped warmly into her brain, he touched her.

She felt the slight brush of his hand, again, on delicate skin, this time at the back of her neck. Her senses were so intensely engaged that she heard the faint pop of the hook parting from the eye. She registered the feel of his hand, felt astounded by the hard, unyielding texture of his skin.

He looked like he was pure business, a banker maybe, a wealthy benefactor, but there was nothing soft about his hand that suggested a life behind a desk, his tools a phone and a computer. For some reason it occurred to her that hands like that belonged to people who handled ropes…range riders, mountain climbers. Pirates. Ah, yes, pirates with all that mysterious charm.

He dispensed with the hook at the top of the zipper in a split second, a man who had dispensed with such delicate items many times? And then he paused, apparently realizing the height of the zipper would make it nearly impossible for her to manage the rest by herself—she hoped he would not consider how much determination it had taken her to get it up in the first place—and then slid the zipper down a sensuous inch or two.

With that same altered sense of alertness Molly could feel cool air on that small area of her newly exposed naked back, and then, though she did not glance back, she could feel heat. His gaze? Her own jumbled thoughts?

Molly fought the chicken in her that just wanted to bolt out the open door. Instead, she turned and faced him.

"There you go," he said mildly, rocking back on his heels. The heat must have come from her own badly rattled thoughts, because his eyes were cool, something veiled in their intriguing silver depths.

"Thank you," she said, struggling to keep her voice deliberately controlled to match the look in his eyes. "I'm sorry to interrupt."

"No, no, Molly," Miss Viv said, and it was a mark of the intensity of her encounter with him that Molly was actually jarred by the fact Miss Viv was still in the room. "I called your office to invite you to meet Mr.

Whitford. I'm going on an unscheduled holiday, and Mr. Whitford is taking the helm."

Molly felt the shock of Miss Viv's announcement ripple down a spine that had already been thoroughly shocked this morning. But even as she dealt with the shock, part of her mused with annoying dreaminess, *helm. Pirate. I knew it.*

"Houston Whitford, Molly Michaels," Miss Viv said. The introduction seemed ridiculously formal considering the rather astounding sense of intimacy Molly had just felt under his touch.

Still, now she felt duty-bound to extend her hand, and be touched again, even as she was digesting the fact *he* was in charge. How could that be? Molly was always in charge when Miss Viv was away!

And Miss Viv was going on a holiday, but hadn't told anyone? Second Chances was a family and far better than Molly's family of origin at providing a place that was safe, and supportive, and rarely unpredictable.

"There are going to be a few changes," Miss Viv said, cheerfully, as if Molly's nice safe world was in no way being threatened. "And no one is more qualified to make them than Mr. Whitford. I expect Second Chances is going to blossom, absolutely go to the next level, under his leadership. I'm thrilled to pass the reins to him."

But Molly felt the threat of her whole world shifting. Miss Viv was stepping down? The feeling only intensified when Houston Whitford's hand—warm, strong, cool—touched her skin again. His hand enveloped her hand and despite the pure professionalism of his shake, the hardness of his grip told her something, as did the glittering silver light in his eyes.

He was not the usual kind of person who worked an

ill-paying job at a charity. His suit said something his hands did not: that he was used to a world of higher finances, higher-power, higher-tech.

The only thing that was higher at Second Chances was the satisfaction, the feeling of changing the world for the better.

The cost of his suit probably added up to their operating budget for a month! He didn't fit the cozy, casual and rather shabby atmosphere of the Second Chances office at all.

She felt the unmistakable tingle of pure danger all along her spine. There was something about Houston Whitford that was not adding up. Change followed a man like that as surely as pounding rain followed the thunderstorm.

Molly, her father had said, on the eve of leaving their family home forever, *there is going to be a change.*

And she had been allergic to that very thing ever since! She wanted her world to be safe and unchanging and that view had intensified after she had flirted with a major life change in the form of Chuck. Since then Second Chances had become more her safe haven than ever.

"What kind of changes?" she asked Miss Viv now, failing to keep a certain trepidation from entering her voice.

"Mr. Whitford will be happy to brief you, um, after you've changed into something more appropriate," Miss Viv said, and then glanced at her watch. "Oh, my! I do have a plane to catch. I'm going to a spa in Arizona, my dear."

"You're going to a spa in Arizona, and you didn't tell anyone?" It seemed unimaginable. That kind of vacation usually should have entailed at least a swimsuit shopping excursion together!

"The opportunity came up rather suddenly," Miss Viv said, unapologetically thrilled. "A bolt from the blue, an unexpected gift from an old friend."

Molly tried to feel delighted for her. No one deserved a wonderful surprise more than her boss.

"For how long?" she asked.

But the shameful truth was Molly did not feel delighted at her boss's good fortune. *Sudden change.* Molly hated that kind more than the regular variety.

"Two weeks," Miss Viv said with a sigh of anticipated delight.

Two weeks? Molly wanted to shout. *That was ridiculous. People went to spas for a few hours, maybe a few days, never two weeks!*

"But when you come back, everything will be back to normal?" Molly pressed.

Miss Viv laughed. "Oh, sweetie," she said. "What is normal? A setting on a clothes dryer as far as I'm concerned."

Molly stared at her boss. What was normal? Not something to be joked about! It was what Molly had never had. She'd never had a normal family. Her engagement had certainly not been normal. It felt as if she had spent a good deal of her life searching for it, and coming up short. Even her pets were never normal.

Molly's life had been populated with the needy kind of animal that no one else wanted. A dog with three legs, a cat with no meow. Her current resident was a bald budgie, his scrawny body devoid of feathers.

"I've been thinking of retiring," Miss Viv shocked Molly further by saying. "So, who knows? After the two weeks is up, we'll just play it by ear."

Molly wanted to protest that she didn't like playing it by ear. She liked plans and schedules, calendars that were marked for months in advance.

If Miss Viv retired, would Houston Whitford be in charge forever?

She could not think of a way of asking that did not show her dread at the prospect!

Besides, there is no *forever,* Molly reminded herself. That was precisely why she had put on this dress. To debunk *forever* myths.

She particularly did not want to entertain *that* word anywhere near the vicinity of him, a man whose faintest touch could make a woman's vows of self-reliance disintegrate like foundations crumbling at the first tremor of the coming quake.

CHAPTER TWO

THE BRIDE FLOUNCED out of the room, and unbidden, words crowded into Houston's brain.

And then they lived happily ever after.

He scoffed at himself, and the words. Yes, it was true that a dress like that, filled out by a girl like Molly Michaels, represented a fairy tale.

But the fact she was stuck in it, the zipper stubborn, her hair wound painfully around the pearls, represented more the reality: relationships of the romantic variety were sticky, complicated, *entrapping.*

Besides, a man didn't come from the place Houston Whitford had come from and believe in fairy tales. He believed in his own strength, his own ability to survive. He saw the cynicism with which he had regarded that dress as a *gift.*

In fact, the unexpected appearance of one of the Second Chances employees in full wedding regalia only confirmed what several weeks of research had already told him.

Second Chances reminded Houston, painfully, of an old-style family operated bookstore. Everyone was drawn to the warmth of it, it was always crowded and full of laughter and discussion, but when it came time to actually buy a book it could not compete with the online giants, streamlined, efficient, economical. Just how Houston liked his businesses, running like well-oiled machines. No brides, no ancient, adorable little old ladies at the helm.

He fought an urge to press the scar over the old break on the bridge of his nose. It ached unbearably lately. Had it ached ever since, in a rare moment of weakness, he had agreed to help out here? This wasn't his kind of job. He dealt in reality, in cold, hard fact. Where did a poorly run charity, with brides in the hallways and octogenarians behind the desks, fit into his world?

"And that was our Molly," Miss Viv said brightly. "Isn't she lovely?"

"Lovely," Houston managed. He recalled part two of his mission here.

Miss Viv had confessed to him she was thinking of retiring. She loved Molly and considered her her natural successor. But she was a little worried. She wanted his opinion on whether Molly was too soft-hearted for the job.

"Is she getting ready for her wedding?" On the basis of their very brief encounter, Molly Michaels seemed the kind of woman that a man who was not cynical and jaded like him—a man who believed in fairy tales, love ever after, family—would snatch up.

He didn't even like the direction of those thoughts. The wedding dress should only be viewed in the context of the job he had to do here. What was Miss Michaels doing getting ready for her wedding at work? How did that reflect on a future for her in management?

The job he hadn't wanted was getting less attractive by the second. A demand of complete professionalism was high on his list of fixes for the ailing companies he put back on the track to success.

"She's not getting ready for her wedding," Miss Viv said with a sympathetic sigh. "The exact opposite, I'm afraid. Her engagement broke off before they even set a date. A blessing, though the poor child did not see it that way at the time. She's not been herself since it happened."

At this point, with anyone else, he would make it clear, right now, he didn't want to know a single thing about Molly Michaels's personal life. But this job was different than any he'd ever taken on before. And this was Miss Viv.

Everybody was a *poor child* to her. His need to analyze, to have answers to puzzles, surprised him by not filing this poor child information under strictly personal, none of his business, nothing to do with the job at hand. Instead, he allowed the question to form in his mind. *If a man believed in the fairy tale enough to ask someone like Molly Michaels to be his wife, why would he then be fool enough to let her get away?*

Because the truth was *lovely* was an unfortunate understatement, and would have been even before he had made the mistake of making the bridal vision somehow *real* by touching the heated silk of Molly's skin, the coiled copper of her hair.

Molly's eyes, the set of her sensuous mouth and the corkscrewing hair, not to mention the curves of a slender figure, had not really said *lovely* to him. Despite the fairy tale of the dress the word that had come to mind first was *sexy.*

Was that what had made him get up from his chair? Not really to rescue her from her obvious discomfort, but to see what was true about her? Sexy? Or innocent?

He was no Boy Scout, after all, not given to good deeds, which was another reason he should not be here at Second Chances.

Still, was his need to know that about Molly Michaels personal or professional? He had a feeling at Second Chances those lines had always been allowed to blur. *Note to self,* he thought wryly, *no more rescuing of damsels in distress.*

Though, really that was why he was here, even if Miss Viv was obviously way too old to qualify as a damsel.

Houston Whitford was CEO of Precision Solutions, a company that specialized in rescuing ailing businesses, generally large corporations, from the brink of disaster. His position used all of his strengths, amongst which he counted a formidable ability to not be swayed be emotion.

He was driven, ambitious and on occasion, unapologetically ruthless, and he could see that was a terrible fit with Second Chances. He didn't really even *like* charities, cynically feeling that for one person to receive the charity of another was usually as humiliating for the person in need as it was satisfying for the one who could give.

But the woman who sat in front of him was a reminder that no man had himself alone to thank for his circumstances.

Houston Whitford was here, at Second Chances, because he owed a debt.

And he was here for the same reason he suspected most men blamed when they found themselves in untenable situations.

His mother, Beebee, had suggested he help out. So, it had already been personal, some line blurred, even before the bride had showed up.

Beebee was Houston's foster mother, but it was a distinction he rarely made. She had been there when his real mother—as always—had not. Beebee had been the first person he had ever felt genuinely cared about him and what happened to him. He owed his life as it was to her *charity,* and he knew it.

Miss Viv was Beebee's oldest friend, part of that remarkable group of women who had circled around a tough boy from a terrible neighborhood and seen something in him—*believed in something in him*—that no one had ever seen or believed in before.

You didn't say *sorry, too busy* in the face of that kind of a debt.

It had started a month ago, when he'd hosted a surprise birthday celebration for Beebee. The catered high tea had been held at his newly acquired "Gold Coast" condominium with its coveted Fifth Avenue address, facing Central Park.

Beebee and "the girls" had been all sparkle then, oohing over the white-gloved doorman, the luxury of the lobby, the elevators, the hallways. Inside the sleek interior of his eleven-million-dollar apartment, no detail had gone unremarked, from tiger-wood hardwood to walnut moldings to the spectacular views.

But as the party had progressed, Miss Viv had brought up Second Chances, the charity she headed, and that all "the girls" supported. She confessed it was having troubles, financial and otherwise, that baffled her.

"Oh, Houston will help, won't you, dear?" his foster mom had said.

And all eyes had been on him, and in a blink he wasn't a successful entrepreneur who had proven himself over and over again, but that young ruffian, *poor child,* rescued from mean streets and a meaner life, desperately trying to live up to their expectation that he was really a good person under that tough exterior.

But after that initial weakness that had made him say

yes, he'd laid down the law. If they wanted his help, they would have to accept the fact he was doing it his way: no interfering from them, no bringing him home-baked goodies to try to sway him into keeping things the very same way that had gotten the charity into trouble in the first place and *especially* no references to his past.

Of course, they hadn't understood that.

"But why ever not? We're all so proud of you, Houston!"

But Beebee and her friends weren't just proud of him because of who he was now. No, they were the ones who held in their memories that measuring stick of who he had once been…a troubled fourteen-year-old kid from the tenements of Clinton, a neighborhood that had once been called Hell's Kitchen.

They saw it as something to be admired that he had overcome his circumstances—his father being sent to prison, his mother abandoning him—but he just saw it as something left behind him.

Beebee and Miss Viv dispensed charity as easily as they breathed, but as well-meaning as they were, they had no idea how shaming that part of his life, when he had been so needy and so vulnerable, was to him. He did not excuse himself because he had only been fourteen.

He still felt, sometimes, that he was their *poor child,* an object of pity that they had rescued and nursed back to wellness like a near-drowned kitten.

Was he insecure about his past? No, he didn't think so. But it was over and it was done. He'd always had an ability to place his life in neat compartments; his need for order did not allow for overlapping.

But suddenly, he thought of that letter that had arrived at his home last week, a cheap envelope and a prison postmark lying on a solid mahogany desk surely a sign that a man could not always keep his worlds from overlapping.

Houston had told no one about the arrival of that letter, not even the only other person who knew his complete history, Beebee.

Was that part of why he was sending her away with Miss Viv? Not just because he knew they could probably not resist sharing the titillating details of his past with anyone who would listen, including all the employees here at Second Chances, but because he didn't want to talk to Beebee about that letter? The thought of that letter, plus being here at Second Chances, made him feel what Houston Whitford hated feeling the most: *vulnerable,* as if that most precious of commodities, *control,* was slipping away from him.

And there was something about this place—the nature of charity, Miss Viv and his history, Molly, sweetly sensual in virginal white—that made him feel, not as if his guard was being let down, but that his bastions were being stormed.

He was a proud man. That pride had carried him through times when all else had failed. He didn't want Miss Viv's personal information about him undermining his authority to rescue her charity, changing the way people he had to deal with looked at him.

And when people found out his story, it did change the way they looked at him.

He could tell, for instance, Molly Michaels would fall solidly in the soft-hearted category. She'd love an opportunity to treat him like a kitten who had nearly drowned! And he wasn't having it.

"Let's discuss Molly Michaels for a minute," he said carefully. "I'd like to have a little talk with her about—"

"Don't be hard on her!" Miss Viv cried. "Try not to judge Molly for the outfit. She was just being playful. It was actually good to see that side of her again," Miss Viv said.

Playful. He liked playful. In the bedroom.

In the office? Not so much.

"Please don't hurt her feelings," Miss Viv warned him.

Hurt her feelings? What did feelings have to do with running an organization, with expecting the best from it, with demanding excellence?

He did give in to the little impulse, then, to press the ridge of the scar along his nose.

Miss Viv's voice lowered into her *juicy-secret* tone. "The broken engagement? She's had a heartbreak recently."

It confirmed his wisdom in sending Miss Viv away for the duration of the Second Chances business makeover. He didn't want to know this, *at all.* He pressed harder. The ache along the scar line did not diffuse.

"A cad, I'm afraid," Miss Viv said, missing his every signal that he did not want to be any part of the office stories, the gossip, the personalities.

Despite his desire to remove himself from it, Houston felt a sudden and completely unexpected pulsing of fury.

Not for the circumstances he found himself in, certainly not at Miss Viv, who could not help herself. No, Houston felt an undisciplined desire to hurt a man he did not know for breaking the heart of a woman he also did not know—save for the exquisite tenderness of her neck beneath his fingertips.

That flash of unreasonable fury, an undisciplined reaction, was gone nearly as soon as it happened, but it still served to remind him that things did not always stay in their neat compartments. He had not overcome what he had come from as completely as everyone believed.

He came from a world where violence was the default reaction.

Houston knew if he was to let down his guard, lose his legendary sense of control for a second—one second—he could become that man his father had been, his carefully constructed world blown apart by forces—fury, passion—that could rise up in a storm that he had no hope of taming.

It was the reason Houston did not even allow himself to contemplate his life in the context of fairy tales represented by a young woman in a bridal gown. There was no room for a compartment like that in the neat, tidy box that made up his life.

There was a large compartment for work, an almost equally large one for his one and only passion, the combat sport of boxing.

There were smaller compartments for his social obligations, for Beebee, for occasional and casual relationships with the rare member of the opposite sex who shared his aversion for commitment. There were some compartments that were nailed shut.

But now the past was not staying in the neat compartment system. The compartment that held Houston's father *and* his mother was being pried up, despite the nails trying to hold it firmly shut.

Houston's father had written his only son a letter that asked nothing and expected nothing. And yet at the same time Houston was bitterly aware that how he reacted to it would prove who he really was.

After nineteen years, his father was getting out of prison.

And it felt as if all those years of Houston outdistancing his past had been a total waste of energy. Because there it was, waiting for him, right around the next bend in time.

The scar across his nose flared with sudden pain, and Houston pressed a finger into the line of the old break, aware he was entering a danger zone that the mean streets of Clinton had nothing on.

"HAVE A SEAT," Houston invited Molly several hours later, after he had personally waved goodbye to Beebee and Miss Viv at the airport.

"Thank you." She took a seat, folded her hands primly in her lap and looked at him expectantly.

It was his second encounter with her, and he was determined it was going to go differently than the first. It was helpful that Miss Viv was not there smiling at him as if he was her favorite of all charity cases.

And it was helpful that Molly Michaels was all business now, no remnant of the blushing bride she had been anywhere in sight. No, she was dressed in a conservative slack suit, her amazing hair pinned sternly up on her head.

Still, it was way too easy to remember how it had felt underneath his hands. He was not going to allow himself to contemplate the fact that even after untangling her from that dress several hours ago he was no closer to knowing her truth: was she sexy? Or innocent?

Not thoughts that were strictly *professional.* In fact, those were exactly the kind of thoughts that made a man crazy.

"I'm sorry about the dress. You must think I'm crazy."

Damn her for using that word!

The nails holding a compartment of Houston's past shut gave an outrageous squeak. Houston remembered the senior Whitford had been made *crazy* by a beautiful woman, Houston's mother.

Who hadn't she made crazy? Beautiful, but untouchable. Both of them had loved her desperately, a fact that had only seemed to amuse her, allowed her to toy with her power over them. The truth? Houston would have robbed a bank for her, too, if he'd thought it would allow him to finally win something from her.

The memory, unwanted, of his craving for something his mother had been unable to give made him feel annoyed with himself.

"Crazy?" he said. *You can't begin to know the meaning of the word.* "Let's settle for eccentric."

She blushed, and his reaction was undisciplined, *unprofessional,* a ridiculous desire, like a juvenile boy, to find out what made her blush and then to make it happen *often.*

"So, you've been here how long?" Houston asked, even though he knew, just to get himself solidly back on the professional track.

"As an employee for several years. But I actually started here as a volunteer during high school."

Again, unprofessional thoughts tickled at him: what had she been like during high school? The popular girl? The sweet geek? *Would she have liked him?*

Houston remembered an incident from his own high school years. She probably would not have liked him, *at all.* He shook off the memory like a pesky fly. High school? That was fifteen years ago! That was the problem with things coming out of their compartments. They could become unruly, pop up unannounced, uninvited, in moments when his concentration was challenged, when his attention drifted.

Which was rarely, thank God.

Since the memories had come, though, he exercised cool discipline over them. He reminded himself that good things could come from bad. His mother's abandonment had ultimately opened the door to a different world for him; the high school "incident" had led to Beebee putting him in boxing classes "to channel his aggression."

Houston was more careful than most men with the word *love,* but he thought he could honestly say he loved the combat sport of boxing, the absolute physical challenge of it, from the grueling cardiovascular warm-up to punching the heavy bags and the speed bags, practicing the stances, the combinations, the jabs and the hooks. He occasionally sparred, but awareness of the unexpected power of fury prevented him from taking matches.

Now he wondered if a defect in character like fury could lie dormant, spring back to life when it was least expected.

No, he snapped at himself.

Yes, another voice answered when a piece of Molly's hair sprang free of the restraints she had pinned it down with, curled down the soft line of her temple.

She'd been engaged to a cad.

Tonight, he told himself sternly, he would punch straight left and right combinations into the heavy bag until his hands, despite punch mitts, ached from it. Until his whole body hurt and begged for release. For now he would focus, not on her hair or her past heartbreaks, but on the job he was here to do.

Houston realized Molly's expression had turned quizzical, wondered how much of the turmoil of that memory he had just had he had let slip over his usually well-schooled features.

Did she look faintly sympathetic? Had she seen something he didn't want her to see? Good grief, had Miss Viv managed to let something slip about him?

Whatever, he knew just how to get rid of that look on her face, the look of a woman who *lived* to make the world softer and better.

A cad could probably spot that gentle, compassion-filled face from a mile away! It would be good for her to toughen up.

"Let me be very blunt," he said, looking at the papers in front of him instead of her hair, the delicate creamy skin at her throat. "Second Chances is in a lot of trouble. I need to turn things around and I need to do it fast."

"Second Chances is in trouble?" Molly was genuinely astounded. "But how? The secondhand stores that provide the majority of our funding seem to do well."

"They do perform exceedingly well. The problem seems to be in an overextension of available funds. Your department?"

Here it was: could she make the kind of hard decisions that would be required of her if she took over the top spot in the newly revamped Second Chances?

The softness left her face, replaced with wariness. Better than softness in terms of her managerial abilities. If that was good, why did he feel so bad?

"You can't run an organization that brings in close to a million dollars a year like a mom and pop store.

You can't give everyone who comes in here with their hand out and a hard luck story everything they ask for."

"I don't!" she said. "I'm very careful what I fund."

He saw her flinch from his bluntness, but at this crucial first stage there was no other way to prepare people for the changes that had to happen. Another little curl broke free of her attempt to tame her hair, and he watched it, sentenced himself to another fifteen minutes on the bag and forged on.

"Two thousand dollars to the Flatbush Boys Choir travel fund? There is no Flatbush Boys Choir."

"I know that now," she said, defensively. "I had just started here. Six of them came in. The most adorable little boys in matching sweaters. They even sang a song for me."

"Here's a check written annually to the Bristol Hall Ladies' Lunch Group. No paperwork. No report. Is there a Bristol Hall Ladies' Lunch Group? What do they do? When do they meet? Why do they get money for lunch?"

"That was grandfathered in from before I started. Miss Viv looks after it."

"So, you're project manager, except when Miss Viv takes over?"

"She is the boss," Molly said uneasily, her defensive tone a little more strident.

"Ah." He studied her for a moment, then said softly, "Look, I'm not questioning your competence."

She looked disbelieving. Understandably.

"It's just that some belt-tightening is going to have to happen. What I need from you as I do research, review files and talk to people is for you to go over your programming in detail. I need exact breakdowns on how you choose programs. I need to review your budgets, I need to analyze your monitoring systems."

She looked like she had been hit by a tank. Now would be the wrong time to remember the sweet softness of her skin under his fingertips, how damned protective he had felt when he heard about the *cad.* Now he was the cad!

"How soon can you have that to me?" he pressed.

"A week?"

A chief executive officer needed to work faster, make decisions more quickly. "You have until tomorrow morning."

She glared at him. That was good. Much easier to defend against than sweet, shocked vulnerability. The angry spark in her eyes could almost make him forget her hair, that tender place at her nape. Almost.

He plunged forward, eager to get the barriers—compromised by hands in hair—back up where they belonged. Eager to find out what he needed to know about her—professionally—so he could make a recommendation when the job here was done and move on.

"I've been sorting through paperwork for a number of weeks," he told her. "I have to tell you, after a brief look, it's quite evident to me that you're going to have to ax some of your projects. Sooner rather than later. I've short-listed a few that are on the block."

"Ax projects?" she said with disbelief. "Some of *my* projects are on the block?"

He nodded. He felt not the least like a knight riding in to rescue the business in distress. Or the damsel. He was causing distress, in fact. The feeling of being the cad intensified even though he knew in the long run this would pay off for Second Chances, guarantee their good health and success in the coming years and possibly decades if this was done right, if they had the right leader to move ahead with.

"Which ones?" She went so pale a faint dusting of freckles appeared over the bridge of her nose.

He was annoyed that his feeling of being the cad only deepened, and that she was acting as if he had asked her to choose one of her children to float down the river in a basket. He was aware of feeling the faintest twinge of a foreign emotion, which after a second or two he identified, with further annoyance, as guilt.

Houston Whitford did not feel guilty about doing his job! Satisfied, driven, take charge, in control. Of course, generally, it would be fairly safe to say he didn't *feel,* period.

He used a reasonable tone of voice, designed to convince either her or himself that of course he was not a cad! "We have to make some practical decisions for the future of this organization."

She looked unconvinced about his cad status, and the careful use of the *we* did not even begin to make her think they were a team.

She looked mutinous, then stunned, then mutinous again. Her face was an open book of emotion.

"Is it that bad?" she finally sputtered. "How can it be? Miss Viv never said a word. She didn't even seem worried when she left!"

He had actually sheltered Miss Viv from how bad things were as he had begun to slug his way through the old gal's abysmal record and bookkeeping systems. Miss Viv—and his mother, Second Chances's largest patron—trusted him to fix this. He would. Neither of them needed to know the extent he had to go to. But Molly Michaels did, since the mantle of it all could quite possibly fall on her slender shoulders.

"Yes, it's bad." He closed the fuchsia cover on one of the project reports, the mauve one on another and put those files on the desk between them. "The Easter Egg hunt is gone. The poetry competition is out. And I'm looking at the prom dress thing, and—"

"Prom Dreams?" she gasped. "You can't! You don't know what it means to those girls."

"Have you ever known real hardship?" he asked her, his voice deliberately cold. This job was not going to be easy no matter how he did it. Hard choices had to be made. And he had to see if she was willing to make them. There was no way she was going to be suited to taking over the top job at Second Chances if she was always going to be blinded by the stars in her eyes.

But cad that he was, his gaze went to the lip that she was nibbling with distraction. He was shocked that out of the blue he wondered if one of his hard choices was not going to be whether or not to taste those luscious lips before he made his escape!

She met his eyes. Stopped nibbling. Things that should be simple, cut-and-dried, suddenly seemed complicated. He wished she wasn't looking at him as if she was remembering, too, that unguarded moment when two strangers had touched and the potential for something wild and unpredictable had arced in the air between them.

"My parents divorced when I was young," she offered, softly. "I considered that a terrible hardship. The only one I've known, but life altering."

Thank God she didn't mention the cad! He could see the pain in her eyes. Houston reminded himself, sternly, that he likely had a genetic predisposition toward allowing women to make him crazy. Because he had no business thinking of trying to change the light in her eyes. But he was thinking of it, of how soft her lips would be beneath his own.

Why would that genetic predisposition toward *crazy* be surfacing now, for God's sake? He'd been around many, many beautiful women. He'd always taken his ability to keep his emotional distance for granted, one of the few gifts from his chaotic childhood.

Don't form attachments. Don't care too deeply.

Except for his business and boxing. Both had rigid guidelines and rules that if followed, produced a predictable result. That made them safe things to care about. An occasional bruised knuckle or fat lip, a skirmish in the business world, those hazards were nothing compared to the minefields of becoming attached to people, where the results were rarely predictable.

No, he knew exactly where he was going to channel his substantial passion and energy.

He was being drawn backward, feeling shadows from his past falling over him, entirely against his will. He blamed the letter from his father and the unfortunate fact it coincided with the past weeks of going over files of people who were as desperate and as needy as his family had once been.

It was his annoyance at himself for allowing those thoughts into his business world that made his tone even sharper than it had to be, even if he was testing her ability to run a million-dollar corporation.

"Have you ever been hungry?" But even as he asked it, he knew that question, too, stemmed not so much from professional interest as from a dark past he thought he had left behind.

"No," she said, "but I think I can imagine the desperation of it."

"Can you?" he said cynically.

Without warning a memory popped over the barrier of the thick, high wall he had constructed around the compartment of his childhood.

So hungry. Not a crumb of food in the house. Going into Sam's, the bakery at the corner of his street, Houston's heart beating a horrible tattoo in his chest, his mouth watering from the smells and the sights of the freshly baked bread. Looking around, it was crowded, no one paying any attention to him. Sam's back turned. Houston's hands closing around one of the still-warm loafs in a basket outside the counter, stuffing it under his thin jacket. Lifting his eyes to see Sam looking straight at him. And then Sam turning away, saying nothing, and Houston feeling the shame of the baker's pity so strongly he could not eat the bread. He brought it home to his mother, who had been indifferent to the offering, uncaring of what it had cost him.

Molly was looking at him, understandably perplexed by the question.

Stop it, he ordered himself. But another question came out anyway, clipped with unexpected anger. "Out of work?"

"I don't suppose the summer I chose to volunteer here instead of taking a paying job counts, does it?"

"The fact you could make a choice to volunteer instead of work indicates to me you have probably not known real hardship."

"That doesn't make me a bad person!" she said sharply. "Or unqualified for my job!"

"No," he said, taking a deep breath, telling himself to smarten up. "Of course it doesn't. I'm just saying your frame of reference when choosing projects may not take into account the harsh realities the people you are helping live with."

Another memory popped over that wall. His father drunk, belligerent, out of work again. Not his fault. Never his fault. His mother screaming at his father. You loser. The look on his father's face. Rage. The flying fists, the breaking glass.

Houston could feel his heart beating as rapidly as though it had just happened. Molly was watching him, silently, the dismay and anger that had been in her face fading, becoming more thoughtful.

He ordered himself, again, to stop this. It was way too personal. But, master of control that he was, he did not stop.

"Have you ever had no place to live?"

"Of course not!"

Homelessness was so far from her reality that she could not even fathom it happening to her. Not that he had any right to treat that as a character defect, just because it had once been part of his childhood reality.

The eviction notice pounded onto the door. The hopeless feeling of nowhere to go and no place to feel safe. That sense that even that place he had called home was only an illusion. A sense that would be confirmed as the lives of the Whitfords spiraled steadily downward toward disaster.

Again Molly was silent, but her eyes were huge and had darkened to a shade of green that reminded him of a cool pond on a hot day, a place that promised refuge and rest, escape from a sizzling hot pressure-cooker of a world.

Her expression went from defensive to quiet. She studied his face, her own distress gone, as if she saw something in him, focused on something in him. He didn't want her to see his secrets, and yet something in her steady gaze made him feel seen, vulnerable.

"You're dealing with desperation, and you're doling out prom dresses? Are you kidding me?"

Houston was being way too harsh. He drew a deep breath, ordered himself to apologize, to back track, but suddenly the look on her face transformed. Her expression went from that quiet thoughtfulness to something much worse. *Knowing.*

He felt as transparent as a sheet of glass.

"You've known those things, haven't you?" she guessed softly.

The truth was he would rather run through Central Park in the buff than reveal himself emotionally.

He was stunned that she had seen right through his exquisite suit, all the trappings of wealth and success, seen right through the harshness of his delivery to what lay beneath.

He was astounded that a part of him—a weak part—*wanted* to be seen. Completely.

He didn't answer her immediately. The part of him that felt as if it was clamoring to be acknowledged quieted, and he came back to his senses.

He had to apply his own rules right now, to set an example for her. Don't form attachments. Don't care too deeply. Not about people. Not about programs.

And he needed to take away that feeling he'd been *seen.* Being despised for his severity felt a whole lot safer than that look she'd just given him.

He was laying down the law. If she didn't like it, too bad. It was his job to see if she was capable of doing what needed to be done. Miss Viv wanted to hand this place over to her. There was absolutely no point doing any of this if six months later soft hearts had just run it back into the ground.

"Prom Dreams is gone," he said coolly. "It's up to you to get rid of it."

She bit her lip. She looked at her shoes. She glanced back at him, and tears were stinging her eyes.

There was no room for crying at work!

And absolutely no room for the way it made him feel: as if he wanted to fix it. For Pete's sake, he was the one who'd created it!

"I can see we are going to have a problem," he said. "You are a romantic. And I am a realist."

For a moment she studied him. For a moment he thought she would not be deflected by Prom Dreams, by his harshness, that despite it she would pursue what he had accidentally shown her.

But she didn't.

"I am not a romantic!" she protested.

"Anyone who shows up for work in a wedding gown is a romantic," he said, pleased with how well his deflection had worked. It was about her now, not about him, not about what experiences he did or didn't know.

"I didn't arrive in it," she said, embarrassed and faintly defensive, again. "It was a donation. It had been put on my desk."

"So naturally you had no alternative but to try it on."

"Exactly. I was just checking it for damage."

"Uh-huh," he said, not even trying to hide his skepticism. "Anyone who wants to buy dresses instead of feeding people is a romantic."

"It's not that black and white!"

"Everything is black and white to a realist. Rose-colored to a romantic."

"I might have been a romantic once," she said, her chin tilted proudly, "but I'm not anymore."

Ah, the cad. He shoved his hands under his desk when they insisted on forming fists.

"Good," he said, as if he were the most reasonable of men. "Then you should have no problem getting on board for the kind of pragmatic changes that need to be made around here."

He knew she was kidding herself about not being a romantic. Despite the recent heartbreak Miss Viv had told him about, it seemed that Molly had hopes and dreams written all over her. Could she tame that enough to do the job Second Chances needed her to do?

"Couldn't we look at ways to increase funding, rather than cutting programs?"

Ah, that's what he wanted to hear. Realistic ideas for dealing with problems, creative approaches to solutions, coming at challenges from different directions, experimenting with angles.

For the first time, he thought *maybe.* Maybe Molly Michaels had the potential to run the show. But he let nothing of that optimism into his voice. It was just too early to tell. Because it couldn't work if she was so attached to things that she could not let go of the ones that were dragging the organization down.

"Believe me, I'm looking at everything. That's my job. But I still want every single thing Second Chances funds to have merit, to be able to undergo the scrutiny of the people I will be approaching for funding, and to pass with flying colors."

"I think," she said, slowly, "our different styles might work together, not against each other, if we gave them a chance."

He frowned at that. He wasn't looking for a partnership. He wasn't looking to see if they could work together. He wanted to evaluate whether she could work alone. He wasn't looking for anything to complicate what needed to be done here. It already was way too complicated.

Memories. Unexpected emotion.

Annoyed with himself, he put Houston Whitford, CEO of Precision Solutions, solidly back in the driver's seat.

"What needs to be done is pretty cut-and-dried," Houston said. "I've figured it out on paper, run numbers, done my homework. A team of experts is coming in here tomorrow to implement changes. Second Chances needs computer experts, business analysts, accounting wizards. It needs an image face-lift. It needs to be run like a corporation, stream-lined, professional."

"A corporation?" she said, horrified. "This is a family!"

"And like most families, it's dysfunctional." *That* was the Houston Whitford he knew and loved.

"What a terribly cynical thing to say!"

Precisely. And every bit of that cynicism had been earned in the school of hard knocks. "If you want Walt Disney, you go to the theater or rent *Old Yeller* from the video store. I deal in reality."

"You don't think the love and support of a family is possible in the business environment?"

The brief hope he'd felt about Molly's suitability to have Miss Viv turn over the reins to her was waning.

"That would assume that the love and support of family is a reality, not a myth. Miss Michaels, there is no place for sentiment in the corporate world."

"You're missing all that is important about Second Chances!"

"Maybe, for the first time, someone is seeing exactly what *is* important about Second Chances. Survival. That would speak to the bottom line. Which at the moment is a most unbecoming shade of red."

She eyed him, and for a moment anger and that other thing—that soft *knowing*—warred in her beautiful face. He pleaded with the anger to win. Naturally, the way his day was going, it didn't.

"Let me show you *my* Second Chances before you make any decisions about the programs," she implored. "You've seen them in black and white, on paper, but there's more to it than that. I want to show you the soul of this organization."

He sighed. "The soul of it? And you're not romantic? Organizations don't have souls."

"The best ones do. Second Chances does," she said with determination. "And you need to see that."

Don't do it, he ordered himself.

But suddenly it seemed like a life where a man was offered a glimpse at soul and refused it was a bereft place, indeed. Not that he was convinced she could produce such a glimpse. Romantics had a tendency to see things that weren't there. But realists didn't. Why not give her a chance to defend her vision? Really, could there be a better way to see if she had what it took to run Second Chances?

Still, he would have to spend time with her. More time than he had expected. And he didn't want to. And yet he did.

But if he did go along with her, once he had seen she was wrong, he could move forward, guilt-free. Make his recommendations about her future leadership, begin the job of cutting what needed to be cut. Possibly he wouldn't even feel like a cad when he axed Prom Dreams.

Besides, if there was one lesson he had carried forward when he'd left his old life behind him, it was to never show fear. Or uncertainty. The mean streets fed on fear.

No, you set your shoulders and walked straight toward what you feared, unflinching, ready to battle it.

He feared the *knowing* that had flashed in her eyes, the place that had called to him like a cool, green pond to a man who had unknowingly been living on the searing hot sands of the desert. If he went there could he ever go back to where—to what—he had been before?

That was his fear and he walked toward it.

He shrugged, not an ounce of his struggle in his controlled voice. He said, "Okay. I'll give you a day to convince me."

"Two."

He leaned back in his chair, studied her, thought it was probably very unwise to push this thing by spending two days in close proximity to her. And he realized, with sudden unease, the kind of neighborhoods her projects would be in. He'd rather hoped never to return to them.

On the other hand the past he had been so certain he had left behind was reemerging, and he regarded his unease with some distaste. Houston Whitford was not a man who shirked. Not from *knowing* eyes, not from the demons in his past.

He would face the pull of her and the desire to push away his past in the very same way—head-on. He was not running away from anything. There was nothing he could not handle for two short days.

"Okay," he said again. "Two days."

Maybe it was because it felt as if he'd made a concession and was giving her false hope—maybe it was to fight the light in her face—that he added, "But Prom Dreams is already gone. And in two days all my other decisions are final."

CHAPTER THREE

MOLLY WAS GLAD to be home. Today easily qualified as one of the worst of her life.

Right up there with the day her father had announced her parents' plan to divorce, right up there with the day she had come home from work to find her message machine blinking, Chuck's voice on the other end.

"Sorry, sweetheart, moving on. A great opportunity in Costa Rica."

Not even the courtesy of a face-to-face breakup. Of course, if he'd taken the time to do that, he might have jeopardized his chances of getting away with the contents, meager as they had been, of her bank account.

A note had arrived, postmarked from Costa Rica, promising to pay her back, and also telling her not to totally blame him. *Sweetheart, you're a pushover. Don't let the next guy get away with pushing you around.* To prove she was not a pushover, she had taken the note directly to the police and it had been added to her complaint against Chuck.

A kindly desk sergeant had told her not to hold her breath about them ever finding him or him ever sending a check. And he'd been right. So far, no checks, but the advice had probably been worth it, even if so far, there had been no *next* guy.

Besides, the emptied bank account had really been a small price to pay to be rid of Chuck, she thought, and then felt startled. It was the first time she had seen his defection in that light.

Was it Houston, with his hard-headed pragmatism, that was making her see things differently? Surely not! For all that he was a powerful presence, there was no way she could be evaluating Chuck through his eyes!

And finding the former coming up so lacking.

Perhaps change in general forced one to evaluate one's life in a different light?

For instance, she was suddenly glad she had never given in to Chuck's pressure to move in with her, that she had clung to her traditional values, that it was marriage or nothing.

She had actually allowed Chuck access to her bank account to take the sting out of that decision, one she'd been unusually firm about even in the face of Chuck's irritation.

Because of that decision today she could feel grateful that her apartment remained a tiny, cozy space, all hers, no residue of Chuck here.

Usually her living room welcomed her, white slipcovers over two worn love seats that faced each other, fresh flowers in a vase on the coffee table between the sofas. The throw cushions were new to pick up the colors from her most prized possession, acquired since Chuck's defection from her life.

It was a large, expensively framed art poster of a flamboyantly colored hot air balloon rising at dawn over the golden mists of the Napa Valley.

There were two people standing at the side of the basket of the rising balloon, sharing the experience and each other at a deep level that the photographer had managed to capture. Tonight, Molly Michaels looked at it with the fresh eyes of one who had been judged, and felt defensive.

She told herself she hadn't bought it because she was a *romantic,* as a subliminal nod to all she still wanted to believe in. No, Molly had purchased the piece because it spoke to the human spirit's ability to rise above turmoil, to experience peace and beauty despite disappointments and betrayals.

And that's why she'd tried on the wedding dress, too?

The unwanted thoughts made her much-loved living space feel like a frail refuge from the unexpected storm that was battering her world.

Hurricane Houston, she told herself, out loud trying for a wry careless note, but instead she found she had conjured an image of his eyes that threatened to invade even the coziness of her safe place.

Which just went to show that Houston Whitford was a man she *really* would have to defend herself against, if the mere remembering of the light in his eyes could make him have more presence here in her tiny sanctuary than Chuck had ever had.

That begged another question. If someone like Chuck—unwilling to accept responsibility for anything, including his theft of her bank account—could devastate her life so totally, how much more havoc could a more powerful man wreak on the life of the unwary?

Molly remembered the touch of Houston's hands on her neck, and shivered, remembering how hard the texture of his skin had been, a forewarning he was much tougher than the exquisite tailoring of the suit had prepared her for.

Have you ever been hungry?

What had she seen in him in that moment? Not with her eyes, really, her heart. Her heart had sensed something, known something about him that he did not want people to know.

Stop it, she ordered herself. She was only proving he was right. Hearts sensing something that the eyes could not see was romantic hogwash.

He had already axed Prom Dreams. That's what she needed to see! She was dealing with a man who was heartless!

Though she rarely drank and never during the week, she poured herself a glass of the Biale Black Chicken Zinfandel from the region depicted on the poster. She raised her glass to the rising hot air balloon.

"To dreams," she said, even though it was probably proving that Houston Whitford was right again. A romantic despite her efforts to cure herself of it. She amended her toast, lifted the wineglass to the photo again. "To hope."

With uncharacteristic uncertainty tormenting her, Molly spent the evening reviewing her projects—alternately defending each and every one, and then trying to decide which ones to take him to in the two days he had reluctantly allotted her.

And she tried desperately to think of a way to save Prom Dreams. They always had lots of donations of fine gowns, but never enough. It had to be supplemented for each girl who wanted a dress to get one. The thought of phoning the project coordinator and canceling it turned her stomach. Hearts would be broken! For months, girls looked forward to the night the Greenwich Village shop, Now and Zen, was transformed into prom dress heaven.

Could she wait? Hope for a change of heart on his part? A miracle?

If she could convince him of the merit of her other projects, would there be a chance he might develop faith in her abilities? Could she then convince him Prom Dreams had to be saved?

She was not used to having to prove herself at work! The supportive atmosphere at Second Chances had always been such that she felt respected, appreciated and approved of! None of her projects had ever come under fire, none had ever been dismissed as trivial! Of course there had been a few mistakes along the way, but no one had ever made her feel incompetent because of them! She had always been given the gift of implicit trust.

That was part of the *soul* of Second Chances. It trusted the best in everyone would come out if it was encouraged!

Could she make Houston Whitford see that soul as she had promised? Could she make him feel that sense of family he was so cynical about? Could she make him understand the importance of it in a world too cold, and too capitalistic and too focused on those precious bottom lines?

But she was suddenly very aware she did not want to think of Houston Whitford in the context of a family.

That felt as if it would be the most dangerous thing of all, as if it would confirm what her heart insisted it had glimpsed in him when he had talked about hunger and hardship.

That he was lonely. That never had a man needed a family more than he did.

Stop it, she told herself. That was exactly the kind of thinking that got her into trouble, made her a pushover as Chuck had so generously pointed out from the beaches of Costa Rica, no doubt while sipping Margaritas paid for with her money! Molly took far too long the next morning choosing her outfit, but she knew she needed to look and feel every inch a professional, on even footing, in a position to command both respect and straight answers.

She had to erase the message that the wedding dress had given. She had to be seen as a woman who knew her job, and was a capable and complete professional.

The suit Molly chose was perfect—Calvin Klein, one-inch-above-the-knee black skirt, tailored matching jacket over a sexy hot-pink camisole. But somehow it wasn't quite right, and she changed it.

"You don't have time for this," she wailed, and yet somehow *looking* calm and confident when that was the last thing she was feeling seemed more important than ever.

She ended up in a white blouse and a spring skirt—splashes of lime-green and lemon-yellow—that was decidedly flirty in its cut and movement. She undid an extra button on the blouse. Did it back up. Raced for the door.

She undid the top button again as she walk-ran the short distance to work. She was going to need every advantage she could call into play to work with that man! It seemed only fair that she should keep him as off balance as he made her.

Only as soon as she entered the office she could see they were not even playing in the same league when it came to the "off balance" department.

The Second Chances office as she had always known it was no more.

In its place was a construction zone. Sawhorses had been set up and a carpenter was measuring lengths of very expensive-zlooking crown molding on them. One painter was putting down drop cloths, another was leaning on Tish the receptionist's desk, making her blush. An official-looking man with a clipboard was peering into filing cabinets making notes. A series of blueprint drawings were out on the floor.

Molly had ordered herself to start differently today. To be a complete professional, no matter what.

Bursting into tears didn't seem to qualify!

How could he do this? He had promised to give her a chance to show him where funding was needed! How could he be tearing down the office without consulting the people who worked there? Without asking them what they needed and wanted? Why had she thought, from a momentary glimpse of something in his eyes, that he had a soft side? That she could trust him? Wasn't that the mistake she insisted on making over and over again?

Worst of all, Prom Dreams was the first of her many projects being axed for lack of funding, and Houston Whitford was in a redecorating frenzy? There were four complete strangers hard at work in the outer office, all of whom would be getting paid, and probably astronomical amounts! Molly could hear the sounds of more workers, a circular saw screaming in a back room.

Calm and control, Molly ordered herself. She curled her hands in her skirt to remind herself why she had taken such care choosing it. *To appear a total professional.*

Storming his office screaming could not possibly accomplish that. Not possibly.

Instead, she slid under an open ladder—defying the bad luck that could bring—and went through the door of her own office. Molly needed to gather her wits and hopefully to delay that temper—the unfortunate but well-deserved legacy she shared with other redheads—from progressing to a boil.

But try as she might, she could not stop the thoughts. *Office renovation? Instead of Prom Dreams?*

Houston Whitford had insinuated there was *no* money, not that he was reallocating the funds they had. She needed to gather herself, to figure out how to deal with this, how to put a stop to it before he'd spent all the money. Saving Prom Dreams was going to be the least of her problems if he kept this up. Everything would be gone!

A woman backed out of the closet, and Molly gave a startled squeak.

"Oh, so sorry to startle you. I'm the design consultant. I specialize in office space and you need storage solutions. I think we can go up, take advantage of the height of this room. And what do you think of ochre for a paint color? Iron not yellow?"

He'd told her there was no money for Prom Dreams, but there was apparently all kinds of money for things he considered a priority.

Foolish, stupid things, like construction and consultants, that could suck up a ton of money in the blink of an eye. How could complete strangers have any idea what was best for Second Chances?

Molly was suddenly so angry with herself for always believing the best of people, for always being the reasonable one, for always giving the benefit of the doubt.

Pushover, an imaginary Chuck toasted her with his Margarita.

She had to make a stand for the things she believed in. Be strong, and not so easy for people to take advantage of.

"The only colors I want to discuss are the colors of prom dresses," she told the surprised consultant.

Molly's heart was beating like a meek and mild

schoolteacher about to do battle with a world-wise gunslinger. But it didn't matter to her that she was unarmed. She had her spirit! She had her backbone! She turned on her heel, and strode toward the O.K. Corral at high noon.

This had already gone too far. She didn't want another penny spent! He had called her favorite program frivolous? How dare he!

She stopped at the threshold of Miss Viv's office, where Houston Whitford had set up shop.

He looked unreasonably gorgeous this morning. Better than a man had any right to look. "Ready to go?" he asked mildly, as if he wasn't tearing her whole world apart. "I need half an hour or so, and then I'm all yours."

Don't even be sidetracked by what a man like that being *all yours* could mean, she warned the part of herself that was all too ready to veer toward the romantic!

Molly took a deep breath and said firmly, not the least sidetracked, "This high-handed hi-jacking of Second Chances money is unacceptable to me."

He cocked his head at her as if he found her interesting, maybe even faintly amusing.

"Mr. Whitford, there is no nice way to say this. Miss Viv left you in charge for a reason I cannot even fathom, but she could not have been expecting this! This is a terrible waste of the resources Miss Viv has spent her life marshalling! Construction and consultants? Are you trying to break her heart? Her spirit?"

She was quite pleased with herself, assertive, a realist, speaking a language he could understand! Well, maybe the last two lines had veered just a touch toward the romantic.

Still, Molly was making it clear to herself and to him that she wasn't *trusting* anymore.

Not that he seemed to be taking her seriously!

"From what I've seen of Miss Viv," he said, with a touch of infuriating wryness, "it would take a little more than a new paint job, a wall or two coming down, to break her spirit."

"Are you deliberately missing my point? This is *not* what Second Chances is about. We are not about slick exteriors! We are about helping people, and being of genuine service to our community."

"Pretty hard to do if you go belly-up," he pointed out mildly.

"Isn't a renovation of this magnitude going to rush us toward that end?"

He actually smiled. "Not with me in charge, it isn't."

She stared at him, unnerved by the colossal arrogance of the man, his confidence in himself, by his absolute calm in the face of her confusion, as if ripping apart people's lives was all ho-hum to him!

"There's someone in my office wanting to know if I like ochre," Molly continued dangerously. "Not the yellow ochre, the iron one. I'd rather have new prom dresses."

"I thought I made it clear the prom dress issue was closed. As for design money for the offices, I've allocated that from a separate budget."

"I don't care what kind of shell game you play with the money! It's all coming from the same pot, isn't it?"

He didn't answer her. He was not even trying to disguise the fact, now, that he found her attempts at assertiveness amusing. She tried, desperately, to make him see reason.

"Girls who are dying to have a nice dress won't get one, but we'll have the poshest offices in the East Village! Doesn't something strike you as very wrong about that?"

But even as Molly said it, she was aware it wasn't all about the girls and their dresses. Maybe even most of it wasn't about that.

It was about turning over control. Or not turning over control. To people who had not proven themselves deserving. Especially handsome men people!

"Actually, no, it doesn't strike me as wrong. Prom dresses in the face of all this need is what's *wrong.*"

Part of her said maybe her new boss was not the best place to start in standing her ground. On the other hand, maybe it was just time for her to learn to stand her ground no matter who it was with.

"This is what's wrong," she said. "How on earth can you possibly justify this extravagance? How? How can you march in here, knowing nothing about this organization, and start making these sweeping changes?"

"I've made it my business to know about the organization. The changes you're seeing today are largely cosmetic." A tiny smile touched his lips. "Sweeping is tomorrow."

"Don't mock me," she said. "You told me I could have two days to convince you what Second Chances really needs."

"I did. And I'm ready to go."

"But you're already spending all our money!"

"Second Chances hasn't begun to capitalize on the kind of money that's available to organizations like this. A charity, for all its noble purposes, is still a business. A business has to run efficiently, this kind of business has to make an impression. Every single person who walks through the front door of this office has the potential to be the person who could donate a million dollars to Second Chances. You have one chance to make a first impression, to capitalize on that opportunity. One. Trust me with this."

Molly suddenly felt like a wreck, her attempt to be assertive backfiring and leaving her feeling regretful and uncertain. Trust him?

Good grief, was there a job she was worse at than choosing whom to trust? She wished Miss Viv was here to walk her through this minefield she found herself in—that she hated finding herself in! Second Chances was supposed to be the place where she didn't feel like this: threatened, as if your whole world could be whipped out from under you in the blink of an eye.

Molly, there are going to be some changes.

"I'll be ready in half an hour," she said with all the dignity she could muster. She was very aware that it rested on her shoulders to save the essence of Second Chances. If it was left to him the family feeling would be stripped from this place as ruthlessly as Vikings stripped treasures from the monasteries they were sacking!

The consultant, thankfully, was gone from her office, and Molly sat down at her desk, aware she was shaking from her heated encounter with Houston, and determined to try to act as if it was a normal day, to regain her equilibrium. She would open her e-mail first.

Resolutely she tapped her keyboard and her computer screen came up. She was relieved to see an e-mail from Miss Viv.

Please give me direction, she whispered to the computer. *Please show me how to handle this, how to save what is most important about us. The love.*

Aware she was holding her breath, Molly clicked. No message—a paperclip indicated an attachment.

She clicked on the paperclip and a video opened. It was a grainy picture of a gorgeous hot air balloon, its colors, purple, yellow, red, green, vibrant against a flawless blue sky, rising majestically into the air. What did this have to do with Miss Viv?

The utter beauty of the picture was in such sharp contrast to the ugly reality of the changes being wrought in her life that Molly felt tears prick her eyes. She had always thought a ride in a hot air balloon would be the most incredible experience *ever.* Just last night she had toasted this very vision.

She squinted at the picture, and it came into focus. Two little old ladies were waving enthusiastically from the basket of the balloon. One of them blew a kiss.

Molly frowned, squinted hard at the grainy picture and gasped.

What was Miss Viv doing living Molly's dream? If this video was any indication, Miss Viv had complete trust in Houston Whitford being left in charge! Apparently she wasn't giving her life back here—or her Second Chances family—a single second thought.

In fact, Miss Viv was waving with enthusiasm, decidedly carefree, apparently having the time of her life. It made Molly have the disloyal thought that maybe she, Molly, had allowed Second Chances to become too much to her.

Molly's job, her career, especially in the awful months since Chuck, had become her whole life, instead of just a part of it.

What had happened to her own dreams?

"Dreams are dangerous," she reminded herself.

But that didn't stop her from envying the carefree vision Miss Viv had sent her. She wished, fervently, that they could change places!

She hit the reply button to Miss Viv's e-mail. "Call home," she wrote. "Urgent!"

CHAPTER FOUR

HOUSTON REGARDED THE empty place where Molly had just stood, berating him, with interest. In terms of the reins of this place being handed over to her one day, it was a good thing that she was willing to stand up for issues that were important to her. She had made her points clearly, and with no ultimatums, which he appreciated.

He would be unwilling to recommend her for the head spot if she was every bit as soft as she looked. But, no, she was willing to go to battle, to stand her ground.

Unreasonable as it was that she had chosen him to stand it with! And her emotional attachment to the dress thing was a con that clearly nullified the pro of her ability to stand up.

Unreasonable as it was that the fight in her had made her just as attractive as her sweetness in that wedding dress yesterday.

Maybe more so. Fights he knew how to handle. Sweetness, that was something else.

Still, for as analytical as he was trying to be, he had to acknowledge he was just a little miffed. He had become accustomed to answering to no one, he had earned the unquestioning respect of his team and the companies he worked for.

When Precision Solutions went in, Houston Whitford's track record proved productivity went up. And revenue. Jobs were not lost as a result of his team's efforts, but gained. Companies were put on the road to health, revitalized, reenergized.

There was nothing personal about what he did: it purely played to his greatest strengths, his substantial analytical skills. Except for the satisfaction he took in being the best, there was no emotion attached to his work.

Unlike Molly Michaels, most people appreciated that. They appreciated his approach, how fast he did things, how real and remarkable the changes he brought were. When he said cut something, it was cut, no questions asked.

No arguments!

They *thanked* him for the teams of experts, the new computers and ergonomically designed offices, and carefully researched paint colors that aided higher productivity.

"Maybe she'll thank you someday," he told himself, and then laughed at the unlikelihood of that scenario, and also at himself, for somehow wanting her approval.

This would teach him to deny his instincts. He had known not to tackle the charity. He had known he was going to come up against obstacles in the casually run establishment that he would never come across in the business world.

A redheaded vixen calling him down and questioning his judgment being a case in point!

But how could he have refused this? How could he refuse Beebee—or her circle of friends—anything? He owed his life to her, and to them. In those frightening days after his father had first been arrested, and his mother had quickly defected with another man—Houston had been making the disastrous mistake of trying to mask his fear with the anger that came so much more easily in his family.

He'd already worked his way through two foster homes when suddenly there had been Beebee. He had been in a destructive mode and had thrown a rock through the window of her car, parked on a dark street.

She had caught him red-handed, stunned him by not being the least afraid of him. Instead, she had looked at him with that same terrible *knowing* in her eyes that he had glimpsed in Molly's eyes yesterday.

And she had taken a chance. Recently widowed, and recently retired as a court judge, she had been looking for something to fill the sudden emptiness of her days. He still was not quite sure what twist of fate had made that *something* him.

And a world had opened up to him that had always been closed before. A world of wealth and privilege, yes, but more, a world without aggression, without things breaking in the night, without hunger, without harsh words.

It was also a world where things were expected of him that had never been required before.

Hard work. Honesty. Decency. She had gathered her friends, her family, her circle—including Miss Viv—around him. Teaching him the tools for surviving and flourishing in a different kind of world.

Houston shook his head, trying to clear away those memories, knowing they would not help him remain detached and analytical in his current circumstances.

Houston was also aware that it was a careful balancing act he needed to do. He needed to save the charity of the women who had saved him. He needed to decipher whether Molly was worthy to take the helm, but he could not afford to alienate her in the process, even if in some way, alienating her would make him feel safer.

It was more than evident to him, after plowing his way through Miss Viv's chaotic paperwork, that Molly Michaels was practically running the whole show here. Would she do better at that if she was performing in an official capacity? Or worse? That was one of the things he needed to know, absolutely, before Miss Viv came back.

He decided delay was not the better part of valor. He didn't want to allow Molly enough time to paint herself into a corner she could not get out of.

He went down the hallway to Molly's office. A ladder blocked the door; he surprised himself, because he was not superstitious, by stepping around it, rather than under it.

She was bent over her computer, her tongue caught between her teeth, a furious expression of concentration on her face.

She hit the send button on something, spun her chair around to face him, her arms folded over her chest.

"I'm hoping," he said, "that you'll give the changes here the same kind of chance to prove their merit that I'm giving you to prove the merit of your programs."

"Except Prom Dreams," she reminded him sourly.

"Except that," he agreed with absolutely no regret. "Let's give each other a chance."

She looked like she was all done giving people chances, residue from her *cad,* and the new wound, the loss of Prom Dreams.

And yet he could see from the look on her face that she was basically undamaged by life. Willing to believe. Wanting to trust. A *romantic* whether she wanted to believe it of herself or not.

Houston Whitford did not know if he was the person to be trusted with all that goodness, all that softness, all that compassion. He didn't know if the future of Second Chances could be trusted with it, either.

"All right," she said, but doubtfully.

"Great. Where are we going first?"

"I want to show you a garden project we've developed."

Funny, that was exactly what he wanted to see. And probably not for the reason Molly hoped, either. That land was listed as one of Second Chance's assets.

He handed her a camera. "Take lots of pictures today. I can use them for fundraising promotional brochures."

THE GARDEN PROJECT would be such a good way to show Houston what Second Chances *really* did.

As they arrived it was evident spring cleanup was going on today. About a dozen rake and shovel wielding volunteers were in the tiny lot, a haven of green sandwiched between two dilapidated old buildings. Most of the people there were old, at least retirement age. But the reality of the neighborhood was reflected in the fact many of them had children with them, grandchildren that they cared for.

"This plot used to be a terrible eyesore on this block," Molly told Houston. "Look at it now."

He only nodded, seeming distant, uncharmed by the sprouting plants, the fresh turned soil, the new bedding plants, the enthusiasm of the volunteers.

Molly shook her head, exasperated with him, and then turned her back on him. She was greeted warmly, soon at the center of hugs.

She felt at the heart of things. Mrs. Zarkonsky would be getting her hip replacement soon. Mrs. Brant had a new grandson. Sly looks were being sent toward Mr. Smith and Mrs. Lane, a widower and a widow who were holding hands.

And then she saw Mary Bedford. She hadn't seen her since they had put the garden to bed in the fall. She'd had some bad news then about a grandson who had been serving overseas.

Molly went to her, took those frail hands in her own.

"How is your grandson?" she asked. "Riley, wasn't it?"

A tear slipped down a weathered cheek. "He didn't make it."

"Oh, Mary, I'm so sorry."

"Please don't be sorry."

"How can I not be? He was so young!"

Mary reached up and rested a weathered hand against her cheek. It reminded Molly of being with Miss Viv when she looked into those eyes that were so fierce with love.

"He may have been young," she said, "but he lived every single day to the fullest. There are people my age who cannot say that. Not even close."

"That is true," Molly said.

"And he was like you, Molly."

"Like me?" she said, startled at being compared to the young hero.

"For so many of your generation it seems to be all about *things*. Bank accounts, and stuff, telephones stuck in your ears. But for Riley, it was about being of service. About helping other people. And that's what it's about for you, too."

Molly remembered sending that message to Miss Viv this morning, pleading for direction.

And here was her answer, as if you could not send

out a plea for direction like the one she had sent without an answer coming from somewhere.

Ever since the crushing end of her relationship with Chuck, Molly had questioned everything about herself, had a terrible sense that she approached life all wrong.

And now she saw that wasn't true at all. She was not going to lose what was best about herself because she'd been hurt.

And then she became aware of her new boss watching her, a cynical look on his face.

For a moment she criticized herself, was tempted to see herself through his eyes. I *am too soft,* she thought. *He sees it.* For a moment she reminded herself of her vow, since Chuck, to be something else.

But then she realized that since Chuck she *had* become something else: unsure, resentful, self-pitying, bitter, frightened.

When life took a run at you, she wondered, did it chip away at who you were, or did it solidify who you really were? Maybe that was what she had missed: it was her *choice.*

"The days of all our lives are short," Mary said, and patted her on the arm. "Don't waste any of it."

Don't waste any of it, Molly thought, being frightened instead of brave, playing it safe instead of giving it the gift of who you really were.

The sun was so warm on her uplifted face, and she could feel the softness of Mrs. Bedford's tiny, frail hand in hers. And she could also feel the hope and strength in it.

Molly could feel love.

And if she allowed what Chuck—what life—had done to her to take that from her, to make her as cynical as the man watching her, then hadn't she lost the most important thing of all?

Herself.

She was what she was. If that meant she was going to get hurt from time to time, wasn't that so much better than the alternative?

She glanced again at Houston. That was the alternative. To be so closed to these small miracles. To know the price of everything and the value of nothing.

She suddenly felt sorry for him, standing there, aloof. His clothing and his car, even the way he stood, said he was so successful.

But he was alone, in amongst all the wonder of the morning, and these people reaching out to each other in love, he was alone.

And maybe that was none of her business, and maybe she could get badly hurt trying to show him there was something else, but Molly suddenly knew she could not show him the soul of Second Chances unless she was willing to show him her own.

And it wasn't closed and guarded.

When she had put on that wedding dress yesterday for some reason she had felt more herself than she had felt in a long time.

Hope filled. A believer in goodness and dreams. Someone who trusted the future. Someone with something to give.

Love.

The word came to her again, filled her. She was not sure she wanted to be thinking of a word like that in such close proximity to a man like him, and if she had not just decided to be brave she might not have. She might have turned her back on him, and gone back to the caring that waited to encircle her.

But he needed it more than she did.

"Houston," she said, and waved him over. "Come meet Mary."

He came into the circle, reluctantly. And then Mary had her arms around his neck and was hugging him hard, and even as he tried to disentangle himself, Molly saw something flicker in his face, and smiled to herself.

She was pretty sure she had just seen his soul, too. And it wasn't nearly as hard-nosed as he wanted everyone to believe.

The sun was warm on the lot and she was given a tray of bedding plants and a small hand spade. Soon she was on her knees between Mrs. Zarkonsky and Mr. Philly. Mrs. Zarkonsky eyed Houston appreciatively and handed him a shovel. "You," she said. "Young. Strong. Work."

"Oh, no," Molly said, starting to brush off her knees and get up. "He's…" She was going to say *not dressed for it,* but then neither was she, and it hadn't stopped her.

He held up a hand before she could get to her feet, let her know that would be the day that she would have to *defend* him, and followed the old woman who soon had him shoveling dirt as if he was a farm laborer.

Molly glanced over from time to time. The jacket came off. The sleeves were rolled up. Sweat beaded on his forehead. Was it that moment of recognizing who she really was that made her feel so vulnerable watching him? That made her recognize she was weak and he was strong, she was soft and he was hard? The world yearned for balance, maybe that was why men and women yearned for each other even in the face of that yearning being a hazardous endeavor.

Houston put his back into it, all mouthwatering masculine grace and strength. Molly remembered the camera, had an excuse to focus on him.

Probably a mistake. He was gloriously and completely male as he tackled that pile of dirt.

"He looks like a nice boy," Mary said, following her gaze, but then whispered, "but a little snobby, I think."

Molly laughed. Yes, he was. Or at least that was what he wanted people to believe. That he was untouchable. That he was not a part of what they were a part of. Somewhere in there, she could see it on his face he was just a nice boy, who wanted to belong, but who was holding something back in himself.

Was she reading too much into him?

Probably, but that's who she was, and that's what she did. She rescued strays. Funny she would see that in him, the man who held himself with such confidence, but she did.

Because that's what she did. She saw the best in people. And she wasn't going to change because it had hurt her.

She was going to be stronger than that.

Molly was no more dressed for this kind of work than Houston. But she went and got a spade and began to shift the same pile of topsoil he was working on. What better way to show him *soul* than people willing to work so hard for what they wanted? The spirit of community was sprouting in the garden with as much vitality as the plants.

The spring sun shone brightly, somewhere a bird sang. What could be better than this, working side by side, to create an oasis of green in the middle of the busy city? There was magic here. It was in the sights and the sounds, in the smell of the fresh earth.

Of course, his smell was in her nostrils, too, tangy

and clean. And there was something about the way a bead of sweat slipped down his temple that made her breath catch in her throat.

Romantic weakness, she warned herself, but half-heartedly. Why not just enjoy this moment, the fact it included the masculine beauty of him? Now, if only he could join in, instead of be apart. There was a look on his face that was focused but remote, as if he was immune to the magic of the day.

Oh, well, that was his problem. She was going to enjoy her day, especially with this new sense of having discovered who she was.

She gave herself over to the task at hand, placed her shovel, then jumped on it with both feet to drive it in to the dirt. It was probably because he was watching—or maybe because of the desperately unsuited shoes—that things went sideways. The shovel fell to one side, throwing her against him.

His arm closed around her in reaction. She felt the hardness of his palm tingling on the sensitive upper skin of her arm. The intoxicating scent of him intensified. He held her arm just a beat longer than he had to, and she felt the seductive and exhilarating *zing* of pure chemistry.

When he had touched her yesterday, she had felt these things, but he had looked only remote. Today, she saw something pulse through his eyes, charged, before it was quickly doused and he let go of her arm.

Was it because she had made a decision to be who she really was that she couldn't resist playing with that *zing?* Or was it because she was powerless not to explore it, just a little?

"You're going to hurt yourself," he said with a rueful shake of his head. And then just in case she thought he had a weak place somewhere in him, that he might actually care, that he might be feeling something as intoxicatingly unprofessional as she was, he said, "Second Chances can't afford a compensation claim."

She smiled to herself, went back to shoveling.

He seemed just a little too pleased with himself.

She tossed a little dirt on his shoes.

"Hey," he warned her.

"Sorry," she said, insincerely. She tossed a little more.

He stopped, glared at her over the top of his shovel. She pretended it had been purely an accident, focused intently on her own shovel, her own dirt. He went back to work. She tossed a shovel full of dirt right on his shoes.

"Hey!" he said, extricating his feet.

"Watch where you put your feet," she said solemnly. "Second Chances can't afford to buy you new shoes."

She giggled, and shoveled, but she knew he was regarding her over the top of his shovel, and when she glanced at him, some of that remoteness had gone from his eyes, *finally,* and this time it didn't come back. He went back to work.

Plop. Dirt on his shoes.

"Would you stop it?" he said.

"Stop what?" she asked innocently.

"You have something against my shoes?"

"No, they're very nice shoes."

"I know how to make you behave," he whispered.

She laughed. This is what she had wanted. To know if there was something in him that was playful, a place she could *reach.* "No, you don't."

He dangled it in front of her eyes.

A worm! She took a step back from him. "Houston! That's not funny!" But, darn it, in a way it was.

"What's not funny?" he said. "Throwing dirt on people's shoes?"

"I hate worms. Does our compensation package cover hysteria?"

"You would get hysterical if I, say, put this worm down your shirt?"

He sounded just a little too enthused about that. It occurred to her they were flirting with each other, cautiously stepping around that little *zing,* looking at it from different angles, exploring it.

"No," she said, but he grinned wickedly, sensing the lie.

The grin changed everything about him. Everything. He went from being too uptight and too professional to being a carefree young man, covered in dirt and sweat, real and human.

It seemed to her taking that chance on showing him who she really was was paying off somehow.

Until he did a practice lunge toward her with the worm. Because she really did hate worms!

"If I tell your girlfriend you were holding worms with your bare hands today, she may never hold your hand again."

"I don't have a girlfriend."

Ah, it was a weakness. She'd been fishing. But that's what worms were for!

He lunged at her again, the worm wiggled between his fingers. He looked devilishly happy when she squealed.

Then, as if he caught himself in the sin of having fun, he abruptly dropped the worm, went back to work.

She hesitated. It was probably a good time to follow

his lead and back off. But, oh, to see him smile had changed something in her. Made her willing to take a risk. With a sigh of surrender, she tossed a shovel of dirt on his shoes. And he picked up that worm.

"I warned you," he said.

"You'd have to catch me first!"

Molly threw down her shovel and ran. He came right after her, she could hear his footfalls and his breathing. She glanced over her shoulder and saw he was chasing her, holding out the worm. She gave a little snicker, and put on a burst of speed. At one point, she was sure that horrible worm actually touched her neck, and she shrieked, heard his rumble of breathless laughter, ran harder.

She managed to put a wheelbarrow full of plants between them. She turned and faced him. "Be reasonable," she pleaded breathlessly.

"The time for reason is done," he told her sternly, but then that grin lit his face—boyish, devil-may-care, and he leaped the wheelbarrow with ease and the chase was back on.

The old people watched them indulgently as they chased through the garden. Finally the shoes betrayed her, and she went flying. She landed in a pile of soft but foul-smelling peat moss. He was immediately contrite. He dropped the worm and held out his hand—which she took with not a bit of hesitation. He pulled her to her feet with the same easy strength that he had shoveled with. Where did a man who crunched numbers get that kind of strength from? She had that feeling again, of something about him not adding up, but it was chased away by his laughter.

"You don't laugh enough," she said.

"How do you know?"

"I'm not sure. I just do. You are way too serious, aren't you?"

He held both her hands for a moment, reached out and touched a curl, brushed it back from out of her eyes.

"Maybe I am," he admitted.

Something in her felt absolutely weak with what she wanted at that moment. To make him laugh, but more, to *explore* all the reasons he didn't. To find out what, exactly, about him did not add up.

"Truce?" he said.

"Of course," she panted. She meant for all of it, their different views of Second Chances. All of it.

He reached over, snared the camera out of her pocket and took a picture of her.

"Don't," she protested. She could feel her hair falling out, she was pretty sure there was a smudge of dirt on her cheek, and probably on her derriere, too!

But naturally he didn't listen and so she stuck out her tongue at him and then struck a pose for him, and then called over some of the other gardeners. Arms over each other's shoulders, they performed an impromptu can-can for the camera before it all fell apart, everyone dissolving into laughter.

Houston smiled, but that moment of spontaneity was fading. Molly was aware that he saw that moment of playfulness differently to her. Possibly as a failing. Because he was still faintly removing himself from them. She had been welcomed into the folds of the group, he stood outside it.

Lonely, she thought. *There was something so lonely about him.* And she felt that feeling, again, of wanting to explore.

And maybe to save. Just like she saved her strays. But somehow, looking at the handsome, remote cast of his face, she knew he would hate it that she had seen anything in him that needed saving. That *needed,* period.

They got back in the car, she waved to the old people. Molly was aware she was thrilled with how the morning had gone, by its unexpected surprises, and especially how he had unexpectedly revealed something of himself.

"How are your hands?" she asked him. He held one out to her. An hour on a shovel had done nothing to that hand.

"I would have thought you would have blisters," she said.

"No, my hands are really tough."

"From?"

"I box."

"As in fight?"

He laughed. "Not really. It's more the workout I like."

So, her suspicions that he was not quite who he said were unfounded. He was a high-powered businessman who sought fitness at a high-powered level.

That showed in every beautiful, mesmerizing male inch of him!

"Wasn't that a wonderful morning?" she asked, trying to solidify the camaraderie that had blossomed so briefly between them. "I promised I would show you the soul of Second Chances and that's part of it! What a lovely sense of community, of reclaiming that lot, of bringing something beautiful to a place where there was ugliness."

She became aware he was staring straight ahead. Her feeling of deflation was immediate. "You didn't feel it?"

"Molly, it's a nice project. The warm and fuzzy feel good kind."

She heard the *but* in his voice, sensed it in the set of his shoulders. Naturally he would be immune to warm fuzzy feeling good.

"But it's my job to ask if it makes good economic sense. Second Chances owns that lot, correct?"

She nodded reluctantly. Good economic sense after the magical hour they had just spent? "It was donated to us. Years ago. Before I came on board it was just an empty lot that no one did anything with."

If she was expecting congratulations on her innovative thought she was sadly disappointed!

"Were there provisos on the donation?"

"Not that I know of."

"I'll have to do some homework."

"But why?"

"I have to ask these questions. Is that the best use of that lot? It provides a green space, about a dozen people seem to actually enjoy it. Could it be liquidated and the capital used to help more people? Could it be developed—a parking lot or a commercial building—providing a stream of income into perpetuity? Providing jobs and income for the neighborhood?"

"A parking lot?" she gasped. And then she saw *exactly* what he was doing. Distancing himself from the morning they had just shared—distancing himself from the satisfaction of hard work and the joy of laughter and the admiration of people who would love him.

Distancing himself from her. Did he know she had *seen* him? Did he suspect she had uncovered things about him he kept hidden?

He didn't like *feelings*. She should know that firsthand. Chuck had had a way of rolling his eyes when she had asked him how he was feeling that had made her stop asking!

But, naive as it might be, she was pretty sure she had just glimpsed the real Houston Whitford, something shining under those layers of defenses.

And she wasn't quite ready to let that go. It didn't have to be personal. No, she could make it a mission, for the good of Second Chances, she told herself, she would get past all those defenses.

For the good of Second Chances she was going to rescue him from his lonely world.

CHAPTER FIVE

"HEY," SHE SAID, "there's Now and Zen."

She could clearly see he was disappointed that she had not risen to the bait of him saying he was going to build a parking lot over the garden project.

"Why don't we go in?" she suggested. "You can look for some gardening shoes."

She was not going to give up on him. He was not as hard-nosed as he wanted to seem. She just knew it.

How could he spend a morning like they had just spent in the loveliness of that garden, and want to put up a parking lot? Giving up wasn't in her nature. She was finding a way to shake him up, to make him see, to make him connect! Lighten him up.

And Now and Zen was just plain fun.

"Would you like to stop and have a look?"

He shrugged, regarded her thoughtfully as if he suspected she was up to something but just wasn't quite sure what. "Why not?"

Possibly another mistake, she thought as they went in the door to the delightful dimness and clutter of Now and Zen. He'd probably be crunching the numbers on this place, too. Figuring out if its magic could be bottled and sold, or repackaged and sold, or destroyed for profit.

Stop it, she ordered herself. *Show him. Invite him into this world. He's lonely. He has to be in his uptight little world where everything has a price and nothing has value.*

She tried to remind herself there was a risk of getting hurt in performing a rescue of this nature, but it was a sacrifice she was making for Second Chances! Second Chances needed for him to be the better man that she was sure she saw in there somewhere, sure she had seen when he was putting his all into that shovel.

That was muscle, a cynical voice cautioned her, *not a sign of a better man.*

Something caught her eye. She took a deep breath, plucked the black cowboy hat from the rack and held it out to him in one last attempt to get him to come into her world, to see it all through her eyes.

"Here, try this on."

Now and Zen was not like the other stores, but funky, laid-back, a place that encouraged the bohemian..

The whole atmosphere in the store said, *Have fun!*

He looked at her, shook his head, she thought in refusal. But then he said, "If I try that on, I get to pick something for you to try on."

She felt the thrill of his surrender. So, formidable as his discipline was, she could entice him to play with her!

"That's not fair," Molly said. "You can clearly see what I want you to try on, but you're asking me for carte blanche. I mean you could pick a bikini!"

"Did you see one?" he asked with such unabashed hopefulness that she laughed. It confirmed he did have a playful side. And she fully intended to coax it to the surface, even if she had to wear a bikini to do it.

Besides, the temptation to see him in the hat—as the gunslinger—proved too great to resist, even at the risk that he might turn up a bikini!

"Okay," she said. "If you try this on, I'll try something on that you pick."

"Anything?" He grinned wickedly.

There was that grin again, without defenses, the kind of smile that could melt a heart.

And show a woman a soul.

He took the hat from her.

"Anything," she said. The word took on new meaning as he set the hat on his head. It didn't look corny, it didn't even look like he was playing dress-up. He adjusted it, pulled the brim low over his brow. His eyes were shaded, sexy, silver.

She felt her mouth go dry. *Anything.* She had known that something else lurked between that oh so confident and composed exterior. Something dangerous. Something completely untamed. Could those things coexist with the better man that she was determined to see?

Or maybe what was dangerous and untamed was in her. In every woman, somewhere. Something that made a prim schoolteacher say to an outlaw, *anything. Anywhere.*

"My turn," he said, and disappeared down the rows. While he looked she looked some more, too. And came up with a black leather vest.

He appeared at her side, a hanger in his hand.

A feather boa dangled from it, an impossible and exotic blend of colors.

"There's Baldy's missing feathers!" she exclaimed.

"Baldy?"

"My budgie. With hardly any feathers. His name is Baldy." It was small talk. Nothing more. Why did it feel as if she was opening up her personal life, her world, to him?

"What happened to his feathers?"

"Stolen to make a boa. Kidding." She flung the boa dramatically around her neck. "I don't know what happened to his feathers. He was like that when I got him. If I didn't take him..." She slid her finger dramatically over her throat.

"You saved him," he said softly, but there was suspicion in his eyes, worthy of a gunslinger, *don't even think it about me.*

No sense letting on she already was!

"It was worth it. He's truly a hilarious little character, full of personality. People would be amazed by how loving he is."

This could only happen to her: standing in the middle of a crazy store, a boa around her neck, discussing a bald budgie with a glorious man with eyes that saw something about her that it felt like no one had ever seen before.

And somehow the word *love* had slipped into the conversation.

Molly took the boa in her hand and spun the long tail of it, deliberately moving away from a moment that was somehow too intense, more real than what she was ready for.

He stood back, studied her, nodded his approval. "You could wear it to work," he decided, taking the hint that something too intense—though delightful—had just passed between them.

"Depending where I worked!"

"Hey, if you can wear a wedding gown, you can wear that."

"I think not. Second Chances is all about image now!"

"Are you saying that in a good way?"

"Don't take it as I'm backing down on Prom Dreams,

but yes, I suppose I could warm to the bigger picture at the office. Don't get bigheaded about it."

"It's just the hat that's making you make comments about my head size. I know it."

She handed him the vest. "This goes with it."

"Uh-uh," he said. "No freebies. If I try on something else, I get to pick something else for you."

"You didn't bring me a bikini, so I'll try to trust you."

"I couldn't find one, but I'll keep looking."

He slipped on the vest. She drew in her breath at the picture he was forming. Rather than looking funny, he looked coolly remote, as if he was stepping back in time, a man who could handle himself in difficult circumstances, who would step toward difficulty rather than away.

He turned away from her, went searching again, came back just as she was pulling faded jeans from a hanger.

He had a huge pair of pink glass clip-on earrings.

"Those look like chandeliers. Besides, pink looks terrible with my hair."

"Ah, well, I'm not that fond of what the hat is doing to mine, either."

She handed him the jeans.

"You're asking for it, lady. That means I have one more choice, too."

"You can't do any worse than these earrings! My ears are growing by the second."

His eyes fastened on her ears. For a moment it felt as if the air went out of the room. He hadn't touched her. He hadn't even leaned closer. How could she possibly have felt the heat of his lips on the tender flesh of her earlobe?

He spun away, headed across the store for one of the

change rooms. She saw him stop and speak to Peggy for a moment, and then he disappeared into a change room.

Moments later, Peggy approached her with something. She held it out to Molly, reverently, across two arms. "He said he picks this," she said, wide-eyed, and then in a lower tone, "that man is hotter than Hades, Molly."

Peggy put her in the change room beside his. The dress fit her like a snakeskin. It dipped so low in the front V and an equally astonishing one at the back, that she had to take it off, remove her shoes and her underwear to do the dress justice. She put it back on and the lines between where she ended and the dress began were erased.

Now, that spectacular dress did her justice. It looked, not as if she was in a funky secondhand store, but ready to walk the red carpet. Molly recognized the intense over-the-top sensuality of the dress and tried to hide it by putting the feather boa back on.

It didn't work.

She peeked out of the dressing room, suddenly shy.

"All the way out," he said. He was standing there in his jeans and vest and hat, looking as dangerous as a gunslinger at high noon.

She stepped out, faked a confidence she wasn't feeling by setting a hand on the hip she cocked at him and flinging the boa over her shoulder.

His eyes widened.

She liked the look in them so much she turned around and let him see the dipping back V of the dress, that ended sinfully just short of showing her own dimples.

She glanced over her shoulder to see his reaction.

She tried to duck back into the change room, but his

hand fell, with exquisite strength, on her shoulder. She froze and then turned slowly to face him.

"I do declare, miss, I thought you were a schoolmarm," he drawled, obviously playing with the outfit she had him in. Isn't this what she'd wanted? To get the walls down? To find the playful side of him? For them to connect?

But if his words were playful, the light in his eyes was anything but. How could he do this? How could he act as if he'd had a front row seat to her secret fantasy about him all the time? Well, she'd asked for it by handing him that hat!

"And I thought you were just an ordinary country gentleman," she cooed, playing along, *loving* this more than a woman should. "But you're not, are you?"

He cocked his head at her.

"An outlaw," she whispered. *Stealing unsuspecting hearts.*

She saw the barest of flinches when she said that, as if she had struck a nerve, as if there was something real in this little game they were playing. She was aware that he was backing away from her, not physically, but the smooth curtain coming down over his amazing eyes.

Again she had a sense, a niggle of a feeling, *there is something about this man that he does not want you to know.*

She was aware she should pay attention to that feeling.

One of the girls turned up the music that played over the store's system. It was not classical, something raunchy and offbeat, so instead of paying attention to that feeling, Molly wanted to lift her hands over her head and sway to it, invite him deeper into the game.

"Would you care to dance?" she asked, not wanting

him to back away, not wanting that at all, not really caring who he was, but wanting to be who she really was, finally. Unafraid. Molly held her breath, waiting for his answer.

For a long moment—forever, while her heart stopped beating—he stood there, frozen to the spot. His struggle was clear in his eyes. He knew it wasn't professional. He knew they were crossing some line. He knew they were dancing with danger.

Then slowly, he held up his right hand in a gesture that could have been equally surrender or an invitation to put her hand there, in his.

She read it as invitation. Even though this wasn't the kind of dancing she meant, she stepped into him, slid her hand up to his. They stood there for a suspended moment, absolutely still, palm to palm. His eyes on her eyes, his breath stirring her hair. She could see his pulse beating in the hollow of his throat, she could smell his fragrance.

Then his fingers closed around hers. He rested his other hand lightly on her waist, missing the naked expanse of her back by a mere finger's width.

"The pleasure is all mine," he said. But he did not pull her closer. Instead, a stiffly formal schoolboy, ignoring the raunchy beat of the music, he danced her down the aisle of Now and Zen.

She didn't know how he managed not to hit anything in those claustrophobic aisles, because his eyes never left her face. They drank her in, as if he was memorizing her, as if he really was an outlaw, who would go away someday and could not promise he would come back.

Molly drank in the moment, savored it. The scent of him filling her nostrils, the exquisite touch of his hand on her back, the softness in his eyes as he looked down at her. She had intended to find out something about him, to nurse something about him to the surface.

Somehow her discoveries were about herself.

That she *longed* for this. To be touched. To be seen. To feel so exquisitely feminine. And cherished. To feel as if she was a mystery that someone desperately wanted to solve.

Ridiculous. They were virtually strangers. And he was her boss.

The song ended. Peggy and the other clerk applauded. His hands dropped away, and he stepped back from her. But his gaze held.

And for a moment, in his eyes, her other secret longings were revealed to Molly: babies crawling on the floor; a little boy in soccer; a young girl getting ready for prom, her father looking at her with those stern eyes, saying, *You are not wearing that.*

Molly had never had these kinds of thoughts with Chuck. She had dreamed of a wedding, yes, in detail she now saw had been excessive. A marriage? No. A vision of the future with Chuck had always eluded her.

Maybe because she had never really known what that future could feel like. Nothing in her chaotic family had given her the kind of hope she had just felt dancing down a crowded clothing aisle.

Hope for a world that tingled with liveliness, where the smallest of discoveries held the kernels of adventure, the promise that exploring another person was like exploring a strange country: exotic, full of unexpected pleasures and surprises. Beckoning. For the first time since Molly had split from Chuck she felt grateful. Not just a little bit grateful. Exceedingly.

She could have missed *this.* This single, electrifying moment of knowing.

Knowing there were things on this earth so wonderful they were beyond imagining. Knowing that there was something to this word called *love* that was more magnificent than any poem or song or piece of film had ever captured.

Love?

That word again in the space of a few minutes, not in the relatively safe context of a bald budgie this time, either.

Pull away from him, she ordered herself. He was casting a spell on her. She was forgetting she'd been hurt. She was forgetting the cynicism her childhood should have filled her with.

She was embracing the her she had glimpsed in the garden, who thought hope was a good thing.

But couldn't hope be the most dangerous thing of all?

Pull back, she ordered herself. *Molly, I mean it!* This wasn't what she had expected when she had decided to live a little more dangerously.

This was *a lot* more dangerously.

Yes, she had decided she needed to be true to herself, but this place she was going to now was a part of herself unexplored.

He was her boss, she told herself. In her eagerness to reach him, to draw him into the warmth of her world, she had crossed some line.

How did you get back to normal after something like that?

How did you go back to the office after that? How did you keep your head? How did you not be a complete pushover?

"Dior," Peggy whispered, interrupting her thoughts.

"I've been saving that dress for Prom Dreams. Do you want to see the poster I'm sending out to the schools to advertise the Prom Dreams evening? It just came in."

Molly slid Houston a look. Whatever softening had happened a moment ago was gone. He was watching her, coolly waiting for her to do what she needed to do.

But she couldn't.

The mention of the probably defunct Prom Dreams should have helped Molly rally her badly sagging defenses, make her forget this nonsense about bringing him out of his lonely world, showing him the meaning of soul.

It was just too dangerous a game she was playing.

On the other hand, she could probably trust him to do what she could not! To herd things back over the line to proper, to put up the walls between them.

OUTSIDE HE SAID to her, no doubt about who was the boss now, "Why didn't you tell her Prom Dreams has been canceled?"

He said it coolly, the remoteness back in his eyes.

She recognized this was his pattern. Show something of himself, appeal to his emotion, like at the garden, and then he would back away from it. There he had tried to hide behind the threat of a parking lot.

This time by bringing up the sore point of Prom Dreams.

He knew, just as she did, that it was safer for them to argue than to chase each other with worms, to dance down dusty aisles.

But despite the fact she knew she should balance caution with this newly awakened sense of adventure, she felt unusually brave, as if she never had to play it safe again. Of course, the formidable obstacle of his will was probably going to keep her very safe whether she wanted to be or not!

She tilted her chin at him. "Why didn't you?"

"I guess I wanted to see if you could do it."

"I can. I will if I have to. But not yet. I'm hoping for a miracle," she admitted. Because that was who she was. A girl who could look at herself in a wedding dress, even after her own dreams had been shattered, even in the face of much evidence to the contrary, a girl who could still hope for the best, hope for the miracle of love to fix everything.

And for a moment, when his guard had gone down, dancing with him, she had believed maybe she would get her miracle after all....

"A miracle," he said with a sad shake of his head. He went and opened the car door for her, and drove back to Second Chances in silence as if somehow she had disappointed him and not the other way around.

A MIRACLE, HE THOUGHT. If people could really call down such a thing, surely they would not waste that power on a prom dress. Cure world hunger. Or cancer. He was annoyed at Molly.

For not doing as he had asked her—a thinly veiled order really—and canceling Prom Dreams, at least she should have told that girl to get ready for the cancellation of it.

But more, for wheedling past his defenses. He had better things to be doing than dancing with her in a shabby store in Greenwich Village.

It was the type of experience that might make a man who knew better hope for a miracle.

But hadn't he hoped for that once?

The memory leaped over a wall that seemed to have chinks out of it that it had not had yesterday.

It was his birthday. He was about to turn fifteen. He'd been at Beebee's for months. He was living a life he could never have even dreamed for himself.

He had his own room. He had his own TV. He had his own bathroom. He had nice clothes.

And the miracle he was praying for was for his mother to call. Under that grand four-poster bed was a plain plastic bag, with everything he had owned when he came here packed in it.

Ready to go. In case his mother called. And wanted him back.

That was the miracle he had prayed for that had never come.

"I don't believe in miracles," he said to Molly, probably way more curtly than was necessary.

"That's too bad," she said sympathetically, forgiving his curtness, missing his point entirely that there was no room in the business world for dreamers. "That's really too bad.

"Why don't we call it a day?" she said brightly. "Tomorrow I'll take you to Sunshine and Lollipops, our preschool program. It's designed to assist working poor mothers, most of them single parents."

Houston Whitford contemplated that. Despite the professionalism of her delivery, he knew darn well what she was up to. She was taking down the bricks around his carefully compartmentalized world. She was *getting* to him. And she knew it. She knew it after he had chased her in the garden with that worm, danced with her.

She was having quite an impact on his legendary discipline and now she was going to try to hit him in his emotional epicenter to get her programs approved. Who could resist preschoolers, after all?

Me, he thought. She was going to try to win him over to her point of view by going for the heart instead of the head. It was very much the romantic versus the realist.

But the truth was Houston was not the least sentimental about children. Or anything else. And yet even as he told himself that, he was aware of a feeling that he was a warrior going into battle on a completely unknown field, against a completely unknown enemy. Well, not completely. He knew what a powerful weapon her hair was on his beleaguered male senses. The touch of her skin. Now he could add dancing with her to the list of weapons in the arsenal she was so cheerfully using against him.

He rethought his plan to walk right into his fear. He might need a little time to regroup.

"Something has come up for tomorrow," he said. *It was called sanity.*

"You promised me two days," she reminded him. "I assume you are a man of honor."

More use of her arsenal. Challenging his *honor.*

"I didn't say consecutively."

She lifted an eyebrow, *knowing* the effect she was having on him, knowing she was chiseling away at his defenses.

"Friday?" he asked her.

"Friday it is."

"See you then," he said, as if he wasn't the least bit wary of what she had in store for him.

Tonight, and every other night this week, until Friday, he would hit the punching bag until the funny *yearning* that the glimpse of her world was causing in him was gone. He could force all the things he was feeling—*lonely, for one*—back into their proper compartments.

By the end of the week he would be himself again. He'd experienced a temporary letting down of his guard, but he recognized it now as a weakness. He'd had a whole lifetime of fighting the weaknesses in himself. There was no way one day with her could change that permanently.

Sparring with Molly Michaels was just like boxing, without the bruises, of course. But as with boxing, even with day after day of practice, when it came to sparring, you could take a hair too long to resume the defensive position, and someone slipped a punch in. Rattled you. Knocked you off balance. It didn't mean you were going to lose that fight! It meant you were going to come back more aware of your defenses. More determined. Especially if the bell had rung between rounds and you had the luxury of a bit of a breather.

She wasn't going to wear him down, and he didn't care how many children she tried to use to do it.

CHAPTER SIX

HOUSTON WHITFORD CONGRATULATED himself on using his time between rounds wisely. By avoiding Molly Michaels.

And yet there really was no avoiding her. With each day at Second Chances, even as he busied himself researching, checking the new computer systems, okaying details of the renovations, there was no avoiding her influence in this place.

Molly Michaels was the sun that the moons circled around. Just as at the garden, she seemed to be the one people gravitated to with their confidences and concerns. She was warm, open and emotional.

The antithesis of what he was. But what was that they said? Opposites attract. And he could feel the pull of her even as he tried not to.

They had one very striking similarity. They both wanted their own way, and were stubborn in the pursuit of it.

Tuesday morning three letters had been waiting for him on his desk when he arrived. The recurring theme of the three letters: *Why I Want a Prom Dress.* One was on pink paper. One smelled of perfume. And he was pretty sure one was stained with tears.

Wednesday there were half a dozen.

Yesterday, twenty or so.

Today he was so terrified of the basket overflowing

with those heartfelt feminine outpourings that he had bypassed his office completely! The Sunshine and Lollipops program felt as if it had to be easier to handle than those letters!

Molly was chipping away at his hardheaded jadedness without even being in the same room with him.

Today children. He didn't really have a soft spot for children, but a few days ago he would have said the same of teenage girls pleading for prom dresses!

Molly was a force to be reckoned with. Houston was fairly certain if he was going to be here for two months instead of two weeks, by the end of that time he would be laying down his cloak over mud puddles for her. He'd probably be funding Prom Dreams out of his own pocket, just as he was donating the entire office renovation, and the time and skill of his Precision Solutions team.

The trick really was not to let Molly Michaels know that her charm was managing to permeate even his closed office door! The memory of the day they had already spent together seemed to be growing more vibrant with time instead of less.

Because she was a mischievous little minx—laughter seemed to follow in her wake—and she would not hesitate to use any perceived power over him to her full advantage!

So, the trick was not to let her know. They hailed a cab when she took one look at his car and pronounced it unsuitable for the neighborhood they were going into.

As someone who had once put a rock through a judge's very upscale Cadillac, Houston should have remembered that his car, a jet black Jaguar, would be a target for the angry, the greedy and the desperate in those very poor neighborhoods.

The daycare center was a cheery spot of color on a dreary street that reminded Houston of where he'd grown up. Except for the daycare, the buildings oozed neglect and desperation. The daycare, though, had its brick front painted a cheerful yellow, a mural of sunflowers snaked up to the second-floor windows.

Inside was more cheer—walls and furniture painted in bright, primary colors. They met with the staff and Houston was given an enthusiastic overview of the programs Second Chances funded.

He was impressed by the careful shepherding of the funds, but how he'd seen people react to her in the garden was repeated here.

Dealing with people was clearly her territory. He could see this aspect of Second Chances was her absolute strength. There was an attitude of love and respect toward her that even a jaundiced old businessman like him could see the value of. Money could not buy the kind of devotion that Molly inspired.

Still, aside from that, analytically, it was clear to him Molly had made a tactical error in bringing him here. He had always felt this particular program, providing care for children of working or back-to-school moms, had indisputable merit. She had nothing to prove, here.

Obviously, in her effort to show him the soul of Second Chances she was trying to find her way to his heart.

And though she made some surprising headway, the terrible truth about Houston was that other women had tried to make him feel things he had no intention of feeling, had tried to unlock the secrets of his heart.

They had not been better women than Molly, but they had certainly been every bit as determined to make him feel something. He dated career women, female versions of himself, owned by their work, interested only in temporary diversion and companionship when it came to a relationship. Sometimes somebody wanted to change the rules partway in, thinking he should want what they had come to want: something deeper. A future. Together. Babies. Little white picket fences. Fairy tales. Forever.

Happily ever after.

He could think of very few things that were as terrifying to him. He must have made some kind of cynical sound because Molly glanced at him and smiled. There was something about that smile that made him realize she hadn't played all her cards yet.

"We're going to watch a musical presentation, and then have lunch with the children," she told him.

The children. Of course she was counting on them to bring light to his dark heart, to pave the way for older children, later, who needed prom dresses, though of course it was the *need* part that was open to question.

"Actually we could just—"

But the children were marching into the room, sending eager glances at their visitors, as excited as if they would be performing to visiting royalty.

He glared at Molly, just to let her know using the kids to try to get to him, to try to get her way, was the ultimate in cheesy. He met her gaze, and held it, to let her know that he was on to her. But before she fully got the seriousness of his stern look, several of the munchkins broke ranks and attacked her!

They flung themselves at her knees, wrapping sturdy arms around her with such force she stumbled down. The rest of the ranks broke, like water over a dam, flowing out toward the downed Molly and around her until he couldn't even see her anymore, lost in a wriggling mass of hugs and kisses and delightful squeals of *Miss Molly!*

Was she in danger? He watched in horror as Molly's arm came up and then disappeared again under a pile of wiggling little bodies, all trying to get a hold of her, deliver messy kisses and smudgy hugs.

He debated rescuing her, but a shout of laughter—female, adult—from somewhere in there let him know somehow she was okay under all that. Delighting in it, even.

He tried to remain indifferent, but he could not help but follow the faint trail of feeling within him, trying to identify what it was.

Envious, he arrived at with surprise. Oh, not of all those children, messy little beings that they were with their dripping noses and grubby hands, but somehow envious of her spontaneity, her ability to embrace the unexpected surprise of the moment, the gifts of hugs and kisses those children were plying her with.

Her giggles came out of the pile again. And he was envious of that, too. When was the last time he had laughed like that? Let go so completely to delight. Had he ever?

Would he ever? Probably not. He had felt a tug of that feeling in the garden, and again in Now and Zen. But when had he come to see feeling good as an enemy?

Maybe that's what happened when you shut down *feeling:* good and bad were both taken from you, the mind unable to distinguish.

Finally she extricated herself and stood up, though every one of her fingers and both her knees were claimed by small hands.

The businesswoman of this morning was erased. In

her place was a woman with hair all over the place, her clothes smudged, one shoe missing, a nylon ruined.

And he had never, ever seen a woman so beautiful.

The jury was still out on whether she would make a good replacement for Miss Viv. So how could he know, he who avoided that particular entanglement the most—how could he know, so instantly, without a doubt, what a good mother Molly would make with her loving heart, and her laughter filled and spontaneous spirit?

And why did that thought squeeze his chest so hard for a moment he could not breathe?

Because of the cad who had made her suffer by letting her go, by stealing her dreams from her.

No, that was too altruistic. It wasn't about her. It was about him. He could feel something from the past looming over him, waiting to pounce.

As Molly rejoined him, Houston focused all his attention on the little messy ones trying so hard to form perfect ranks on a makeshift stage. It was painfully obvious these would be among the city's neediest children. Some were in old clothes, meticulously cared for. Others were not so well cared for. Some looked rested and eager, others looked strangely tired, dejected.

With a shiver, he knew exactly which ones lay awake with wide eyes in the night, frightened of being left alone, or of the noises coming from outside or the next rooms. He looked longingly for the exit, but Molly, alarmingly intuitive, seemed to sense his desire to run for the door.

"They've been practicing for us!" she hissed at him, and he ordered himself to brace up, to face what he feared.

But why would he fear a small bunch of enthusiastic if ragamuffin children? He seated himself reluctantly in terribly uncomfortable tiny chairs, the cramped space ringing with children's shouts and shrieks, laughter. At the count of three the clamor of too enthusiastically played percussion instruments filled the room.

Houston winced from the racket, stole a glance at Molly and felt the horrible squeeze in his chest again. *What was that about?*

She was enchanted. Clapping, singing along, calling out encouragement. He looked at the children. Those children were playing just for her now. She was probably the mother each of them longed for: engaged, fully present to them, appreciative of their enthusiasm if not their musical talent.

And then he knew what it was about, the squeezing in his chest.

He remembered a little boy in ragged jeans, not the meticulously kept kind, at a school Christmas concert. He had been given such an important job. He was to put the baby Jesus in the manger at the very end of the performance. He kept pulling back the curtain. Knowing his dad would never come. But please, Mommy, please.

Hope turning to dust inside his heart as each moment passed, as each song finished and she did not enter the big crowded room. His big moment came and that little boy, the young Houston, took that doll that represented the baby Jesus and did not put him in the waiting crib. Instead, he threw it with all his might at all the parents who had come. The night was wrecked for him, he wanted to wreck it for everybody else.

Houston felt a cold shadow fall over him. He glanced at Molly, still entranced. He didn't care to know what a good mother she would be. It hurt him in some way. It made him feel as he had felt at the Christmas play that night. Like he wanted to destroy something.

Instead, he slipped his BlackBerry out of his pocket, scanned his e-mails. The Bradbury papers, nothing to do with Second Chances—all about his other life—had just been signed. It was a deal that would mean a million and a half dollars to his company. Yesterday that would have thrilled him. Filled him.

Yesterday, before he had heard her laughter emerge from under a pile of children, and instantly and without his permission started redefining everything that was important about his life.

He shook off that feeling of having glimpsed something really important—maybe the only thing that was important—he shook it off the same way he shook off a punch that rattled him nearly right off his feet. Deliberately he turned his attention to the small piece of electronics that fit in the palm of his hand.

Houston Whitford opened the next e-mail. The Chardon account was looking good, too.

MOLLY CONGRATULATED HERSELF on the timing of their arrival at the daycare program. The concert had been a delight of crashing cymbals, clicking sticks, wildly jangling triangles. Now it was snack time for the members of the rhythm section, three and four year olds.

They were so irresistible! They were fighting for her hands, and she gave in, allowed herself to be tugged toward the kitchen.

She glanced back at Houston. He was trailing behind. How could he be looking at his BlackBerry? Was she failing to enchant him, failing to make him *see?*

Well, there was still time with her small army of charmers, and Molly had never seen a more delightful snack. She felt a swell of pride that Second Chances provided the funding so that these little ones could get something healthy into them at least once a day.

Healthy but fun. The snack was so messy that the two long tables were covered in plastic, and the children, about ten at each long, low table, soon had bibs fashioned out of plastic grocery bags over their clothes.

On each table were large plastic bowls containing thinly cut vegetables—red and green peppers, celery, carrots—interspersed with dips bowls mounded with salad dressing.

The children were soon creating their own snacks—plunging the veggies first into the dressing, and then rolling the coated veggie on flat trays that held layers of sunflower seeds, poppy seeds, raisins.

Though most of the children were spotlessly clean beneath those bibs and the girls all had hairdos that spoke of tender loving care, their clothes were often worn, some pairs of jeans patched many times. The shoes told the real story—worn through, frayed, broken laces tied in knots, vibrant colors long since faded.

Molly couldn't help but glance at Houston's shoes. Chuck had been a shoe aficionado. He'd shown her a pair on the Internet once that he thought might make a lovely gift from her. A Testoni Norvegese—at about fifteen hundred dollars a pop!

Was that what Houston was wearing? If not, it was certainly something in the same league. What hope did she have of convincing him of the immeasurable good in these small projects when his world was obviously so far removed from this he couldn't even comprehend it?

She had to get him out of the BlackBerry! She wished she had a little dirt to throw on those shoes, to coax the happiness out of him. She had to make him *see* what was important. This little daycare was just a microcosm of everything Second Chances did. If he could feel the love, even for a second, everything would change. Molly knew it.

"Houston, I saved you a seat," she called, patting the tiny chair beside her.

He glanced over, looked aghast, looked longingly—and not for the first time—at the exit door. And then a look came over his face—not of a man joining preschoolers for snack—but of a warrior striding toward battle, a gladiator into the ring.

The children became quite quiet, watching him.

If he knew his suit was in danger, he never let on. Without any hesitation at all, he pulled up the teeny chair beside Molly, hung his jacket over the back of it—not even out of range of the fingers, despite the subtle Giorgio Armani label revealed in the back of it—and plunked himself down.

The children eyed him with wide-eyed surprise, silent and shy.

Children, Molly told herself, were not charmed by the same things as adults. They did not care about his watch or his shoes, the label in the back of that jacket.

Show me who you really are.

She passed him a red pepper, a silly thing to expect to show you a person. He looked at it, looked at her, seemed to be deciding something. She was only aware of how tense he had been when she saw his shoulders shift slightly, saw the corners of his mouth relax.

Ignoring the children who were gawking at him, Houston picked up a slice of red pepper and studied it. "What should I do with this?"

"Put stuff on it!"

He followed the instructions he could understand,

until the original red pepper was not visible any longer but coated and double coated with toppings.

Finally he could delay the moment of truth no longer. But he did not bite into his own crazy creation.

Instead, he held it out, an inch from Molly's lips. "My lady," he said smoothly. "You first."

Something shivered in her. How could this be? Surrounded by squealing children, suddenly everything faded. It was a moment she'd imagined in her weaker times. Was there anything more romantic than eating from another's hand?

Somehow that simple act of sharing food was the epitome of trust and connection.

She had wanted to bring him out of himself, and instead he was turning the tables on her!

Molly leaned forward and bit into the raisin-encrusted red pepper. She had to close her eyes against the pleasure of what she tasted.

"Ambrosia," she declared, and opened her eyes to see him looking at her with understandable quizzicalness.

"My turn!" She loaded a piece of celery with every ingredient on the table.

"I hate celery," he said when she held it up to him.

"You're setting an example!" she warned him.

He cast his eyes around the table, looked momentarily rebellious, then nipped the piece of celery out of her fingers with his teeth.

Way too easy to imagine this same scenario in very different circumstances. Maybe he could, too, because his silver-shaded eyes took on a smoky look that was unmistakably sensual.

How could this be happening? Time standing still, something in her heart going crazy, in the middle of the situation least like any romantic scenario she had ever imagined, and Molly was guilty of imagining many of them!

But then that moment was gone as the children raced each other creating concoctions for their honored guests. As when his shoulders had relaxed, now Molly noticed another layer of some finally held tension leaving him as he surrendered to the children, and to the moment.

They were calling orders to him, the commands quick and thick. "Dunk it." "Roll it." "Put stuff on it! Like this!"

One of the bolder older boys got up and pressed right in beside Houston. He anchored himself—one sticky little hand right on the suit jacket hanging on the back of the chair—and leaned forward. He held out the offering—a carrot dripping with dressing and seeds—to Houston. Some of it appeared to plop onto those beautiful shoes.

Molly could see a greasy print across the shoulder lining of the jacket.

A man who owned a suit like that was not going to be impressed with its destruction, not able to see *soul* through all this!

But Houston didn't seem to care that his clothes were getting wrecked. He wasn't backing away. After his initial horror in the children, he seemed to be easing up a little. He didn't even make an attempt to move the jacket out of harm's way.

In fact he looked faintly pleased as he took the carrot that had been offered and chomped on it thoughtfully.

"Excellent," he proclaimed.

After that any remaining shyness from the children dissolved. Houston selected another carrot, globbed dressing on it and hesitated over his finishing choices.

The children yelled out suggestions, and he listened and obeyed each one until that carrot was so coated in stuff that it was no longer recognizable. He popped the whole concoction in his mouth. He closed his eyes, chewed very slowly and then sighed.

"Delicious," he exclaimed.

Molly stared at him, aware of the shift happening in her. It was different than when they had chased each other in the garden, it was different than when they had danced and she was entranced.

Beyond the sternness of his demeanor, she saw someone capable of exquisite tenderness, an amazing ability to be sensitive. Even sweet.

Molly was sure if he knew that—that she could see tender sweetness in him—he would withdraw instantly. So she looked away, but then, was compelled to look back. She felt like someone who had been drinking brackish water their entire life, and who had suddenly tasted something clear and pure instead.

The little girl beside Houston, wide-eyed and silent, held up her celery stick to him—half-chewed, sloppy with dressing and seeds—plainly an offering. He took it with grave politeness, popped it in his mouth, repeated the exaggerated sigh of enjoyment.

"Thank you, princess."

Her eyes grew wider. "Me princess," she said, mulling it over gravely. And then she smiled, her smile radiant and adoring.

Children, of course, saw through veneers so much easier than adults did!

I am allowing myself to be charmed, Molly warned herself sternly. And of course, it was even more potent because Houston was not trying to charm anyone, slipping into this role as naturally and unselfconsciously as if he'd been born to play it.

But damn it, who wouldn't be charmed, seeing that self-assured man give himself over to those children?

I could love him. Molly was stunned as the renegade thought blasted through her brain.

Stop it, she ordered herself. She was here to achieve a goal.

She wanted him to acknowledge there was the potential for joy anywhere, in any circumstance at all. Bringing that shining moment to people who had had too few of them was the soul of Second Chances. It was what they did so well.

But all of that, all her motives, were fading so quickly as she continued to *see* something about Houston Whitford that made her feel weak with longing.

He couldn't keep up with children hand-making him tidbits. In minutes he had every child in the room demanding his attention. He solemnly accepted the offerings, treated each as if it was a culinary adventure from the five-star restaurant he was dressed for.

He began to really let loose—something Molly sensed was very rare in this extremely controlled man. He began to narrate his culinary adventure, causing spasms of laughter from the children, and from her.

He did Bugs Bunny impressions. He asked for recipes. He used words she would have to look up in the dictionary.

And then he laughed.

Just like he had laughed in the garden. It was possibly the richest sound she had ever heard, deep, genuine, true.

She thought of all the times she had convinced Chuck to do "fun" things with her, the thing she deemed an in-love couple should do that week. Roller-skating, bike riding, days on the beaches of Long Island, a skiing holiday in Vermont. Usually paid for by her of course, and falling desperately short of her expectations.

Always, she had so carefully set up the picture, trying to make herself feel some kind of magic that had been promised to her in songs, and in movies and in storybooks.

Molly had tried so hard to manufacture the exact feeling she was experiencing in this moment. She had thought if she managed this outing correctly she would show Houston Whitford the real Second Chances.

What she had not expected was to see Houston Whitford so clearly, to see how a human being could shine.

What if this was what was most real about him? What if this was him, this man who was so unexpectedly full of laughter and light around these children?

What if he was one of those rare men who were made to be daddies? Funny, playful, able to fully engage with children?

"I told you, you don't laugh enough," she whispered to him.

"Ah, Miss Molly, it's hard for me to admit you might be right." And then he smiled at her, and it seemed as if the whole world faded and it was just the two of them in this room, sharing something deep and splendid.

Molly found herself wanting to capture these moments, to hold them, to keep them. She remembered the camera he had given her, took it out and clicked as he took a very mashed celery stick from a child.

"The best yet," she heard him say. "To die for. But I can't eat another bite. Not one."

But he took one more anyway, and then he closed his eyes, and patted his flat belly, pretending to push it out against his hand. The children howled with laughter. She took another picture, and Molly laughed, too, at his antics, but underneath her laughter was a growing awareness.

She had thought bringing Houston to her projects would show her the real Houston Whitford. And that was true.

Unfortunately, if this laughing carefree man was the real Houston, it made her new boss even more attractive, not less! It made her way too aware of the Molly that had never been put behind her after all—the Molly who yearned and longed, and ultimately *believed.*

"Will you stay for story time?"

No. Nothing that ended happily-ever-after! Please! She suddenly wanted to get him out of here. Felt as if something about her plot to win his heart was backfiring badly. She had wanted to win him over for Second Chances! Not for herself.

He was winning her heart instead of her winning his, and it had not a single thing to do with Second Chances.

"Not possible," Molly said, quickly, urgently. "Sorry."

It wasn't on the schedule to stay, thank goodness, but even before the children started begging him, it seemed every one of them tugging on some part of him to get him up off the floor, his eyes met Molly's and she knew they weren't going anywhere.

With handprints and food stains all over the pristine white of that shirt, Houston allowed himself to be dragged to the sinks, where he obediently washed his own hands, and then one by one helped each of the children wash theirs.

After he washed "Princess's" face, the same child who had sat beside him at snack, she crooked her finger at him. He bent down, obviously thinking, as Molly did, that the tiny tot had some important secret to tell him.

Instead she kissed him noisily on his cheek.

Molly held out the camera, framed the exquisite moment. *Click.*

He straightened slowly, blushing wildly.

Click. She found herself hoping that she was an accomplished enough photographer to capture that look on his face.

"Did you turn me into a prince, little princess?" Houston asked.

The girl regarded him solemnly. "No."

But that's not how Molly felt, at all. A man she had been determined to see as a toad had turned into a prince before her eyes.

Again she realized that this excursion was not telling her as much about Houston Whitford as it was telling her about herself.

She wanted the things she had always wanted, more desperately than ever.

And that sense of desperation only grew as Molly watched as Houston, captive now, like Gulliver in the land of little people, was led over to the story area. He chose to sit on the floor, all the children crowding around him. By the time they were settled each of those children seemed to have claimed some small part of him, to touch, even if it was just the exquisitely crafted soft leather of his shoe. His "little princess" crawled into his lap, plopped her thumb in her mouth and promptly went to sleep.

Molly could not have said what one of those stories was about by the time they left a half hour later, Houston handing over the still sleeping child.

As she watched him, she was in the grip of a tenderness so acute it felt as if her throat was closing.

Molly was stunned. The thing she had been trying to avoid because she knew how badly it would weaken her—was exactly what she had been brought.

She was seeing Houston Whitford in the context of family. Watching him, she *felt* his strength, his protectiveness, his *heart.*

She had waited her whole life to feel this exquisite tenderness for another person.

It was all wrong. There was no candlelight. It smelled suspiciously like the little girl might have had an accident in her sleep.

Love was supposed to come first. And then these moments of glory.

What did it mean? That she had experienced such a moment for Houston? Did it mean love would come next? That she could fall in love with this complicated man who was her boss?

No, that was exactly what she was not doing! No more wishing, dreaming! Being held prisoner by fantasies.

No more.

But as she looked at him handing over that sleeping little girl, it felt like she was being blinded by the light in him, drawn to the power and warmth of it.

Moth to flame, Molly chastised herself ineffectively.

"Sorry she's so clingy," the daycare staff member who relieved him of her said. "She's going through a rough time, poor mite. Her mother hasn't been around for a few days. Her granny is picking her up."

And just like that, the light she had seen in his face snapped off, replaced by something as cold as the other light had been warm.

Selfishly, Molly wanted to see only the warmth, especially once it was gone. She wanted to draw it back out of him. Would it seem just as real outside as it had in? Maybe she had just imagined it. She had to know.

She had to test herself against this fierce new challenge.

As they waited for a cab on the sidewalk, he seemed coolly remote. The electronic device was back out. She remembered this from yesterday. He came forward, and then he retreated.

"You were a hit with those kids." She tried to get him back to the man she had seen at lunch.

He snorted with self-derision, didn't look up. "Starving for male attention."

"I can see you as a wonderful daddy someday," she said.

He looked up then, gave her his full attention, a look that was withering.

"The last thing I would ever want to be is a daddy," he said.

"But why?"

"Because there is quite a bit more to it than carrot sticks and storybooks."

"Yes?"

"Like being there. Day in and day out. Putting another person first forever. Do I look like the kind of guy who puts other people first?"

"You did in there."

"Well, I'm not."

"You seem angry."

"No kidding."

"Houston, what's wrong?"

"There's a little girl in there whose mom has abandoned her. How does something like that happen? How could anybody not love her? Not want her? How could anybody who had a beautiful child like that not devote their entire life to protecting her and making her safe and happy?"

"An excellent daddy," she said softly.

"No, I wouldn't," he said, coldly angry. "Can you wait for the cab yourself? I just thought of something I need to do."

And he left, walking down the street, fearless, as though that fancy watch and those shoes didn't make him a target.

Look at the way he walked. He was no target. No victim.

She debated calling after him that she had other things on the agenda for today. But she didn't. This was his pattern. She recognized it clearly now.

He felt something. Then he tried to walk away, tried to reerect his barriers, his formidable defenses, against it.

Why? What had happened to him that made a world alone seem so preferable to one shared?

"Wait," she called. "I'll walk with you."

And he turned and watched her come toward him, waited, almost as if he was relieved that he was not going to carry some of the burden he carried alone.

CHAPTER SEVEN

HOUSTON WATCHED MOLLY walking fast to catch up with him. The truth was all he wanted was an hour or so on his punching bag. Though maybe he waited, instead of continuing to walk, because the punching bag had not done him nearly the good he had hoped it would last night. Now it felt as if it was the only place to defuse his fury.

That beautiful little girl's mother didn't want her. He knew he was kidding himself that his anger was at *her* mother.

From the moment he'd heard Molly laughing from under the pile of children a powerless longing for something he was never going to have had pulled at him.

You thought you left something behind you, but you never quite left that. The longing for the love of a mother.

The love of his mother. She was dead now. He'd hired a private detective a few years back to find her. Somehow he had known she was dead. Because he'd always thought she would come back. He would have left Beebee's world in a minute if his mother had loved him and needed him.

It had been a temporary relief when the private eye had told him. Drugs. An overdose.

Death. The only reasonable explanation for a mother who had never looked back. Except, as the P.I. filled in the dates and details, it wasn't the explanation he'd been seeking after all. She'd died only a few years before he made the inquiries about her—plenty of time to check in on her son if she had wanted to.

She hadn't.

And he was powerless over that, too.

There was nothing a man of action like Houston hated so much as that word. *Powerless.*

Molly came and walked beside him. He deliberately walked fast enough to keep her a little breathless; he knew intuitively she would have a woman's desire to *talk,* to probe his wounds.

He could feel his anger dispersing as they left the edgier part of the Lower East Side and headed back to where Second Chances was in the East Village.

"This is where I live," she said as they came to a well-kept five-story brownstone. "Do you want to stop for a minute? Meet Baldy? Have a coffee?"

She obviously intended to pursue this thing. His *feelings.* He was not going to meet her bird, enter her personal space and have a coffee with her!

On the other hand, the punching bag had not been working its normal magic. He hesitated. And she read that as a yes. In the blink of an eye she was at the door with her key out.

He still had a chance to back away, but for some reason he didn't. In fact, he ordered himself to keep walking, to call after her, *Maybe some other time.* But he didn't.

Instead, feeling oddly *powerless* again, as if she might have something he was looking for, he followed her up the three flights of stairs to her apartment.

"Close it quick," she said, as he came through the door behind her. "Baldy."

And sure enough out of the darkness of the apartment a tiny missile flew at them, a piece of flesh-colored putty with naked wings. It landed on her shoulder, pecked at her ear, turned and gave him a baleful look.

"Good grief," he said, but he was already glad he had come. The bird was so ugly he was cute. The tiny being's obvious adoration for Molly lightened something in Houston's mood. "ET call home!"

Still, there was something about that bird, looking as if it, too, would protect her to the death, that tugged at a heart that had just faced one too many challenges today.

The bird rode on her shoulder as she guided him into the apartment which looked to be all of five hundred square feet of pure feminine coziness.

The bird kissed her cheek and made a whimpering noise that was near human. She absently stroked his featherless body with a tender finger. The bird preened.

"Just have a seat," she said. "I'll make coffee."

But he didn't have a seat. Instead he questioned his sanity for coming in here. He studied the framed poster of a balloon rising over the Napa Valley in California. He turned away from it. How was it her humble five hundred square feet felt like *home* in a way he had never quite managed to achieve?

It must be the fresh flowers on the coffee table between the two sofas.

"Nice flowers," he heard himself say.

"Oh, I treat myself," she called from the kitchen. "There's a vendor on the way home from work."

He went and stood in the doorway of her tiny kitchen, watched her work.

"No boyfriend buying you flowers?"

That's exactly why it had been a mistake to accept her invitation into her personal space. This was going too far. He'd chased her with a worm. And danced with her. He'd felt the exquisite plumpness of her lip on his finger when he'd fed her from his hand. Now he was in her house.

In high school, he scoffed at himself, that might count as a relationship. But for a mature man?

"Believe me," she muttered, "the boyfriend I had never bought me flowers."

"Really?" he said, and some of his dismay at that must have come through in his tone. What kind of cad wouldn't buy her flowers? He would buy her flowers if he was her boyfriend.

Now that was a dangerous side road his mind had just gone down!

Her tongue was caught between her teeth as she concentrated on putting coffee things on a tray. She pressed by him in the narrow doorway, set the tray on the coffee table by the flowers.

It all looked very cozy. He went and sat down.

She poured coffee. "He was more than my boyfriend. My fiancé."

"Ah." He took a generous gulp of coffee, burned his mouth, set it down and glared at it.

She took a tiny sip of hers. "His name was Chuck. We were supposed to get married and live happily ever after. Instead, he emptied my bank account and went to live on a beach in Costa Rica. That's what finished me for being a romantic."

Why was she telling him this? He got it very suddenly. They were going to share confidences.

"Now I see it as a good thing," she said. "It got me ready for you."

He stared.

"Hardened me," she declared. "So that I'm not a romantic anymore. So that I can handle all the changes at work."

And he wasn't aware he had stopped breathing until he started again. For a suspended moment in time, he had thought she was going to say losing her fiancé had freed her to love him. What would give him such a notion?

Still, it was very hard not to laugh at her declaration that she was *hardened.* "But there's such a thing as being too hard," she went on.

"I guess there is," he agreed warily.

"I'd like you to trust me. Tell me why the situation at the daycare with the little girl and her mother made you so angry today?"

Her perception—the feeling that she could see what he least wanted to be seen—was frightening.

What was even more frightening was the temptation that clawed at his throat. To take off all the armor, and lay it at her feet. Tell her all of it. But the words stuck.

"When I was little," she told him, still thinking it was a confidences exchange, "my mom and dad fought all the time. And I dreamed of belonging to a family where everyone loved each other."

"Ah," he said, unforthcoming.

"Do you think such a family exists?"

"Honestly? No."

"You're very cynical about families, Houston. Why?"

She wanted to know? Okay, he'd tell her. She probably wasn't going to be nearly as happy to know about him as she thought she was going to be!

"Because I grew up in one just like yours. Constant fighting. Drama. Chaos. Actually it would probably make yours look like something off a Christmas card.

And it made me feel the opposite of you. Not a longing for love. An allergy to it."

"Isn't that lonely?"

He didn't answer for a long time. "Maybe," he finally said. "But not as lonely as waiting for something that never happens. That's the loneliest."

"What did you wait for that never happened?"

This was what he had come here for. For her to coax this out of him.

He was silent.

"Trust me," she said quietly.

And he could not resist her. Even though he pitted his whole strength against it, he heard himself say, his voice a low growl of remembered pain, "Once, when I was quite small, I was in a Christmas concert."

And somehow he told her all of it. And with every single word it felt like a chain that had been wrapped hard around his heart was breaking apart, link by link.

Somehow, when he was finished, she had moved from the couch across from him to the place right beside him. Her hand was in his. And she was silent for the longest time.

"But why didn't she come?" she finally asked.

"I don't know," he said. "I don't remember."

"Was it just that once that she didn't come?"

Here she was dragging more out of him.

"No, it was all the time."

"Because she couldn't care about anybody but herself," Molly said sadly. "Did you think it was about you?"

As she spoke those words Houston knew a truth he did not want to know. Of course he had thought it was about him.

It was not his father he had never forgiven. Not entirely.

Somewhere in him, he had always thought the truth was that he was a person no one could care about. Not if tested. Not over time. If his own mother had found him unworthy of love, that was probably the truth.

It was not his mother he had not forgiven, either.

It was himself he had never forgiven. For not being worthy of love. For not being a person that his mother and father could have at least tried to hold it all together for.

Molly reached up and guided his hand to her face. It was wet with her tears. It was such a tender powerful gesture, without words.

Something in him surrendered. He allowed himself to feel something he had not felt for a very long time. At home. As if he belonged. As if finally, in this world, there was one place, one person who could accept him for what he was.

He contemplated the temptation to tell her more, not sure if a man could put things back the way they used to be after he had experienced such a thing as this.

And it felt like a weakness that he could not fight and that he was not sure if he wanted to.

Damn it, he wanted to. He could not give in to this.

But then, his hand that rested on the wetness of her cheek went, it seemed of its own volition, to the puffiness of her lip. He traced the fullness of it with his thumb, took in the wideness of her eyes, the gentle puff of her breath touching his thumb.

I'm going to kiss her, he thought, entranced. Dismayed.

He snapped back from her, dropped his hand from the full and exquisite temptation of her lips.

But she wasn't having it. When he pulled away, she stretched forward. She had clearly seen what he would have loved to have kept hidden. In every sense.

Her lips grazed his. Tender. Soft. Supple.

Sexy.

It took every ounce of his considerable discipline to pull away from her. He got to his feet, abruptly, aware if he stayed on that couch with her he was not going to be fully in control of what happened next.

"That shouldn't have happened," he said gruffly.

"Why?" she said softly.

She knew why. She knew she was crashing through his barriers faster than he could rebuild them.

"It was inappropriate. I apologize."

"I think it was me who kissed you. And I'm not apologizing."

"Molly, you have no idea what you are playing with," he told her softly, sternly.

"Maybe I do."

As if she saw him more clearly than he saw himself! Just because he had told her one thing. He didn't like it that he had told her that. That brief moment of feeling unburdened, not so damned lonely, was swiftly changing to regret.

"I have work to do," he said, hardened himself to what these moments had made him feel, turned and walked away, shutting the door firmly behind him.

But he didn't go back to Second Chances, despite his claim he had work to do. He also had no work at home, not even his laptop. He didn't even feel compelled to check his BlackBerry. Life could go on without him for one evening.

He was sitting out on his terrace, overlooking Central Park.

The terrace was as beautifully furnished as his apartment, dark rattan furniture with deep white cushions, plants flowering in a glorious abundance of color under the new warmth of the spring sun.

Houston was sipping a glass of wine, a Romanée-Conti from the Burgundy region of France. The wine was so rare and sought after it had to be purchased in boxes that contained a dozen bottles of wine, only one the coveted Romanée-Conti, the other eleven from other domains.

For as spectacular as the wine was, it occurred to him this was the kind of wine that seemed as if it would lend itself to romance.

Over the sounds of the traffic, he could hear the pleasant *clip clop* of the hooves of a horse pulling a carriage.

For the second time—unusual since Houston was not a man given to romantic thoughts—his mind turned to romance. He wondered if young lovers, or honeymooners, in New York for the first time—were riding in that carriage.

He wondered if they were full of hope and optimism, were enjoying the spring evening, snuggled under a blanket, the world looking brighter because they were seeing it through that lens of love. He resisted an impulse to go give them the remainder of that exquisite bottle of wine.

Houston realized, not happily, that he felt lonely. That the merest touch of Molly's lips had unleashed something terrifying in him.

He realized, too, that he usually kept his life crammed full enough that he could avoid feelings like that—a sudden longing to share a moment like this one with someone else.

Molly Michaels if he wanted to get specific. The truth was they had shared some moments that had forged an instant sense of bonding, of intimacy. It was hard to leave it behind. That was all. It was natural to feel this way.

But it wasn't natural for *him* to feel this way.

He realized he still had Molly's camera in his pocket, and he took it out, scanned idly through the pictures.

He stopped at the one where *Princess* was kissing his cheek.

Something had changed for him, Houston acknowledged, in that exact moment. Because at that moment, he had surprised himself. He had surprised himself by so clearly seeing—no, not just seeing, *knowing*—the need in those children. But the biggest surprise had come when he had embraced that need instead of walking—no, running—away from it.

Everything had become personal after that.

It hadn't been about helping out Beebee and Miss Viv anymore, doing his civic duty, get in, get out, goodbye.

Those kids in that daycare, wistful for the fathers and mothers they didn't have, had hurt him, reminded him of things long buried, which made the fact he'd embraced their need even more surprising to him.

They called to who he had once been, and he wondered if there was something in that self he had left behind that had value.

"I doubt it," he muttered, wanting a beer out of a bottle being a prime example. The fact that, even though he was doing nothing else tonight, he was avoiding answering the letter from his father, being another example.

Houston wished, suddenly, wearily, that he had delegated the whole Second Chances project to someone else. It was bringing things to the surface that he had been content to leave behind for a long time.

He scanned through more pictures on the camera, stopped at the one of Molly that he had taken in the garden. She was leaning on the shovel, a smudge of dirt on her cheek, her hair wild around her, her eyes laughing, the constant wariness finally, finally gone from them.

Some tension she always held around him had relaxed in that garden. The playful part that he had glimpsed the first time he had seen her—in a bridal gown at work—had come back out at the garden. And at the preschool.

People loved her. That was evident in the next picture, her in the very middle of a line of ancient grandmothers, unaware how her youth and vitality set her apart, how beautiful she looked with her head thrown back in laughter as she kicked her leg up impossibly high. And in another of her at Sunshine and Lollipops, of her laughing, unaware there was salad dressing in her hair.

Ah, well, that was the promise that had been in her eyes all along. That she could take a life that had become too damned serious and insert some fun back in it.

What would she add to an evening like this one? Would she be content to sit here, listening to spring sounds? Or would she want to be out there, part of it?

Houston thought of the taste of her lips beneath his—raindrop fresh—and felt a shiver of pure longing that he killed.

Because the bigger question was what *price* would he pay to know those things? Would it be too high?

"Ah, Houston," he said. "The question isn't whether the price you would pay would be too high. It's what price would be asked of her, and if it would be more than she was willing to pay?"

Because to satisfy his curiosity by inviting her into his life would only invite trouble. Eventually she would want things he could not give her.

Because you could not give what you did not know. What you had never known. Though he felt how disappointed Beebee would be to know that even her best efforts had not taught him the lesson she most wanted to give him. That a life well lived was rarely lived alone.

And certainly not without love.

She had really come along too late. He'd been fourteen, his life lessons already learned, his personality long since shaped.

He tossed back a wine that was meant to be savored. He did not want to even think the word *love* on the same day he had told her things he had never told another living soul.

Told her? Ha! Had it dragged out of him!

He got up abruptly, went inside, closed the French doors on the sounds of spring unfolding relentlessly all around him.

He thought of her guiding his hand to the tears slipping down her cheeks, and something happened that hadn't happened to him since he had learned his mother was dead.

A fist closed in his throat, and something stung behind his eyes.

That's what he needed to remember about love, he told himself sternly. It hurt. It hurt like hell. It could make a strong man like his father weak.

Or a strong man like him.

A man needed to approach these kinds of temptations with a plan, with a road map of how to extricate himself from sticky situations.

And so when he saw her next, he would be coolly professional. He would take a step back from all the lines that had been crossed. He would not think of chasing her with a worm, or dancing with her, or holding her and telling her one small secret. He would not think of how it had felt to open his world just a little bit to another human being.

He steeled himself against the temptation to go those few steps down the hall to her office, just to see her, make small talk, ask about the stupid budgie.

So, when she arrived in the doorway of his office just before lunch the next day, he hardened himself to how beautiful she looked in a white linen suit, a sunshine-yellow top, her hair already doing its escape routine.

He had one more week here, and then he was never going to see her again. He could suck it up for that long.

"They finished painting my office yesterday," she said, cheerfully, as if her lips had not touched his. "The ochre isn't that bad."

"That's good." Apparently she had decided she could suck it up for that long, too. Keep it professional, talk about paint, not revisit last night. *Is that why it had taken her so long to come and see him today?*

"I was at the Suits for Success auction this morning."

As if he had asked why he hadn't seen her!

"How was it?"

"Great."

They stood on a precipice. Were they going to go deeper? Were they going to remember last night or move on?

She jumped off it.

"My bird likes you," she said, and then she smiled. "He doesn't like everybody."

Her bird liked him? Wasn't she thinking about that kiss? Had it been a sympathy kiss, then? Good grief!

"That's good." How ridiculous was it to preen slightly because her bird liked him? And didn't like just anybody? Houston fought the urge to ask her if the bird had liked Chuck, as if he could use that to judge the bird's true skill.

"I want you to know it meant a lot to me. The whole day yesterday. Letting me show you the soul of Second Chances." Her voice dropped lower. "And then showing me a bit of yours."

"I don't like pity, Molly."

"Pity?" She looked genuinely astounded, and then she laughed. "Oh, my God, Houston, I cannot think of a man who would inspire pity less than you."

And he could tell that she meant it. And that the kiss had not been about pity at all. And she was so beautiful when she laughed.

Houston knew he could not spend another day with her. She made him too vulnerable. She opened something in him that was better left closed. He could not be with her without looking at her lips and remembering.

The research portion of the job at Second Chances was done. He knew exactly what each store brought in, he knew what their staffing and overhead costs were, he'd assigned a management team to go in and help them streamline, improve their efficiency, develop marketing plans.

One week left. He could suck it up for that long if he avoided her. If he stayed in Miss Viv's newly revamped office with the door firmly shut and the Do Not Disturb sign out.

Houston Whitford had built a career on his ability to be in control.

But this week was showing him something different about himself. And that version of himself could not refuse what she was offering.

One week. There were really two ways of looking at it. He could avoid her. Or he could engage with her.

Why not give himself that?

Because it's dumb, his more reasonable self said, *like playing with fire.*

But he felt the exquisite freedom of a man who had just ripped up his plan and thrown away the map. Like he could do anything and go anywhere.

For one week.

"Do you want to go for lunch?"

Molly was beaming at him. The late-morning light was playing off her hair, making the copper shimmer with flame and reminding him what it was like to play with fire, why children were drawn to sticks in campfires. Because before fire burned, it was irresistible, the temptation of what it offered wiping out any thought of consequences.

MOLLY DIDN'T TASTE one single bite of the five-star meal she had ordered. She didn't think of Miss Viv, or Prom Dreams or what the future of Second Chances was going to look like with him as the boss.

When she left him after lunch, she felt as if she was on pins and needles waiting to see him again, *dying* to see him again. Thinking uncontrollable thoughts of how his lips had felt beneath hers.

Was he feeling it, too?

When her phone rang, and it was him, she could hear something in his voice.

"I noticed that boys' soccer team we sponsor are playing on the Great Lawn fields at Central Park tonight. That's close to home for me. I wouldn't mind going."

With me?

"With you."

There was a momentary temptation to manufacture an exciting full schedule to impress him, to play hard to get, but she had played all the games before and knew they were empty. What she wanted now was real.

"I'd love to join you," she said.

And that's how they ended up spending most of the week together. The soccer game—where she screamed until she was hoarse—led to dinner. Then he said he had been given tickets for *Phantom of the Opera* for the next evening. Though it was the longest running show in Broadway history, Molly hadn't seen it, and was thrilled to go with him.

After, she was delighted when he insisted on seeing her home. And then said, "If I promise to be a perfect gentleman, can I come in and see Baldy?"

He came in. She made coffee. Baldy decided to give him a chance. She was not sure she had ever seen anyone laugh so hard as when Baldy began to peck affectionately on Houston's ear.

Being with Houston was easy and exhilarating. She found herself sharing things with him that she had rarely told anyone. She told him about the pets that had preexisted Baldy. She told him things from her childhood, anecdotes about the long chain of stepfathers. Finally it was he who remembered they both had to work in the morning.

He hesitated at her door. For a moment she thought he would kiss her, again, and her life as she had known it would be over because she knew they were reaching the point where neither of them was going to be able to hold back.

But clearly, though the struggle was apparent in his face, he remembered his promise to be a gentleman.

At work the next day, she appreciated his discipline. It was hard enough to separate the personal from the professional without the complication of another kiss between them.

But even without that complication her life suddenly felt as if it were lit from within.

They had gone from being combatants to being a team. They were working together, sharing a vision for Second Chances. Houston could make her laugh harder than she had ever laughed. He could take an ordinary moment and make it seem as if it had been infused with sunshine.

There was so much to be done and so little time left to do it as they moved toward the reopening of the office, the open house unveiling party set for Friday afternoon. The personal and the professional began to blend seamlessly. They worked side by side, late into the night, eating dinner together. He always walked her home when they were done.

She was beginning to see how right he had been about Second Chances, it could be so much better than she had ever dreamed possible.

And her personal life felt the same way. Life could be so much better than she had ever dreamed was possible!

It seemed like a long, long time ago, she had tried on that wedding dress, and felt all that it stood for. In this week of breathtaking changes and astounding togetherness, Molly had felt each of those things. *Souls joined. Laughter shared. Long conversations. Lonely no more.*

Was she falling in love with her boss? She had known the potential was there and now she evaluated how she was feeling.

If falling in love meant feeling gloriously alive every minute you spent together, then yes. If falling in love meant noticing a person's eyes were the exact color of silver of moonlight on water, yes. If falling in love was living for an accidental brush of a hand, yes.

If falling in love made the most ordinary things—coffee in the morning, the phone ringing and his voice being on the other end—extraordinary, then yes.

She glanced up to see him standing in her office doorway, looking at her. Something in his face made a shiver go up and down her spine.

"Tomorrow's the big day," she said, smiling at him.

But he didn't smile back.

"Molly, I need to show you something."

There was something grim about him that stopped the smile on her lips. He ushered her outside to a waiting cab, and gave the driver an address she didn't recognize.

But somehow her gut told her they were going somewhere she did not want to go.

CHAPTER EIGHT

HOUSTON KNEW SOMETHING that Molly didn't. Their time together was ticking down. Only Houston was so aware now that the week he had given himself didn't seem like enough. He was greedy. He wanted more. A woman like her made a man feel as if he could never get enough of her. Never.

Giving himself that week had made him feel like a man who had been told he only had a week to live: on fire with life, intensely engaged, as awake as he had ever been.

But there was that shadow, too. A feeling of foreboding from knowing that thing that she didn't. Nothing good ever lasted.

He realized the thought of not seeing her was like putting away the sun, turning his world, for all its accomplishments, for all he had acquired, back into a gray and dreary space, not unlike this neighborhood they were now entering.

He was not sure when he had decided to take this chance, only that he had, and now he was committed to it, even though his spirits sank as they got closer to the place that he had called home, and that somehow, he had never left behind. This was the biggest chance of his life.

What if he let her know the truth of him? All of it?

"I want to show you something," he said to her again

as the cab slowed and then stopped in front of the address he had given the driver. He helped her out of it. She was, he knew, used to tough neighborhoods. But there were certain places even the saints of Second Chances feared to go.

"This is Clinton," he said, watching her face. "They don't call it Hell's Kitchen anymore."

The cab drove away, eager to be out of this part of town.

"You've found us a new project?" she asked. She had the good sense to frown at the cab leaving.

Maybe a project so challenging even Molly would not want to take it on.

"Not exactly. This is where I grew up."

"This building?"

He scanned her face for signs of reaction. He was aware pity felt as though it would kill him. But there was no sign of pity in her face, just the dawning of something else, as if she knew better than him why he would bring her here.

Why had he? A test.

"Yes. I want to show you something else." He walked her down the street. "This didn't used to be a liquor store," he told her quietly. "It used to be a bank."

She waited, and he could tell she knew something was coming, something big. And that she wanted it to come. Maybe had waited for this. He plunged on, even while part of him wanted to back away from this.

"When I was fourteen my dad lost his job. Again. My mother was her normal sympathetic self, screaming at him he was a loser, threatening to trade up to someone with more promise."

Again, he scanned her face. If *that* look came across

it, the drowned kitten look, like he needed rescuing by *her,* they were out of here.

"He took a gun, and he came down here and he held that gun to the teller's nose and he took all the money that poor frightened woman could stuff into a bag. On his way out, a man tried to stop him. My father shot him. Thankfully he didn't kill him.

"He went to jail. Within a week my mother had traded up as promised. I never saw her again."

"But what happened to you?" Molly whispered.

"I became the kind of bitter man who doesn't trust anyone or anything."

"Houston, that's not true," she said firmly. "That's not even close to true."

He remembered the first day he had met her, when he had talked about being hungry and out of work and not having a place to live, had talked about it generically but her eyes had still been on his face, *knowing.*

"What is true then?" he asked her roughly. What if she *really* knew? He was aware of holding his breath, as if he had waited his whole life to find out.

Her eyes were the clearest shade of green he had ever seen as she gazed at him. A small smile touched her lips, and she took a step toward him, placed her hand on his chest, her palm flat, the strength of her *knowing* radiating from her touch.

"This is true," she whispered. "Your heart."

And the strangest thing was that he believed her. That somewhere in him, safe from the chaos, his heart had beat true and strong.

Whole.

Waiting.

"Did you think this would change how I feel about you?" she asked softly.

It was a major distraction. How *did* she feel about him?

"I always knew there was something about you that made you stronger than most people," she said.

He suddenly knew why he was here. He was asking her, *are you willing to take a chance on me?* And it was only fair that she knew the whole story before she made that decision. Still, he made one last-ditch effort to convince her she might be making a mistake.

"There's nothing romantic about growing up like this, Molly. Maybe it makes you strong. Or maybe just hard. I have scars that might never heal."

"Like the one on your nose?"

"That's the one that shows."

"I think love can heal anything," she said quietly, and somehow it felt as if she had just told him how she felt about him, after all.

Something felt tight in his chest. She was the one who believed in miracles. And standing here at the heart of Clinton, seeing the look in her eyes, it occurred to him that maybe he did, too.

"There's something else you should know," he said stubbornly. *Tell her all of it.*

"What's that?" she said, and she was looking at him as if not a single thing he could ever do or say could frighten her away from him.

Houston hesitated, searching for the words, framing them in his mind.

My father's getting out of prison. I don't know what to do. Somehow I feel that you'll know what to do, if I let you into my world. Did she want to come into this?

He drank her in, felt her hand still on his heart. The softness in her face, the utter desire to love him, could make a man take a sledgehammer to his own defenses, knock them down, not be worried about what got out.

Wanting to let something else in. Wanting to let in what he saw in her eyes when she looked at him.

A place where a man could rest, and be lonely no more. A place where a man could feel cared about. A place where he could lay down his weapons and fight no more. A place where he could be seen. And *known.* For who he was. All of it. She would want him to answer that letter from his father. He knew a man who was going to be worthy of loving her would be able to do that.

Would be able to believe that love could heal all things, just as she had said.

For a moment he was completely lost in thought, the look in her eyes that believed him to be a better man than Houston Whitford had ever believed himself to be. A man could rise up to meet that expectation, a man could live in the place that he found himself. Funny, that he would come this close to heaven in Clinton.

Suddenly the hair on the back of his neck went up. He was aware of something trying to penetrate the light that was beginning to pierce his darkness. And then he realized he was not free from darkness. This world held a darkness of its own, not so easy to escape, and he foolishly had brought her here.

They weren't alone on this street. The hair rising on the back of his neck, an instinctual residue from his days here, let him know they were being watched.

He glanced over Molly's shoulder, moved away from her hand still covering his heart. With the focused stare of a predator, a man in a blue ball cap nearly lost in the shadow of the liquor store's doorway was watching them. He glanced away as soon as Houston spotted him.

What had Houston been thinking bringing her here? Flashing his watch and his custom suit like a neon invitation. He knew better than that! He should have known better than that.

That man pushed himself off the wall, shuffled by them, eyed Houston's watch, scanned his face.

Houston absorbed the details. The man was huge, at least an inch taller than Houston, and no doubt outweighed him by a good fifty pounds. He had rings on his hand, a T-shirt that said Jay on it, in huge letters. His face was wily, lined with hardness.

"What's going on?" Molly asked, seeing the change in Houston's face. She glanced at the man, back at him.

But Houston didn't answer, preparing himself, his instincts on red alert.

"Got the time?" "Jay" had circled back on them.

The certainty of what would happen next filled Houston. Mentally he picked up the weapons he had thought it was safe to lay down. Without taking his eyes off Jay he noted the sounds around him, the motion. The neighborhood was unusually quiet today, and besides, people here knew how to mind their own business.

Molly was looking up at the thug, smiling, intent on seeing the good in him, just as she was intent on seeing the good in everyone. *Even a man who had come into her life to bring changes she hadn't wanted.*

Except falling in love. She'd wanted that. The bridal gown should have warned him. He should have backed away while he still could have. Because Molly was about to see something of him that he had not intended to show her. That he thought he had managed to kill within himself.

She looked at her wrist, gave "Jay" the time. Houston was silent, reading the predatory readiness in that man's body language, the threat.

Silently he begged for Molly to pay attention to her

intuition, to never mind hurting anyone's feelings if she was wrong. He wanted her to run, to get the hell out of the way. To not see what was going to happen next.

"How 'bout a cigarette?" the man asked.

The first doubt crossed Molly's features. Houston could feel her looking at him for direction, but he dared not take his eyes off "Jay," not for a second.

"I don't smoke," she said uneasily.

Adrenaline rushed through Houston. In one smooth move he had taken Molly and shoved her behind his back, inserted himself between her and the threat.

"He doesn't want a cigarette, Molly," he said, still not taking his eyes from the man.

"Ain't no watch worth you dying for," the man told him, and Houston saw the flash of a silver blade appear in his palm.

"Or you," Houston said.

Molly gasped. "Just give him the watch."

But if "Jay" got the watch, then what? Then the purse? Then the wallet? Then Molly?

The watch might not be worth dying for. But other things were.

"Just give it up," the man was saying in a reasonable tone of voice. "No one has to get hurt."

Something primal swept Houston. He went to a place without thought, a place of pure instinct. Years on the speed bag had made him lightning fast.

He knew his own speed and he knew his own strength, and there was nothing in him that held back from using them both. He was outgunned, the man both taller and heavier than him. There could be no holding back. None.

He was aware his breath was harsh, but that he felt calm, something at his core beyond calm. Still. It felt strangely as if this was the moment he'd prepared for his entire life, all those hours at the bag, running on cold mornings, practicing the grueling left right combinations and jabs.

All for this. To be ready for this one moment when he had to protect Molly.

"Hey, man," the guy said, "give it up, I tell you."

But the phrase was only intended to distract. Peripherally Houston registered the silvery flash in the young thug's hand, the glitter of malice in his eyes. Houston was, in a split second, a man he had never wanted Molly to see, a man he had never wanted to see himself, even as he'd been aware of the shadowy presence within him.

This was what he had tried to outrun, the violence of his father, the primitive ability to kill thrumming through his veins. He was a man who had never left these streets behind him at all, who was ready now to claim the toughness, the resilience, the resourcefulness that a person never really left behind them.

His fists flashed. Left jab. Straight right. The man slashed at him once, but his heaviness made him less than agile, and Houston's fury knew no bounds. Jay went down under the hail of fists, crashed to the sidewalk.

Houston was on top of him, some instinct howling within him. *Don't let him get up. Not until you see the knife. Where is it?*

Pounding, pounding in the rhythm to the waves of red energy that pulsed through him. The fury drove his fists into the crumpled form of Jay over and over.

Slowly he became aware that Molly was pulling at him, trying to get him off him, screaming.

"Stop, Houston. You're going to kill him."

"Where's the knife?"

And then he saw it, the silver blade under Jay's leg. The man had probably dropped it the minute he'd been hit.

Still, Houston was aware of his reluctance, as he came back to her, made himself stop, rose to his feet, tried to shake it off.

He was aware he had come here to show Molly where he was from, to see how she reacted to that.

Instead, he had found out who he really was. A thug. Someone who could lose control in the blink of an eye. He'd brought Molly down here to see if she could handle *his* reality. He was grateful this test that not even he could have predicted or expected had come.

They were not going to move forward. There was no relationship with Molly Michaels in his future.

What if he got this angry at her? The way his father had gotten angry at his mother? And claimed it was love.

And if anybody asked him why he had just pulverized that young man, wouldn't that be his answer, too?

Because he loved her.

And he would protect her with his very life.

Even if that meant protecting her from himself.

He had come so close to believing he could have it all. Now watching that dream fade, he felt bereft.

The man rolled to his side, scrambled drunkenly to his feet, sent a bewildered look back, blood splashing down a nose that was surely broken onto a shirt. The knife lay abandoned on the sidewalk.

Only when he was sure that Jay was gone did Houston turn to her. She stared at him silently. And then her face crumpled. A sob escaped her and then another. She began to shake like a leaf. She crept into him, laid her head against his chest and cried.

Just the shock of the assault? Or because she had seen something in him that she couldn't handle and that love could not tame, had no hope of healing?

Houston took off his jacket and wrapped it around her shoulders, pulled her close into him, aware of how fragile she was, how very, very feminine, how his breath stirred her hair.

There was that exquisite moment of heightened awareness where it felt as if he was breathing her essence into his lungs.

To savor. To hold inside him forever. Once he said goodbye.

And then, out of nowhere, heaven sent, a cab pulled up and he shoved her in it.

"B-b-but shouldn't we wait for the police?"

The police? No, when you grew up in these neighborhoods you never quite got clear of the feeling that the police were not your friends.

Besides, what if some nosy reporter was monitoring the scanner? What a great story that would make. CEO of successful company wins fight with street thug. But just a bit of digging could make the story even more interesting. A nineteen-year-old story of a bank robbery.

Loser, his mother had screamed when there was another lost job, another Friday with no paycheck. The look on her face of such disdain.

And the look on his father's.

I will win her. I will show her. I will show them all.

Except he hadn't. His father had been his mother's hero for all of two hours, already drunk, throwing money around carelessly. The police had arrived and taken him. An innocent bystander shot, but not, thank God, killed, during the bank robbery his father had committed. *Nineteen years of a life spent for an attempt to win what Houston realized, only just now, could not be won.*

"No police," he said firmly. "Give the driver your address."

It was a mark of just how shaken she was that she didn't even argue with him, but gave her address and then collapsed against him, her tears warming his skin right though his shirt. His hand found her hair. Was there a moment in the last few days when he had not thought of how her hair felt?

Touching it now felt like a homecoming he could not hold on to. Because in the end, wasn't love the most out of control thing of all?

And yet he could not deny, as he held her, that that's what the fierce protectiveness that thrummed through him felt like. As if he would die protecting her if he had to, without hesitation, without fear.

A feeling was coming over him, a surge of endorphins releasing like a drug into his brain and body.

He would have whatever she gave him tonight. He would savor it, store it in a safe place in his heart that he could return to again and again.

Once it was over. And it would be over soon enough. He did not have to rush that moment.

He helped her up the stairs to her apartment. Her hands were shaking so badly he had to take the keys from her.

"Do you have something to drink?" he asked, looking at her pale face.

"Zinfandel," she said. "Some kind of chicken zinfandel."

"And I always thought wine was made with grapes."

He hoped to make her laugh, but somehow his tone didn't quite make it. Tonight he had gone down there with an expectation of *maybe* there being some kind of chance for them.

For him to build a life different than the one of unabating loneliness he had always known. A life different than what his family had given him.

But that fury resided in him. And he was not sharing that legacy with her. Someday, if he followed that look in her eyes, there would be children, too. They did not deserve the Whitford legacy, either. Innocent. His unborn children were innocent, as once he had been innocent.

The ugly truth now? He had *liked* the feeling of his fist smashing into that man's face.

He would have liked to just leave, but he could tell she was quickly disintegrating toward shock.

"I think we need something a little stronger than chicken zinfandel," he suggested.

"I think there might be some brandy above the fridge. Chuck drank…" she giggled "…everything."

She was staring at him with something hungry in her eyes. She reached out and touched him, her hand sliding along the still coiled muscle of his forearm. There was naked appreciation in her touch.

He recognized in her a kind of survivor euphoria. He felt it sometimes after a sparring match. A release of chemical endorphins, a hit of happiness that opened your senses wide.

Tomorrow she would wake up and think of his hands smashing into that man, and feel the fear and doubt that deserved.

Tonight, she would think he was her hero.

He pulled his arm away from her, poured her a generous shot of brandy, made her drink it, but he refused one for himself.

One loss of control for the night was quite enough.

"Houston." She took a sip, stared at him, drank him as greedily as the brandy. And he let her. Drank her back, saved her every feature, the wideness of her eyes and the softness of her lips.

"I think you're bleeding," she gasped suddenly.

He followed her gaze down. A thin thread of red was appearing above the belly line on his white shirt. So, the knife had not dropped instantly. At some level, had the physical threat triggered his rage?

Excuses.

"You're hurt," she said, frightened.

If he was, adrenaline was keeping him from feeling it. "Nah. A little scrape. Nothing. A long way from the heart."

If his arm was hanging by a thread at the moment he suspected he would do the manly thing and tell her it was nothing.

"Let me see."

"No, I'm okay."

But she pointed at a chair, and because he was going to savor every single thing she gave him tonight—he sat there obediently while she retrieved the first aid kit. "Take off your shirt," she told him.

Who had he been kidding when he'd said his injuries were not close to the heart? It was all about the heart. The walls he had tried to repair around it were crumbling again, faster than he could build them back up.

Now his heart was going to rule his head. Because he knew better than to take off that shirt for her. He was leaving. Why drag this out?

And he did it anyway, aware he was trying to memorize the kindness of her face, and the softness in her eyes, the hunger in her.

He undid the buttons with unreasonable slowness, dragging out this moment, torturing himself with the fact it would not be him who fed that hunger. He let the shirt fall open. He didn't need to take it off, but he did, sliding it over his shoulders, holding it loosely in one hand. The tangy scent of his own sweat filled the room, and he watched her nostrils flare, drinking him in.

She knelt in front of him, and her scent, lemony and clean, melted into his. Even though she was trying to be all business, he could see the finely held tension in her as her eyes moved over his naked chest.

It seemed like a long time ago that he had first seen her, known somehow she would change something about him.

Make him long for things he could not have.

But he could have never foreseen how this moment of her caring for him would undo him. Her tenderness toward him created an ache, a powerful yearning that no man, not even a warrior, could fight.

Not forever.

And he had been fighting since his hand had first tangled in her hair, had found the zipper on her wedding dress.

"Oooh," she said, inspecting the damage, a tiny thin line that ran vertically from just below his breastbone to his belly button. "That's nasty."

He glanced down. To him it looked like a kitten scratch.

"Are you sure we shouldn't call the police?" she said. "You've been stabbed."

"No police."

"I don't understand that."

"You wouldn't understand it," he said harshly. "All it would take would be for one snoopy reporter to be monitoring the police channel, and it could be front page news. What a nice human interest story. Especially if anyone did any digging. The son of an armed robber foils an armed robbery."

"Your father's shame isn't yours."

"Yes, it is," he said wearily. "You know after my dad was arrested, and my mom left, I got a second chance. A great foster home. For the first time in my life I had food and clothes and security.

"Then in high school there was a dance. I danced with a cheerleader. Cutest girl in the school. And some guy—maybe her boyfriend, or just a hopeful, I don't remember—came and asked her what she was doing dancing with a thug.

"And I nearly killed him. Just the way I nearly killed that man tonight. And I liked the way it felt. Just the way my dad must have liked the way it felt when he was hitting people, which was often."

"I don't believe that," she said uncertainly. "That you liked it. You just did what you had to do. He was huge. Any kind of holding back might have turned the tide in his favor."

He laughed, aware of the harsh edge to it. "That was the first two punches. He was already done when he hit the ground."

"Houston, you did an honorable thing tonight. Why are you trying to change it into something else?"

"No," he said softly. "Why are you?"

"I'm not."

"Yes, you are. Because you always want to believe the best about everybody even if it's not true."

"How come you haven't spent your life beating people up if you like it so darn much?"

"I learned to channel my aggression. Boxing."

"There you go."

"Not because I wanted to," he said, "but because I didn't like the way people looked at me after that had happened."

"You want to be a bad guy, Houston. But you're just not."

He got up even though she wasn't finished. He could not allow her to convince him. He knew what he was. He knew what he had felt when he hit that man. Satisfaction. Pure primal satisfaction. He tugged his shirt on. "I have to go."

"Please don't."

That man could see through her veneers as ruthlessly as he had disposed of his own. That man saw everything that she wanted to hide.

Her need was naked in her eyes, in the shallowness of her breath, in the delicate color that blossomed in her cheeks, in the nervous hand that tried to tame a piece of that wild hair.

Her gaze locked on to his own, her green eyes magnificent with wonder and hunger and invitation.

He was aware of reaching deep inside himself to tame the part of him that just wanted to have her, own her, possess her, the two sides of his soul doing battle over her.

He took a step toward the door. She stepped in front of him. Took his shoulders, stood on her tiptoes.

Her lips grazed his lips. He had waited for this moment since he had tasted her the first time. He felt the astonishing delicacy of her kiss, and the instant taming of that thing in him that was fierce.

Not all the strength of his warrior heart could make him back away. He had promised himself he would take whatever she offered tonight, so he would have something to savor in the world he was going back to.

So he took her lips with astounding gentleness and a brand-new part of him, a part he had no idea existed, came forward. It met her tenderness with his own. Exploring what she offered to him with reverence, recognition of the sacredness of the ritual he had just entered into.

This was the dance of all time. It was an ancient call that guaranteed the future. It was a place where ruthless need and tender discovery met, melded and became something brand-new.

His possession of her deepened. With a groan, he allowed his hands to tangle in her hair, to draw her in nearer to him. He dropped his head from the warm rhapsody of her mouth, and trailed kisses down the slender column of her throat, to the hollow at the base of it.

With his lips, he could feel her life beating beneath that tender skin.

"Please," she whispered, her hands in his hair, on his neck.

Please what? Stop, or go forward?

His lips released her neck, and when that contact stopped, it was as if the enchantment broke. Some rational part of him—the analytical part that had been his presenting characteristic, his greatest strength, his key to his every success—studied her.

The half-closed eyes, the puffiness of the lips, the pulse beating crazily in her throat.

Storing it.

But an unwelcome truth penetrated what he was feeling. He could not take what she had to offer, for just one night. You didn't just kiss a woman like her and walk away from it unscathed, as if it was nothing, meant nothing, changed nothing.

She would be damaged by such a cavalier *taking* of her gifts.

Besides, she was not fully aware of what she was offering. The brandy on top of the shock had made her vulnerable, incapable of making a rational decision. If there was ever a time the rational part of him needed to step up to the plate it was now.

He was not the hero she wanted to see.

"I'm going," he said.

"Please don't," she said. "I'm scared. I know it's silly, but I feel scared. I don't want to be alone."

Perhaps he could be a hero for just a little while longer, though it would take all that was left of his strength.

It was so hard to press her head into his chest, let his hands wander that magnificent hair. It was hard to move to the couch, to allow her to relax into him, to feel her shallow breathing become deep and steady, to let her feel safe.

He had another fault then, as well as fury that years had not tamed. He was no hero, but a thief, because he was going to steal this moment from her.

Steal it to hold in his heart forever.

After a long time, her grip relaxed on his hand, her lips opened and little puffed sighs escaped. She had gone to sleep on him. He slipped out from underneath her sweet weight, laid her on the couch, looked for something to cover her with.

He tucked a knitted afghan around her, looked at her face, touched her hair one more time.

He glanced around her apartment, noticed the poster on the wall, and was mesmerized by it for a moment.

He took a deep breath and moved away from all it represented.

Though he was now beyond weariness, he went back to his office, the one he would turn over to Miss Viv tomorrow.

There was a new stack of letters in defense of Prom Dreams. Just in case he wasn't feeling bad enough, he read them all.

A picture fell out of the last one. It was of a beautiful young woman, at her university convocation. The podium she was standing by said Harvard.

Dear Mr. Whitford:
I recently heard that Second Chances was thinking about canceling their Prom Dreams program. I would just like you to know that five years ago, my school was chosen to participate in that program. You may find this hard to believe, but being allowed to choose that beautiful dress for myself was the first time in my life that I ever felt I was worth something.

He set the letter down.

No, he came from the very neighborhood her school had been in. He knew how hard it was to feel as if you were worth something.

He knew, suddenly, that was as important as having a full belly. Maybe more. Because filling a belly was temporary. Making a person feel as if they were worth something, even for a moment, that was something they carried in them forever.

He could not have Molly. He had decided that tonight.

But still, he could live up to the man she had hoped

he was. It could be a standard that he tried to rise to daily. Even as it was ending, something in him could begin.

It could start with leaving a note to Miss Viv, telling her that Molly should lead this organization into its new future, that she had gifts greater than his to give Second Chances. The ability to analyze was nothing compared to the ability to love that she poured into this place.

It could start with a few prom dresses.

And it could start with an answered letter to his father.

CHAPTER NINE

IT WAS WAY too soon to love him, Molly thought, walking up the street toward the office the next morning.

But there was no doubt in her mind that she was in love. Totally. Irrevocably. Wonderfully.

The whole world this morning felt different, as if rain had come and washed it clean, made it sparkle.

He had brought her to the place of his birth, thinking he risked something by showing her everything. Instead, she had seen him so completely it made her heart stand still, awed to be in the presence of a soul so magnificent, so strong.

She smiled thinking of how he thought it said something *bad* about him that he had dispensed with that horrible young mugger so thoroughly.

She suspected she would spend the rest of her life performing alchemy on him, showing him what he thought was lead was really gold.

Molly shivered when she thought of him last night *protecting* her. Prepared to die to protect her if he had to. And then running that act of such honor and such incredible bravery through the warp of something in his own mind, and making it *bad*.

He said he had lost control. But she didn't see it that way. He'd stopped. If he'd truly lost control, "Jay" would never have gotten up and scrambled away.

Houston didn't lose control.

If he did, last night would have ended much differently! Molly was aware of feeling a little singing inside of her as she contemplated the delightful job she was going to have making that man lose control.

She was pretty sure it was going to involve lots of lips on lips, and that she was up for the job. Even thinking about it, her belly did the most delightful downward swoop, anticipating seeing him today.

Maybe she'd dispense with the niceties, just close his office door and throw herself at him.

Wantonly. There was going to have to be an element of taking him by surprise to make him lose control.

Then again, today was a big day for them, a milestone, the unveiling of the new Second Chances that they had created together, that they would continue to create together.

Maybe she would hold off taking him by surprise until the open house was over. But she'd tease him until then. The odd little touch, her eyes on him, a whisper when he least expected it.

Her life felt so full of exciting potential. She could barely believe her life had gone from that dull feeling of same-same to this sense of invigorated engagement in such a short time.

That's what love did.

Brought out the best. Empowered. Made all things possible. And healed all things, too.

Molly could feel her heart beating a painfully quick tattoo within her chest as she mounted the stairs, and went in the front door of the office.

Another day together. A gift. If things had gone differently last night they might not have this gift. It was a reminder to live to the fullest, to take the kind of chances that made a life shimmer with glory.

Tish was already at her desk. She looked up, beaming. "There's a surprise for you."

Molly's eyes went to the huge bouquet of pink lilies on Tish's desk. She started to smile.

When she'd woken last night and found he had slipped away, she had thought maybe he planned to try to fight this thing. She put her nose to the flowers, and let subtle scent engulf her.

But no, they were on the same page. He was going to romance her. It was probably going to be hard for a realist like him, too! Because lovely as they were, flowers weren't going to cut it. They were the easiest form of romance.

Tish laughed. "Those aren't for you, silly. Those are from the next door neighbor congratulating us on our reopening. Your surprise is in Miss Viv's office."

He was waiting for her, then. Had some surprise to make up for the disappointment of a kiss not completed, of not staying the night with her.

She went to the closed office door, knocked lightly, opened it without waiting for an answer.

A sight that should have filled her heart to overflowing greeted her. Miss Viv sat behind her own desk.

Molly bit back the wail, *Where is he?* and rushed into the arms that were open to her. She had to fight back tears as Miss Viv's embrace closed around her.

"My word," Miss Viv said. "Isn't this incredible? Isn't the office incredible? You'll have to show me how to use this."

"I thought you didn't like computers?" Molly teased.

"There isn't anything here I don't like," Miss Viv declared happily.

"Where's Houston?" Molly asked, casually.

"I'm not sure," Miss Viv said. "I haven't seen him.

Do you press this button to put the camera on? Molly, help me figure this out!"

Molly complied, pulled a chair up to Miss Viv's desk. Part of her was fully engaged in showing Miss Viv how to use the computer, hearing tidbits about her trip and the wonderful time she'd had.

Part of her listened, waited. Part of her asked, *Where is his office going to be, now that Miss Viv is back?*

She waited for the sound of the voice and the footsteps that did not come. For some reason, she thought of the time he had told her about waiting at the concert for his mother. This, then, was how he had felt.

The waiting was playing with her game plan. She was not going to be able to contain herself when she finally saw him. She was surely going to explode with joy. Everyone was going to know.

And she didn't care.

But by lunch he still had not come. Molly tried his cell phone number. She got the recording.

She listened to his voice, *greedily,* hung up because she could not think of a message to leave that could begin to say how she was feeling.

Eventually she and Miss Viv joined the rest of the office in getting ready for the open house. The flowers on Tish's desk had only been the first of many arrangements that arrived: from friends of Second Chances, neighboring businesses, well-known New York business people and personalities.

The caterers arrived and began setting up food, wine and cheese trays, while Brianna went into a tizzy of last minute arranging and "staging," as she called it.

At three, people began to trickle in the door. Invited guests, curious people from the neighborhood, the press. Information packets had been prepared for all of them: what Second Chances did, complete with photographs. Though no mention of a donation was ever made, each packet contained a discreet cream envelope addressed to Second Chances.

Molly felt as though she was in a dream as that first trickle of people turned into a flood. She was there, and not there. She was answering questions. She was engaged with people. She was laughing. She was enjoying the sense of triumph of a job well done. She was sipping the champagne that had been uncorked, nibbling on the incredible variety of cheeses and fresh fruits.

But she was aware she was not there at all.

Watching the door. Waiting.

Where was he? Where was Houston? This was his doing, the success of this gathering—and there was no doubt it was a success—was a tribute to his talent, his hard work, his dedication, his leadership. How could he not be here to reap the rewards of this, to see that basket on Tish's desk filling up with those creamy white envelopes?

Finally Miss Viv asked for everyone's attention. She thanked them all for coming, and invited them to watch a special presentation with her.

The lights were lowered, the voices quieted.

A screen came down from the ceiling.

Music began to play.

The office designer who had been in Molly's office closet the first day stood beside Molly. "Wait until you see this," she said. "Mr. Whitford always does the most incredible presentations." Then she cocked her head. "Hey, he's changed the music. That's interesting. It was Pachelbel before."

But it wasn't Pachelbel now. It was a guitar, and a single voice, soulful, almost sorrowful, filling the room, as black-and-white pictures began to fill the screen, one melting into the next one.

"You told me," the music said, "that I would know heaven."

But the pictures weren't of heaven. They were of dark streets and broken windows, playgrounds made of asphalt, boarded over businesses. They were of the places, that Molly had found out yesterday, where he had grown up.

The places that had shaped that amazingly strong, wonderful man.

The voice sang on, "You promised me a land free from want..."

And the pictures showed those who had newly arrived, the faces of immigrants, wise eyes, unsmiling faces, ragged clothes.

> "I expected something different than what I got,
> Oh, Lord, where is my heaven, where is my heaven?"

The pictures were breathtaking in their composition: a young man crying over the body of a friend in his arms; a little boy kicking a can, shoulders humped over, dejection in every line of him; a woman sitting on steps with a baby, her eyes fierce and afraid as she looked into the camera.

Then the pictures began to change, in perfect sync with the tempo of the music changing, the lyrics suspended, a single guitar picking away at the melody, but faster now, the sadness leaving it.

The pictures showed each of the stores, Peggy laughing over a rack of clothes at Now and Zen, the ultra-sophisticated storefront of Wow and Then, a crowded day at Now and Again. Then it showed this office before the makeover, walls coming down, transformation.

And that voice singing, full of hope and power now, singing, *If we just come together, if I see you as my brother, Lord, there is my heaven, there is my heaven.*

Now there was a photograph of the green space that Molly recognized as her garden project, the only color in a block of black and white, the children at the daycare, the Bookworms bus.

Emotion was sweeping the room. Brianna was dabbing at her eyes with a hankie. "Oh, my God," she whispered, "he's outdone himself this time."

Something in Molly registered that. *This time.* Brushed it away like a pesky fly that was spoiling an otherwise perfect moment. Except it wasn't perfect. Because he wasn't here.

"Where is Houston?" Molly whispered to Brianna. She *needed* him to be here, she needed to be sharing this with him.

"Oh," Brianna said, "he never comes to the final day."

"Excuse me? What final day? He's the boss here." *We are going to be building a future together.*

And hopefully not just at work.

But Brianna was clapping now, keeping time. Every one was clapping, keeping time as that voice sang out, rich and powerful, full of promise, *"There is my heaven."*

A final picture went across the screen.

It was that little girl, the princess, kissing Houston on the cheek.

And Molly thought, as that picture froze in its frame, *there is my heaven.*

Over the thunder of applause, she turned to ask Brianna what she meant, about the final day. About Houston never coming to the final day.

Other thoughts were crowding her memory. She realized he had a relationship with all those workers who had come in, with Brianna. He hadn't just met them when he took over, hadn't just hired contractors and designers and computer geeks.

He'd known them all before.

He *never* came to the final day. He's outdone himself *this time.*

Houston Whitford had done all this before. That's why he'd been brought in to Second Chances. Because he'd done it all before. And done it well.

The applause finally died down. Miss Viv stood at the front of the room, beaming, dabbing at her eyes.

As she spoke, Molly felt herself growing colder and colder.

"First of all, I must thank Houston Whitford for donating his time, his expertise and his company, Precision Solutions, to all of us here. I know his team does not come cheaply. His donation probably rates in the tens of thousands of dollars."

The cold feeling increased. He'd been donating all the renovations? He'd let her believe he was taking the money from Prom Dreams?

No, he'd never said that. He'd probably never told Molly an out-and-out lie. The more subtle kinds of lies. The lies of omission.

"Houston's not here today," Miss Viv said. "With any luck he's back to his real job. Personally I wish Precision Solutions was consulting with the president of the United States about getting this country back on track."

A ripple of appreciative laughter, only Molly wasn't laughing. There. It was confirmed. He was not an employee, not the new head of Second Chances. He had never planned to stay, he had known all along they were not building a future of any kind together.

The only one, apparently, who had not known that was her.

Little Molly Pushover. Whose record of being betrayed by every single person she had ever loved was holding.

Miss Viv was talking about the holidays she had just gone on, and how it had made her rethink her priorities. She had decided to retire. Then Miss Viv was thanking everyone for their years of support, hoping they would all show the same support and love to the new boss as they had shown to her.

"I'd like to introduce you now to our new leader," Miss Viv said, "the person I trust to do this job more than anyone in the world."

So, he was here after all. Molly allowed relief to sweep over her. She must have misunderstood. He was leaving Precision Solutions to head up Second Chances. Molly could feel herself holding her breath, waiting to see him, *dying* to see him.

So relieved because as the afternoon had worn on and he had not shown up, a feeling of despair had settled over her. She had known *exactly* what he had felt like at that Christmas concert when his mother had not come.

He would not make someone else feel like that. Not that he cared about. He wouldn't. She thought of the look of fierce protectiveness on his face last night. He would never be the one to hurt her. He had almost died to keep her safe!

But now he was here. Somewhere. She craned her neck, waiting for Miss Viv to call his name. After the crowds had thinned, she would laugh with him about her misunderstanding. Kick closed that office door, and see what happened next.

But Miss Viv didn't call his name.

Her eyes searched the people gathered around her, until she finally found Molly. She smiled and held out her hand.

"Molly, come up here."

Molly tried to shrink away. Oh, no, she did not want to be part of introducing the new boss. She thought her feelings would be too naked in her face, she felt as if there was no place for her to hide.

But Miss Viv did not notice Molly trying to shrink away. She gestured her forward even more enthusiastically. She thought Molly not coming was because of the press of the crowds, and gave up trying to get her to the front.

The crowd opened for her. Somebody pushed her from behind.

Molly had no choice but to go up there.

"I'd like to introduce you to the new head of Second Chances," Miss Viv said gleefully. "Molly Michaels."

Molly stood there, stunned. There was no happiness at all. Just a growing sense of self-scorn. Until the very last minute, she had believed in him, believed the best in him. Just like always.

No doubt she'd be getting another postcard from some far off exotic place soon. To rub her face in her own lack of discernment.

Her own Pollyanna need to *believe.*

She had been lied to by the man she thought she had seen more truly than anyone else. He wasn't the boss and he wasn't going to be part of her future here.

Or anywhere else.

"I don't know that I'm qualified," Molly managed to say through stiff lips, in an undertone to Miss Viv.

"Oh, but you are, dear. That's one of the things our darling Houston was here to do. To find out if you were ready to take over for me."

Our darling Houston.

Molly had been falling in love, and he'd been conducting a two-week job interview?

The front door opened, and a delivery man walked in, barely able to see over his arms loaded with long, white boxes. "Where should I put—" He stopped, uncomfortably aware he was the center of attention. "The dresses?"

"What dresses?" Tish asked.

"I hate to break up the party, but I got a truckload of prom dresses out there, lady, and I'm double parked."

Miss Viv put a hand to her heart. "Oh," she said, and her eyes filled with fresh tears. "My Houston."

And again, Molly felt no joy at all. *Her Houston. Darling Houston.* Houston Whitford was Miss Viv's Houston.

They had a relationship that preexisted his coming here. He had never thought to mention that in two weeks, either. Nor had Miss Viv mentioned it when she had first introduced him.

Molly had been lied to, not just by him, but by the woman she loved more than any other in the world?

Somehow Molly managed to get through the gradual wind-down of the festivities. She begged off looking at the dresses that had arrived. Someone else could do it. Prom Dreams seemed like a project suited to a desperate romantic, which she wasn't going to be anymore.

And she meant that, this time. That moment in the

garden when Molly had thought she knew who she really was wavered like the mirage that it was.

Though there were still people there, Molly tried to get out the door unnoticed.

Miss Viv broke away from the crowd and came to her. "Wait just a sec. Houston left something for you."

She came back moments later with a long, narrow box, pressed it into Molly's unwilling hands.

"Are you all right?"

She was not ready to discuss the magnitude of how not all right she was. "Just tired," she said.

"Are you going to open it?"

Molly shook her head. "At home." The fact that it was light as a feather should have warned her what was in it.

She opened the box in the safety of her apartment with trepidation rather than enjoyment.

There was the feather boa she had worn on that day when they had danced at Now and Zen. Baldy's feathers. One of those fancy dresses, a diamond ring, flowers, somehow she could have handled a gift like that. Expensive. Impersonal somehow. A *thanks for the memories* brush off.

But this?

Molly allowed the tears to come. What she should have remembered when she was nourishing the ridiculous fantasy of him as the lone gunslinger who saved the town, was how that story always ended.

With the hero who had saved the town riding away as alone as the day he had first ridden in.

An hour ago watching Houston's face flash across the screen, that child kissing his cheek, Molly had thought, *there is my heaven.*

How was it that heaven could be so close to hell?

CHAPTER TEN

HOUSTON AWOKE WITH the dream of her kiss on his lips. If he closed his eyes again, he could conjure it.

It had been a month since he had felt her lips under his own, since he had known he had to say goodbye to her. Why were the memories of the short time they had shared becoming more vivid instead of fading?

Probably because of the choice he had made. He might have chosen to walk away from Molly—for her own good—but he had also chosen not to walk away from her lesson.

Every day he tried to do one thing that would make her proud of him, if she knew, one thing that somehow made him live up to the belief he had seen shining in her eyes.

He had sent a truckload of brand-new shoes to Sunshine and Lollipops. He had arranged scholarships for some of those girls who had written the earnest letters in defense of Prom Dreams.

Yesterday, he had rented an apartment for his father. It was just down the block from the garden project that would never become a parking lot. After he had rented the apartment, he had wandered down there, and looked at the flowers and the vegetables growing in cheery defiance of the concrete all around them, and he had known this would be a good place for his father to come to.

Then Houston had seen Mary Bedford working alone, weeding around delicate new spinach tops. He had gone to her, and been humbled by her delight in seeing him. He had told her his father would soon be new to the neighborhood. He had not told her anything that would bring out the drowning kitten kind of sympathy—for his father would hate that—but he had asked her if she could make him welcome here.

His phone rang beside the bed.

"Houston, it's Miss Viv."

"What can I do for you, Miss Viv?" *Please, nothing that will test my resolve. Don't ask me to be near her.*

"It's about Molly."

He closed his eyes, steeling himself to say no to whatever the request was.

"I have a terrible feeling she's involved herself in an Internet affair. You know how dangerous those can be, don't you?"

"What? Molly? That doesn't sound like Molly." Even though his heart felt as if it was going to pound out of his chest, he forced himself to be calm. "What would make you think that?"

"After I came back from my holiday, Molly just wasn't herself. She didn't seem interested in work. She wouldn't accept the position as head of Second Chances and seemed angry at me, though she wouldn't say why. She lost weight. She had big circles under her eyes. She looked exhausted, as if she may have been crying, privately."

Not an Internet affair, he thought, sick, *a cad.*

"But then, about a week ago, everything changed. She started smiling again. I didn't feel as if she was angry with me. In fact, Houston, she became radiant.

Absolutely radiant. I know a woman in love when I see one."

In love? With someone other than him? This new form of torture he had not anticipated.

"Then, just out of the blue, she announced she was going on holidays. I just know she's met someone on the Internet! And fallen in love with them. Houston, she's foolish that way."

I know.

"Did she say she'd met someone?" he asked, amazed by how reasonable he made his voice sound.

"She didn't have to! She said she's done experiencing her dreams through a picture on her living room wall! She said she was going to California for a while."

"What do you want me to do?" he asked.

"I don't know," Miss Viv wailed. "But I need to know she's safe."

That's funny. So did he.

"I'll look after it," he said.

"But how?" This said doubtfully. "California is a big place, Houston!"

He thought of the picture on Molly's living room wall. "It's not that big," he said.

MOLLY SIGHED WITH absolute contentment, and looked over the incredible view. The sun was setting over the Napa Valley. It was as beautiful as she had ever dreamed it could be.

Of course, maybe that was because she was in love.

Finally.

With herself.

Molly sat on a stone patio, high up on a terraced hillside that overlooked the famous vineyards of the Napa Valley in California. The setting sun gilded the grapevines in gold, and the air was as mild as an embrace. She was alone, wearing casual slacks and a T-shirt from a winery she had visited earlier in the day.

She had the feather boa wrapped around her neck.

In front of her was a wineglass of the finest crystal, a precious bottle of Cabernet Sauvignon this Valley was so famous for producing.

For a while after Houston had gone, she had thought she would die. Literally, Molly had thought she would curl up in a ball in a corner somewhere in her apartment and die.

But she didn't. She couldn't.

Baldy needed her.

And then one day she went to Sunshine and Lollipops to do a routine visit for a report that needed to be filled out for a grant.

All the children, every single one of them, were wearing new shoes.

"An anonymous donor," one of the staff told her. "A whole truckload of them arrived."

Something in Molly had become alert, as if she was reaching for an answer that she couldn't quite grasp.

The next day there had been an excited message on her answering machine.

"Miss Michaels, it's Carmen Sanchez." Tears, Spanish mixed with English, more tears. *"I got a scholarship. I don't know how. I never even applied for one."*

And that feeling of alertness inside Molly had grown. And then, when the second call came, from another one of the girls who had written a letter for Prom Dreams, the alertness sighed within her, *knowing.*

And with that knowing had come a revelation: she had always known the truth about Houston Whitford.

It was her own truth that she had not been so sure of.

Even though he would never admit it, she could clearly see he understood love at a level that she had missed.

It didn't rip down. It didn't tear apart. It didn't wallow in self-pity. It didn't curl up in a corner and die.

Those who had been lucky enough to know it gave back. They danced with life. They embraced *everything:* heartbreak, too. They never stopped believing good could come from bad.

She had told *him* that love could heal all things.

But then she had not lived it. Not believed it. Not ever embraced it as her own truth.

Now she was going to do just that. She was going to be made *better* by the fact, that ever so briefly, she had known the touch and the grace and the glory of loving. She was going to take that and give it to a world that had always waited for her to *see.*

Herself.

So, she watched with a full heart as the light faded over the Napa Valley. She felt as if the radiance within her matched the golden sun.

Headlights were moving up the hill toward the bed-and-breakfast where she was staying, and she watched them pierce the growing blackness, marveled at how something so simple could be so beautiful, marveled at how a loving heart could *see.*

The car pulled into the parking lot, below her perch, and she watched as a man got out.

In the fading light and at this distance, the man looked amazingly like Houston, that dark shock of hair, the way he carried himself with such masculine confidence, grace.

Of course, who didn't look like Houston? Every dark-haired stranger made her heart beat faster. At first, in her curl-up-in-the-corner phase, she had hated that. But as she came to embrace the truth about herself, she didn't anymore.

It was a reminder that she had been given a gift from him. And when she saw someone who reminded her of him now, she allowed herself to tenderly explore what she felt, and send a silent blessing to him.

To love him in a way that was pure because it wished only the best for him and asked for nothing in return.

It wasn't the same as not expecting enough of someone like Chuck, because really getting tangled with someone like Chuck meant you had not expected enough of yourself!

The man disappeared inside the main door far below the patio she sat on, and Molly allowed the beating of her heart to return to normal. She took another sip of wine, watched the vineyards turn to dusky gold as the light faded from the sky.

"Hello."

She turned and looked at him, felt the stillness inside her, the *knowing*. That love was more powerful than he was, than his formidable desire to fight against it.

"Hello," she said softly, back.

"Surprised to see me?"

"Not really," she said.

He frowned at her. "You made yourself damnably hard to find, if you were expecting me."

She smiled.

"Miss Viv was worried that you were having an Internet affair."

"And you? Were you worried about that?"

"Impossible," he whispered.

"Then why did you come?"

He sighed and took the chair across from her. "Because I couldn't *not* come."

They sat there silently for a moment.

"The feathers look good on you," he said after a while.

"Thank you."

"Where's Baldy?"

"I left him with a neighbor."

"Oh."

Again the silence fell. She noticed it was comfortable. *Full,* somehow.

"I owe you an apology," he said.

"No," she said, "you don't. I learned more from you walking away than I could have ever learned from you staying."

He frowned. "That's not what I was going to apologize for. We both know you're better off without me."

We do?

"No, I wanted to apologize for bringing you to the old neighborhood that night. And then for losing it on that guy, the mugger. For not being able to stop. I might have killed him if you hadn't stopped me."

She chuckled, and he glared at her.

"It's not funny."

"Of course it's funny, Houston. I weigh a hundred and thirteen pounds. And I could have stopped you? Don't be ridiculous. You stopped yourself."

"I'm trying to tell you something important."

"I'm all ears."

"I come from chaos," he said. "And violence. That is my legacy. And I am not visiting them on you."

"Why?" she asked softly.

He glared at her.

"Why are you so afraid to visit your legacy on me?"

"Because I love you, damn it!" The admission was hoarse with held in emotion.

"Ah," she said softly, her whole world filling with a light that put the gold of the Napa Valley sunset to shame. "And you're afraid you would hurt me?"

"Yes."

"You told me you hit a boy in high school once."

"True," he said tautly.

"And then what, fourteen or fifteen years later you hit another person? Who was attacking you?"

"I didn't feel like he was attacking me. I felt as though he was attacking you."

"And so defending me, putting your body between me and that threat, taking care of it, that was a *bad* thing? A pattern?"

"I lost control."

She would have laughed out loud at how ludicrous that assessment of himself was, except she saw what he was doing. He was trying to convince himself to climb back on that horse and ride away from her, back to those lonely places.

The thing was, she wasn't letting him ride off alone. That's all there was to it. Somewhere, somehow, this incredible man had lost a sense of who he really was.

But she saw him so clearly. It was as if she held his truth. And no matter what was in it for her, she was leading him back to it. Because suddenly, she understood that's what love did.

"He had a knife, Houston. He was huge. Don't you think you did what you had to do?"

"Overkill," he said. "Inexcusable."

"I'm not buying it, Houston."

He looked her full in the face.

"You're afraid of loving me."

"Yes," he whispered.

"You're afraid I will let you down, just like every other person who should have loved you has let you down."

"Yes," he admitted.

"You're afraid you will let yourself down. That love will make you do something crazy that you will regret forever."

"Yes," he said absolutely.

"There is a place," she said ever so softly, "where you do not have to be afraid anymore, Houston. Never again."

He looked at her. His eyes begged for it to be true.

She opened her arms.

And he came into them. She reached up and touched his cheek, with reverence, with the tender welcome of a woman who could see right to her gunslinger's soul. She could feel the strong beat of his good, good heart.

"You are a good man, Houston Whitford. A man with the courage to take every single hard thing life has handed you and rise above it."

He didn't speak, just nestled his head against her breast, and he sighed with the surrender of a man who had found his way down from the high and lonely places.

Over the next few days, they gave themselves over to exploring the glory of the Napa Valley.

They took the wine train. They went for long walks. They drove for miles exploring the country. They stopped at little tucked-away restaurants and vineyards, book shops and antique stores. They whiled away sun-filled afternoons sipping wine, holding hands, looking at each other, letting comfortable silences fall.

They laughed until their sides hurt, they talked until their voices were hoarse.

Molly remembered the day she had first met him, looking at herself in that wedding dress, and yearning for all the things it had made her feel: a longing for love, souls joined, laughter shared, long conversations. Lonely no more.

It was their final morning in California when he told her he had a surprise for her. It was so early in the morning it was still dark when he piled her into the car and drove the mazes of those twisting roads to a field.

Where a hot air balloon was anchored, gorgeous, standing against the muted colors of early morning.

It seemed to pull against its ropes, its brilliant stripes of color—purple, red, green, yellow—straining to join the cobalt-blue of the sky.

She walked toward it, her hand in Houston's, ready for this adventure. Eager to embrace it. She let Houston help her into the basket.

As the pilot unleashed the ropes and they floated upward to join the sky, she leaned back into Houston.

"I have waited all my life for this," Molly whispered.

"For a ride in a hot air balloon?"

"No, Houston," she said softly.

For this feeling—of being whole and alive. In fact, it had nothing to do with the balloon ride and everything to do with love. Over the last few days, it had seeped into her with every breath she took that held Houston's scent.

The hot air heater roared, and the balloon surged upward. The balloon lifted higher as the sun began to rise and drench the vineyards and hillsides in liquid gold. They floated through a pure sky, the world soaked in misty pinks and corals below them.

"Houston, look," she breathed of the view. "It's wonderful. It is better than any dream I ever dreamed."

She glanced at him when he didn't respond. "Is something wrong?"

"I was wondering—" he said, and then he stopped and looked away. He cleared his throat, uncharacteristically awkward.

"What?" she asked, growing concerned.

"Would you like some cheese?"

He produced a basket with an amazing array of cheese, croissants warm from the oven.

"Thank you," she said. "Um, this is good. Aren't you going to have some?"

He was working on uncorking a bottle of wine.

It was way too early for wine. She didn't care. She took a glass from him, sipped it, met his eyes.

"Houston, what is wrong with you?"

"Um, look, I was wondering—" he stopped, took a sudden interest in the scenery. "What's that?" he demanded of the pilot.

The pilot named the winery.

"Are you afraid of heights?" she breathed. This man, nervous, uptight, was not her Houston!

"No, just afraid."

Only a few days ago he wouldn't have admitted fear to her if he'd been dropped into a bear den covered in honey. She eyed him, amazed at his awkwardness. He was now staring at his feet. He glanced up at her.

"I told you," she reminded him gently, "that there is a place where you don't have to be afraid anymore."

"What if I told you I wanted to be in that place, with you, forever?"

His eyes met hers, and suddenly he wasn't fumbling at all.

In a voice as steady as his eyes, he said, "I was wondering if you would consider spending the rest of your life with me."

Her mouth fell open, and tears gathered behind her eyes. "Houston," she breathed.

"Damn. I forgot. Hang on." He let go of her hand, fished through the pocket of the windbreaker he had worn, fell to one knee. He held a ring out to her. The diamonds turned to fire as the rays of the rising sun caught on their facets.

"Molly Michaels, I love you. Desperately. Completely. With every beat of my heart and with every breath that I take. I love you," he said, his voice suddenly his own, strong and sure, a man who had always known exactly what he wanted. "Will you marry me?"

"Yes," she said. Simply. Softly. No one word had ever felt so right in her entire life.

It was yes to him, but also yes to herself. It was *yes* to life, in all its uncertainty. It was *yes* to disappointments being healed, *yes* to taking a chance, *yes* to being fully alive, *yes* to coming awake after sleeping.

And then they were in each other's arms. Houston's lips welcomed her.

Their kiss celebrated, not the miracle of a balloon rising hundreds of feet above the earth, defying gravity, but the absolute miracle of love.

He kissed her again with tenderness that *knew* her. And just like that they were both home.

At long last, after being lost for so long, and alone for so long, they had both found their way home.

EPILOGUE

HOUSTON WHITFORD SAT on the bench in Central Park feeling the spring sunshine warm him, his face lifted to it.

The park was quiet.

Peripherally he was aware of Molly and his father coming back down the park path toward him. They had wandered off together to admire the beds of tulips that his father, the gardener, loved so much.

Houston focused on them, his father so changed, becoming more shrunken and frail every day. Molly's arm and his father's were linked, her head bent toward her beloved "Hughie" as she listened to something he was telling her.

Houston saw her smile, saw his father glance at her, the older man's gaze astounded and filled with wonder as if he could not believe how his daughter-in-law had accepted him into her life.

This is what Houston had learned about love: it could not heal all things.

For instance, it could not heal the cancer that ate at his father. It could not heal the fact that he woke from his frequent sleeps with tears of regret sliding down his face.

Love, powerful as it was, could not change the scar left on a nose broken by a father's fury, or the other scars not quite as visible.

No, love could not heal all things.

But it could heal some things. And most days, that was enough. More than enough.

Once, his father had looked at Molly, and said sadly, "That's the woman your mother could have been had I been a better man."

"Maybe," Houston had said gently, feeling that wondrous thing that was called forgiveness. "Or maybe I'm the man you could have been if she had been a better woman."

Now, the baby carriage that Houston had taken charge of while Molly took his father to look at the tulips vibrated beneath where his fingertips rested on the handle, prewail warning. Then his daughter was fully awake, screaming, the carriage rattling as her legs and arms began to flail with fury.

Like her mother in so many ways, he thought with tender amusement, redheaded and bad-tempered.

At the sound of the cry, Houston's father quickened his steps on the path, breaking free of Molly's arm in his hurry to get to the baby.

He arrived, panting alarmingly from the small exertion. He peered at the baby and every hard crease his life and prison had put in his face seemed to melt. He put his finger in the carriage, and the baby latched on to it with her surprisingly strong little fist.

"There, there," his father crooned, "Pappy's here."

The baby went silent, and then cooed, suddenly all charm.

For a suspended moment, it seemed all of them—his father, Molly, the baby, Houston himself—were caught in a radiance of light that was dazzling.

"I lived long enough to see this," his father said, his

voice hoarse with astonishment and gratitude, his finger held completely captive by the baby.

"A good thing," Houston said quietly.

"No. More. A miracle," his father, a man who had probably never known the inside of a church, and who had likely shaken his fist at God nearly every waking moment of every day of his life, whispered.

Houston felt Molly settle on the bench beside him, rest her head on his shoulder, nestle into him with the comfort of a woman who knew beyond a shadow of a doubt that she was loved and cherished above all things.

"How's my Woman-of-the-Year?" he asked.

"Oh, stop," she said, but kissed his cheek.

She had taken Second Chances to the next level, beyond what anyone had ever seen for it, or dreamed for it. He liked to think his love helped her juggle so many different roles, all of them with seeming effortlessness, all of them infused with her great joy and enthusiasm for life.

Houston put his arm around her, pulled her in closer to him, touched his lips to her forehead.

His father was watching him, his eyes went back to Molly and then rested on Houston, satisfied, content, *full*.

"A miracle," he said again.

"Yes, it is," Houston, a man who had once doubted miracles, agreed.

All of it. Life. Love. The power of forgiveness. A place to call home. All of it was a miracle, so sacred a man could not even contemplate it without his heart nearly bursting inside his chest.

"Yes," he repeated quietly. "It is."

* * * * *